LINDSAY EVANS
and
KAYLA PERRIN

*The CEO's Dilemma &
Undeniable Passion*

ISBN-13: 978-1-335-45843-8

The CEO's Dilemma & Undeniable Passion

Copyright © 2019 by Harlequin Books S.A.

The publisher acknowledges the copyright holders of the individual works as follows:

The CEO's Dilemma
Copyright © 2019 by Lindsay Evans

Undeniable Passion
Copyright © 2019 by Kayla Perrin

Recycling programs for this product may not exist in your area.

This edition published by arrangement with Harlequin Books S.A.

For questions and comments about the quality of this book, please contact us at CustomerService@Harlequin.com.

Printed in U.S.A.

www.Harlequin.com

"Your apology is not worth the air you took to say it." She blinked hard and jerked her gaze toward the windows behind him.

For a horrific moment, Roman thought she would cry, but Aisha drew herself up to her full height on already high heels and visibly clenched her teeth. "You may be doing this just to spite your old man, but you're also screwing over someone else. Me. It's not fair what you're doing. I—I worked hard on that design and I was the top choice. I won't let you erase my career the way you're obviously intent on erasing your father."

Every word she spoke was like a punch to his gut.

"Ms. Clark, this decision is not about you, so please don't take it personally."

Those words came easily to his mouth, but Roman couldn't stop the pulse of sympathy, of regret, that threatened to turn his lunch against him. Sorry as he was, he wouldn't change his mind. He wouldn't allow his father to trap his mother in death the way he had in life.

"How can I do anything but take this personally, Mr. CEO?" Her words were scornful.

Distantly, Roman heard the outer office door open and a low voice talking to his assistant. Aisha looked over her shoulder through the open door and seemed to gather herself. Her tongue wiped over her lower lip and Roman's stomach dipped as he stared, unable to look away. She grabbed the letter on his desk, neatly folded it and put it back in her purse. She looked at him one last time before sailing out of his office, her heels stabbing the floor with each step.

Lindsay Evans was born in Jamaica and currently lives and writes in Atlanta, Georgia, where she's constantly on the hunt for inspiration, club in hand. She loves good food and romance and would happily travel to the ends of the earth for both. Find out more at www.lindsayevanswrites.com.

Books by Lindsay Evans

Harlequin Kimani Romance

Visit the Author Profile page at Harlequin.com for more titles.

CONTENTS

THE CEO'S DILEMMA

Lindsay Evans

Dear Reader,

When Aisha Clark runs into Roman Sykes in a coffee shop, she's smitten and imagines dating the handsome hunk. But it turns out that Roman is more than eye candy. He's also the CEO of the firm threatening to take away the professional prize for the building design she's worked hard for. The bitter truth of who he really is should turn Aisha all the way off, but she finds herself wanting to find out more about him.

Roman has to prove himself in his new leadership role at his father's firm. It means handing down tough decisions that are not always popular. He finds himself facing disapproval from Aisha when he rules on her project.

Aisha and Roman will find themselves battling it out in a test of wills. And wondering if love will prevail?

Best,

Lindsay

Chapter 1

The bell above the door jangled as Aisha pushed her way inside the bakery. Smiling wide, she let out a sigh of pleasure at the rush of delicious scents pouring from Baked Good, an indie bakery and coffee shop, aka a little slice of heaven in the Grant Park neighborhood of Atlanta.

"Hmm, this place is so yummy!" Aisha looked over her shoulder at her sister, Devyn, walking in behind her.

"I know you think so." Devyn rolled her eyes but was smiling back. "You and Mom love this place, which is so weird since you two are all about healthy eating."

"There's nothing unhealthy in this place. It all smells too good." Aisha headed directly for the front counter to join the long line already there.

"You're talking about a boatload of carbs, Aisha."

"Carbs get a bad rap," she said. "Just you wait. In a few years, everyone will be on the anti-paleo whatever diet and kicking themselves for missing out on the basic human right of fresh baked bread for so long."

Baked Good was one of Aisha's favorite places in the world, aside from home or anyplace with her family. Like a kid in a candy store, she wriggled with excitement from the back of the line six people deep.

More than anything else the bakery carried, she loved their cupcakes. Her favorite, the red velvet with cream cheese frosting, she could literally eat every single day and not get tired of them.

"You're ridiculous," Devyn said, laughing. "But I'm glad you could spare me a little bit of your Saturday morning so we could celebrate you winning the freakin' Sylvia Sykes Architectural Prize." She said the name of the award in a tone of awe and admiration that made Aisha blush and smile even wider.

It was kind of a big deal, wasn't it? Aisha thought with pride. But she kept her cool.

"Oh my God, you know I won the thing months ago and celebrated maybe a little too much back then." Well, maybe it hadn't been *too* much. Just enough fun with plenty of drinks, her proud family and a guy she'd been seeing at the time. Drinks, the people she loved around her and a little nookie at the end of the night. Kind of perfect, actually.

"Well, I was so caught up in my own craziness that I didn't congratulate you properly," Devyn said with an apologetic bump of Aisha's hip.

"Okay, none of that talk." She leaned in and smoothed the delicate skin on her sister's brow. "We're in the presence of cupcakes."

"Of course!" Devyn gave a little laugh and her pretty eyes sparkled. "I don't want to blaspheme."

Aisha slung an arm around her sister's waist and squeezed her tight. It was so good to see Devyn laughing and enjoying life again. She'd been going through a lot with her former boss at the art gallery where she used to work. Now she was free of that controlling witch and, in a few weeks, would open her own gallery. This was a dream she'd had since forever. It didn't hurt that Devyn also had a brand-new husband warming her cockles every night.

Her sister wore her happiness well. Always a fashionable dresser, Devyn now exuded confidence and cutting-edge style in everything she wore. Today's iron-gray dress with slashes of red at the waist and shoulders was no different. The purse she carried, probably a gift from her yummy hubby, was an art piece in itself. It looked like the color wheel done in leather and was big enough to brush her hip from its elegant drape over her arm.

Dev looked amazing. She looked content.

"Seriously though, thanks for bringing me here," Aisha said. "Obviously you know this place is my favorite."

Devyn laughed again. "Obviously."

Aisha and their mother loved absolutely everything about Baked Good. From its owner, Aspen, a girl barely twenty-five who was making her own way in the world despite a million challenges, to its location near a ton of other stores to visit on a Saturday afternoon, including a yoga studio, an early morning farmers market and a little pet shop that hosted animal adoptions a few times a month.

Aisha loved the neighborhood where she lived with her family and couldn't imagine residing anywhere else.

Aisha and Devyn moved up further in the line. Devyn patted her purse and gestured to the bakery case full of drool-worthy pastries. "Order whatever you want, sister dear. My treat."

"Ooh, big spender!"

When it was finally their turn at the counter, Aisha picked two red velvet cupcakes and a glass of sparkling water while Devyn got herself a savory scone and a cup of coffee. Aisha eyed the coffee the woman behind the bar poured for Devyn with more than a little java lust.

But no, she didn't need any more caffeine for the day. It was barely ten o'clock and by the time Devyn had come by her house to pick her up less than half an hour ago, she'd already had two cups.

Just as Devyn finished paying, a bistro table by the window in the back of the café opened up. They quickly took it before anyone else could.

At the table, they arranged the plates so they could share their treats.

Aisha slowly unwrapped her cupcake and sank her teeth into the corner, getting an explosion of flavor from both frosting and cake on her tongue.

"God, this is so, so good." She moaned around the dessert with closed eyes.

"You know people are staring at you, right?" Devyn sipped her coffee.

"I don't care." She licked away the bit of frosting she could feel at the corner of her mouth and made another pleased sound. "This cupcake makes all the worries of the world float away."

"As if you have any worries right now." Devyn smiled over the rim of her mug.

Once upon a time that comment would have been tinged with envy, but now, swimming in her own happiness after years of thinking she'd made nothing but wrong moves, her sister looked as happy as Aisha felt. Although Devyn would probably feel even better with a cupcake in her hand, she thought.

"I do have a few worries," Aisha said once she finished chewing the delicious bite.

She thought of her bosses at Wainwright and Tully, two old men with outdated ideas about women in the workplace despite having hired her and two other women. Even though she'd been over the moon with happiness when she'd first got hired by one of the best architectural firms in the country, now her feet were firmly on the ground. After five years of having her plans get passed over time and time again in favor of those belonging to men—and white men at that—she realized that her dream job had turned into a nightmare. It was time for her to wake up.

Although Devyn already knew all about that, Aisha reminded her.

Her sister held the coffee mug in both hands, elbows on the table. The steam from the coffee rose up, hot and fragrant, between them. "The Sykes Prize is a game changer. With that on your résumé, you can tell those backward-thinking guys stuck in their high castle to kiss your behind."

"That's not very PC of you, sister," Aisha said, but she giggled at the image of Albert Tully at his desk, wrinkled mouth all puckered up and ready to smooch her rear end as she slammed her resignation letter down on his desk.

"What they've been doing to you isn't very PC." Anger snapped briefly in Dev's eyes. "They should be sued for the number of times they passed you over when your project was obviously better."

"It's fine," Aisha said, though it wasn't. "Like you

said, getting the Sykes Prize has already changed some things for me. I haven't even put out any résumés yet and a firm from London has already reached out to me." She'd been shocked when she'd opened the email, although, in the end, not too impressed with that they were offering.

"That's fantastic! Are you going to take it?" Devyn took another sip of her coffee, obviously enjoying her drink the way Aisha enjoyed her cupcake. It was just cruel of her sister to drink that in front of her when she knew Aisha was cutting back on her caffeine intake.

"Maybe." She eyed her sister's quickly emptying mug. "Listen, I'm going to grab a cup of coffee before I snatch yours and gobble it down." She stood and grabbed her purse.

With a flash of her laughing smile, Devyn shoved a ten-dollar bill in her hand. "No need for that. Take the cash. I told you everything is my treat today."

If she thought her sister would let her get away with it, Aisha would push the money back in Devyn's hand. Even with the foolishness at work, she still made more money than what Dev took home every month.

She took Devyn's ten. "Fine, I'll be right back."

As she headed toward the front counter, the bell over the door chimed. She got in line behind two other people just as someone else stepped there. Aisha looked up and nearly choked on her next breath.

Wow.

The man who walked up to the line was, in a word, scrumptious. Much taller than her five feet ten, he stepped close with a sexy walk and straight back, frowning down at his phone before shoving the device into the pocket of his gray workout pants. Despite the frown, his deeply set eyes had laugh lines around them and the corners of his defined mouth were gently creased. Like icing on a cake she wanted to devour with both hands, a glinting silver frosted the temples of his neatly trimmed back hair.

He was basically every daddy fantasy Aisha never knew she had come to life.

Like a greedy kid facing a second helping of cake, she licked her lips. God, to have a taste of that…

With his height, people probably asked him if he played basketball—if basketball players walked around with bagged yoga mats slung over a wide shoulder and wore tank tops advertising the Bilbao Guggenheim Museum. She idly noticed that he wore the same black Nike high-tops her brother had. And, thankfully, no wedding ring.

Wow, Aisha thought again, her throat drying up.

"Are you all right?" Hot Yoga Daddy asked in a deep and luscious voice, directly meeting her eyes.

She had to swallow a couple of times to stop herself from stammering like a complete idiot. "Um…yeah. Just shook by all your sexy." *Brilliant, Aisha. He probably thinks you were dropped on your head as a child.* Aisha cleared her throat and stuck out her hand. "Hi, I'm Aisha."

A smile slipped into the creases around his mouth and eyes. "And you're forward."

The line moved up a little as the person in front ordered and stepped aside to wait.

"If you don't ask for what you want in this life, you never get it," she said, smiling back into his eyes. There was something in his face that reminded her of gargoyle statues perched atop Notre-Dame. His features were too strong to be called handsome, but the strength in them was also what made her want to grab on to his wide shoulders and never let go.

Down, girl.

"You realize you're young enough to be my kid?" He arched an eyebrow in her direction.

"Only if you started procreating in middle school," she said.

He huffed a laugh. "Now that's a disturbing thought."

"Exactly. Which is why you should stop saying that to girls trying to get your number."

"Is that what you're trying to do?"

Giving up any lingering subtlety, she gave his toned arms a long and appreciative look. "Absolutely."

"What can I get for you?"

Aisha turned around to face the woman at the counter. Damn, she wasn't ready to let this conversation go. "A large coffee, please, with a shot of French vanilla and room for cream."

When the woman moved away to make her coffee, Aisha turned back to Hot Yoga Daddy with a flirtatious smile.

"You're very, very sweet," he said with a regretful shake of his head, still smiling down at her. "But a little too tender for me."

"That'll be four dollars even." The woman came back with the coffee, looking with interest between Aisha and the man she wanted to be the father of her children.

Hot Yoga Daddy slid a five across the counter before Aisha could move. "Let me get your coffee instead of that number you want."

So not an equal trade.

Chuckling, the woman snatched up his money and put the change in the tip jar at his nod in that direction.

Swallowing her disappointment, Aisha picked up her coffee and slowly stepped back so the man could get to the business of ordering whatever he'd come for. "A pity you're not up to the challenge," she said once he'd placed his order for half a dozen assorted cupcakes and a large hot chocolate with cayenne pepper and whipped cream.

His eyes widened at the dare in her voice and his smile grew, making the crinkles at the corners of his eyes sexier than they had any right to be. Normally she wasn't into older men. Too many control issues. Too much baggage. But his incongruities intrigued her.

Yoga mat. Cupcakes. Muscular arms. A sense of humor. All that put together was practically her catnip.

"Maybe another lifetime," he said, toasting her with his hot chocolate as he headed out the door.

Aisha shamelessly watched his muscular butt shift and flex under the gray sweatpants as he walked away. "Damn, he's fine."

"You can say that again," the woman behind the counter agreed with a low chuckle. "Good for you for trying, though."

Tried but failed. It wasn't every day Aisha got told no. But into every life a little rain must fall. It really was too bad that it had to be this time.

Aisha sipped her coffee and watched through the bakery's glass door as the man strolled across the full parking lot. A silver Acura was parked nearby. He reached into his pocket for a set of keys, but instead of opening the Acura as she'd expected, he unlocked the antique, apple-green Ford truck parked next to it.

Wow. Nothing about him was what she expected. Another jolt of disappointment settled in her belly as she watched him drive away and out of her life.

"Aisha." Her sister's voice came from just behind her, warm and teasing. "What kind of trouble are you starting now?"

Chapter 2

If Aisha killed Oliver Jeffries, she probably wouldn't get away with it.

Muttering under her breath, she slammed her front door shut and threw her keys toward the ceramic bowl on the bookshelf. She missed. With a discordant clang, the keys clipped the bowl, skidded over the polished mahogany shelf and fell on the floor. Her black cat, Eloise, who'd been napping on the couch, gave a frightened yowl and took off like a shot.

Great. Just like the rest of her day was going.

That bastard Tully.

Her boss damn well knew Jeffries had stolen elements of her design. Days ago, she'd showed Tully her plan for the bank building in downtown Valerian, the town where her parents had been born and lived before moving down to Atlanta.

Aisha's hand clenched around the stack of envelopes and flyers she'd just picked up from the mailbox.

The project had been a special one to her. Thoughts of making her mother really proud of her for designing a bank that would sit proudly in downtown Valerian with her name on the plans had been ringing in her mind as she'd lovingly and carefully designed the two-story, mid-19th-century red-brick building. The design had fit the architecture of the historic downtown but had all the necessary modern conveniences on the interior.

Before the final meeting with Tully, she'd slipped out to get a quick cup of coffee that had turned into a mini-counseling session in the dining room—God forbid they call it a "break room"—and when she got back to her office, she'd been just in time to see Oliver Jeffries slipping out the door. Like a naive fool, she'd left her plans for the bank spread out on her drafting table.

Two days after her meeting with both Albert Tully and Wallace Wainwright, Jeffries had his. Magically, his design not only had the same type and shape facade, but even the enclosed courtyard with benches and green space for its employees to use.

Screw all of those guys. Every single one.

Snarling at the empty air, she dropped her purse and the mail on her sofa. At two o'clock on a Thursday afternoon, her house was quiet just as she normally liked it. But at home wasn't where she was supposed to be.

Her shoes tumbled to the hardwood floor when she kicked them off.

Aisha loved her work. Creating incredible, or even just useful, structures conceived in the palace of her mind was what she'd always dreamed of doing as a kid. And now the stupid idiots at Wainwright and Tully were turning her dream against her.

Like she always did when she was feeling upset, she grabbed the phone to call her sister and headed for the kitchen. She needed some coffee right now. When Dev answered, she jumped right in.

"They did it again." Her voice was rough from holding back a scream. "They gave another man at the firm a project that was supposed to be mine."

"What…? Damn. Are you sure?" Before Aisha could reply, Dev said something to someone else, the muffled words a sign she'd covered the phone. Then she heard the sound of high heels on a hardwood floor and a door closing.

It sounded like Dev was at the site of her new gallery. Devyn Clark Galleries wasn't officially open yet, still in the throes of putting the finishing touches in place.

"Crap. I'm sorry," Aisha apologized. "You're at work. Where I should be. We can talk later." Ugh, she was a mess.

"Don't be ridiculous. I'm in my office now. What happened?"

In the kitchen and fiddling with the fancy new coffeemaker her brother got her for her last birthday, she told Dev the entire story.

Her sister sounded shocked. "They can't do that, can they? Legally, I mean."

With a fresh cup of coffee in her favorite mug, Aisha wandered to the window looking over her landscaped backyard. Although she was too young to remember living in Valerian, she often imagined what her days would have been like there. Of all the things she'd seen during the family visits over the years, she loved the big trees with swings hanging from them the most.

So she'd recreated a little bit of that in her own back-yard. The tree wasn't massive like the ones she'd played under in Valerian, but her large magnolia was strong enough to hold a swing on one of its big branches and a small sitting hammock on another.

Being out there would probably do her a world of good now. She needed that calm.

"I'm not sure about the legality, honestly," she said. "But I do know it's not fair. If anyone looks closely at the firm's designs for the last however many years, they'll see that most, if not all, of the buildings we designed were done so by the male architects. When I got to the firm, I thought I'd show them what good things a fresh perspective could bring, but they're not passing over my designs for the same tired structures the good old boys are coming up with, they're actually stealing my sh—" She bit off the curse and slammed her hand on the dark granite of her kitchen counter.

The sting was oddly satisfying.

Aisha burned from the injustice of what her bosses had done, but was even angrier at herself for not con-fronting Jeffries when she'd seen him scurrying out of her office that day.

"Don't break your hand over there, Aisha." Her sis-ter made a tsking sound. "Just make your moves. Send out those updated résumés you've been holding on to. Or, hell, take the job in London. It's better than having those guys take advantage of you over and over again."

"Yeah…" A sigh blew past her lips. "I need to do something instead of holding out hope they'll change.

At least the Sykes Prize is something I can hold on to in the meantime."

"Exactly. You have a lot of good things going on right now. Just go out there and make them even better. One thing I'm so glad about is that you're not like me. You don't take anything lying down, and I'm so proud of that. Any challenges that come your way are just obstacles for you to overcome. You never see them as roadblocks." Aisha could hear the smile in her sister's voice. "That's why I know you'll blow these guys out of the water and show them what a mistake they made treating you like this."

A smile touched Aisha's lips. Sometimes it seemed that her sister—hell, her whole family—had more faith in her than she did. But it felt good to know they supported her so completely and trusted in her strength to do what she needed to be happy.

The sound of someone knocking on a door came through the phone.

"Hold on," Dev said. "Someone's—"

"No, no! Go back to work. I know you're busy. We can talk later when you're free." She had to stop being so selfish. Her sister had the gallery she was getting ready to open. She didn't need Aisha talking her ear off in the middle of the afternoon. "Love you, Dev. We'll talk soon."

"Okay…if you're sure."

"Hang up the phone and get back to work. Bye!" Aisha disconnected the call and dropped the cell in her dress pocket.

Coffee in hand, she went back into the living room and sank into her comfy leather couch. She sighed, curving her hands around the warm mug. Dev was right. She needed to make some moves. London wasn't a real option since that would mean living too far from her family, but she was open to nearly anything else.

She merely had to find a new firm she wanted and simply make them want her back. With the latest addition of the Sykes Prize to her résumé, that shouldn't be too hard. Who wouldn't want an architect who graduated top of her class, interned for one of the best firms in the United States and won the Sykes Prize the first time she entered?

No one, that's who.

She grinned into her cup and took another yummy sip.

Okay, implosion averted.

Now that her head wasn't about to explode over her situation at work, she could focus on other things. Like getting her house back in order.

Ugh. What do you live in, a pigsty?

She had to laugh at herself. Her entire house was museum neat, an easy modern design centered around her gorgeous caramel leather couch and accent walls of various shades of green. Because the house was so neat, whenever one thing was out of place, everything seemed chaotic. Like the jumble of mail she'd grabbed from the mailbox and not put in its right place.

But she might as well open it all.

Catalogs. Coupons from stores in the neighborhood. A postcard from one of her friends who'd just left for a year in Japan.

What's this?

An envelope stood out from the rest of them. Crisp and white with a blue logo in the upper left-hand corner. The return address was for Sykes Global Corporation in midtown.

She'd already been to the glam party where she'd accepted the trophy for the prize then danced the night away with a bunch of executives and banker types she'd probably never see again. The cash prize was in her bank account, untouched, part of her "Screw-It Money" in case Wainwright and Tully tried her patience enough to make her quit before finding another job.

She opened the envelope and pulled out the single sheet of paper inside.

Dear Ms. Clark,
It is with regret that we inform you that the Sylvia Sykes Architectural Prize you previously won has been revoked. The planned use for the building and the stated design requirements were proposed in error. This revocation is through no fault of your own. As a token of our regret, you may keep the funds that were awarded with the prize.
Office of Roman Sykes, CEO
Sykes Global Corporation

Aisha felt sick. She blinked at the letter clenched between her trembling fists. Then she read it again as her stomach roiled and her face flushed with angry heat.
No. They can't do this.
She'd worked too hard for the prize for them to just take it away. The days she'd spent researching Sylvia Sykes, the late wife of the company's CEO, to find out exactly what kind of building would do the woman's life justice. She'd even researched the CEO himself to find out what kind of design a man like him would want.

Then Aisha had used hours and hours of her own time after work—months of hours—to perfect the design she'd eventually entered into the competition. Two male colleagues from Wainwright and Tully had also entered the competition and it had given her sweet validation when she'd beaten them out. Winning the award had been proof that she wasn't just paranoid in suspecting her bosses of passing over her designs for reasons other than the quality of her work.

Aisha shot to her feet, still clutching the letter. Her knees gave out, no doubt from shock, and she slammed into the coffee table.

"Oh!" She gasped from the pain a second before the nearly full cup of coffee tilted and fell over with a crash. Hot liquid rushed over the coffee table, soaking the mail she'd already sorted through then dripping to the rug.

"Dammit!"

But she wasn't seeing the spilled coffee. She didn't see hot brown liquid soaking into the white envelopes on her antique table. No. She was seeing all the plans she'd made, all the options she had after leaving the firm curl up at the edges, wither and die.

Then her sister's words washed over.

You don't take anything lying down... Any challenges that come your way are just obstacles for you to overcome.

She crumpled the letter in her fist.

Her sister was right. This letter threatened to crush her career and the future she saw for herself, but she wouldn't let it. Like Dev said, she wasn't going to take this lying down. She had a new obstacle to overcome and she'd be damned if it ended up trapping her at Wainwright and Tully with thieves like Oliver Jeffries and bosses who consistently undermined her work and didn't support her.

With trembling hands, she smoothed out the letter

then, after folding it carefully into a neat square, tucked it into her purse.

There was only one thing she could do now.

Her pulse thudded fast and hard in her neck. Her heart raced as she shoved her feet back into her shoes, grabbed her purse and flew out the door, locking it quickly behind her.

If this ass of a CEO thought she'd accept him wrenching the Sykes Prize out of her hand without a fight, she had some bad news for him.

Chapter 3

"Thanks very much, Eileen."

"You're welcome, Mr. Sykes."

While the woman from the building's restaurant walked out with the remnants of his sushi lunch and closed the door behind her, Roman turned to the wide window of his new office and stared out at the Atlanta skyline.

The city was glittering and beautiful spread out before him. Youthful and compelling under the steady caress of the late afternoon sun.

Very much like the woman he'd met at the Grant Park bakery this past Saturday. Days after the encounter, Roman still couldn't get her out of his mind. Yes, he'd dismissed her as being too young at the time, but something inside him had woken up as she'd flirted with him. He hadn't wanted to leave her in that bakery and that was what had made him rush out of there like his ass was on fire.

He should be thinking about his father dead in the grave, not this *girl*. But until his father dropped the responsibility of Sykes Global squarely on his shoulders, Roman had had time enough to pursue women, although he'd never before had such a spark with one so young.

Damn, she'd been gorgeous. Not that simple-minded prettiness of college girls at the bars his brother sometimes dragged him to. No, she was…interesting.

The challenge in her eyes had ignited something inside him. Never before had a woman approached him so aggressively. But, to be fair, she wasn't even a woman, just a girl who looked too young to even date his little brother, Lance.

Roman blew out a chagrined breath and scratched the corner of an eyebrow. He had to stop thinking about her.

He shook his head and turned from the window back to his desk. The same desk where his father had spent the last thirty-plus years of his life, the desk where he'd died. Now, a month in his grave, his father was shackling Roman to the desk, too, all but ensuring he had the same lonely and pathetic life. And death.

A low growl left his throat. His hands trembled and heated from the sudden desire to break something. He wanted to howl his frustration at the ceiling. But he kept his hands loose at his sides, his mouth shut, and breathed long and deep, summoning ujjayi breath to guide him through the rage rattling his bones and unsettling his foundation.

He'd known what he was getting into before sitting behind this desk. He'd known all too well.

That was why, over the weekend before his first day

of work, he'd spent the last time he would have for himself doing the things he'd wanted. On Friday evening, he drove up to Lake Lanier with Merrine, his best friend and the one who knew him best now that his mother was dead.

He and Merrine had spent the night at one of those weird "glamping" campsites she loved. They watched the stars, drank kombucha and talked about what they wanted for their lives. They talked about everything.

Then on Saturday morning, he'd taken a session at the yoga studio in Grant Park he'd always meant to try but had never made it to before. He bought Merrine some cupcakes and then, standing in the bakery that smelled like all the combined pleasures of the world, he'd faced what had felt like the greatest temptation of his life.

Although—

Enough, he told himself. He had to get back to work.

Roman settled behind his desk and, on his laptop, pulled up the contracts he'd been looking over before Eileen had knocked at his office door with lunch. Just then, the digital to-do list on his phone popped up with a notification. He dismissed it with a quick tap.

That task was already finished, completed before his first hour in the office. There was still a massive amount of things on his plate for the day, near the end of his first week as CEO of his father's company. He didn't completely suck at the job, though. The list had been much bigger when he'd started on Monday.

The work hadn't been difficult. In fact, although he largely left the day-to-day running of things to people he trusted and paid well, even more so now that he had taken on responsibility of Sykes Global full time, it wasn't much different from what he did running his own business, a chain of yoga and Pilates studios around the United States as well as the yoga annual retreat. He did know a little bit of what he was doing.

In the end, knocking things off the Sykes Global to-do list had been energizing, enervating, intoxicating in a way he hadn't expected. And that scared him.

If that was how his father felt running the multibillion-dollar construction corporation he'd founded, no wonder the man had been practically chained to his desk twenty-four hours a day. Being in control of this powerful beast was a high like no other Roman had ever experienced.

He cursed.

"Carolyn." He opened a line to his assistant through the speakerphone. "The Briggs contract looks sound but I want to talk to both brothers before we finalize anything."

"Your father usually lets his lawyer handle that," Carolyn said with disapproval in her voice.

She'd been doing the same thing all week and four days of her nonsense didn't make him take any more kindly to it. Roman firmed his voice. "Make the appointment with the Briggs brothers, Carolyn. Please. You have my calendar."

A pause. "Very well, Mr. Sykes."

"Thank you." Jaw working in annoyance, he ended the call.

He wasn't the only one who had to accept that his father was dead and there was a new CEO in charge. Even if it was temporary. Roman only planned on being behind the CEO's desk for as long as it took to transition his brother, Lance, to the job. Otherwise he'd hire a new assistant and tell Carolyn to take her objections to Roman and his methods far away from Sykes Global.

But just for the few weeks or months of his time behind the big desk, it wasn't worth the trouble, especially if his brother would only turn around and hire his own assistant.

"I want to see him right now!"

A commotion just outside his office door jerked his attention away from his thoughts. Suddenly his office door burst open and a woman blew in, a whirlwind in a green dress. Behind her, Carolyn sat at her desk, watching with a cool expression. It didn't look like she'd done much to stop the woman from barging into his office.

Roman's jaw clenched. He stood. "Can I help you, miss?"

The woman drew closer to his desk, giving Roman his first good look at her. He took a rough breath, realizing several things at once. The woman who stood aggressively in his office looked barely out of college. Her hair, thick and natural and blooming around her face, was like the petals of a dark flower. He also realized he'd seen this woman before.

She stumbled to a halt in front of his desk, her eyes wide. "You!" Before Roman could respond to that non-question, she yanked a piece of paper from her purse and slammed it down on his desk with the sound of a shot. He noticed her five slender fingers and six tiny gold rings. "I don't care how hot you are, you can't do this to me."

The door behind her gaped wide open and his assistant didn't seem in any hurry to close it or to usher the woman from his office.

"What exactly is going on here?" Because his legs couldn't exactly support him anymore, Roman sat behind his desk.

It was her. The woman—the girl—from the coffee shop. The why and how of it spun in his head for a few seconds before he could focus on what she was talking about.

"I won the Sykes Prize. You know, to design the building the CEO wanted." Hands on her hips, she stared him down, then her eyes darted between the plaque on the desk with Roman's name and the mysterious letter she'd slammed down. "And I've seen him before. You're not him. You're so not him."

He plucked up the letter and quickly read it. His mouth tightened. Ah, yes.

How could he forget?

Every three years the company—through the Sylvia Sykes Foundation—sponsored a prize open to architects worldwide. In the beginning it had been a ploy of his father's to attract and potentially employ some of the best architects with vision and promise to help visually spread the Sykes Global Corporation's footprint all over the world. This year had been special because it was a building his father had planned to put up right here in Atlanta and in so-called honor of his late wife.

By the time this "honor" occurred to him, she'd already been dead a year.

Emotionally unable to sprinkle his wife's ashes out in the woods like Sylvia Sykes had requested, his father had kept the ashes in a silver urn in his bedroom. Under lock and key.

Roman had asked his father again and again to let his mother's ashes go, but his father wouldn't listen. Even though Langston Sykes hadn't loved his wife enough in life to spend time with her the way she'd always asked and deserved, he'd been selfish in her death. His possession of Sylvia's ashes wasn't something he allowed anyone to question.

And finally, *finally*, when his father had decided to let his mother's ashes go, the bastard had commissioned a damn skyscraper of a library in midtown with a statue of Sylvia Sykes on its roof, her ashes enshrined in the statue's belly. It was obscene.

It was like seeing his mother still trapped by Langston Sykes's idea of what a wife should be.

Roman had been in India when he'd first heard of his father's plan. And had vehemently opposed it.

How dare he build this *mausoleum* for his mother who'd only wanted to live in the world and drink it all up? She would have hated for her ashes to be entombed in another one of his father's monuments to his wealth. The building he'd planned was not about her. Nothing his father had ever done was done with his mother in mind. She died knowing that, and back then Roman thought he'd had to live with it. His father was the CEO and what he decided was law.

But not anymore.

A flare of renewed rage at his father heated his spine, but he tamped it down and released yet another calming breath. At this rate, he'd be hyperventilating before the day was through. He leaned back in the too comfortable leather chair and rested his linked fingers on the desk. The woman who stood above him, Aisha Clark, according to the letter he'd just read, stood with her full mouth pulled tight and her hands shoved in the pockets of her dress. Her dark eyes snapped with anger.

She was just as tempting as he remembered. But he couldn't afford that kind of temptation.

"My father is dead. He was the CEO you met."

"Oh! I'm—I'm sorry to hear that." She drew back, her teeth pressing into her lower lip, the aggression in her stance turning to contrition. "I didn't know." Her lashes fell low to brush her cheeks and she blinked, looking away from him. "I should have known, though. Damn."

Roman dismissed her self-flagellation. "It's just a fact. I'm not telling you to get your sympathy or make you kick yourself. His death was…expected." A man couldn't work himself to death and arrive at that death with anyone being surprised. "He's been mourned and we're moving on."

Two heart attacks, consistently high blood pressure and the refusal to change his lifestyle gave the family enough warning that Langston Sykes wouldn't live forever. He'd held on longer than anyone thought, though, by all appearances as strong as a bull until he'd fallen over at his desk late one night.

The announcement of his father's death had been handled with discretion, but because of the size of the company, it had flared briefly in the news before being quietly snuffed out by the company's PR team. Sykes Global was privately held, with most of its board members being family or close friends of his father's who'd invested in the company early on and stayed on to reap the benefits of its success. There had been some panic with his father's passing, till Roman quelled it.

Everyone knew Roman wasn't interested in the business and Lance, though he very much wanted to run the company, was the younger son. Things had to pass through Roman's hands first.

"Wow. Okay, then." Aisha shifted her stance to look down at him again. "I guess you're not that broken up about it. Especially since you're trying to erase one of his big decisions now that he's no longer behind that desk. How very Trump of you."

Roman felt his eyebrows jerk up. "This has nothing to do with trying to erase anything about my father. The letter states it very clearly. The building my father intended is nothing my mother would have wanted built to honor her. I apologize again for the error and that my father's judgment is negatively impacting you."

Even just talking about the building made his stomach muscles tighten.

"No. This is *your* judgment impacting me. You're the one who's done this. You can change it if you want to."

"I've already made up my mind, Ms. Sykes. Again, I apologize, but nothing you say will change my stance." He hadn't yet made an official announcement canceling the year's prize along with the construction of the building itself, but it was on his to-do list.

"Your apology is not worth the air you took to say it." She blinked hard and jerked her gaze toward the windows behind him. For a horrific moment, Roman thought she would cry, but Aisha drew herself up to her full height on already high heels and visibly clenched her teeth. "You may be doing this just to spite your old man, but you're also screwing over someone else. Me. It's not fair what you're doing. I—I worked hard on that design and I was the top choice. I won't let you erase my career the way you're obviously intent on erasing your father."

Every word she spoke was like a punch to his gut.

"Ms. Clark, this decision is not about you, so please don't take it personally."

Those words came easily to his mouth but Roman couldn't stop the pulse of sympathy, of regret, that threatened to turn his lunch against him. Sorry as he was, he wouldn't change his mind. He wouldn't allow his father to trap his mother in death the way he had in life.

"How can I do anything but take this personally, Mr. CEO?" Her words were scornful.

Distantly, Roman heard the outer office door open and a low voice talking to his assistant. Aisha looked over her shoulder through the open door and seemed to gather herself. Her tongue wiped over her lower lip and Roman's stomach dipped as he stared, unable to look away. She grabbed the letter on his desk, neatly folded it and put it back in her purse. She looked at him one last time before sailing out of his office, her heels stabbing the floors with each step.

"Whoa!" His brother Lance, dressed in khakis and an untucked dress shirt the color of a clear sky, quickly moved to the side to avoid clipping Aisha's shoulder with his.

"Excuse me!" Aisha kept going until she was past Roman's useless assistant and yanking open the outer door. The rapid sounds of her high heels were loud accusations aimed firmly at Roman's conscience.

"The first week and already you have drama." Chuckling, Lance closed the office door. He jerked a thumb behind him. "What's up with her?"

Roman drew in a breath of badly needed air. "Nothing you need to concern yourself with. Have a seat. I have a few things to go over with you."

Very deliberately, he didn't think about Aisha and the deep ache she'd left in his conscience. And in other places.

Chapter 4

"Thanks for taking the time to see me, Roman." Avery Betts, a partner in the law firm that had been handling the Sykes's family business for decades, waved Roman to the thick leather sofa in his office.

"I could hardly say no," Roman replied, undoing the single button of his suit jacket and taking a seat. "However, your message did come at the perfect time. There's something I want to discuss with you, as well."

"Good." Avery got up from behind his desk and took a seat in the wingback chair adjacent to the sofa. His reddish hair and mustache along with his pale brown eyes captured bits of the late afternoon sun.

If Roman let his imagination get away from him, he would think the large office smelled like generational wealth and rich old men wagging their fingers from the grave. Like his father was about to do once Roman told Avery what he wanted.

"Can I get you anything?" Avery asked. "Coffee? Mineral water? Whiskey?"

Roman almost laughed. This was the kind of life he was living now. Being offered a stiff drink before five o'clock on a Friday afternoon.

"Room temperature bottled water, if you have it," he said.

A woman appeared a few seconds later with a bottle of Voss and a glass on a small tray. She poured the water for him then slipped from the office, gently closing the door behind her.

A little creepy, but okay.

He took a sip from the glass then, after putting aside the water on the nearby table, sat back in the sofa. The leather was warm and firm under him.

"Why don't you tell me what's on your mind first, Roman?" Avery sat ramrod-straight with a manila folder and blank legal notepad balanced on top of a crossed knee.

The lawyer was probably at least five years younger than Roman's thirty-seven years but carried himself like an octogenarian. It wasn't as though he was physically weak but instead seemed like a man who'd seen and heard too much and now just wanted to cut through the bull. Ever since their first meeting ten years ago, he'd always been up-front with Roman and now Roman wanted to return the courtesy.

"I don't want this thing," Roman said baldly. "And I think you know that."

He appreciated that Avery didn't pretend to not know what Roman was talking about.

"You're the one your father wanted at the helm of Sykes Global, Roman."

"But that's not what I want."

"All right, then what exactly is it that you do want?" Avery asked.

Roman barely stopped himself from blowing out a sigh of frustration. The past week behind his father's big desk had been full of more responsibility than he'd ever known, and also more success than he'd previously challenged himself to attain. It was addictive. Potent.

After having a taste of what his father had long threatened him with, he only wanted more. Which was another reason why he had to step away from the feast and leave the CEO position behind.

"Lance should have the company," Roman said. "That's why I'm here. I want you to draw up the papers to transfer the CEO position to him." It was the right thing to do. For everyone.

"Okay. I can do that for you, but let me be transparent with you first." Avery's narrow features became pinched. "There are conditions to what you're asking."

Of course there were. "Tell me."

Once his father died, there had been a rush to make sure Sykes Global didn't suffer a single financial loss during the transfer of power. And as much as Roman bucked against taking over the company, his father had groomed him well enough all his life that it had been a relatively seamless transition.

Avery rested his hand flat on top of the legal pad and folder on his knee, his narrow face becoming even sterner, something Roman never thought was possible. "If you give up the CEO position now, your brother will get nothing."

Roman jerked in surprise. "Excuse me? He's the one I'll be passing on the position to."

"Listen, Roman." Avery paused as if searching for the right words to explain his remark. "Your father had some rather firm stipulations in his will regarding the business."

The will had been read a few days before and held few surprises. Roman received half his father's estate along with control of the company. Lance had been given the other half of the estate along with the family house he currently lived in, which had been in the Sykes family for four generations. Roman had never cared for his father's ostentatious style, nor had he cared to live so close to the man himself. Once he'd been able to be on his own, he'd bought a simple four-bedroom bungalow in Virginia–Highland.

"What stipulations?"

Wordlessly, Avery passed Roman the manila folder. Inside were three typed legal pages, all in Langston Sykes's distinctive voice. Each word Roman read stiffened his spine and threw gasoline on the anger that already raged in him against his father. The pages were signed and witnessed by both partners in the law firm.

"If you don't keep the CEO position of Sykes Global for at least a year, all of your brother's material wealth, including the home he lives in now, will go to charity." Avery summed up what Roman read, his voice coolly neutral. "It's a charity that your father clearly stipulated in the attached documents."

He made the unspoken clear. Roman couldn't create a nonprofit to be the beneficiary, a nonprofit that would also happen to be run by Lance.

With each word Avery spoke, Roman felt the noose around his neck getting tighter. "Does Lance know anything about this?" He finished reading, tucked the papers back in the folder and passed it back to the lawyer.

"No, he doesn't." Avery collected the folder and positioned it back on his raised knee, once again under the blank notepad. "Nothing will change if you tell him, so it's your decision whether or not to share that information."

Roman cursed. Ever since his brother could talk, he'd wanted to run the company. Between his affairs with models and minor actresses, he'd gone to business school and even had some future plans for the company he'd been keeping to himself, saying that Roman would find out when it was time. In Lance's mind, Sykes Global was already his.

Roman had been all set to make that a reality. Now, though... "An entire year, huh?" He'd read the words in the folder himself but still had to ask.

"At minimum," Avery said firmly.

Roman cursed again, grabbed the glass of water and finished it all in a few gulps. "Lance isn't going to like this."

The day before when Lance walked into the office, he'd come in like it already belonged to him. And why not since Roman had essentially promised that it would soon be?

"Lance's feelings weren't your father's main concern. He wanted the company to last past your generation, not die shortly after he does."

"What does that mean? My brother will take care of Sykes Global. He's been preparing for this job his entire life."

"Your father, and the other members of the board, didn't think he's had sufficient preparation." From Avery's tone, he felt the same. "In many ways, your brother is still a child eager to play with a new toy. That can't be the attitude of the new CEO."

It felt like they were talking about two separate people. Lance was ready and willing to take on all the responsibilities of being CEO to one of the largest, privately held construction corporations in the world. He had his business school degree. He was on the Sykes Global board of directors and was a major decision-maker at the Sylvia Sykes Foundation. Long ago, he'd even made the responsible decision to live in Atlanta instead of running off to more exciting parts of the world.

The look on Avery's face didn't invite any disagreement and Roman didn't feel like banging his head against a brick wall trying to convince the man of something he was already closed off to.

"All right," he said with a heavy sigh. "I'll commit to the year and I'll just…I don't know…corral Lance toward something else." Although his brother would fight him tooth and nail on that one. Lance was convinced he already knew everything about running Sykes Global and just needed to step into the role. "I don't want him to know his own father didn't trust him to run the company he's prepared his entire life for."

Avery was unfazed. "As I said, it's your decision whether or not to inform Lance."

"Okay, I suppose that's it then." Roman stood then remembered that Avery had his own reason for the meeting. "Apologies. What is it that you wanted to talk to me about?"

"You already brought it up on your own, actually. A convenient coincidence." Avery tapped his fingers against the still blank legal pad.

"My father's blackmail you mean?" Roman wasn't in the mood to be generous.

"If you want to call it that."

"That's what it is." Roman could feel himself getting worked up, the blood pumping faster in his body, rushing through him like a high and threatening tide. Taking a deep and quiet breath, he buttoned his jacket. "Thank you for your time, Avery. I'll see myself out."

"Very well." The lawyer made a noncommittal gesture. "If you need anything else regarding this or any other matter, please don't hesitate to contact me." He rose and left the empty notepad and folder on the chair, heading toward his desk, apparently trusting Roman to indeed see himself across the massive office and out the door. "My regards to your brother."

Roman grunted.

On the slow descent in the elevator, neither his temper nor his unease about what his father had done to Lance managed to simmer him down. He needed something else besides the deep, slow breaths that were definitely not doing him any good.

Less than fifteen minutes later he was walking into his favorite teahouse in the city. The place was a fusion of Asian cultures that had the tranquility of a bonsai garden, the culinary variety of a Thai food market and the faint scent of honeysuckle blossoms.

Just entering brought his shoulders down from where they'd been tensed up around his ears. His breathing automatically settled.

"Mr. Sykes." The hostess greeted him with a smile. "It's good to see you again."

"It's good to be seen, Kiyoshi. Do you have a table for me?" The teahouse was already full of the Friday after-work crowd, most of whom had probably left their offices early. Despite that, the large room still retained its air of temple-like quiet and tranquility.

"Always." She picked up a menu. "Please, follow me." She led him to the only remaining free table.

Unbuttoning his suit jacket, he sat at the low table beside the wide windows with a view onto the quiet street.

"Will you be having the usual?" Kiyoshi asked.

Roman opened his mouth to say yes then changed his mind. "Actually, room temperature water with lemon slices for now, please. Let me take a look at the menu and see if I can switch it up."

"A little change does a life good," she said, settling the menu in his hands. "I'll have your server come by with some water right away."

"Thank you."

She disappeared in a swish of skirts while Roman tried to pair his mood with one of the dishes on the menu. A steady presence at the window brought his head up and his eyes collided with a very familiar gaze. He swallowed heavily in an uncontrollable reaction. The dark eyes outside the window widened before narrowing with speculation and then disappeared.

What were the odds?

This neighborhood was far enough away from where he'd met the outspoken girl-woman before that seeing her now felt as odd as meeting a unicorn in space. Or anywhere for that matter.

Great. Now she had him thinking about things that didn't exist.

The menu claimed his attention again after far too long thinking about unique, magical creatures and what this girl might have in common with them when a slim shape slid into the chair across from him.

Aisha Clark's smile was more shark than pixie, but that didn't stop Roman from nearly swallowing his tongue at the sight of her.

"Good afternoon, Mr. CEO." She looked far too pleased to have caught him by surprise. "Funny running into you in a place like this."

Chapter 5

Aisha settled into the chair across the table from Roman Sykes and wanted to laugh at the look of shock that showed briefly on his face.

"Funny isn't quite the word I would use," he said with a frown.

She airily waved away his grumpiness. "What are we having tonight? All the food I passed by on my way in here looks good."

"Everything here is good," he said.

"Excellent! That should make our choices easy then."

Aisha slid her purse onto the small table for two and propped her chin in her palm. After that quick moment of naked surprise, Roman Sykes's granite face turned calm, his eyes level and cool. And even though his calm pricked her temper even more, part of her admired his steel in the face of her potential craziness.

After getting the letter canceling the Sykes Prize, she'd been livid with rage. That rage had carried her through their clash in his office and the many hours after that. A day later she was only just beginning to calm down and think of the next steps when, wandering the quiet in-town neighborhood after work, she'd seen him in the restaurant window.

Instantly all her calm had crumbled. With anger fueling her, she'd acted without thinking, storming into the quiet restaurant and plopping herself down at his table.

Truth be told, she was a little shocked by her own behavior, but she was committed now.

Ugh. Where was the waiter? Her dry mouth and lips begged for a glass of water to soothe them.

Clenching her shaking hands together in her lap, she arranged her face into a look of defiance and faced Roman Sykes head-on.

She'd never let him know the surprise she'd felt at seeing the Sykes heir at the teahouse in the part of Atlanta she'd always considered her own. She'd already revealed too much of how she'd felt at seeing Hot Yoga Daddy from Baked Good transform into the three-piece-suit-wearing CEO intent on destroying her dreams.

She still couldn't believe those two men were the same. A part of her had died inside when she'd seen Roman the CEO sitting behind that big desk, his appealing face and those warm laugh lines at the corner of his eyes all subdued in that massive office. But the man she'd seen also belonged there in that room of power and wealth. He just did not belong to her.

At the thought, she winced and looked around the crowded teahouse. Despite the people, it was so quiet.

Across from her, Roman Sykes heaved a sigh loud

enough for the neighboring table to hear it. "Ms. Clark, I don't think it's very produ—"

"Good evening, sir. Ma'am." A waiter in a dark shirt and pants, what Aisha assumed was the uniform of the place, smiled at her and Roman Sykes. He put a glass of water and a small saucer of sliced lemons on the table before Roman and then poured water with ice into the empty glass in front of Aisha. "What else can I get you to drink tonight?"

She immediately grabbed the water and drank half of it in one go.

Sykes raised an eyebrow at Aisha and put his menu on the table. The challenge was obvious in his gaze. Did he think she would back down?

"What are you having, darling?" She drawled out the last word. "By the time you tell him what you want, I should be ready." Aisha grabbed up his discarded menu and made a show of looking at it, tracing each item on the list of small plates while Sykes glowered at her.

"Of course, miss." The waiter gave her a gentle smile then turned to Sykes. "Sir, do you know what you'd like?"

Sykes's look said he'd like for Aisha to get out of there and allow him to eat his dinner in peace, but that wasn't about to happen.

"Actually," she said, warming up to her gate-crasher role, "I'd love some tea. Is there something you can recommend?" The question was for the waiter but, surprisingly, it was Sykes who answered.

"A pot of the TranquiliTea would be a good place for us to start, actually," he said, his gaze flickering briefly to Aisha. "Lightly sweetened."

"Certainly, sir. And that's okay with you, ma'am?"

"Who can resist TranquiliTea?" She gave the waiter

a playful smile and when he rushed away to put in their order, she wiped the smile off her face. "Is that what you're offering me tonight instead of the Sykes Prize that I put my soul into and won fair and square?"

Sykes braced his arms on the table, linking his fingers and resting them just below his mouth.

"What can I do for you, Ms. Clark?"

"You know damn well what you can do for me," she snapped.

"And I already told you, that's impossible. The decision has already been made." He looked completely implacable. Untouchable. So unlike the man at the bakery. But she wasn't just after a phone number tonight.

"Why have you done this?" Her hand turned into a fist on top of the table. "Why? Did I do something to you and don't know it? Is it because I asked for your phone number that afternoon?"

He winced and that single show of emotion made her glad.

"This has nothing to do with what happened between us on Saturday. I didn't know who you were then and I certainly would never punish someone for...going after what they want."

"Even if what they want is you?"

"Even then."

"So what's the issue? You're not out to get me because I want to see you naked. Then what is it?" She bit down on her lip to stop herself from screaming at him. But he must have caught something in her expression.

His mouth tightened. "Have you thought about meditating?" he asked her, looking so serious she wanted to crack his calm in two. "You're really worked up about this."

"Worked up?" She let out a breath of disbelief. "You'd be this passionate, too, if someone just made a decision that affected your entire career. The only reason you're sitting there calm as can be is because you're completely in control of yourself and all your millions. Someone didn't just pull the rug from under your life."

A strange look came over his face. He brushed his chin with the pad of a large thumb, his eyes slipping into the middle distance. Back and forth went that thumb. The anger that simmered in her blood changed into something else altogether.

Damn him. She squeezed her thighs together and prayed for strength. She only wanted to hate him. But that spark that had flared between them in the bakery now burned hotter than ever. She wanted to replace that brushing thumb with her own finger and then her lips. Her mouth was once again painfully dry and she was thirsty for a drink of Roman Sykes.

Okay, Aisha. Focus. This man is your enemy. Not any sort of dream lover, no matter how many times he's actually appeared in your dreams. Naked.

Finally, Sykes pursed his lips and brought himself back from whatever place he'd slipped off to. "Your entire career, really?" he asked.

"Yes, really. Why is that so hard for you to believe?"

"Actually, it's pretty easy for me to believe. It's just that—" He broke off to squeeze a lemon slice into his water and then take a drink.

"What, you think your problems define the scope of everyone else's?" Aisha asked scornfully. "Please don't tell me you're another one of those self-centered types."

He didn't seem like one of those, but as much as she wanted to get to know him, she didn't.

"One person's self-centeredness is another's self-care," he said with a raise of his eyebrow.

That damn eyebrow. Raising it at her was a sure sign he was saying something she didn't want to hear. What she wanted him to say was that he'd made a mistake and was giving her the prize after all. So far those words hadn't left his mouth.

Hell, she had to accept that they never would.

Just then the waiter came back with a tea service that he carefully placed in the middle of the table. Sykes had ordered it lightly sweetened, which didn't at all sound appealing, but she wasn't enough of an ass to tell him, now that the tea was in front of them, that she preferred hers without sugar. Once the waiter left with their dinner orders, Sykes poured tea into the small, Japanese-style teacups for them both. His fingers were broad and wide around the delicate blue porcelain. Very masculine, very strong.

Aisha swallowed and looked away. This was a complication she didn't need. She cleared her throat and put the tea to her lips.

Hmm. Not bad. The sweetness was light and added to the aroma of lavender and mint that rose from the small cup. It wasn't exactly what she'd call tranquility in a cup but it tasted just like what she needed. Aroma and flavor combined perfectly with each sip.

"Okay, Mr. CEO." The fine gold rings on her fingers winked in the light as she put down her teacup. "Since you're so set on telling me no, can you at least let me know the reason you don't want this building built?"

"It's personal." His low voice was deep, its sensual registers rippling over her senses despite her determination to treat him as the enemy.

"If it's so personal, why have you let it affect this business decision?" She gave him back a raised eyebrow. "Because, make no mistake, this decision you've made has impacted my business life in a very dangerous way."

"Aren't you being a little dramatic here?"

"Uh-uh. You don't get to minimize what's important in my life, Mr. CEO."

His abyss-dark eyes looked into hers. They were so intent that she wanted to look away but forced herself to face him unflinchingly.

"That's not my name, Ms. Clark."

"I know very well what your name is, Mr. Sykes." His name was on the prize she wanted—no, the prize she *needed*. Even now that name was on her résumé, waiting to be erased.

"That's not my name, either. It's Roman. The name my mother gave me."

Damn. Why did he have to mention his mother?

"Okay, Roman." Unable to help herself, she licked her lips, enjoying the intimate feel of his name in her mouth. "In that case, the name my friends and enemies call me is Aisha. Can you at least do me the courtesy of telling me why you're doing this?"

"Okay, Aisha," he parroted back at her.

His large hand picked up the teacup but he didn't drink. He shifted the cup to the other hand and then finally took a sip. The cup thudded gently against the table when he set it down.

"My mother is the reason," he finally said then frowned. "My father wanted to put her ashes somewhere in that monstrosity he approved. That's not something she would have ever wanted for herself."

Aisha bit her tongue. She wanted to bulldoze over him

when he called her building a "monstrosity" but decided this wasn't a point she wanted to argue. Not yet anyway.

"She only ever wanted to be free," he continued. "Having her ashes trapped inside a building, no matter how nice-looking, is not her way." He shook his head, his eyes briefly closing. "It wasn't her way."

The way he spoke about this mother made it seem as if she was still there with him, not gone nearly two years like the Wikipedia page had told her.

Earlier Aisha had thought that once she'd gathered herself she'd show Sykes—no, Roman—her design and convince him her building was still worthy of being built and supported by Sykes Global. But now she wasn't so sure. She sighed softly in relief when the waiter came back with their food. A curried chicken salad on a bed of mixed spring greens for her and vegetarian *banh mi* for him.

She started to eat. "Oh, this is really good!" Not the biggest fan of Asian food, she'd assumed that the curry chicken salad would be the safest thing for her to eat but the flavors brought out in the curry, with raisins and the surprising hazelnuts, made it the best chicken dish she'd eaten in a long time. "Really, really good."

A low chuckle left Roman's lips and she dipped her head to stop staring at their sensual shape as he slowly chewed a bite from his sandwich. When did a man chewing his food become sexy?

"Well, okay then!" She felt like an idiot with her nonsensical words that should've stayed stuffed in her mouth along with the food. This man was turning her emotions all kinds of upside down.

Aisha dove into her food while the remains of their tea stayed hot on the single flame, which looked just like a tea light to her, built into the elegant tray supporting the pale green iron pot. The food was good and the scent of the tea in her cup rose around her. The restaurant itself smelled like something peaceful and she didn't fully appreciate its calming properties until she noticed how much more relaxed Roman seemed.

In a drool-worthy three-piece suit, his body was a loose invitation in the chair, the shape of his lips a match to the lines of laughter around his eyes. Even after she'd sat and started harassing him.

She complimented him on the choice of place and made a mental note to come back sometime soon. Then he told her it was his sanctuary of sorts.

She winced, feeling like an ass for destroying his peaceful evening, but he smiled and waved off her apology, interspacing bites of his sandwich with sips of his tea. God, he really was the most compelling man.

Once they both finished their meal and the waiter whisked away their plates, they regarded each other once more over refreshed cups of tea. Aisha tapped a fingernail against the fragile teacup.

"Um, I think we can find a solution to both our problems," she said.

"Oh, do you?" He leaned back in his chair, looking like he built his entire world on a bedrock of doubt.

"Oh, yes. I'm a born optimist and natural problem solver." She flashed him a smile. "Or at least that's what my résumé says."

"Do you have a solution yet?" Again, she detected no confidence in his deep gaze though a hint of a smile touched his mouth.

Gah! She needed to stop staring at his lips as if the

solutions to all her problems, or at least the ones having to do with her dead sex life, lay there.

She cleared her throat. "Not yet, but now that I know you're open to it— You are open to it, right?" At his nod, she forged forward again. "Now that you're open, I'll put some real thought into a solution instead of poking that voodoo doll I have of you."

"Ah, that's why I've been feeling like needles have been jabbing my back the last couple of days."

A soft laugh bubbled from her without her permission and she bit her lip to stop it. That was such a weak joke. Why had she laughed?

But that was just one of the many questions left unanswered by the time they finished their tea and paused outside the doors of the teahouse, about to go their separate ways.

"I'll be in touch with my new plan," she said, shaking the hand he offered. Her knees went a little weak at how large and warm it felt around hers, how his direct and piercing gaze had her wondering if he'd be equally intense in bed.

Down, girl.

"I'm sure you will, Aisha," he said with a soft laugh. "You know where to find me."

"That I do, Mr. CEO."

"It's Roman. Remember?"

As if she could ever forget.

Chapter 6

Aisha Clark was young and beautiful. But mostly young.

Roman had tried to ignore one of those two very obvious facts while they were eating together in the teahouse.
The casual way she tossed around contemporary slang
and, unlike many of the women he'd been with in the
past, made it obvious that she found him attractive but
didn't push the issue. If anything, she'd been hyper-
focused on the reason she'd sat with him in the first place.

The Sylvia Sykes Architectural Prize.

While he stood near the doorway of the teahouse, he'd
watched her walk away, cursing her youth but admiring
the way she approached him, fearless and determined.
After he got home he indulged in his curiosity and looked
her up online.

It was easy to find her on social media. Her Instagram,
Snapchat and Twitter had updates every day about one

thing or another. There were photos of her hanging out with her brother, retired basketball player Ahmed Clark. "Snaps" of her pretending to snatch off her sister's large diamond engagement ring. Plus a few photos of her cat Eloise, which she seemed to treat like a princess or her own child. And, finally, there was her professional page.

After all that searching, he finally found out her age. She was twenty-four.

Not jailbait but still much too young for a thirty-seven-year-old man like him. He'd always thought less of men who ended up with women much younger than them. What was wrong with them that they couldn't attract and keep a woman their own age? A woman who would provide an equal partnership, inside jokes about the songs that were popular when they were younger or the ridiculous fashion from back in the day.

No, Roman had no respect for men like that. And he definitely didn't want to become one, either. So he had to stay away, no matter how interesting or smart Aisha Clark was.

He told himself that all of Friday night and Saturday. By the time Saturday evening and the party the company was throwing him in celebration of his new position came around, he almost believed it.

"So, I'll just meet you here?" With the cell phone to his ear, Roman got out of his black Mercedes in front of the venue and handed the keys to the valet.

On the other end of the line, Merrine gave him the answer he was waiting on. "Yes. And don't think because you're all of a sudden a CEO that you can start bossing me around."

"I wouldn't dream of it," Roman said, chuckling then ending the call. He slipped the valet ticket in his pocket and jogged up the half dozen stairs into the elegant, early twentieth-century hotel.

"Good evening, sir." The doorman greeted him with a nod and held the door for him to pass through.

"Thanks and good evening to you, too." He strode through the lobby, the marble floors ringing under his dress shoes. An elegant sign in script pointed toward The Sykes Event and the ballroom down an impressive double staircase.

He huffed a soft breath of amazement. This was his life now. Everything else was far behind him. Or at least it would be for another year.

He paused on the staircase. In the massive ballroom, classical music played. Voices rippled with laughter and conversation. The heavy chandelier made of thousands of crystals glittered overhead and threw sparks of light on the beautifully dressed crowd. Tuxedos. Ball gowns. Cocktail dresses. Diamonds and plenty of vintage pearls.

An orchestra, fronted by a fourteen-year-old cello prodigy, played music on the raised bandstand. The boy's high and thick afro swayed with his slow and elegant movements. Around him, people were dancing or watching him play, their eyes full of wonder.

Money well spent, Roman thought.

From his position at the top of the staircase, he could see his assistant, his brother and several people he'd worked with during the week he'd been officially in charge. Roman would rather be in his backyard, stretched out on the grass and watching the sky. But Merrine had convinced him he had to go since the party was for him. He couldn't wait for her to get there.

He knew the sooner he joined the party, the sooner he

could leave and go back to what he wanted to be doing tonight. Which was nothing.

Here we go. Time to join the fray.

Hand on the marble balustrade, he quickly made his way down into the crowd.

Immediately, Lance drifted away from his conversation with one of the company lawyers. "Ah, here he is, the man of the hour." A flash of envy sharpened his brother's face.

Of course, Lance wished that it was him being celebrated tonight. Roman did, too.

"Enjoying yourself?" he asked Lance.

His brother snagged a glass of champagne from a passing waiter and pressed it into Roman's hand. "Yes and no."

At least he was being honest. Lance never apologized for wanting more. He just demanded it and, if it didn't come to him, he went after it with a ruthlessness that sometimes surprised Roman.

These days, he was putting a lot of his energy into sponsoring race car drivers and extreme sports athletes. He usually financed winners who made him back the money he invested in them plus more.

Roman wished their father had seen that and done right by his younger child. It would be a relief to hand the reins over to his brother when the time came. It would feel like righting a wrong.

"What's the 'no' part of that?" Roman put the glass of champagne to his mouth then changed his mind at the last minute about drinking it.

He'd just showered and made his way to the hotel ballroom after an intense session of hot yoga. His body felt almost divinely strong, flexible and pulsing with power, the closest to ecstasy he could feel without having sex. He didn't want to ruin the feeling with alcohol.

Lance shrugged, the tuxedo over his narrow shoulders moving elegantly with his body. "Just wondering if these same people will be here next year celebrating me when it's my turn."

Although he hadn't told Lance the particulars of their father's will, Roman had let him know they had to wait a year to transfer the company's leadership from Roman's hands to his.

"They will be here." Roman handed his untouched champagne off to another passing waiter. "You're a Sykes, after all, and most of them have nothing but loyalty and respect for the family."

"For you and Dad, you mean." Lance sneered. It wasn't a good look on his otherwise handsome face.

"Your time will come." Roman tried to pacify him. "They just don't know you yet. You haven't had a chance to prove to them what you can do."

"You've never had to prove a thing to them, though, have you?"

"They've been used to the idea of me taking over, that's all," Roman said, looking around the room. "When I was a kid, I was here nearly every day, remember?"

His brother only grunted.

He didn't know what else to say to Lance. As much as Roman had distanced himself from the business and from his father in his twenties, while growing up he'd paid strict attention to everything his father had wanted to teach him. He'd watched and learned and, despite himself, had been impressed with everything Langston Sykes had done to make Sykes Global a formidable name in large-scale construction worldwide.

As much as he didn't want to follow in those work-aholic footsteps, he had nothing but respect for the incredible legacy his father left behind. He wanted that to continue with Lance and with any children they both managed to have.

"If it isn't the guest of honor." Nelson Stearns, an old friend of his father's and the company's chief financial officer, came out of the woodwork to pat Roman on the back. "Your old man would've been very proud of you. Only a week in and you've already impressed the board."

"They like to see money, that's all," Roman said with a quick smile, aware of his brother's watchful gaze.

"You say that like it's a bad thing." Nelson chuckled. "Whatever you're doing, keep up the good work, and welcome to the place where your father always meant for you to be." Then he was gone.

Lance raised his glass of champagne in mocking salute.

Nelson's appearance was the first of the night but not the last. By the time Roman had fended off over a dozen offers of congratulations, Lance had thankfully wandered somewhere else. Then Merrine finally arrived.

"My CEO BFF," she laughed at Roman as she came up to him, elegant in a skintight tuxedo and bright red lipstick, a Naomi Campbell lookalike with just a little more meat on her bones. Her hair was loose and long around her face and down her back. "Just how much are you ready to crawl out of your skin?"

"I'm ready to leave, if that answers your question," Roman said.

Merrine drew close to him with the scent of flowers and chocolate, kissing him on each cheek like she'd gotten used to from the last few years living in Europe. With another teasing laugh, she handed him a bottle of sparkling water. "The crowd looks ready to eat you alive."

"You already missed the feast," he said. "They're happy I'm making them more money already."

"Ooh, you miracle worker!" She teased him with an upward flicker of ruthlessly pruned eyebrows.

"You know better than anyone how fickle those numbers can be. It's a coincidence that they'd surged so high while I've been here. It's only been a week."

"As much as you'd like to think you're just some beach bum who loves to take yoga classes and Zen out in his lawn chair, you're not." Merrine lightly stroked a nail along his jawline. "I'm sorry to have to tell you that you are a little bit of a business genius."

"Stop talking your foolishness and come dance with me," he said. He didn't want to talk any more about business and what anyone expected of him.

He grabbed Merrine's hand and led her off to the dance floor, the one spot in the ballroom not many people seemed to be making use of. The two open bars were crowded. The comfortable chairs arranged at different places in the room held the weight of elegantly dressed women and men, and the balconies had their fair share of smokers and people who just snuck away for some peace and quiet.

The orchestra had stopped playing and the DJ now stood behind a complicated setup on one of the small interior balconies overlooking the ballroom, safe from anyone who even had the smallest thought of making a request. Music from the seventies throbbed from the speakers.

"This is nice," Merrine said once they were dancing to the Ohio Players.

It actually was. As much of a loner as he was, Roman was enjoying some parts of his evening. The music and food, yes. But also seeing his brother hide that smirk of his and try to make real connections. Once Lance was CEO, they'd remember moments like this.

Roman spun Merrine around, laughing when she did a shimmy and nearly gave the guy dancing near them a heart attack. Then he froze.

"Everything okay?" Merrine turned to stare in the direction he was looking. "Oh! She's gorgeous."

They both watched the woman glide into the room like she was some sort of woodland creature skating gracefully across a frozen lake. Her walk was a slow and sensual movement that was all woman, her legs hidden by the shimmering rainbow skirts of her floor-length, mermaid-style gown. The fabric hugged her body just perfectly. Thighs. Hips. The subtle curves of her breasts. Her hair was a midnight halo around her beautiful face and floated around her with each step.

Aisha Clark.

"Hands off, she's taken," he said before he could do better. Then he dug himself in deeper when he saw the gleam of sensual interest in his best friend's eyes. "By me."

With a hand on the crook of his elbow, Merrine had the nerve to laugh. "Is she?"

"Yes," Roman said.

Aisha wasn't his, though. He wanted her to be, but what he wanted wasn't possible and it certainly wasn't right. Even now, his palms itched to touch her soft skin. His mouth longed to take a sip of desire directly from hers. Since their meeting in the bakery, his body clamored for a closeness to hers. And the desire had only grown more insistent since their impromptu meal together at the tea shop.

Merrine's soft laughter brought him back to himself. "Does this lovely morsel know that she's already taken?"

Roman shrugged, figuring it was better not to say anything than lie to his best friend. "She's probably here to see me," he said instead, because he couldn't imagine her being at this party for any other reason. This uptight gathering didn't seem quite her thing.

Briefly, he told Merrine about meeting Aisha and what she wanted from him.

"Interesting," his best friend said.

Aisha moved gracefully through the crowd, gliding closer to Roman although she obviously hadn't seen him yet. Inexplicably nervous, he wiped his damp palms on his slacks.

Merrine looked at him in surprise. "If I didn't know any better, I'd swear you were falling for this girl."

"But you do know better," Roman said softly, still watching Aisha move through the ballroom, steady and focused.

It looked like she was searching for someone, her eyes roving from face to face, visually dismissing the people she saw but didn't want. And then she noticed him. Aisha didn't hesitate. She smiled, a soft and secretive thing, before beginning her purposeful glide his way. Roman's heart threatened to punch its way out of his chest.

"You're definitely not falling for anybody." The laughter was obnoxiously obvious in Merrine's tone.

Would it be rude to tell his best friend to shut up?

But then it was too late to do anything but smile as Aisha appeared at Roman's side.

"Roman Sykes." She smiled up at him first then turned

to Merrine. "And friend." Her grin was cheeky and bold and, God help him, Roman loved it.

He could drown in the liquid depths of her eyes. "If I didn't know better, I'd swear you were stalking me," he said.

"Do you know better?" Some shocked look must have broken through his calm facade because she laughed. "I'm just joking."

"Let me cut through your foreplay to introduce myself." Merrine extended a hand to Aisha. "This one calls me his best friend but you can just call me Merrine."

"Hi, Merrine. A pleasure to meet you." Aisha leaned forward the same moment that Merrine did and Roman watched with surprise as the two women naturally exchanged a double kiss on the cheeks. "I should have known that my Hot Yoga Daddy would be interesting enough to have a woman as his best friend."

Merrine practically choked on her laughter. "Hot Yoga Daddy?" Her eyes shone with mirth as she looked over at him.

"That's what I've been calling Roman in my head since we met at that cute little bakery in Grant Park." Aisha quickly told the whole story, though it was a version Roman wasn't completely sure he agreed with. "When he didn't give me his name that day, what else could I call him?" The mischief made her glow.

"I can see that," Merrine said, just about guaranteeing she was giving up the role as his best anything except pain in the butt. "The touch of gray in his hair, the hot body. And he is very bendy from all that yoga."

Aisha chortled. "I wish I could find out just how bendy but he keeps pushing me away."

Heat rose up Roman's spine but he clenched his teeth

against it. That didn't stop him from imagining just how much he could show her about what he could do with this body he'd honed to a fine machine from years of discipline.

Merrine snuck him a look from the corner of her eyes. "I don't think he's doing much pushing today. Give him a try and see."

Roman glared at her. He had to separate these two devils, and fast. "Would you like to dance, Aisha?"

"I'd love to, Roman." Her grin told him she knew exactly what he was doing.

"And that's my cue to move on to the open bar." Merrine waved at Aisha. "See you around, darling. And as for you—" she laughed at Roman some more "—talk with you later on tonight." Then she was gone, slipping through the crowd of dancers that had started gathering on the dance floor.

"Well, she's nice," Aisha said as she moved into the circle of Roman's arms.

His brain scrambled, Roman moved into position for a waltz, then flushed with embarrassment when he finally heard the tempo of the song. He was about to correct himself when Aisha slipped her hand in his, effortlessly matching his posture like it was the most natural thing. Then they were waltzing to Bootsy Collins.

Roman was in trouble. *So* much trouble.

He cleared his throat. "Yes, she is. Or at least she was until tonight."

Aisha smiled and looked past his shoulder toward where Merrine disappeared. "The two of you act the way my brother and sister do with each other. You're all growly and teasing, but it's obvious there's love between you."

"I do love her," Roman admitted.

A smile swam up from somewhere and took over his face. He felt it and tried to move it off to someplace more appropriate but it refused to budge. Completely out of step with the psychedelic funk, he and Aisha continued their traditional waltz. He shouldn't date her. He couldn't. But if he could, she was perfect. No other woman he'd ever been interested in had taken it at face value that he and Merrine were just friends.

Before getting into anything serious, he always told his would-be lovers how he and Merrine met years ago—in kindergarten when they got into a shoving match after giving the same girl a valentine—and how she'd stood by him when he'd said he wanted nothing to do with the family business and instead wanted to make his own way.

She was the epitome of platonic love to him. Although they didn't share blood, she was his sister and he'd do just about anything for her. The jury was still out on killing for her, though. She was reckless enough that he could imagine one of her many enemies tempting him to do just that.

The music changed to something faster and happier, but he and Aisha continued to move to their own shared rhythm.

"So why are you really here?" Roman asked as they turned in a tight circle to avoid the flailing arms of someone doing the Dougie.

"Well, I was honest with you earlier. I wasn't stalking you, per se, but I'm only here to speak with you. I can dance and drink in my own living room. Or my brother's since his living room is about the size of this place." She briefly cast her gaze around them with a fond smile. The love she had for her brother, for her family, blazed as bright as the sun from her captivating eyes.

"Is that right?" Roman murmured, unable to look away from them.

"Mmm-hmm."

"And so what do you want to talk to me about?"

"The Sykes Prize, of course."

The disappointment that rolled through Roman took his breath away. He cleared his throat. "Okay, Miss Aisha Clark. What's on your mind?"

Chapter 7

For Aisha, keeping focused on the reason she'd tracked Roman down to this fancy party in his honor was harder than she thought.

Sure, she was more attracted to him than she'd ever been to any other man. Yes, he was gorgeous and lit up the world when he smiled. But she had a mission, dammit. Operation: Save Aisha's Career. It was stupid to let an ill-advised attraction drain all the sense out of her brain.

But, damn, he looked amazing in a tux.

When she mentioned the reason she was there, his face shuttered, wiping away the traces of warmth and animation he'd had before Merrine had left them alone.

Aisha licked her lips. "Well, I thought for a long time about the building your father wanted and also what you said about your mother."

"Yes?"

The music was nostalgic. Songs she remembered her parents playing and dancing to when she was young. Even Dev and Ahmed loved this music. The energy was contagious but she didn't want to move any faster and lose the palm-to-palm connection she had with Roman.

"Yes. Um. I thought I'd change the focus of the design. Like you said, you don't think she would've wanted to be trapped in a building in death like she'd been in life."

Through their connection, she felt him flinch. Whatever had happened between his parents affected him so strongly, so deeply. In that moment with the music around them, she still felt a little sadness radiating from him. Aisha pressed her lips together and moved closer to him, still waltzing with him but now close enough that he could feel the heat of her body. It felt like he needed warmth just then.

"I'm listening," he said softly.

"Okay, good." She suppressed the surge of optimism threatening to overwhelm her good sense. "Let me change my design to something you think your mother would've liked. I've read about her, but what the internet didn't tell me was what made you love her, what made her the person you remember."

His face shuttered even more.

She rushed to reassure him. "I don't mean give me intimate details about your mother-son times or anything." Ugh, could she be any more of an ass? "But special things about her that the public wouldn't know. Things that would help me accurately imagine a space in her honor." But Roman wasn't having it. Through their skin-to-skin contact, she felt his reluctance. She plunged on. "Obviously if you don't like it, you can torpedo the idea. But all I'm asking is for you to keep an open mind. I don't want to do anything to tarnish her memory. You know I want to keep the prize and give my résumé the padding I need to—" she broke off; he didn't need to know her situation at work "—to look better to potential employers."

"Potential employers? You're already working at one of the best firms in the country. I know some seasoned architects who'd give just about anything to be where you are."

Aisha knew exactly how they felt. Before getting the job, she'd been in the same position. "Not everything is as it seems, Roman."

He hummed a noncommittal response. The music changed again and segued to a smooth R&B rhythm with a strong baseline. Now, *this* song she loved. Aisha threw her head back and swayed her shoulders to the beat, rocked her hips. Roman let go of her hands but stayed close, his hips moving against hers, keeping the same rhythm.

They didn't exchange any words, just a look that transformed their waltz into something more sensual, more earthy. His eyes dipped down her body and heat flared within them. Aisha bit her bottom lip and put her hands on his chest, just resting them there as their bodies moved together.

So damn sexy.

His arms slid around her waist and she tilted her head back to look up at him. Oh, his body was like a furnace against hers. All heat and strength and power. They moved together, their thighs brushing. His palms resting lightly against her lower back sent tiny shivers through her. He looked at her as if he wanted to devour everything he saw.

It would take only the barest movement from both of them for their lips to join. All she had to do was to rise a couple of inches on her tiptoes. Or for him to lean down.

Aisha's whole body throbbed. Possibility made her lick her lips and tensed her belly. She felt her fingers curl into the soft fabric over his chest. Roman huffed a breath of surprise and she opened her mouth to apologize, inadvertently sucking in that breath of his.

A low moan left her throat and his gaze locked on her mouth. She licked her lips again and saw him mimic the motion.

They danced still, bodies rocking against each other. Aisha's panties clung intimately to her and every movement against Roman rubbed her just the right way. The breath shuddered in her throat and she clung more tightly to him. The proof of his desire was firm and hot against her belly through their layers of clothes.

Aisha bit her lip and pressed back into him then, mapping the shape of his sex with her clenching stomach muscles. His moan vibrated against her palms and she melted at the sound.

God, she wanted him. More than she'd ever wanted any other man.

She just about gnashed her teeth when her more logical side asserted itself. It told her they shouldn't be doing this here, not in such a public space, and especially not in front of people he worked with.

A quick flick of her gaze reassured her that not many people were paying attention to them. Besides, what was there for anyone to see? Just a man and a woman dancing. Hell, they'd made more of a scene waltzing to the hip-hop song than they were now.

Still, Aisha flattened her palms against his chest and

forced herself to stop thinking about how his body would feel naked against hers.

She cleared her throat. "About my idea, Roman. What do you think?"

Eyes blinking, he looked like he was coming out of a trance. A deep breath shook his powerful frame. "All right. I think… Let's try it. Design something else and we'll see where we go from there."

The feeling of triumph she expected didn't come. Only a sense of an anticlimax. Of something left dangling like temptingly ripe fruit on the vine.

"Okay. Great. Thank you." Because it seemed like the right thing to do, she dropped her head on his chest and heard the furious thumping of his heart. Startled, she eased back, but his expression was as neutral as ever with absolutely no sign of the fervor she felt in his chest.

"Don't thank me yet," he said. "All I'm giving you is time to do more work than you planned."

Aisha didn't mind more work. Although she grew up with a virtual silver spoon in her mouth thanks to her brother's wealth and generosity, the things that meant the most to her—her credentials as an architect, the two other languages she spoke, the closeness she maintained with her family—she'd worked hard for. She drew in a breath of relief when she realized just what his agreement meant.

"So when do you want to get together again?" She eased back even further until they were no longer touching. They became like two separate islands on the dance floor while the dancers moved around them. "To discuss the project, of course."

The look on Roman's face—part surprise, part chagrin—said he hadn't thought too much about what he'd agreed to before that moment. She bit the inside of her lower lip to stop herself from grinning. But because he was a man more than her equal, he didn't back down.

Eyebrow raised in that way she was becoming intimately familiar with, he gave her the smallest of smiles. "Let me look at my calendar and let you know," he said. "It'll be sometime soon."

"My, my. Are you arranging a hookup on company time, Roman?" A low and mocking voice came from over Aisha's shoulder before a man moved into view.

He was the man she'd almost bumped into that afternoon in Roman's office a couple of days before.

The man was more slender than Roman, younger, maybe her age, but with cynicism in his opaque eyes. Although he wasn't as attractive as Roman, he was good-looking enough and carried himself like he knew it. The general shape of his face and his height told her he was related to Roman somehow.

"This is party time, if anything," Roman said, hands in his pockets. "The company doesn't own me like that yet." He nodded to Aisha, that small smile of his still intact. "Aisha, allow me to introduce you to my younger brother, Lance. Lance, this is Aisha Clark."

"A pleasure to meet you," his brother said and kissed the back of Aisha's hand.

Only the barest of good manners that her mother had drilled into her stopped her from dragging her hand away from him and wiping it off on the back of her dress. Weren't these hand kisses supposed to be a dry, barely-there touch of mouth to hand? Whatever it was, she didn't like him doing it. She bared her teeth in what she hoped passed for a smile.

"Hi there." She wasn't polite enough to lie and say it was nice to meet him. There was something about him she didn't like. Maybe it was because he seemed like every other entitled rich man she'd ever met.

Lance's gaze volleyed between her and Roman. "Sorry to break up your make-out session but I just wanted a few words with my brother."

"You can have as many as you want," Aisha said. "I'm heading out anyway. I have a date with my sibs and a pint of rum-raisin ice cream." She touched Roman's arm through the sumptuous tuxedo jacket. "We'll talk soon, okay?"

He gave her a brief nod although his gaze said he wanted to say more to her but not in front of his brother. "I'll be in touch," Roman said.

She wondered if the brother had the same thoughts about the Sykes Prize and the decision their father had made. Not that it mattered since Roman was the one she had to deal with.

"I hope it wasn't something I said." Lance Sykes looked amused. "I wouldn't want to break up—" he waved an arm, encompassing both Roman and Aisha "—whatever you two have going on here."

"You didn't," Aisha assured him. He didn't matter enough to her. Although from the look of concern on Roman's face as he looked at Lance, what he thought and did mattered a lot to his older brother.

With a careless wave, Aisha turned and left them to it.

"Who's that woman?" she heard Lance ask as she walked away. "I've seen her somewhere before."

"Who she is, is none of your business, little brother," Roman answered but with a hint of fondness.

Hmm. Did that mean he wanted to keep her to himself for a little while? The thought made her smile.

Chapter 8

"Hey, is anybody home?" Aisha dropped her purse and her keys on the table in her brother's entryway.

It was a rhetorical question since she knew he was home, along with his wife and maybe with Dev, too. It was their planned "night in." She'd been too keyed up after leaving Roman's party to call either of her siblings. The short drive from midtown had been filled with nothing but her own thoughts. All in a conflicted jumble over Roman Sykes's hot, complicated, yoga-toned ass.

"Come on through," her brother called out. "We're in the living room watching a movie."

When she got to the living room, though, whatever they were watching on the ridiculously large TV screen had been paused. Her brother and his wife sat together on the couch, Ahmed's arm draped around Elle, who leaned into him looking as entranced by her husband as she had been the first time Aisha had seen her and Ahmed together. They were disgustingly in love.

Devyn sat cross-legged on the floor, leaning into the couch opposite her brother and digging into a bowl of popcorn. Their mother sat, queenlike, in the hunter-green armchair nearby, a glass of wine in hand.

"Hey, y'all," Aisha greeted. "What are you doing? Because I don't see a movie on."

"We were watching something—" Devyn looked briefly at the TV screen "—but that was just an excuse to wait for you. How did the party go? Did he agree to everything you asked for?"

Aisha had told them all about the ridiculousness of the Sykes Prize and how much she wanted it, and that it wasn't hers anymore.

"It went okay, I guess. Roman did agree to look at some alternative designs of mine."

Her brother gave a whoop of triumph. "If anybody could convince that guy, I knew it would be you."

She dropped down into the sofa Dev leaned against and gave her sister's shoulder a quick squeeze. "Nothing's certain. He's just not outright saying no to me right now."

"You'll impress him. I know you will." So very ladylike, Dev plucked a few kernels of popcorn from the bowl and popped them in her mouth one by one.

Reaching down, Aisha dug her entire hand into the bowl and pulled out a fistful of popcorn to shove into her mouth. "We'll see. The best part was getting to see him again." Around mouthfuls of popcorn, she told them all about her brief evening with Roman. Then she sighed. "I can't believe he's the same Hot Yoga Daddy from the bakery. What are the odds?"

"Interesting." Dev pursed her lips and gave Aisha an

encouraging look, not that she needed any encouragement to chase after what she wanted.

"It sounds like you're about to get yourself into trouble," Ahmed said. "Don't mix business with pleasure, Aisha. Things can go left real quick."

"There's nothing wrong with a little healthy mix," his wife said with a teasing smile. "It might make things more interesting for Aisha." Elle was the co-owner of some sort of romance-facilitating service. Aisha wasn't clear on the details but she knew whatever it was, her sister-in-law was good at it and her business made enough money to satisfy her.

"Nope. Too messy," Ahmed said.

Dev waved off their brother's concern. "She met him before she knew he was the guy in charge of the Sykes Prize. Plus, he's sexy."

"Well then, never mind." Ahmed rolled his eyes and got an elbow in the ribs from Elle for his trouble.

Aisha knew what she wanted to do. It may have been stupid, but when she'd walked into that office and seen another version of Hot Yoga Daddy, she'd been so thankful to get another chance with him that she'd nearly forgot what she'd gone to his office for.

She was a natural flirt. She loved dating and she loved men. But there was something special about Roman. She couldn't ignore her attraction to him even if she tried. Yes, she wanted the Sykes Prize. It would make the business moves she had planned so much easier. But…

Biting her lip, she looked up at her mother. "Mom, what do you think I should do?"

Holding the glass of red wine between her slender fingers, her mother warmly met her gaze. "Follow your heart, darling."

Devyn laughed. "I don't think it's her heart that she's listening to right now, Mom."

"Dev!" Aisha stared at her sister while Ahmed and Elle nearly bust a collective gut cackling at Aisha's embarrassment. "It's not like that."

Her mother gave a slow nod. "Well, whether these feelings stem from your heart or a little farther south, do what you sense is right for you, love. Life is too short to deny yourself pleasure."

It was a motto her mother firmly believed in. Although Aisha was too young to remember everything about her parents when her father was alive, she knew her mother had loved him. She'd adored him. They had adored each other.

After his death, she'd shut herself off from everyone but her children. Yes, she'd gone to work and done all the things necessary to keep the house. She'd come home after every workday and sit with her children, feed them, love them. But Aisha could never forget walking by her mother's bedroom late one night and hearing the sound of her desperate, open-throated sobbing.

When her mother finally pulled herself from the fog of grief, at least the one that had her crying alone in her room every night, she'd started to date. She'd exercised to get herself in shape. She'd started going out with her friends. She'd started having a life again. There hadn't been anyone serious enough for her to bring home to her children, but she wasn't a nun.

Devin plucked a runaway popcorn kernel from her lap. "I can tell you like him already, probably way too much to pull back now."

"Maybe." What Aisha hadn't told them was that she'd been gone for Roman since the moment he'd bought her that coffee. She loved how honest he'd been with her that morning in the bakery. No sugar-coating. No BS. Maybe it had been the unfamiliar rejection. Maybe it was the position of the moon the previous night. Whatever it was, Aisha wanted Roman Sykes and she was on a shameless mission to get him. Mostly.

"It's such a bad idea." She pressed the shiny material of her dress between her thumb and index finger, the bits of glitter embedded in the cloth rough to the touch. "Things are getting worse at work every day."

The resulting silence in the room was profound enough for Aisha to hear each of her own uncertain breaths.

"This isn't like you to doubt yourself, darling," her mother said long moments later.

"Yeah." Ahmed frowned. He'd been one of her biggest champions over the years. And her biggest motivation for going after the things she wanted.

"I'm not doubting myself, you guys, I'm just being cautious," Aisha said, although the uncertainty in those words was painfully obvious.

She hated it. She hadn't come this far in her career or her life by making reckless decisions and, as much as she wanted Roman, she wasn't about to start now. The trouble was, she wasn't sure which of the decisions would be the more reckless one. Follow this brilliant ribbon of possibility with Roman. Or let this potentially complicated mess go. He thought she was too young. She was hurting him by challenging him about his mother's memory. The obvious conflict of interest for him threatened to make whatever happened between them end in disaster.

"I know it's complicated, Aisha, but it's not an impossible situation," Dev said. She'd recently come through her own complicated situation with her now husband,

Bennett, so she would know. "Why don't you try to find some other alternatives to getting this Sykes thing so you can have him where you want him?" Dev waggled her eyebrows. "In your bed, obviously."

Aisha looked at her sister, an idea forming. Could it really be that simple?

The "getting him into bed" part could be that simple. But finding something like the Sykes Prize to help her escape Wainwright and Tully? That was where she needed the luck.

It wasn't completely impossible. Was it?

Chapter 9

She's too young for you.

Don't stir up this already complicated situation.

Roman's thoughts tumbled around one after the other, telling him it was better to leave Aisha alone. But he owed her an honest explanation about the fate of the Sykes Prize, especially after their last conversation. Right?

Yeah, because phones don't exist on the same plane as your ridiculous infatuation with a girl young enough to be your kid.

With the one-sided conversation buzzing in his head, Roman stepped up to the reception desk in the spacious lobby of the high-rise that housed the offices of Wainwright and Tully.

"Is Aisha Clark available?" he asked.

The man behind the desk looked up from his computer at Roman, quickly scanning him from head to foot. In his dark blue, three-piece Zegna suit, Roman knew he didn't read like some rando off the street, but that was exactly how the guy looked at him.

"Do you have an appointment?" the receptionist asked, voice edging from neutral to suspicious.

"Not at all." He rested a hand on the low but wide desk. "Just tell her Roman is here to see her, please."

That quick body scan again and the receptionist pressed a button and spoke into the Bluetooth attached discreetly to his ear. "Ms. Clark? There's a Roman, no last name given, in the lobby wanting to see you." He listened for a few seconds. "Of course." He ended the connection. "If you'll just take a seat, she'll be right out."

Hands in his pockets, Roman stepped away from the desk and strolled to the row of uncomfortable-looking chrome-and-leather chairs in the light-filled lobby. With the framed photographs of buildings that architects in the famous firm had no doubt designed, a massive gray rug underfoot and wide windows looking over midtown Atlanta, the space gave off an ambience of subtle luxury, exclusivity and meticulous care. Shades of white, permutations of gray and a wide stripe of black running through the middle of the pale wall made the place seem cold. And he'd thought the lobby of Sykes Global was a little full of itself. It was downright homey compared to this.

"Roman? This is a surprise."

He'd been so busy critiquing the lobby's design that he hadn't noticed Aisha's appearance. He turned and had to stifle a smile. She looked so much herself, a creature of warmth and passion, despite the cold and unwelcoming workplace. Her gorgeous hair was pulled back into two thick braids, the ends fastened by a bright red flower clip.

A white blouse complemented the rich color of her skin and her slacks echoed the red of her hair clips.

"A good surprise, I hope."

"I'm not sure about that yet." Her eyes dipped to take in the receptionist who was watching them both with avid curiosity. "Come back to my office."

He followed her out of the lobby and through a maze of cubicles to a small office. It was just large enough for her desk, a visitor's chair and a drafting table. The single window overlooked a narrow alley and the side of a neighboring building.

"Have a seat, please," she said.

Roman strolled to her window and glanced down into the alley before turning back to her. "Actually, I'm here on the chance that you haven't had lunch yet." She stared at him as if he was speaking a foreign language she didn't understand. "Have you?"

"What?"

"Eaten lunch." He teased her with his raised eyebrow. "You know, something you put in your mouth and chew. Usually ingested in the middle of the day."

"Um. No." She blinked and shook her head. "I'm sorry. You caught me completely off guard."

To be honest, that was sort of his plan. At every step since they'd met, it seemed like she was the one keeping Roman on his toes. He'd wanted to turn the tables for once. And, he had to admit to himself, be in the presence of her refreshing beauty one more time. Sure, she was young, but there was nothing wrong with him basking in her incredible energy and borrowing some of that energy to power him through the rest of his workday.

"Well, the last time we saw each other, we talked about an alternate design based on new information you learn about the marvelous Sylvia Sykes." He felt his mouth curve up with his mother's name. "There's no better time to discuss such things than over lun—"

A brisk knock on the door cut off his words. Aisha barely opened her mouth to respond to whoever it was before the door opened.

A gray head poked in. "Ms. Clark, I heard you have a guest. Is it Roman Sykes, perhaps?" From his position at the window, Roman watched the man come uninvited into Aisha's space, his eyes taking in everything that his manner said all belonged to him. "Ah, Mr. Sykes. Welcome to Wainwright and Tully." He fully ignored Aisha now. "Is there something the firm can help you with?"

Although Sykes Global primarily dealt with its own in-house architects, there had been a few times over the years when the company had done some outsourcing. Roman had no doubt the man was in here nosing around to see what could be done to elevate Wainwright and Tully. Which in theory meant he should have allowed Aisha to handle Roman.

"I already have all the help I need," Roman said to the man who could only be Albert Tully according to the information he'd gotten from the firm's web site. "As you know, Ms. Clark is the winner of the latest Sykes Prize." He tipped his head at Aisha. "As such, she and I have some things to discuss."

Tully took a couple more steps into the office and straightened his already immaculate tie. "Well, not to minimize the work Aisha has done for you, but we have much more experienced architects here who would be glad to speak with you about future projects."

Was that how things worked here? "Ms. Clark has everything I need." He emphasized her last name and the respect it carried. "You can go and close the door behind you."

Tully was goggle-eyed. Roman watched him visibly struggle for something to say, but nothing apparently came to him because he nodded stiffly and backed out of the office, closing the door with a sharp click.

"His professionalism leaves something to be desired." Roman ambled away from the window and approached Aisha's desk. "So are you ready for lunch? My treat."

She quickly bounced back from the unpleasant surprise of her boss's visit, making Roman think this wasn't a single instance of disrespect. He was starting to see Aisha's reason for wanting to turn her back on this place. After grabbing her purse and with her keys in hand, she waved him out in front of her then locked her office door.

"It's been a while since I've been in this area," Roman said as she double-checked the door lock. "Any restaurant recommendations?"

They ended up at a small Indian place at the end of a dead-end street. With water and crispy *papadum* in front of them, Roman brought up some light topics of conversation. Once the main meal came, he asked the waiter not to disturb them then launched into the reason he'd ostensibly come to see Aisha about.

"Have you given any more thought to a new design?" He dipped a piece of garlic naan in the creamy *saag paneer* he'd ordered and bit into it with a sigh of pleasure.

If he didn't know any better, he'd swear that Aisha watched him nervously as she picked up her glass of mango *lassi*.

"I have," she said. "But putting my designs on paper would be premature. After all, we haven't made the time to talk about your mother and what elements you think she would love in a structure honoring her life." Her tongue swiped across her lower lip and Roman almost knocked over his glass of water.

For something constructive to do with his hands, he picked up his fork, only to put it back down. He was eating with his hands anyway.

"You're right. We should do that soon. I don't think an hour's lunch is enough time." He folded another piece of naan slathered with the creamy spinach into his mouth and finished chewing. "Since you and I talked at the party, I realized that you're right. In the last few years, I've been doing my own thing and not paying too much attention to what Sykes Global has been up to. The prize has become almost an institution, something life-changing for the architect who wins, and has also cemented a damn good reputation for the company. I won't win any respect as the new CEO if I get rid of something that obviously has benefitted the company for years."

He felt humbled to tell Aisha this, but it was only the truth.

She teased him with a look. "So you admit you were a bit shortsighted in rescinding the prize? Stubborn even?"

"Let's not get ahead of ourselves here," Roman said, but he felt the smile taking over his face.

"Okay, fine. So what does that mean for me?"

"Basically, the same thing we discussed. You'll create something more suited to its intention and we move on from there. I never put out a press release about canceling the prize, so we'll just go on as before."

"The press already has my design, though." As if that decision had given her permission to finally eat, Aisha picked up a piece of tandoori chicken with her fingers and bit into it, her red lips latching onto the deliciously spiced and scented piece of meat. "They already know exactly what the structure is supposed to look like." Aisha licked the spices from her mouth and continued eating.

Under the table, Roman's thigh jumped. She was actively trying to kill him. There was no other explanation for what she was doing to him. Unless, of course, he admitted that he'd done this to himself when he'd barged into her office. Either way, he realized she may get knocked off guard for a bit, but she always came back harder than before.

And speaking of hard...

Thumb rubbing the underside of his jaw, he dragged his gaze away from her.

He cleared his throat. "That's true. But once you finish the new one, the prize committee will send out a press release with a new design created by the winning architect and that'll be that. You've already proven that you're talented and capable when the committee approved your design as one of the final five."

From what Roman could find out, the process was relatively fair as far as contests based on aesthetics went. After the prize committee received the thousands of entries, they narrowed it down to the best five and then the CEO of Sykes Global, his father in this case, chose the winner from the select few.

"Nobody should have a problem with that," Roman finished.

"I certainly don't," Aisha said with a grin. "I approve of this method, CEO Roman."

"Good," he said dryly. "I wouldn't want to risk your actual disapproval."

To his surprise, he realized just how true that was.

Aisha stuck her tongue out at him, her eyes glittering like jewels in the restaurant's overhead lights.

Despite her youth, despite how very different she was from him, despite everything that put up Don't Go There in flashing neon lights in front of his eyes, Aisha had Roman snared and he couldn't get loose. Sitting in front of her as she smiled and licked the tandoori spices from her fingers, he wasn't even sure that he wanted to get free.

Tethered at the ends of her long and elegant fingers, at that moment, seemed like the perfect place to be.

Damn, he was so screwed.

Chapter 10

After she and Roman finished their lunch and he headed back to his office, Aisha walked into her office building still a little dazed that he'd visited her. And that he'd told her the prize was still hers.

She wanted to celebrate. She wanted to call her family and tell them the good news. But, of course, she had to get back to work first.

She'd only been in her office about three minutes before Wallace Wainwright buzzed her phone, wanting to see her in his office. Aisha was tempted to ignore him but she had a cat to feed.

In his office, she closed the door behind her and sat in the chair in front of his desk.

"Sir?"

Wainwright regarded her with steepled hands resting on the desk, his gaze penetrating. Taller than his partner and with dark hair only touched slightly by silver, despite being in his mid-fifties, Wallace Wainwright was often the crush of the new interns in their office. They got over it once they got to know him.

"Has Sykes approached you about working on something else?" He got straight to the point.

It's none of your damn business, she wanted to say. "Not at all. We're ironing out some details about the design I submitted." She pressed home without a smile. "The winning design."

Was it her imagination or did Wainwright wince?

"Well, I'm sure Albert mentioned it when he came to your office earlier, but we want to make the most of the talent of the firm. So on any future projects Mr. Sykes proposes to you—or if you're making changes to the design of yours he already has—feel free to use the vast talent pool here in the office. Quite a few of the senior architects would leap at the chance to work with Sykes. They also have more experience dealing with large-scale projects." He paused. "No offense."

Much offense taken. "I can handle this one on my own," she said, her linked fingers draped over her crossed knee. "I'm only working on the fuel station redesign and that's just about finished. I have plenty of time to deal with whatever Mr. Sykes needs from me." And because she knew he wouldn't hesitate to do something crazy like drag out her work on the gas station, she added, "The drafting table I have at home doesn't get nearly enough use so I'll be working on any Sykes-related project at home and during my time away from the office."

The sides of Wainwright's mouth pinched tight. "Very well. But don't forget that just because the project you have on your table is only a gas station doesn't mean it doesn't deserve your full attention."

"I'd never think that, sir." She smiled placidly at him while he watched her as steadily as a hawk, probably trying to find some way to stick her with some more busywork.

"All right, then. Good luck working with him. Since he just took over the reins from his father, he's an unknown element over there at Sykes. Don't be reluctant to lean on me or any of your senior colleagues for this project."

"Of course." She gave her boss another smile.

"All right, then. Thank you for coming in. I'll let you get back to your work."

"Thank you, sir." She stood, brushed off the back of her slacks once and walked out of his office.

Prick.

At her desk, she finished the grunt work she'd been stuck doing the past week. She would have finished it sooner, but from the project list the partners had shared in their weekly office meeting, all she had waiting for her was more scut work she could get done while juggling eggs and listening to her weekly Mandarin podcast. They'd hired her because she was capable and smart, but they treated her like a drooling idiot.

With Roman's visit and the good news he'd given her over lunch, the day passed quickly. Come five o'clock, she was one of the first to leave the office, nearly jogging in her eagerness to escape for the weekend.

"Oh, Aisha." As she neared the front desk, Harry, the receptionist, called out to her.

"Hey, I hope you'll have a better weekend this time," she said to him.

The thin young man grimaced. "I hope so, but it's

not looking good." He made a dismissive gesture. "But that's not what I wanted to talk to you about." He pulled a business envelope from a tray on his desk. "A courier dropped this off for you a few minutes ago."

The envelope was plain white with nothing but her name scrawled across it. "I'm not expecting anything but I'll take it," she said.

"Hopefully it's from a hot man about to liven up your weekend," he teased with a grin. "That way, I can live vicariously through you."

"I wish," she said then immediately thought about Roman and the lunch they'd had, how easy it had been with him both today and the day they'd accidentally had dinner together.

"That look on your face says there's a distinct possibility." He winked. "Go ahead, girl."

Aisha laughed. "I'll let you know." She slid the envelope into her bag then waved at him as she headed toward the revolving doors. "I'll see you next week."

"See you."

The envelope was a light addition to her purse but the weight of it felt significant as she walked to the parking deck. Once in her car, she couldn't wait. She grabbed the envelope and, after taking a quick breath, carefully opened it.

Inside was a one-page letter and a business card.

Aisha,
No time to begin like the present, right? If you're
open to it, let's begin our research this weekend.
Be ready tomorrow morning at seven and dress
to get wet.
Roman

The card in the envelope had his name in a simple print, along with his phone number. Before she could find an excuse to refuse him—not that there was any reason in the world why she wouldn't hang out with him—she programmed his number into her phone and sent him a text.

I don't plan to get wet for just anyone. See you tomorrow.

A giggle escaped her and she sank back into the leather seat of her little yellow Fiat with a sigh.

Oh, Roman. You have no idea what you're in for.

Chapter 11

Aisha opened the front door of her house on Saturday morning and almost lost her breath.

Okay, maybe *she* wasn't the one who didn't know what she was in for.

Roman stood on her doorstep with a smile and a large cup of coffee that smelled like French vanilla and cream. The cup he had at his lips was smaller and probably not as delicious as what he'd brought for Aisha.

"I think I might love you," she said, greedily reaching for the cup.

He laughed and the lines around his eyes spread out like rays of sunshine. "Good morning to you, too."

The coffee was like the whipped cream on top of the delicious vision he was in his designer waterproof shoes, thin jeans and T-shirt. The shirt was loose, but every time he moved, it draped over some bit of muscle, some graceful line of him, that made her want to sigh like an infatuated teenager.

"Come in," she said with her hands wrapped firmly around the coffee cup. "I'm almost ready."

It was 7:06 a.m.

Her cat, Eloise, slinked close to see what was going on, her gold eyes trained curiously on Roman, who gave her a smile.

"Hey, there," he said her way before closing the door behind him.

Aisha took a sip of the coffee—perfectly prepared with the right ratio of cream and French vanilla flavoring. Oh, God, if Roman was into it, she was so going to marry him.

What else was she going to do with a man who remembered the way she liked her coffee after seeing her order it once?

"Let me just get my shoes." She wriggled her bare toes against the hardwood floor and then dashed off down the hall to her bedroom. Behind her, Eloise crept closer to Roman with a curious meow.

In her bedroom, she grabbed the socks and shoes she'd already laid out, glorified shoe-liners and her waterproof Mary Janes. A quick look in the mirror verified that the two tight braids she'd re-twisted barely an hour before were still in place. Her yellow T-shirt was plain and she wore her thickest and most comfortable yoga pants that hooked under the arch of her feet like ballet tights. In her opinion, she looked casual and cute, totally ready to be swept off her feet by a yoga-loving CEO.

Aisha laughed softly to herself.

After a stroke of lip gloss, she was all set. Aisha grabbed the waterproof mini-pack that already held some money, her phone and a change of socks. She added her lip gloss, grabbed her coffee off the dresser and went out to meet him.

"I'm ready!"

"Yes, you are." Roman looked up from the cat purring away in his lap.

Aisha tried not to blush too much from the way he slid his eyes over her, a glow of appreciation in them. "We're not going bungee jumping, are we?"

"Only if you want to," he said.

Very gently, he moved Eloise from his lap and onto the space beside him on the couch. "Later, puss."

Eloise meowed at him, batting a friendly paw against his thigh and tried to crawl back on top of him. Like Aisha, she obviously couldn't get enough of Roman.

After an apologetic scratch behind the cat's ears, he picked up his coffee. "I'll drive."

"Of course you will."

His green truck waited for them in her driveway, gleaming apple-bright in the early morning sun. The sight of it made Aisha smile. Never too far away, a memory of him resurfaced—him walking to the truck the day they'd met, the confident and sexy flex of his butt under those thin pants, that quick smile like a secret between them even while he was rejecting her.

"Oh, this is gorgeous." Her hands groped the brightly colored curves of the antique truck. "I'd expected a Mercedes or something like that from a CEO." Although, this beauty was perfect for a Hot Yoga Daddy who fueled dreams she was almost embarrassed about the next morning.

"I haven't always been a CEO," he said, opening the

passenger door for her. "Besides, a Mercedes couldn't handle the roads where we're going." His eyes twinkled.

Aisha climbed into the roomy truck and buckled her seat belt. Outside, it was all nostalgia and apple pie. Inside, though, it was surprisingly modern. He'd installed airbags and a Bluetooth connection, and, as she wriggled in the seat, the leather was butter-soft and she felt like she was sitting on a cloud.

"How perfect is this truck? Antique and up-to-date at the same time." She ran her hands over the chrome dash, inhaling the scent of sun-warmed leather and man. A glance toward the driver seat confirmed he was watching her. "From the outside, this sweet ride is definitely not all that it seems."

"I'd like to think that goes for more than just my truck." Tossing her one last look, he started the engine.

Roman navigated the gleaming creature around Aisha's circular driveway and out onto the main road.

"Well, so far, the appearance of things is fine by me," she said. And was it ever.

Aisha knew that what she was doing with Roman was stupid. It didn't have a chance in hell of ending well. Not with the Sykes Prize and his insistence on seeing her as "too young." But she had every intention of enjoying him as much as she could before things blew up in their faces.

"Good to know" was all Roman said.

They drove for a few minutes, past the streets leading to her mother's house and then Ahmed's.

"This area is beautiful," he said as he skillfully handled the truck along the tree-lined street. "The land is nice-looking, green and so well maintained." He gave the view an appreciative glance. "I can easily imagine having a yoga retreat here. Lots of space."

"Glad you think so. This whole area belongs to my family, actually, and we love it." Aisha explained how Ahmed had bought the large acreage of land years ago and built houses for each of them, creating a large compound that was like their own urban park complete with jogging trails, a pond and the occasional wild animal that wandered in. "We love living so close, but there's enough space between us that we don't see each other unless we want to."

"That's a nice idea," Roman said with a touch of envy in his voice. "Nothing that would work for me and Lance, but it's nice."

"Why wouldn't it work for you and your brother?" *Maybe because Lance is an ass*, Aisha thought then could've pinched herself for making snap judgments about someone she didn't know.

"He likes his houses big and tends to have lots of parties. I prefer walking for miles or skinny-dipping in the pond without worrying about anybody coming around."

A swift heat rose inside her at the thought of him naked and wet, rising from the water with clear rivulets dripping along his bare body, his muscles gleaming and hard under the sun. "You can always come over here and skinny-dip in our pond, if that's what you're after."

He glanced at her, one hand deftly steering the truck while the other lifted the coffee cup to his mouth. "That's not exactly what I'm after," he said. Then a quick look crossed his face, as if he regretted his words.

Before she could think better of it, Aisha brushed a hand over his thigh, intending to soothe him. Then she froze, realizing what she'd done. She cleared her throat. "You can always tell me what you want," she said instead of the apology she'd hastily swallowed. Her coffee tasted sweet and creamy on her tongue. A dangerous sort of pleasure with Roman sitting so close to her.

Driving onto the highway with easy skill, Roman didn't take his eyes off the road in front of them. "That seems like the fastest way for me to get into trouble," he said with a twitch of his lips.

Aisha smiled around the edge of her coffee cup. "Did I ever tell you trouble is my middle name?"

"I don't doubt that for a minute."

Roman drove on. During the long ride, they fell into a smooth banter that made Aisha laugh, squirm and tease Roman until he laughed. It was so easy being with him. Before she knew it, nearly an hour had passed.

"We're here." Roman pulled the truck into a parking area with a half dozen other cars.

The signs around them said they were near the Chattahoochee River. The sound of the river was a gurgling whisper, soothing Aisha despite the giant cup of coffee she'd basically inhaled on the ride.

Tall trees swayed in the early morning sunlight, a light wind played through the leaves, and the fresh smell was all river water and clean outdoors.

Around them in the parking lot, people wrestled with brightly colored boats that they pulled from their trucks and car roofs. Roman got out of the truck and firmly closed the door. It was only then that she realized he, too, had a boat strapped into the back of his truck.

Huh. I really wasn't paying attention to much this morning, was I? Besides Roman.

"What exactly are we doing out here?" Aisha asked as she eyed the area. Everyone around them looked like outdoor types in waterproof clothes and boat shoes, carrying skinny backpacks. A couple in matching bicycle shorts and tight, long-sleeved shirts carried a boat toward the dock.

"We're going kayaking."

Wasn't that a travel web site or something?

"Are you going to drown me in revenge for challenging you about the prize?" She backed away from the boat as he unsnapped the cords tying it down and pulled it out of the truck. The muscles of his arms bulged and stretched and Aisha wet her lips, unable to look away.

Roman didn't look like he had any difficulty at all as he put the boat, a bright blue hard plastic thing with room for two, on the ground next to the truck. "There would be easier ways to get my revenge, believe me." His mouth twisted. "If I were the vengeful sort, which I'm not, by the way."

"Okay..."

Laughing, he locked up the truck. "Your backpack is waterproof, right?" When Aisha nodded, he tossed the keys her way.

She slipped them into the main compartment and put it on her back. "Okay. Since you seem determined to do this, just tell me what to do."

"Tell you what to do? Hmm. I could get used to that."

She tossed a pebble at him.

By the time Roman had gotten through all the instructions, nearly everyone who'd come before them into the parking lot was gone, already sailing down the river that rippled gently under the morning sun. The scene looked very peaceful.

"Oh, I almost forgot." Roman reached into the truck bed and pulled out a pair of bright yellow life vests. "Here. One for you and one for me."

"I can swim," she said. "I don't need one."

Roman put on his own vest and fastened it. "It's not about being able to swim. It gets a bit rocky downriver and if you fall out and hit your head, at least you won't drown before I can drag you to safety."

The images those words put in Aisha's imagination made her stomach cramp with sudden alarm.

She reached for the vest he held out and quickly put it on.

He carried the boat to the dock and put it to water. Even though Aisha didn't have a single clue of how to get in, he helped her make a smooth transition from earth to water.

The kayak glided noiselessly through the river, Roman behind her, being what he called "the anchor" and pretty much doing everything to pilot the boat even though she paddled the way he'd taught her. The river was calm, an early morning mist rising from its surface and diffusing in the air, giving their ride a surreal feel. It was... beautiful.

Except for her four years in a French university, Aisha had lived in Atlanta her whole life. While the city was known for its green spaces and the seamless way the urban and the natural worlds intersected, she'd always been more interested in the city. Skyscrapers. Bright lights. The rush of a thousand pairs of feet across the sidewalks. That was the part of Atlanta she loved.

But she could easily see the appeal of a place like this.

They glided on the glasslike surface of the river, past deep green trees, under a blue sky and cottony clouds.

"My mother loved the water," Roman said. He continued to paddle. "She loved it up here."

His voice was a soothing rumble behind her, low and rich, another beautiful part of the landscape and the unexpected perfection of the morning. She paused her paddling to dip her fingers into the water. Aisha shivered at its coolness and sighed.

"I can see why," she said.

"Lance was never a big fan of the river or even the outdoors." Roman paused, laughing at what seemed a private memory. "He was always worried about ticks, ever since we watched that documentary about hiking the Appalachian Trail where the guys ended up checking each other over for ticks every night."

Aisha shuddered. "Should I even ask where they had to check?"

He laughed again. "I'm sure you can use your imagination."

"Ugh." She shivered dramatically again and that earned her another laugh from him.

"Even though he wasn't a fan of the tick-checking part, I know he still likes to camp, just like I do."

Aisha imagined his brother was more into "glamping" than actually making up a tent and sleeping only two or three pieces of fabric removed from the ground. "When was the last time you went camping?" she asked.

"A couple of weeks ago," he said, and the rhythm of his strokes in the water briefly faltered. "Though, to be fair, it wasn't *camping* in the strictest sense of the word. Just a semi-luxurious night under the stars to clear my mind. I came up here with Merrine to have one last weekend as myself before the responsibilities of being CEO of Sykes swallowed my life."

She frowned, swept her fingers through the water, back and forth. "Are you that much of a workaholic?"

"Why?"

"Well, I get wanting to have some time to yourself

away from this huge job that you have now, but it's possible to find balance, isn't it? Not every person in your position is out there having early heart attacks just because they're rich and successful and have to manage a profitable company."

"That's a great thought, and I wish it could be the case. But the only example of that kind of success was my father who was basically married to the job and considered the profits to be his children. The real ones had to mostly fend for themselves."

Oh. That sounded awful. And lonely for his family. Aisha glanced quickly over her shoulder, nervous about turning around and risking overturning the kayak. "I'm sorry to hear that," she said.

"I was sorry to live it. But all that's over now."

His paddle moved through the water and she paddled along with his strokes, trying to match his rhythm. Birds sang through the trees. Up ahead, she could see the smooth heads of rocks cresting the water. The river itself, she realized, had gradually begun to run a bit more swiftly.

"Do you plan on doing anything to make sure you don't end up living and dying like your father?"

She felt rather than saw his smile, a slow relaxation in his big body. "Absolutely. For one thing, I plan on coming out to the river any chance I get."

"Good. You seem happy here. Everyone should make time for their own happiness, no matter what they do during the week." She peeked over her shoulder at him. "Well, unless they're a serial killer or some other really crappy human being who likes doing crappy things."

His soft laugh rumbled from behind her. "I'll keep that in mind."

The current swept them faster along the river, gliding between rocks that suddenly appeared. Moments later a thick tree limb tumbled across a mini waterfall the small boat maneuvered through.

Wow. Roman was really, really good at this kayaking stuff.

When the conversation lulled to a comfortable silence, broken only by the low sounds of the natural world around them—the subtle splash of his paddle in the water, the easy, deep inhale and exhale of him behind her—Aisha allowed her imagination to roam.

She imagined the straining muscles in Roman's arms as he propelled them skillfully through the water and down the rapidly rushing river. The bunch of his pectoral muscles under the T-shirt. The sensual straining in his back.

A shiver rippled through her entire body. Fireflies of desire lit up her insides.

Control yourself.

But she couldn't. It felt like she was in high school all over again, fluttering all over the place because of her crush on a popular boy she had no hope of winning. But this boy—no, this man—was behind her and she could practically feel the sweat of his exertions, the huff of his breath on the back of her neck.

Twisting around in the kayak, Aisha opened her mouth to speak. But the little boat jerked.

"Be careful!" But Roman spoke too late because she turned too hard and too fast and the kayak tilted. Before she could stop herself Aisha spilled out into the river. Her paddle went one way and she went another.

"Oh my God!" Despite the summer heat, the river slid icy fingers under her shirt, her pants, over her face.

In the cold, deep water, she gasped in a breath. "Roman!" Her life jacket kept her afloat. Thank God, Roman had insisted she wear it.

About ten feet away from her, Roman swam toward her, his paddle in hand as he fought the current. "Grab my paddle!"

Aisha gasped in relief to see him and swam in the direction of the paddle he held out. Then suddenly the kayak was there, inches from her head. Cold water splashed over her face. She gasped and bucked out of the way. But not fast enough. The kayak clipped her shoulder and she hissed from the pain then grabbed it so it wouldn't float away like her paddle.

This little boat was something Roman valued. She wouldn't let it be lost. Not because of her own carelessness. The plastic boat was both rough and slippery under her arm as she grabbed it, keeping it close while she swam one-handed toward Roman.

"It's okay!" she called out to him, gulping water and fighting against the current that hadn't seemed so strong a few minutes ago. "Grab the boat. Throw the paddle inside!"

"Let go of the boat!" Roman yelled at her.

The current swept her along, right into a rock. Pain slammed through her arm and shoulder but she didn't let go of the kayak. Instead she pushed away from the rock, her shoes easily finding purchase.

"The shore!" she gasped and swam as much as she was able to against the current.

A quick glance over her shoulder confirmed that Roman was right behind her, swimming quickly toward her. The rocks near the shore slithered under her shoes.

The kayak slid against her arm and side, bumping into her with her every movement.

"Come on." Suddenly, Roman was on the shore, holding the paddle out to her and helping to pull her up onto the rough bank and dry land.

How did he get there so fast? His fingers were strong around hers, his breathing rough as he dragged her all the way to him and against his chest.

"Damn, Aisha…" he gasped against her ear. "You scared the hell out of me."

Even wet and shaking, he felt good. Aisha licked her lips and held tighter to him, not ready to let go yet. "I told you I can swim."

The kayak dropped out of her grip and dropped to the ground. Roman pulled away, his brows lowered as he stared at her.

"I told you to let go of the boat," he growled at her. "I can buy another one but I could never replace you."

His frown deepened as he seemed to realize what he'd just said. Aisha smiled up at him. "Well, now you don't have to replace either one."

"Christ." He dragged her against him again, his big chest heaving with the effort of swimming so quickly to shore, and maybe with something else, too. "Don't ever do that again." His gaze was intense on hers, with a frantic edge. Water dripped down his face, his gasping lips.

Kiss me, she thought with an edge of desperation. *Please, kiss me.*

As if obeying her directive, his mouth swooped down and captured hers. Firm and hot, a contrast to the cold water, making her shiver. Then Roman stiffened and pulled back, his face a study in shock at what he'd just done. But Aisha didn't want his regret. She wanted his heat. She wanted his desire.

With a low moan, she shot onto her tiptoes and pressed her lips to his. Once. Twice. For a moment he just breathed against her, still as a statue, while she twined her arms around his neck and crushed his mouth with her hungry kisses. Then he shuddered, a full quiver of his entire body that she felt deep inside hers. He groaned like he was in pain and latched his arms around her waist and kissed her back.

Oh hell yes.

It didn't matter that she was soaking wet and about to catch her death of cold. His body against hers felt so right, so good. Her knees buckled when he tongued her lips apart, tenderly exploring her mouth, the intimate place that she swore from now on would only be his to taste, his to make love to.

Oh God. Oh God.

Somehow she knew it would be like this. Once she tasted him, there would be no going back. Not from this. Never.

"Woohoo!" A wild whistle from a passing kayak jerked them apart.

Aisha forced a smile and waved at the pair of kayakers. Roman cursed and licked his gorgeous lips. Even though he stood a foot or so away from her, his eyes were still on her mouth, so Aisha bit her bottom lip, wanting him to see just how much she wanted him, too.

He cleared his throat and jerked his gaze away from her. "We need to go."

"Where? And how?" They were a long way from his truck and she couldn't imagine them paddling upstream against the current. Not to mention they were both dripping wet. She shivered.

After another quick look at her, Roman grabbed the kayak, easily lifting it above his head. "Come on. I know a place where we can dry off at least."

He hefted the kayak over one shoulder then briefly touched the small of Aisha's back. "This way."

Chapter 12

It wasn't supposed to go like this.

The plan was a morning kayak ride on the river to show Aisha one of the things his mother loved, maybe lunch on the way back into the city. And that was it.

If there was one thing that the last few weeks of Roman's life proved, though, it was that things didn't always go as planned.

"It's not too far." With the kayak on his shoulder, Roman risked a darting glance to make sure she was still behind him on the path. He'd prefer her walking in front, but she didn't know the way and he wanted to get there as soon as possible and get her out of those wet clothes.

Wait. The picture his imagination supplied wasn't exactly what he had in mind. Her bare skin, slowly being revealed to him as she shed the wet garments one at a time.

But once the thought came, his mind latched onto it

and wouldn't let go. He clenched his teeth and tried to will away the tightening in his crotch. Just in time, the cabin appeared.

"Right there," he called over his shoulder to her as he pointed ahead.

Two-story and A-frame, the cabin's blond wood glowed under the late morning sun. It was a cabin his mother'd had custom-built for those times she didn't want to rush back to her life in the city. Over the years, he'd made sure to keep a caretaker for it. One who came in twice a month to ensure the cabin was clean with everything in working order and ready to be used at a moment's notice.

Roman climbed the short four steps to the porch and, after sliding the kayak off his shoulder and to the floor, opened the door with the key hidden in a wooden decoration built into the railing. He held the door open for Aisha and, once she stepped inside, closed it behind them.

The cabin wasn't anything luxurious. His mother, despite the fact that she'd been born into money and had married even more money, preferred her luxuries in other things. Travel. Yoga classes and retreats. A well-rounded education for her sons instead of the hyper-focus on business schools and classes her husband insisted on. So, no, this cabin wasn't a mini palace like the one his father owned high in the Blue Ridge Mountains or the French Alps. This one had a small living room with a couch, two chairs and a plain rug gathered around the fireplace, along with a serviceable kitchen, a lofted sleeping space above them and a bedroom with an attached bath down the hall.

After a quick check to make sure everything was in

order, he turned on the power, water heater and everything else that lay dormant between his visits.

Roman and Lance had visited the place with their mother many times. His mother had brought him a few times while he was in high school and later in college. He'd come on his own since his mother died two years ago but never stayed more than a night or two.

The cabin was always cozy. But with Aisha breathing softly near him, he felt all at once its intimacy. She looked around her with curious eyes and then got her hands in on the exploration, running her fingers over the pale wooden walls then leaning against the fireplace to peer up at the framed photographs on the mantel. She seemed especially interested in the one of his mother by herself, her hair a thick fall of mostly gray dreadlocks to the middle of her back.

It was a photo Roman had taken one summer. It captured her wading into the river from its rocky edge, the hem of her long, teal dress gathered in one hand as she looked down to see where she was stepping. Scattered rocks rose large and smooth around her, the river gushing in mini waterfalls around and over them.

Next to that photo was one of his mother with him and Lance when they were teenagers. The third framed photo was of him and his brother taken at Roman's business school graduation. When Aisha's fingers touched the silver box next to the photographs, the breath froze in his lungs. She moved on and he breathed easily again.

Roman cleared his throat.

"The bathroom is down there," he said, pointing to the hallway. "You can have the first shower. There's a dresser in the bedroom with some clothes that might fit you."

"Oh, okay." Aisha turned away from her close study

of the photos. "This place is really something. So unexpected up here." She waved a hand at the photos. "Your mother?"

"Yes."

She nodded and didn't say anything else, only took a slow and scenic meander toward the bathroom. A breath left his open mouth as she closed the door behind her. His knees felt weak, his entire body too battered from his battle with the river's current to properly make sense of what the hell he was doing. After a few cleansing breaths, he managed to get it together.

He stripped off his wet shirt, shoes and socks, keeping on only the pants until Aisha came out of the bathroom and he could use the shower himself. He threw the clothes in the washing machine but didn't turn the machine on just in case Aisha wanted to have her clothes washed, too.

In the kitchen, he put on the coffee and started the kettle for tea.

By the time Aisha came out of the bedroom, the coffee was made and the water for tea ready.

"It's all yours," she said.

She smelled like the lemon body wash he kept in the bathroom and she was wearing an oversize T-shirt and loose pants. One of the many pieces of clothing his mother had kept at the cabin. With her body sweet-smelling from her shower and a faintly nervous smile on her face, Aisha looked delectable. Irresistible. Young.

Roman nearly broke his neck rushing out of the room.

"There's coffee and tea in the kitchen," he said over his shoulder before firmly closing the bathroom door behind him.

Instantly he regretted his decision to rush off so quickly. He should have waited until the scent of her had dissipated from the bathroom. Now, trapped in the small room full of steam and the scent of woman, Roman was hard as river rock.

All too easy, the image of her in that room came to him. Nude and stepping into the glassed-in shower, the steam swirling around her slender body. His own body betrayed his desire. Oh so very easily. His hand drifted down, palmed his hardness through his damp pants. A groan spilled from his lips.

Stop. If he didn't stop the easy grip of his hand right now, he didn't know if he'd be able to.

He yanked his hand away from his hardness and quickly stripped. When he stepped under the shower spray, it was still cold. Roman made quick and efficient work of cleansing himself with one of the small cloths and the same lemon soap that now seasoned Aisha's body.

Despite the cold water and his efficient movements, his body was still ready for hers when he got out of the shower. In the bedroom, he dressed in some of his own clothes and, after taking a deep and calming breath meant to center him and get rid of his lingering arousal, went back into the living room.

While he'd been gone, Aisha had opened the blinds in the kitchen and living room. Sunlight spilled over every surface, over her. In the borrowed clothes that shouldn't have made her seem so damn sexy, she sat on a bar stool at the rustic countertop, drinking what smelled like coffee. When she saw him, she looked up with a warm smile.

"Coffee or tea?" she asked.

Roman's big mouth opened before his brain could kick in. "Isn't there traditionally a third choice in that question?"

Her eyes widened then her pretty mouth curved up in

a slow, seductive smile. Roman noticed how the corners of her eyes were smooth, years away from acquiring any wrinkles. Unlike his.

"I didn't know you were interested in that part of the menu," Aisha said. "But it's very definitely available to you."

Roman swallowed hard, the effort he'd put into calming his body going completely to waste at the look in her long-lashed eyes. Without his permission, his feet took him to the kitchen. The smell of brewed coffee was rich there. And underneath it, the tempting scent of Aisha's newly washed body. Lemons. Woman. Temptation.

Because he was a man who always believed in follow-through, no matter who started it, he went to Aisha, crowded her even as she backed away, a slow and enticing movement of her long legs, until her back hit the kitchen counter.

"You don't know how happy it makes me to hear you say that," he said before lowering his mouth to hers.

Kissing her at the river had been a reckless mistake. She'd been wet from her unplanned swim and gorgeous, the water clinging to her skin, dripping down her eyelashes and her soft cheeks. Although he couldn't remember who'd kissed whom, the meeting of their lips had seemed almost a natural consequence of his fears being unfounded, at being relieved he hadn't accidentally killed her.

That moment had almost been beyond his control.

Now, though, he didn't have that excuse.

"God, you're beautiful."

Did he say that?

His fingers slipped under her thick, damp hair to press into the delicate heat of her scalp then down the back of her neck. Aisha groaned into his mouth. She shifted against him and he could smell the lemon soap against her skin. And knowing that she smelled of the same thing he did seemed like the greatest intimacy. The ultimate knowing.

Heart knocking loud in his chest, he kissed the corners of her mouth, her cheek, the slope of her neck, seeking out more of that skin-warmed scent. "You smell delicious," he groaned, unable to help himself.

"I smell like you." She laughed, low and sensual, just before he returned his lips to hers.

And then her laughter tapered off into a soft moan. She stretched against him, pressing her breasts, belly and thighs into him.

Roman's fingers clutched, digging into her soft hips. His senses reeled.

"Yes…" she breathed against his lips. "Touch me."

Aisha gasped again when he cupped her ripe behind and gripped her tight against him, moving their bodies until they were rocking together against the countertop as their tongues mated, their breaths mixed and their moans and sighs ribboned through the kitchen.

"Like this?" He slid a hand under the back of the pants she wore and encountered naked flesh. His heart thundered loudly in its cage.

"Yes," she groaned again.

He wanted her. No matter how young he thought she was. No matter how complicated their involvement would be. He wanted her with a ferocity that elicited a growl from his throat and ignited the savage desire to claim her for himself so she wouldn't so much as glance at another man.

No. That was wrong. That wasn't how he acted with the women he wanted.

Normally he was a much more civilized man. A more courteous man.

But with every sweep of his tongue inside her mouth, every brush of her long fingers under his shirt, he was turning into someone else. A man who would do anything to have her. Even ignore the obvious and the wrong and the complicated.

She overruled his mind. His sense of right.

Roman gripped Aisha to him, pressing his aching hardness into her.

"Oh!" she gasped into his mouth, a hot sound of delight. Sharp nails clenched into the flesh of his butt through the two layers of clothing.

She seemed to want him just as much as he wanted her.

But he couldn't. They couldn't.

Slowly, Roman pulled back.

"We shouldn't," he said, his breath unsteady. "I shouldn't."

But that was his other voice talking, some long holdout of a conversation he'd had with himself days ago when he'd first thought of having her the way he wanted. Now all the ideas of "shouldn't" were like ruins under his feet. Antiquated. Irrelevant.

"Why not?" Her lips were soft and swollen, well-kissed. "We're not hurting anyone."

Maybe not *anyone*. Just his rational mind and any chances for him to be fair where the Sykes Prize was concerned.

"You know why not," he said, trying to hold on to his reason. He couldn't quite get his breathing under control, but he tried. He also couldn't stop touching her, his hands trailing down her back and under the oversize shirt.

Her skin was so warm, so soft.

"I want you," she said, putting a hand over his aching hardness, gently squeezing. The firmer pressure from the narrow gold rings on her fingers made him groan. "You want me, too. That's all that matters here."

His flesh throbbed under the light touch of her hand. Roman wanted her, too. God, he wanted her so very, very much.

"Aisha—" he began.

She fell to her knees in front of him and, like a river's powerful current, swept the rest of his words away.

Her tongue was soft on him, a light and fluttering touch. Her hands rested on his thighs, her fingers lightly tugging down his pants to his knees while her mouth played havoc with his senses. He groaned her name. Gasped it as she brought him the sweetest pleasure of his life, stroking and kissing him until all he could do was fight to breathe.

The pleasure rolled through him, hot and rhythmic, with every slide of her mouth, every caress of her fingers. She was relentless and he couldn't stop her. Nor did he want to. Then it all came to a head too soon, a lightning strike at the base of his spine and lower, his hips moving and her hands encouraging him, until he exploded in the wet heat of her mouth, gasping her name.

Roman sagged back against the countertop. His body slackened with the aftershocks of his completion that shuddered through him, all of his flesh tingling and aware. So alive.

It had never been like this before. Effortless and complete; his senses swimming in the pleasure but also feeling finally awake, like he'd just had a shot of caffeine directly to a vein.

Still gasping from the incomparable pleasure she'd just given him, he dragged Aisha to her feet and kissed her. Deep and long and hard, groaning at the taste of him on her lips, at the way she moved sensuously against him, nipples hard and scoring his chest, her fingers sinking into his heaving sides.

"You're incredible," he gasped into her mouth between kisses, hungry and grateful.

"I think that's my line," she laughed breathlessly.

Roman reversed their positions, grumbling an apology when the cupboard behind her rattled from the force of him slamming her against it.

"No," she moaned. "More. I like it," she gasped. "I like you like this."

And that was all it took to sweep away any lingering hesitation from him. He dragged down her pants, slid a hand between her thighs.

"You're so wet," he growled.

"Just for you."

Fingers against the swell of her womanly flesh, he circled lightly. She gasped into his mouth, her hips already moving, demanding more. "Please. Please!"

"You don't have to beg me," he groaned. "Anything you want. Anything." Then he stopped giving her words and instead gave her body what it demanded.

Sighing with pleasure, he plunged his fingers deep and rubbed her, shifting his movements until he found the perfect rhythm to make her scream.

"Roman!" She tore her mouth away from his. "Oh! Right there… Oh!"

"Like this?" He moved his fingers slickly inside her. "Do you like it like this?"

"I love it! Please. Don't stop! Don't!"

But the only way he would stop was if he dropped dead in that moment.

This was pleasure. This was sharing. Why had he denied her this? Why had he denied *himself*? Aisha in the throes of her pleasure was beautiful. Her head thrown back, her thighs wide and tensed. His name gasped from her parted lips and her eyelashes fluttering wildly.

"You feel so good," he moaned into her throat just as she screamed his name one last time.

He felt her clench powerfully around his fingers. Her long thighs quivered. Her nails gouged into his back through his shirt. Aisha chanted his name as her internal muscles rippled around his fingers and the button of her pleasure swelled even more under the swift and sure movements of his thumb.

Roman only stopped when she weakly shoved at his hand, whimpering that the sensations were too much. Sighing, he pulled his fingers from her intimate place and then, as she watched, licked them dry.

Aisha whimpered again and bit her already raw-looking bottom lip. "You're a very wicked man," she said breathlessly. "And I can't wait to get you in a bed."

"That isn't what I had in mind when I brought us here," Roman said, although he wouldn't change a thing about what had just happened between them.

With his green tea and Aisha's coffee, they sat on the couch after they'd showered again. Feet bare, warm mugs in hand, their heads rested on opposite ends of the thickly cushioned sofa, their legs slotted neatly together. It was cozy, even more intimate in a way that the sex hadn't been.

"I'm glad it happened anyway." Smiling gently at him, Aisha sipped her coffee. "So why did you bring me here? Do you know?"

Nearly half an hour after his orgasm, his body was still loose but oddly energized. He wanted more of her. It had taken a surprising amount of willpower not to invite her into the bedroom for a long day lingering in their mutual pleasure. He still wasn't sure if that was a strength or a weakness.

"Other than to dry off so we don't catch pneumonia on the long and wet drive back into the city? I don't know what I wanted to do here," he said honestly.

They probably would have dried off in the sun with the windows open and the summer breeze buffeting them from both sides of the truck. But some part of him had wanted the day to linger.

"Well, I for one am glad to not be sun-drying in a truck while this much better option existed," she murmured between sips of her coffee. "Having my clothes dry on me is not a good look. So, thank you."

"It was my pleasure," Roman said then fought a flush of heat in his cheeks at his choice of words.

Aisha's grin was all kinds of dirty. "That was my intention. I'm very happy my efforts paid off."

A reluctant laugh burst out of him. Funny and unpredictable, she was a woman who crackled with energy and fire that often caught him off guard. He loved it and couldn't get enough. In the beginning, he remembered his mother had been like that, too.

"What made you frown just now?" Aisha poked him with her toe.

"Nothing important."

"I doubt that. Tell me. I promise not to take out an article in the paper and advertise how the notoriously closed-off CEO actually spilled some of his inner thoughts to me."

"Closed off? That's not me at all." Was it?

"Are you making a joke?" Aisha laughed because obviously she found his comment to be funny. Then she waved a hand in his direction. "Never mind, gorgeous. Are you going to tell me what's on your mind or not?"

He wanted to repeat his earlier dismissive comment. There was nothing on his mind that he wanted to share. "My father would probably approve of the closed-off man you think I am."

"But not you?"

He shrugged. "No. It's not something I want to be. A closed fist shuts out the world, the good things as well as the bad."

"Very true." She nodded. "And there are a lot of good things out there to let in."

"That sounds like something my mother would say." Although she hadn't been able to interact enough with the world to allow the good things to come in and sweep away the bad. It was as if she'd been convinced she'd had to give up the life she'd led to be with his father. Even now, after years of seeing his parents together, and two years after her death, he still didn't have a good enough answer as to why she'd let her husband change her. "She was the one who taught me about yoga when I was a kid."

"Nice. So not only is she responsible for creating your beautiful exterior self, but she's also the reason for your whole hot yoga CEO vibe."

He laughed. "I guess you could say that."

They'd spent so much of his childhood and his later years doing yoga together and then, when he'd started his string of yoga studios and the annual retreats in different parts of the world, she'd supported him wholeheartedly. She'd even attended some of them with him when she'd been able to drag herself away from the emotional abyss that being unhappily tethered to his father had left her in. She'd supported his interest in yoga, his need to have something separate from his father. But she'd also never let him forget his birthright and the leadership role he would eventually be handed at Sykes Global, whether or not he decided to accept it. Roman said as much to Aisha.

"So you weren't being honest with me before," she said with a teasing grin.

"What do you mean?"

"When you said you weren't always a CEO. You've always been a CEO. Growing up knowing Sykes Global was going to be yours, even when you turned your back on it in your twenties to churn out trendy yoga studios all over the country."

"I wouldn't put it like that." Something about that didn't quite sit right with him. The idea he'd been born with everything he had now and hadn't had to earn it.

"No, no. Don't look like that. I mean you were born to lead and you're doing it now. From what the papers are saying, you're doing it very well behind that big desk."

She was reading up about him? The idea of it blew a warm breeze all the way through Roman's soul. He bared more of it to Aisha.

"That makes me happy to hear." In such a short time, he'd come to enjoy his new role as head of his father's company. "Reluctant or not, I'm doing my best to make sure the board doesn't regret my father's decision to turn over the reins of Sykes Global to me. The company does a lot of good work and has a tremendous impact on the world overall."

Aisha's cheeks creased in a sympathetic smile. "Even though it sounds like the company wasn't exactly your mother's favorite thing, I think she'd be proud of you for stepping up like that."

"I hope so." He inhaled the steam from his recently refilled green tea, remembering suddenly all the times he and his mother had sat in this very room, drinking tea and just talking. "Damn, I miss her."

His words echoed in silence for a moment.

"What do you miss, exactly?" Aisha asked.

And Roman told her. All about the person his mother was and the legacy she'd left him. In turn, Aisha told him about her family. Her stubborn brother who got married a year before to the type of woman he never expected. Her sister's upcoming new art gallery and her own plans for the future.

"My family gave me a lot," she said. "They gave me every advantage a young Black girl growing up in this country could have, but I want to do more. I want to do amazing things and make them proud of me. I want them to know their investment in me hasn't been wasted."

"I'm sure they already know that," Roman said. "I mean, look at all you've already done on your own."

"I can be better," she replied with a determined look.

Aisha, he was beginning to realize more and more, was an incredible woman. He felt lucky to know her.

Roman tumbled deeper into his own thoughts, falling silent. Aisha was quiet, too.

They sat in the silence of the room while the sun

spilled through the windows. Aisha's body was stretched out and relaxed on the sofa.

Yes, Roman remembered what it was like to make love to her with his fingers, and he wanted to do more than that. To touch her and make her shudder and gasp his name. But this moment was enough, the two of them simply sharing space and marinating in the quiet of a Saturday afternoon far away from the things that complicated who they were to each other.

In the end, they didn't leave the cabin until late. Hours of talking on the couch with refilled cups of tea and coffee. A friendly game of Scrabble and then Aisha's initial thoughts on the Sykes Prize redesign.

It was a perfect day, almost too perfect. Even with his body still heavy and content from the various pleasures they shared, Roman couldn't help but wonder when this thing between them would come to an end.

Something this good always had an expiration date.

Chapter 13

After the perfect day she and Roman had had at the river and then later in the cabin, it felt only natural for her to invite him to Dev's official gallery opening a week later. Aisha didn't have any real excuse to offer him the invitation. She just wanted to see him again. When he immediately said yes during one of their evening phone calls, she was surprised.

"Yes?" she asked, her hand clenched nervously in her lap. Next to her on the couch, Eloise meowed and stared at the phone with wide yellow eyes, like she was asking Roman the same question.

"Yes," he said into the phone, his voice soft with gentle laughter. "I'd love to be your plus one."

So he showed up at her house to pick her up on Saturday evening, seven thirty on the dot. Nervous and excited, she shot up off the couch where she'd been chatting on WhatsApp with one of her girlfriends from college.

"Gotta go, Jeanie," she said in a rush of breath while butterflies attacked her stomach. "I'll tell you how it goes."

Jeanie wished her luck and shooed her off the line.

Then Aisha tucked the phone in her handbag and went to the door. "Hi," she said as she opened the door. "You're right on time."

Aisha swallowed hard at the sight of him.

From foot to crown, Roman looked like temptation in the flesh. Matte-black Italian leather shoes. Tailored dark slacks that showed off his lean lower body. A button-down shirt with the sleeves rolled up, revealing his muscled and veined forearms. A button left undone at the throat gave a hint of the muscled flesh she'd felt pressed against her during their passion-filled Saturday afternoon. He was freshly shaved and wore a scent with hints of leather, oranges and dark liquor.

"See something you like?" he teased with a smile tugging at his firm lips.

"You know I do," Aisha said, her voice rough in appreciation.

He didn't look unimpressed himself. Her sister had said "cocktail casual" was the dress code. She wasn't trying to get everyone to dig up old prom dresses or turn out like they were about to attend the Met Gala. So Aisha had thrown on a dress she'd had forever but never worn. Knee-length. Pale yellow with cap sleeves that drooped over her shoulders like fall leaves and sparkled a little in the right light. The dress hugged her curves without telling all her secrets. Plus, it had pockets.

"Good to know I'm not the only one," he said then lifted a hand. He stopped the movement with his fingers just inches from her waist. "May I?"

"Yes. Please."

He completed the movement, sliding his big hand around her waist and tugging her over the threshold and into his arms. His entire body was hard and warm. "You look beautiful. Tonight and every time I've ever seen you."

"So you mean, I just look regular tonight?" She pursed her lips, palms braced against his hard chest. His heart beat hard and steady beneath her touch.

"You, young lady, couldn't be regular even if you tried."

Despite the tripping of her heart, that surprised a laugh out of her. "Why thank you, Hot Yoga Daddy."

She felt him shiver. In the deep pool of his eyes, she saw her own desire reflected there. His gaze dropped to her lips and she knew he was going to kiss her. She held herself steady, hands braced, heart racing, and waited to be kissed. But he only brushed his mouth against her jaw, right below her ear.

"We should go," he said. "Otherwise I'd try my damnedest to convince you to stay here with me all night."

Aisha shivered, her legs growing weak, her panties wet. That didn't sound so bad. But then she found her senses.

If she missed the gallery's grand opening, Devyn would kill her and then cry.

"Okay." The breath shivered from her lungs.

Reaching behind her, she grabbed the doorknob and pulled the door closed. The lock clicked and she tucked her little purse more firmly under her arm. "Let's go."

Roman's green truck sat in the driveway, gleaming under the security lights. Seeing it reminded her of the day they'd spent on the water and then in the cabin. Of the way he'd tasted and the delight he'd taken in bringing her to the edge of pleasure and beyond. That day, the conversation had flowed between them like sweet, dark wine.

He opened the door for her and, after making sure she was safely inside, firmly closed her into the cool interior. Once he got in and started the engine, he took a long and appreciative look at the sculpted French roll she'd had done earlier that day. Then he leaned across her to wind up the manual window halfway.

"I wouldn't want to mess up your hair," he said while still draped across her, his powerful arm slowly working the window crank.

The smell of the truck's vintage leather seats, Roman's natural, masculine scent and the musky notes of his aftershave all settled a wild heat in Aisha's lap.

God, he was making it hard to not jump his bones.

When he finally drew back to his side of the truck, she breathlessly thanked him, squeezed her thighs together and prayed he couldn't detect how badly she wanted him.

"Where are we heading?" he asked.

Aisha told him the address. "Do you want me to put it in the GPS?"

"No," he said. "I'm familiar with that part of town."

Feminist to the core, she didn't realize how sexy it was for a man not to need directions until she watched him confidently head for the highway and point the truck toward her sister's new gallery. Less than a half hour later, they pulled into the parking lot of the gallery, laughter filling the truck as they finished their conversation about alien architecture in movies they'd both seen.

The parking lot serviced the cluster of six businesses in a row of two-story buildings. It was typical for the north

Atlanta neighborhood with its restaurants, yoga spots and boutiques vying for attention from the steady foot traffic.

In the middle, the gallery would have been just like its neighbors except for the pair of twenty-foot-high wings rising above it made of reinforced and laminated multicolored glass. Even in the light of evening, they glistened like they'd been plucked from the back of a giant firebird, drawing the eye in and then down to the small gallery protected by them.

"This is an incredible building." Roman pulled the truck to a complete stop, already looking out at the glassed-in, two-story gallery in front of them.

"Isn't it, though?" Aisha kept the gallery in her sights as she left the truck without waiting for Roman to open the door for her.

Every time she saw it, it made her smile.

During the day this part of town was casual, Atlanta-wealthy chic. Now Aisha could see a significant portion of the foot traffic, dressed in cocktail casual as Dev had suggested, making its way to the glittering wings. The warm night sang with the sound of conversation and laughter.

Roman locked the truck and came around the front to join Aisha. "Ready?"

"Of course." She tucked her arm through his and they walked toward the gallery together. The clear glass doors automatically parted to let them in, then stayed open, allowing the people behind them in, as well. Cool air from inside the large space brushed over Aisha's face and bare arms, and she shivered and smiled.

It all felt very fresh, very new. The ceiling was high and soaring and led the eye to the lofted space above. It, too, was glassed in, but because the glass was reflective and UV repellant, no one outside could see in. And, most important, artwork stored up there was in the safest possible place. The entire building was light and airy and gave the paintings on display room to breathe, to be seen. It was perfect.

Beautiful people wove their way through the gallery. Soft jazz played from the speakers and wait staff circulated with champagne in flutes. Along the walls, Aisha noticed some paintings already had red dots next to them, indicating that they were sold.

God, Dev must be so happy!

As if she'd conjured her sister out of thin air, Aisha saw Dev across the room. Partially hidden from view behind a sculpted steel tree, her sister whispered intimately with her husband. Bennett's pale gray, three-piece suit was the perfect complement to Dev's black dress and high heels. They even *looked* like they belonged together.

Bennett's hand lingered on Dev's waist, his mouth close to her ear as they stood in a pool of golden light meant to illuminate the sculpture. Their love for each other was so obvious, it was blinding.

Aisha let out a low sigh of mingled happiness and longing as she watched them. *This* was what she wanted for herself one day.

But Dev's guests weren't about to allow her time with her husband. Despite the intimacy of her stance with Bennett, a man tapped her on the shoulder, clearing asking her a question only she had the answer to. Waving away his wife's look of disappointment, Bennett dropped a kiss to the inside of her wrist and left her to her adoring crowd.

"Tonight is going to be amazing for her." Aisha leaned

into Roman with the joy for her sister's success fizzing in her chest.

"I agree," he said, his eyes glowing down into hers. "The turnout is as impressive as the place itself."

"Yes, it is."

Suddenly, Aisha heard Dev call her name. She forced herself to look away from Roman's dark eyes and the sensuous curve of his faintly smiling lips.

"There you are!" Her sister walked quickly toward her, dragging a besotted-looking man in her wake. The man who'd interrupted her and Bennett. "This is my sister, Aisha. She designed the building."

Smiling wide, Dev swept Aisha into a tight embrace. She smelled of success and champagne. "There's someone I'd love for you to meet, Aisha." She indicated the man at her side. "This is Sidney Dubois from that architectural magazine I mentioned the other day. He called as soon as I announced the opening, begging for an invitation so he could come to gawk at the inside of the building." With a teasing look, she turned to Sidney, a flush of success on her high cheeks. "Aisha is the brilliant architect who helped make tonight possible."

Aisha's own cheeks grew warm. "You did all the work, Dev. I just gave you the only gift you'd allow me to."

Before Dev made the gallery happen mostly on her own, Aisha had offered her some money to get it started, to help buy the building and begin the process of acquiring art. But her sister had fought her tooth and nail, wanting to do it all on her own and not accept what she'd thought of at the time as charity.

So Aisha had done what she could. Before Dev had even told her she had the money from another source to get the gallery off the ground, Aisha had jumped into action. She'd drafted the building and, with her brother's help, had bought the property—after asking Dev some pointed questions about what her ideal space would be like—and then started the construction. While designing it, she'd known the exterior had to represent her sister's dreams finally taking flight. Which was why it had the wings, glittering and protective and attention-grabbing.

Once Dev had finally decided to push forward with plans to open her own gallery, Aisha had presented her with the gift. And now, here they were.

Ignoring Sidney, she grabbed Dev again. "Congratulations, sister." Aisha hugged her tight. "*You* made this happen for yourself. *You* deserve all of this."

When they pulled back from each other, Devyn's eyes were wet, too. "It's been so incredible. God! I feel so blessed. So lucky."

"You'll get nothing less when you follow your dreams," Aisha said. She gestured to the building around them and the wings rising outside where they stood, the skylight above them open and looking up into the starry night threaded with wisps of clouds. It was like they were being lifted by the wings up into the sky. "You'll fly."

"Stop! You're going to make me cry again." But Dev was already crying anyway. Good thing she'd worn her waterproof mascara.

Over her shoulder, Aisha saw a couple moving purposefully toward Dev. "Your people are coming for you." She gently wiped the tears from her sister's face and gave her a quick kiss. Then she quickly introduced Roman before the couple arrived to claim her sister. "Now go be awesome."

"Devyn," the man said as he drew close, "how did you

manage to get such an impressive collection so quickly? I want to buy absolutely everything."

With an encouraging smile, Aisha waved her sister off and moved into the crowd. Roman kept step at her side.

"So you're the one who designed this place." He swept his gaze around them, eyes lingering on different parts of the space, as if he was somehow trying to connect it with Aisha.

"Yes, I did." She heard the pride in her voice and tried to pull it back, not wanting to seem too boastful. But she'd worked hard on the design, a part of her reminded. "I'm just glad she ended up loving it. Nothing like giving someone a present they hate."

A waiter paused near them as they made their way through the crush of people. Roman took a pair of champagne flutes and passed one to Aisha. "This design is creative and eye-catching. I can't imagine anyone not loving it. Like I said outside, it's damn incredible."

She flushed with pleasure and bit her lip on a smile. "Thank you."

As they passed an empty high table, Aisha put down her glass of untouched champagne.

"Trying to stay sober tonight?"

"Not really. I just don't drink champagne," Aisha said. "Makes my nose itch. And next day, no matter how little I drink, I have a headache from hell."

"Ah…" Roman nodded and sipped from his glass. "This is nice," he said, eyeing the champagne and the bubbles that danced inside the golden liquid.

"I'll take your word for it." Actually, she was pretty sure it was excellent. Probably imported from some small, centuries-old, family-run vineyard in the Champagne region of France. Bennett, Devyn's husband, had taken care of all the food and drinks for the opening and, like Aisha, he wanted and no doubt got only the best for Devyn. As for Aisha, she'd never been able to stand champagne, no matter how expensive, no matter how much the people she dated tried to convince her she just hadn't tasted the right one yet. "For now, I'll leave it to people who can appreciate it."

"I'll appreciate it for both of us then," Roman said with one of his eye-crinkling smiles.

It wasn't long before they found Ahmed and his wife. They stood in front of a painting, Ahmed's arm around Elle's waist, her head leaning against him. They were arguing, as only lovers could, about what image they were supposed to be seeing in the abstract work.

"I think it's a penis with legs," Elle said, wrinkling her brow. She brought her half-finished glass of white wine to her lips and dared her husband with a look. "And you can't tell me it's anything else."

"Back in the day, that would've been describing my brother to a T." Aisha slipped between them to give her sister-in-law a quick hug then teased her brother by nudging him even further away from his wife with her hip. "A *giant* penis with legs."

"I know you think you're funny, Aisha. Hate to break it to you, but you're not."

Her brother poked her waist and Aisha giggled, jumping away before his tickling could get any more aggressive. "Stop! It's not my fault you don't have a sense of humor."

Elle squeezed Aisha's waist and pointedly jerked her chin at Roman, who patiently waited to be introduced. Aisha mentally crossed her fingers that her brother wouldn't do anything to embarrass her. She beckoned

Roman forward, fingers curling into his belt loops when he was close enough to touch him. "Let me introduce you guys to Roman." She shot her brother a warning glare. "Roman, this is my brother, Ahmed, and his wife, Elle."

"A pleasure." Roman shook hands with Ahmed and, when Elle looked at him with her open expression, leaned down to give her a brief hug. "It's good to meet you both," he said. "Aisha hasn't told me a thing about you."

Ahmed let out a shout of laughter. "I think I'm going to like this one, Aisha."

Roman grinned. "Seriously, though. Props to you for all the good work you're doing in the community. Saving Black kids and Black schools should be a priority for more people."

Ahmed nodded, his face growing serious. "I can't imagine doing anything else." When Elle shifted next to him, her face soft with pride, he took her hand in his. "Other than loving my wife, of course."

"Ugh! You guys are so gross." Aisha made a gagging noise.

Elle giggled and her brother lunged forward to tickle her again. "Stop being such a baby, Aisha."

Aisha rolled her eyes. For all her antics and teasing, she was so proud of Ahmed. Not only for being such a role model in their community but also for shifting his world view in a way that opened him up to love. A few years ago she could never have imagined him doing something like this—holding a woman's hand in public and showing how he felt about her. Some days, parts of her ached with jealousy for what he'd found. Mostly though, she was just very happy for him.

She felt a warm weight settle on her back, soothing her through the thin material of her dress. Roman. She dipped her gaze to watch him from the corner of her eye. A smile touched his face and he seemed relaxed next to her, sipping his champagne and taking everything in.

Even just taking up space, he was beautiful to look at.

"—job, Aisha."

"What?" Elle had said something and Aisha had missed it completely.

Her sister-in-law gave a knowing smile. "I was saying how beautiful the building is and it's so perfect for Devyn. You did an amazing job finding the space and designing it."

"Oh! Thank you." Her cheeks warmed as she waved aside the compliment. "It's the only present she's getting from me this year so she better enjoy it."

Elle laughed and Ahmed rolled his eyes. Again.

Suddenly, Roman's hand disappeared from Aisha's back. Immediately she missed its warmth. Then she shivered when he pulled her close and dipped his mouth to her ear. His lips brushed the side of her neck and he drew back with an apologetic smile.

"Excuse me. I see someone I need to say hello to." Once he got Aisha's trembling response, he nodded at Elle and Ahmed. "I'm sure I'll see you guys again later." Then he was off, slipping between the clusters of strangers to make his way to the other side of the room.

Aisha shamelessly watched him. The broad sweep of his shoulders, his narrow waist, the way the slim fit of the slacks hugged his butt. She bit her lip and barely suppressed a sigh of lust.

"He's the Sykes Global guy, isn't he?"

"Huh?"

Elle's soft peals of laughter dragged her attention off Roman's ass. "That answers my question."

"What are you talking about?" But the color rushed furiously to Aisha's cheeks.

She knew exactly what her sister-in-law meant. The only way she would have been more obvious about her infatuation with Roman Sykes was if she wrote it across the sky in giant, passion-red letters.

"He's cute," Elle said with a dip of her shoulder and a smile. "I can see why you're all aflutter."

"I'm not 'aflutter' about him," Aisha said, her blush only getting worse.

"I don't even know what the hell 'aflutter' means, but I agree a hundred percent that you're gone for this guy," Ahmed muttered. "So much for taking it easy where he's concerned."

Oh God. Must he do the whole big brother thing right now?

Elle tapped her husband's arm. "I'm pretty sure *you* told her to take it easy, love. She didn't exactly agree that was going to be her strategy."

"Are you both ganging up on me now?" Ahmed looked between Aisha and his wife, and Aisha couldn't help but laugh.

"Excuse me. Are you Aisha Clark?"

The sound of the low, cultured voice nearby made her turn. A woman walked up to where she, Ahmed and Elle were talking, confident in a black dress that draped loosely around her body and brushed the floor. Her lipstick was a deep red and her hair the darkest tone Aisha had ever seen on a person in real life. It shone under the gallery's lights, jewel-like. Something about this woman was familiar.

"Yes, I am." Aisha offered her hand. "And you are?"

"Emersyn." The woman clasped her hand in a cool and confident greeting. "Pleased to meet you."

The man with her nodded, a motion that was at once warm and elegant. He was beautiful, with smooth skin, a keenly intelligent face and eyes that missed nothing. After the nod, he didn't offer his hand.

"Patrick," he said by way of introducing himself. "It's a pleasure for me, as well. You designed this building, yes?"

In his rich Nigerian accent, the question was more a statement.

Aisha felt more than saw her brother and his wife exchange puzzled looks. "Yes, I did."

"It's very well done," Emersyn said with a smile. "The building, even with the wings, fits nicely into the old space but doesn't at all blend in."

"Very lovely. Very functional. Wonderful use of the glass. It reminds me of a cathedral. And it's obvious you had it in mind to house this gallery all along."

"Thank you," Aisha said, puzzled but pleased.

"Do you mind very much showing us around the building? It really is quite unique." Patrick swept an approving glance around them, smiling in a way that was both oddly cool and warm.

"It's my sister's gallery opening and it's her space. I'd suggest you speak with her. She'd be happy to talk with you about it."

"*You* wouldn't be happy to talk about it?" Emersyn asked, her head tilted in a way that made it seem like she was examining Aisha for more than just her answer to that particular question.

"Stop teasing the woman, Emersyn." Still smiling, Patrick tugged at the light scarf around his neck, resettling it into a configuration that was no different from the original. "She's teasing," he said to Aisha. "We've already spoken with your sister and she's very charming, but she's also busy with selling the art and enjoying her golden moment. We thought it would be lovely to get a different view of things from you."

Patrick and Emersyn weren't obnoxious, exactly, but they seemed almost *too* interested in talking with her. What was going on here?

But this was Devyn's moment, and it made sense that her sister was busy doing what she was meant to, namely enjoy her success and all the people who'd come out to see her. Aisha was still uncertain, though. "Ah...sure."

"I'll come with you." Ahmed put a light hand on her arm. "I'd love to hear more about this building. It's nice to look at but what more is there?"

Elle's deceptively soft eyes skimmed over the couple wanting Aisha's time. "I'll come along, too."

Patrick's eyes glinted with amusement. The two weren't fooling anyone. "The more, the merrier."

Emersyn laughed outright. "Come along, then."

Ahmed and Elle walked just behind them, never too far behind, quietly talking to each other but always keeping an eye on how the strangers interacted with Aisha.

It wasn't until they had seen the building from nearly every angle—inside, outside in the warm night air so they could appreciate the rainbow of lights glowing in the wings, and now upstairs to the lofted space that ran the entire second level—that things began to fall into place. Emersyn and Patrick's accents. The questions they were asking. Even the rapt attention they each paid to her every answer. "Emersyn Rankin and Patrick Sebastian." Aisha barely stopped herself from saying their names in a kind of awe.

The corners of Patrick's mouth curved up and Emersyn laughed for the second time in an hour. "Those are our names, yes," she said.

They were two-thirds of Rankin, Sebastian and Ziegler, one of the most powerful and influential architectural firms in the world.

When Aisha had first thought of going after the very best firm, she'd considered applying with them. But they'd only had offices in Tokyo, Dubai, Accra and Paris at the time. It was only since she'd been at Wainwright and Tully that they had opened an office in Atlanta.

By that point, being with Wainwright and Tully had drained a lot of her spirit and, embarrassingly enough, she'd even lost some of her earlier self-confidence. Yes, WT had offered her an office, but it seemed to come with the understanding that the tiny room was all she would get and all she deserved while churning out designs of gas stations or completing the finishing touches to another architect's work in the firm while he—and it was almost always a *he*—went on to do something more important.

"What are you both doing here?" Aisha asked then could've smacked herself in the forehead. She bit her tongue but kept going. "I thought you both worked out of one of the foreign offices."

"We do," Emersyn said. "But then we heard about an interesting new talent right here in our American backyard and had to investigate for ourselves."

Oh my God!

A moment later Aisha realized that her mouth was hanging wide open. She snapped it shut with an embarrassingly loud click. "You're talking about me, aren't you?"

Emersyn's dark eyes flashed with amusement. "Yes, we are, Ms. Clark."

Behind her, she heard the whispered conversation of her brother and his wife, noticed them falling back a bit more to offer her the privacy she now needed. Her cheeks felt hot and her heart pounded a thousand beats a minute. Emersyn Rankin and Patrick Sebastian, here, and interested in her and the building she'd designed.

If somebody didn't pinch her quick, she was going to pass out. Dev would never forgive her if she took a header off the loft and went splat, humiliating her at her own gallery opening.

"There you are, Aisha." Roman suddenly appeared at her side. "I was beginning to think I'd have to send a search party after you." His eyes narrowed as he locked gazes with Aisha who, she was sure, looked shocked and about to vomit. He put a protective hand on the small of her back. "Is everything all right here?"

At the sound of Roman's deep, soothing voice, the hurricane-force winds of wild emotions drained away, leaving Aisha as limp as a rose in the heat of a Georgia summer. Immediately, Roman's firm arms tightened around her, keeping her on her feet, and she leaned all the way into him.

Her nose immediately sought out the cool and spicy scent of his aftershave.

God, this man is magic.

"I'm more than fine," she finally managed to say even though her voice sounded breathy and high, doing a damn good impression of a Southern belle having an attack of the vapors. "I'm now *officially* freakin' awesome."

Chapter 14

When she thought about Roman, Aisha tried not to grin like an idiot.

Although they hadn't made any promises to each other, she and Roman had been texting each other a few times every day with jokes and random observations about their days. Once Roman even sent her the link to the yoga retreat his company was planning for the next year in South Africa, asking what she thought of the trip. Their connection was unexpected and powerful. Something Aisha never had before with a man.

After Devyn's successful gallery opening and the shock of Emersyn and Patrick's interest in her work, the night had seemed too incredible to be real. Afterward, she and Roman had sat in his truck in the parking lot and watched the lights flash and glow in the building. They'd talked about a million little things, including his surprise at seeing his best friend, Merrine, at the opening.

In the end, Aisha and Roman had been too tired to do more than kiss like horny but exhausted teenagers in her doorway before he drove away at nearly four in the morning. He and Merrine already had plans to meet up at the crack of dawn for a mountain hike.

Friday evening Aisha sat at her drafting table, frowning down at her new plans for the Sykes Prize, pencil in hand.

She nearly jumped out of her skin when the phone rang. Still looking at the design spread out on the drafting table, she fumbled in the pocket of her robe for the phone.

"Hello?" At best, the only people she expected to call at this time of night were her family. Or, not as nice, boundary-less work colleagues. Senior architects from the firm had taken to calling her at all hours lately, demanding more and more ridiculous things she was sure were designed to take her time from the Sykes project.

"You sound distracted," Roman said to her through the phone.

Oh. Just that quickly, she wasn't distracted at all.

"I'm not now." Smiling, Aisha put the pencil down and tied the silky robe more securely around her waist. "To what do I deserve the honor of your call at—" she looked at the wall clock she passed on the way to the living room from her office "—eight thirty at night?"

"It's not booty call hours yet, is it?" he asked with laughter in his voice.

"You tell me. I'm not the kind to make or get those types of phone calls, Mr. Sykes."

"For some reason, I don't believe you."

"Well, I'm just telling you about my life now, not before." Aisha sat on the sofa and stretched out her legs. It should scare her that she'd already clearly delineated her life in terms of after Roman and before. Eloise came out of nowhere, purring her head off. She leaped onto the sofa and made herself comfortable on Aisha's lap.

Aisha nearly sighed like an infatuated school girl at the sound of Roman's warm, deep laughter.

"Well, I'm not calling you for that, just to talk. Your record of no booty calls since we met is still safe."

"Too bad," she said, grinning up at the ceiling. "So if not my booty, what's on your mind?" Eloise uncoiled herself in Aisha's lap and the cat walked up to her chest, meowing as if she knew her favorite new man was on the phone. With her feline hearing, she probably knew very well it was Roman on the line. Aisha ran a hand down the cat's sinuous back.

Roman's low sigh ribboned out of the phone to brush her ear. "It's been a long day and I've already bothered Merrine about my life for the moment, so I thought of you."

"I'm second place, am I?"

"Never. Just someone I want to talk to instead of bitchin' about something you've already heard about a million times." The sound of glass on glass came at her through the phone, then liquid being poured.

"Fair enough, but just so you know, I've been known to have open and nonjudgmental ears to a round of bitchin'. In fact, I'll say that said bitchin' only makes you human and not some yoga god sent to us mere mortals from a super-flexible alternate universe."

He laughed again. "Why don't you tell me about your day instead?"

"Nice deflection." Aisha smiled into the phone. "My day was my day. Boring and filled with work. Although

I did make a detour to that teahouse where you and I met up the other day. I had a very relaxing few hours just thinking about nothing."

"Good. I'm happy you did. That place is great. It's saved my sanity a few times."

"And today, what kind of insanity did you deal with?"

His laughter was rueful. "You're determined to get me to spill my guts, aren't you?"

"I am. And I won't even be subtle about it."

"Fine." He blew out a low breath. "It's my assistant. Or I should say my father's assistant? She's being more of a burden than a help. Although there's no point in replacing her, she's pressing all my buttons lately."

"Why do you think there's no point in replacing her?"

He paused as if he wasn't sure about telling her that much about his life. Aisha's belly sank. She just opened her mouth to tell him "never mind" when he spoke again.

"I won't be CEO of Sykes for more than a year. My brother will take over the company soon and will likely choose his own assistant. I don't want to hire someone who might only have the job for less than a year."

What? "Are you stepping down?"

"I am, yes. Circumstances beyond my control will force me to stay on longer than I'd like, but I'm passing the company to Lance as soon as I'm able."

Wow. Aisha frowned. For some reason, the thought of Lance Sykes as the head of Sykes Global wasn't a comforting one. But it wasn't her company. She turned her thoughts back to what Roman had said.

"No matter how short your time in the CEO chair, you shouldn't inconvenience yourself because of someone else." Aisha scratched behind Eloise's ears, smiling when her cat began to purr even louder. "A good assistant can help things in your office run more smoothly, which makes your time in that office more effective. If you won't replace her for yourself, get rid of her for the company's sake."

"I was afraid you'd say something like that," he said.

"Ah, I see. You know exactly what to do then. You just want someone to talk you out of it."

"Something like that." Roman laughed.

"Well, that won't be me. Sometimes I'm actually very sensible." She grinned down at the purring Eloise, remembering just how intensely she had pursued Roman despite how much sense it made not to. "But only sometimes."

His agreement hummed through the phone. "Sensible days or not, I enjoy talking to you. Every time." His voice was low and intimate, hinting at other things he enjoyed about her. Every syllable he uttered melted her a little bit more.

"Damn, why does this have to be a non-booty call?" Aisha groaned.

The sudden silence on the other end of the line threatened to give her stomach a cramp of anxiety.

"Things can change, you know," Roman finally said.

Aisha swallowed thickly and shoved down the part of herself that warned her against being too bold, too straightforward. "Does this mean you've given up the idea that I'm too young for you?"

"Not at all," Roman said, his voice a deep growl. "It just means I'm weak and completely susceptible to your charms." He paused again. "I want you, Aisha. Come to me. Please."

"I can be at your place in less than an hour," she said, already lifting Eloise off of her. If that made her desperate, she couldn't find it in herself to care.

Chapter 15

Although Aisha had lived in Atlanta for most of her life, this was her first time driving through the back roads of stately and moneyed Virginia–Highland, the area away from the restaurants, trendy shops and artisanal pubs that made up the popular strip. After breaking the speed limit leaving her house, she forced herself to drive more sensibly, especially when she arrived in the maze of houses that was the Virginia–Highland neighborhood. The houses looked homey and unassuming, but she knew the property values were high. Many, with modest wooden gates shielding the homeowners from the naked glare of the street, loomed high on hillocks with lights glowing from inside. That was one of the houses that Roman lived in.

Before he'd given her his address, she'd assumed he'd resided in a midtown penthouse. A high tower of glass overlooking the city and with an uneclipsed view of the sun's movement across the sky.

Now as she pulled up into the small, semicircular drive framed by well-manicured grass and small, smooth-barked trees, she was surprised. She shut the engine off and wiped nervous palms on her thighs. She felt every touch of her hands through the thin dress she wore. But she only had a moment to suffer in her nervousness before the front door, up a short incline and at the top of a half dozen steps beyond a screened-in porch, opened. Roman stepped out.

"I'm glad you're here," he said.

She sighed out a breath.

He was understated and handsome in a gray tank top and workout pants. Both were loose on his body but did nothing to hide the muscles of his chest, the thickness of his sex and the power in his firm thighs.

Damn. "I'm not here yet, just—" she huffed out a deep breath, unable to hide her nervousness for once "—just making my way in." This was just sex anyway. It wouldn't make or break what was between them. But even as she told herself that, she didn't believe a single word.

Forcing herself forward on the course she'd decided on, she grabbed her oversize leather bag and left the car to meet him.

Roman pushed the door open wider and held out a hand. "Come in."

Trembling deep inside, she grasped that big, warm hand of his and stepped over the threshold. "Thank you."

"For having you?" he teased. He took her bag and hung it on the nearby coatrack.

The living room was dim. Aisha had a vague impression of dark furniture, wide windows and pale walls before Roman reclaimed all of her attention. She bit her lip and smiled. "I guess you're in a playful mood, huh?"

"Right now, I'm in a few different moods." He scratched at the faint stubble on his jaw and closed the door behind them. The door took his weight as he leaned back and, with her hand still in his, tugged her against his broad chest. "Including uncertain as hell." His hands rested on her waist, lightly caressing her from ribs to hips. "I shouldn't want you like this, but…" Through their clothes, he felt like a furnace. A hard, beautiful furnace. "I'm weak."

"You're not weak." Still trembling, but for a different reason now, she shook her head and leaned more into him. "You're gorgeous, you're strong, you're sexy." Her truth spilled from her lips and all over him. "You're all that and more, and you're right, maybe what we're doing isn't the smartest thing. But I'm too selfish to let you go."

"Thank God for your selfishness and my foolishness," he said just before their lips met in a kiss.

It started gently. An exploration of firm flesh, a soft sigh of welcome and then the kiss quickly became more. Urgent. Needy. Hot.

Under her hands, the gray tank top bunched up and she splayed her fingers over the muscles of his abdomen and up to his pecs. He groaned when she pinched a nipple and she felt his sex jerk against her. God, he was so gorgeous. She opened her mouth to take in more of him and he captured her tongue, sucking on it in a way that flooded her with wetness. Her fingers curled into him. A hot throbbing between her legs made her breathless.

"I want you," he gasped.

"Then take me."

With another deep groan, he lifted her and she wound her legs around his hips, hissing when she felt the firm press of his arousal against the hot place where she needed it desperately. Her hand fumbled down between them and she felt how hard he was. He grunted her name.

"If you don't stop—" Another harsh sound punched out of him when she traced the shape of him through the soft pants.

And that was probably why they didn't make it too far. In the dark of the living room, Roman raised Aisha higher against him and then the back of the sofa was under her butt and he was crowding against her again, dragging down the straps of her dress to bare her braless breasts.

"So gorgeous," he gasped a moment before latching his mouth to a nipple. Then his head popped back up. "You're pierced here?"

"Very observ—" She lost her words as his mouth went back to work, this time with even more passion, more suction. More heat. He moaned like he was starving for her.

"Roman…" His other hand kneaded the previously neglected breast, his thumb working her nipple while his mouth, hot and wet, sucked the other in his mouth, teeth tugging at the barbell through her nipple, tongue working the combination of the metal and her tender flesh.

Aisha gasped and undulated against him. She was highly sensitive there, which was why she'd gotten both nipples pierced. The intensity of his mouth, the single-minded way he sucked and pleasured her, his hands grasping her thighs and keeping her from touching him, brought her to the breaking point.

The throbbing between her legs grew and grew. The

hot tingle becoming the beginnings of something she couldn't control. "Roman!"

The orgasm roared through her. Aisha shuddered against him. Wailed his name. And let the sensations take her completely over.

He lifted his head, a look of amazement on his face. "Did you just…?"

Breathless, Aisha licked her lips. "Maybe."

With a rough groan in the damp line of her throat, he lifted her into his arms. What was left of Aisha's world tilted and she clung to him, her arms and thighs—hell, all of her—still trembling from her bliss. When she opened her eyes, they were in a bedroom dim from the shroud of evening but softly lit with a row of lights above the bed.

He gently put her on the bed but he had no such gentleness left for himself. Roman yanked off his shirt and pants before coming to claim her, his body large and warm. His aroused flesh nudged between her legs and he immediately kissed her, devouring her breathless cries. The thickness of his sex was intoxicating and she traced his length with her fingers.

"I want this," she breathed into his mouth.

"You're driving me crazy!" he ground out. "I can't think when I'm like this." His groan sounded as if he was being tortured.

Instead of giving her what she wanted, what she needed, Roman reached over to the bedside drawer and yanked out a strip of condoms. He made short work of rolling one onto his thick length. "Aisha… Aisha." He focused on her breasts again, his mouth, his hands, his breath pulling her already intense arousal higher. "What are you doing to me?"

She gripped his muscular shoulders as he held on to

the thickness of his sex and slowly guided it inside her. "Anything you can stand," she breathed as the hot stalk of his maleness fully penetrated her. Wet with desire, she took him in and latched her legs around him, moving against him, eager to show him how much she needed him.

He groaned again and slowly started to move.

The feel of him inside her had her eyes rolling back in her head. So thick, so powerfully male. She groaned his name and dug her nails into his back, meeting him slow thrust for slow thrust.

His lips moved against her ear. "I love how you feel around me." He plunged inside her, deep and strong, then retreated before taking her again. Rhythmic and sweet. His words continued, a low and hot stream of delicious murmurings in her ear that spurred Aisha on. The pleasure stung her all over. Made her shiver and moan and cry out and beg for more.

The headboard knocked against the wall, combining with her shouts that echoed in the bedroom.

"Aisha." He grunted her name with each deep thrust inside her, and she welcomed him.

The headboard knocked faster against the wall and he moved harder and deeper inside her. She shouted until her throat was raw as orgasm overwhelmed her again.

Roman's rhythm faltered and his words fell away and became only sounds, rough and desperate grunts that told her he was close. Closer. He levered himself on his arms, the muscles trembling and damp with sweat, his hips pumping relentlessly between hers. His eyes burned with desire. The breath tumbled roughly from him.

"Come for me," she gasped, encouraging him with her words and the rhythmic squeeze of his thickly muscled glutes. "You're so gorgeous. I love how you look. I love how you fill me up."

"Damn!" He threw his head back and shouted out again, and she felt every ecstatic pulse of his flesh deep inside her as he emptied himself into her.

His trembling arms gave way and he sagged down onto her for a moment, the heavy and damp weight of him pressing her into the bed before he let out a breath and rolled onto his back beside her.

He swore and ran a trembling hand over his face, his breath coming ragged and hard to match hers.

God, he was beautiful. Propped on her arm, Aisha watched the heaving breaths agitate his sleek pecs, the tight muscles of his belly, his sex still thick against his thigh in the condom. All of him was gorgeous.

He stirred enough to pull off the condom and discard it in a nearby trash can. She heard the gentle thump seconds before he flopped back down next to her on the bed.

When he finally opened his eyes again, she grinned down at him, feeling loose and sinfully good. "So, does this mean you're inviting me to stay for breakfast?" she asked.

His deep-set eyes stared up into hers as he curled fingers around the back of her neck and drew her down for a slow kiss. When they pulled apart, there was a world of mystery in those eyes of his. He licked his damp lips then slowly traced his thumb along her jaw and her lower lip. She sucked the thick digit into her mouth and caught it between her teeth.

"You can stay here as long as you want," he whispered, and sent her foolish heart soaring.

Chapter 16

"Is that a baton under the sheet or are you glad to see me?"

Roman slowly woke to the sound of Aisha's soft laughter and her gentle weight against his naked body. His body stirred first, hips juddering under the sweet weight before his mind caught up with what he was doing. Aisha, resting on top of him, watched him with laughter in her eyes while her body matched his movement.

With a low groan, he pushed the thickness of his morning desire between the welcoming spread of her thighs.

"What if I said it was both?" he murmured. Her waist was warm under his hands. Slowly he swept his palms up her back to the slender line of her neck.

"Then I'd call you a liar, sir." Aisha moved against him again. "No dead piece of wood ever felt like this."

Another helpless sound leaked out of him from her sensual antics and she giggled, dropping her face to his chest. Her breath huffed against his skin and he couldn't stop smiling.

"That's quite a thing to accuse a man of being when you're lying in his bed."

She nipped his chest then licked away the sting before he even realized there was any pain. "I guess that makes me some kind of liar, too."

Roman laughed then groaned when that hot mouth migrated to his nipple and sucked. "Aisha…" His hips bucked under her. "Unless you want to stay in the bed all morning, you should stop what you're doing." There were a few things on his schedule for the day but, at the moment, he couldn't recall any of them.

Another soft breath blew against his skin and a hot tongue skimmed over his nipple. "And if I don't stop?" She sucked the nub into her mouth and Roman just about jerked off the bed from the force of the pleasure licking through him.

"Then—" He abruptly lifted her light weight and flipped them over in the bed. Her squeal of surprise burst into the room and then her light and contagious laughter. She wriggled against him and Roman gripped her hips, slid down her body until the humid flower of her sex was open right in front of his hungry mouth. "Then, I'm going to start my breakfast a little early today."

They ended up staying in bed through breakfast and part of lunch, sharing stories and laughter until the insistent growl of her stomach drove them to the kitchen. There, with her dressed in one of his shirts and Roman wearing a pair of workout pants, he made them breakfast for lunch. His special whole grain pancakes with maple syrup and scrambled eggs. She shook her head at the pancakes and instead asked for some of the eggs. She ate them, covered in ketchup, from a bowl while he watched in horror.

"More pancakes for me," he said and poured on the maple syrup.

"Perfect." She moaned with pleasure around a forkful of eggs. "I knew we were perfect for each other."

With his fork halfway to his mouth, Roman froze, but only for a moment. He didn't think Aisha had noticed at all.

But he couldn't stop thinking about her words the rest of the day. While they'd finished eating and stood side by side washing and drying the dishes. In bed again less than an hour later while they'd kissed, their lips inseparable as she slowly rode him, taking her pleasure with slow and perfect rolls of her hips. Later still, in the shower, while they'd washed each other and teased and laughed again.

Perfect. Together.

Were they?

No. It was impossible. There was too much between them. Her youth. The prize. The fact that there were other men out there closer to her age that she could have with just a crook of her finger. Roman couldn't afford to consider what they had as more than a temporary thing.

Too soon, it was time for her to go.

On his porch, she hitched her bag over a shoulder with one hand and held tight to him with the other as they kissed one last time. "This has been the best Saturday I've had in a long time," she said, smiling up at him.

It was the same for Roman, too, but he said, "You must not get out much."

"Well, if you recall, we didn't get out much today, either." It was nearly five in the evening. The sun was high but it was too late to get much of anything done. "Not that I'm complaining, obviously. It was my absolute pleasure to stay in with you."

Roman decided to fess up instead of letting her think the day hadn't been as good for him. "I've enjoyed myself, too. I've enjoyed you. You rescued me from a very boring weekend."

"I know." Mischief sparkled in her eyes.

A sound of a car pulling into the driveway tugged Roman's attention from Aisha. His brother's copper-colored Porsche stopped behind Aisha's Fiat. She glanced over her shoulder.

"Looks like you have company." Her lips brushed his one final time. "I'll leave you to them. Until next time."

She pulled away from him, her slender fingers falling from his. Roman followed her out the screen door and watched as she ambled down the steps, hips twitching from side to side. Then, with a casual wave at Lance, she climbed into her bright yellow car and drove away, going just a little too fast in the tight, semicircle of the driveway.

"Who's that?" His brother hopped up the front steps and Roman stepped back to let him pass. "Oh, wait. That's the woman you were practically making out with on the dance floor at the company party."

For some reason Lance had a hard time referring to that event as Roman's welcome party. He idly wondered why that was.

Roman stepped into the living room, quickly scanning the tidy area for signs of what he and Aisha had been up to. Not that his brother needed anything as obvious as a pair of misplaced underwear as an excuse to start talking mess.

"That was Aisha, yes," he said, simultaneously relieved and sad that she hadn't left anything behind.

"What, that's the third time you've hung out, isn't it?" Lance headed directly for Roman's kitchen and started making himself an espresso from the machine Roman barely used. "She's sexy, even if she looks a little young for you. Young doesn't mean innocent, though, Roman." A delicate espresso cup clicked against the granite countertop when Lance took it down from the cupboard. "Most of the women you've ended up with usually wanted something from you. I remember that much about your sad love life."

"Aisha isn't like anyone else I've been with before." Roman immediately dismissed the idea of Aisha wanting anything from him, although that dismissal wasn't without the familiar pang of anxiety. "She's an architect with a great career ahead of her. She doesn't need or want anything from me."

The espresso bean grinder growled. "Architect?" Lance looked over his shoulder at Roman. "Aisha Clark? The architect who won the canceled Sykes Prize?" His brother shook his head. "Are you kidding? She could want a lot from you."

Hell. Roman could've thumped himself in the forehead.

He'd been so busy thinking about what Aisha might or might not have left behind that he hadn't thought about the information his brother didn't need to know. He loved Lance more than he loved himself some days, but that didn't mean he was oblivious to how malicious his brother could be.

"There's nothing about Aisha you need to worry about, Lance." Hadn't he already had this conversation with his brother? Roman passed the mess Lance was making and headed for the kettle. "What brings you to my side of town on your biggest party night of the week?"

"I'm actually meeting a friend near here and thought I'd stop by," Lance said.

"Really?"

Roman refilled the kettle with water from the tap and put it on a high flame, waiting for the other shoe to drop. The espresso machine trickled the strong beverage into the small cup, breaking the silence between them.

"Well, actually, I wanted to make sure you're still planning on handing the company over to me next year." Looking deliberately nonchalant, Lance leaned back against the countertop and sipped his coffee.

Roman watched the steam rise from the cup and wreathe his brother's face. "That's the plan," he said, grabbing a mug for tea from the dish drainer near the sink.

"Okay, good."

"Why, what's up?"

"You didn't see the company profile in *Forbes* magazine?"

Forbes? The only reading Roman had done since agreeing to take on the responsibility of the company was of reports, contracts and, as of his conversation early last night with Aisha, a headhunter's web site to get used to the idea of finding a new assistant.

"I think you already know the answer to that. What's in there I should see?" Roman asked, but he wasn't that curious. Some games his brother played just weren't that interesting to him.

There was something, though, that had obviously unsettled Lance. His brother moved restlessly around the large kitchen, touching things as he passed—Aisha's mug in the dish drainer, the silver tea tin that had belonged to their mother, the handle of a drawer. All the while, he sipped his espresso, saying nothing. Maybe waiting for Roman to break the silence.

Roman had patience to spare, though. He pulled the tea tin toward him and waited.

Finally, Lance spoke again. "There's a profile about Sykes Global in the magazine. A kind of puff piece that the PR department obviously okayed. Said you were doing a pretty decent job for the short amount of time you've been at the helm."

"That was nice of them." And quick. Roman hadn't known there was any PR massaging in the works about him coming on as the new CEO.

"Yes. It's good for you. I just—you know—don't want you to get a swollen head now that they say you're not too bad at this CEO thing and forget about what you promised me."

"I haven't forgotten," Roman said and watched the relief take over his brother's face, spreading across fine features that were so much like their mother's. "The most important thing is to do what's best for the company, no matter what the magazines decide to write about."

The teakettle began to wail behind him, sounding like an alarm he couldn't ignore.

Chapter 17

"Hey, Aisha! Over here."

Aisha adjusted the picnic basket she carried and searched the hilly park for the voice that called out to her. It was a Sunday in Piedmont Park and it seemed like everyone and their mother was out. At least that was true for her and her siblings. It took her a few seconds to spot them. Devyn, Ahmed and their mother on the huge, psychedelic-print picnic blanket Elle had bought her husband as a joke. They sat out in the open and away from trees, basking in the hot sun. Aisha waved.

Because of the long Friday night and then part of Saturday she'd spent with Roman, she hadn't finished her Sykes project. So, when her mother had suggested the picnic, she'd told them to go ahead while she made some last-minute changes. She'd spent all of Saturday evening and early Sunday morning on the project. The work had been swift and easy, all the things she'd learned about Roman's mother swimming in her head. It had gone so well that she'd sent him the design she'd created, which he'd approved with an unequivocal response. "This is perfect."

A gigantic smile on her face, she'd sent the updated plans to the Sykes Prize Committee for final approval before throwing the fried chicken and potato salad into her basket. She made it out to the park only half an hour after her family.

If she didn't have her hands full, she'd pat herself on the back.

"You look happy," Dev said as Aisha got close.

"I am happy!" She flopped onto the blanket and dropped the food down beside her. "It's a beautiful day and I get to see you guys." She crawled across the blanket to hug them one by one.

Her siblings exchanged a look. "You must have gotten some last night," Dev said with a grin.

"Not *last* night, no." Aisha stuck out her tongue at her sister.

"Respect, please. Your mother is sitting right here." Her mother laughed as she reached for the picnic basket and unloaded what Aisha had brought.

"Oh, good! I was ready to kill for some good fried chicken." Devyn pounced on the container, immediately taking out a drumstick. Only she could make attacking fried chicken seem ladylike. She nibbled on the drumstick and sighed in bliss. "Thanks, sister."

"My pleasure." Aisha reached for the pound cake she knew her sister had spent the morning making although she'd initially claimed to be too swamped with gallery stuff to bake. "Thanks for making the cake. I love you more and more every day," she said seriously.

Dev giggled and kept on eating.

Ahmed leaned back in the sun, his arms bared in a tank top, his face peaceful. There was a half-finished glass of orange juice settled on a cup holder next to him in the grass.

"So aside from the obvious, how's your project going for Sykes?" he asked.

"Actually, I finished it late last night and sent it off this morning before leaving the house."

"Word?" Her brother looked impressed. "Congrats!"

"Thanks." Aisha could feel her entire face breaking out in the biggest smile. "I love how it turned out. It went so well toward the end." She told them about the ideas that had come to her, how easy it had felt, almost dream-like, to delve into the life of a woman who'd made such an indelible mark on one of the most powerful men she knew. "It was actually kind of amazing."

Dev bagged up the chicken leg she'd gnawed to the bone. "Things with Roman must be going amazing, too. Right?"

Even though they talked about things like this all the time and Aisha was never shy about sharing tales of her sex life, a blush scorched her from hairline to breast.

"Leave her alone. Can't you see she's in love?" Her mother reached over to smooth Aisha's hair. "It's a surprise, but it's very sweet. You deserve this, honey."

Aisha ducked her head to escape her mother's all too probing look. Last night, as she'd gone over the final details of the Sykes design, she realized that this thing with Roman was more than she'd ever thought it could be. Yes, she'd set her sights on him, and her heart had quickly followed.

Aisha was in love with him.

For better or worse.

She looked up and caught Dev's eye, noticing her sister's look of sympathy and empathy. Dev had gone through something similar a few months ago with her now husband. Aisha had been there for most of it and had been amazed by her sister's constant state of discombobulation. It felt very different now that it was her turn.

"Mom, don't think I haven't seen that hot young boy who keeps driving up and down the road to your house," Dev said, making Aisha forever grateful that her sister had her back.

"Mom, really!" How could Aisha have missed this? "Who is he?"

"Mind your own business, both of you," their mother said, reaching for the carafe of water sitting in an ice bucket. Now she was the one blushing.

"I've seen that guy," Ahmed said. "He's definitely a young one. Maybe even younger than you, Aisha."

"No!" Aisha and Dev laughed.

"That's enough, you three! Who's the parent here?"

Aisha and her siblings just laughed harder.

They had a great time at the park, catching up with what they'd missed in each other's lives during the week. Elle was off at some romance-related business conference. Dev's husband was down in Miami on business, and their mother was working on a project aimed at helping the homeless in town. But she didn't mention a thing about her new boy toy, whoever that was.

When the picnic wrapped up hours later, Ahmed and their mother took the same car home while Dev and Aisha stayed behind to sunbathe and chat. They stripped down to their bikinis and laid themselves out on the blanket.

"I know how obnoxious we can be all at once," Dev

said, adjusting the sunglasses over her eyes. "Hopefully, you didn't feel like we ganged up on you."

"I did, but that's normal for us." Aisha shrugged. It was her family and she loved them. They weren't strangers. She knew how they could be. Everything was done in love, but sometimes the love was rough. "And it's okay, anyway. I know you guys care."

"We do."

It was silent between them for a few more minutes.

"Things are good with you and this Roman guy for real, then?"

"Yes, very good. My Hot Yoga Daddy is all that and more."

Dev nearly choked on her laughter. "I'm not sure I'm ready to hear all that, but it's good. You deserve to be happy in every part of your life, little sister."

Aisha joked with her sister but it was so true. She was happy with Roman. They'd talked on the phone while she'd driven to the picnic and not once had he referred to her age. Between the amazing sex and the very adult conversations they'd had, he'd begun to see her as more his equal and she loved it. She was relieved that he was allowing himself to be happy with her, free of the baggage he'd heaped on their relationship because of her imagined youth.

Yes, she was younger than him, but so what?

"Something is bothering you, though." Dev rolled over on the blanket and faced her. The sun haloed her face, making it hard for Aisha to see her expression.

Dammit. She'd half hoped to avoid this part of the conversation. Or maybe she needed to talk it over with her sister. She pressed her lips together and thought about what had been bothering her on and off through the night.

"It's about the prize," she finally said.

"I thought you guys worked it out. That's why you were able to finish it and send it off, right?"

"It's more than just getting the chance to impress the prize committee." She nibbled on her lip. "The Sykes Prize is a huge deal and, when I won, it felt like the achievement of a lifetime. Now, though, even though Roman is going ahead with the award, it adds too much complication to our…thing. I'm not sure it's worth it."

Dev sat up and her face came back into sharp focus. "What do you mean? Do you want to give the prize back?" She looked horrified, as if Aisha had said she was giving up the career and city she loved to have babies and live in a hut someplace.

"Hell no." She laughed at the look on her sister's face. "No. I just… I just want to think this whole thing through, maybe even think of some options. This prize could come between us and the thought of that is scaring the crap out of me."

"Your worries are pretty valid," Dev said after a few careful moments.

"Exactly." Aisha sighed.

"Okay, then. This is a problem. But you don't want it to be. What are you going to do?"

Aisha bit her lip again. "I wish I knew."

Chapter 18

Roman's office was thankfully quiet at eight fifteen on a Tuesday morning.

After a long day of work that had ended at a reasonable hour, last night he'd gone home to dinner and a glass of mineral water at his dining table, with Aisha on speakerphone. Separated by the miles, they still managed to eat dinner together and talk, sharing stories about their pasts and about their families that had him smiling long after they hung up.

They'd had over a week and a half of incredible sex, mind-blowing emotional connection and unexpected bursts of laughter that left his stomach aching. He wanted to see her every single day, but with their schedules it wasn't possible.

Two days ago.

That was the last time he'd had her in his home, in his bed. And today, he would get to have her there again.

For the morning, though, he had a long list of meet-ings plus an unpleasant discussion with one of the com-pany's lawyers. But being CEO wasn't all high-powered luncheons and limitless expense accounts. Or women who threw themselves at him, hoping he'd be the next Christian Grey.

Chuckling at the thought of him being into anything resembling BDSM, he turned on his computer. His in-box was an insurmountable Everest most days, which was why he preferred to get started early. He clicked the first message and started to work his way through them.

He'd dealt with most of them that had come in over-night when a subject heading caught his eye.

Re: Cancellation of the Sylvia Sykes Architectural Prize

Frowning, he quickly scanned the message, which was apparently just an FYI. There was an attached press re-lease that had gone off early that morning to notify media outlets that the winning entry no longer mattered since the prize itself had been nullified.

What the hell was this? Anger set off a pounding rhythm in his gut. Roman scanned the press release again to make sure he wasn't seeing things and tapped a but-ton on his desk phone.

"Carolyn, would you come here a moment, please?"

"Of course, Mr. Sykes."

She appeared in the open doorway of his office a few moments later.

"The press release about the Sykes Prize. Who autho-rized it and when?" He spoke carefully, trying his best to calm his anger.

"It was your brother, sir. At the end of last week."

Lance? Why would his brother...?

"And you didn't think it was something I needed to be apprised of?"

Her eyes widened but she crossed her arms and firmed her features. "You were busy with other things, sir. More important things. I didn't think the prize committee matters merited your attention."

"*Everything* with my name on it deserves and gets my full attention." He grated the words out, the muscle in his jaw pulsing in his anger.

Despite how furious he was, he couldn't do anything about the press release. It had been sent out. The company would look disorganized and indecisive if he pulled the news now and said it was all a mistake. No, it was too late. If it hadn't already, it would soon be picked up by all the papers, including everyone with a blog or Twitter account.

Aisha.

A cold fist clenched his belly at the thought of what would go through her mind if—no, when—she saw the news.

"My apologies, sir." But Carolyn didn't sound like she was apologizing. She didn't sound sorry in the least.

This was ridiculous. And he had no one to blame for this but himself. "Apology accepted," he told her. But then he added coolly, "If you would, please clean out your desk." He was done with her. "Security will escort you down."

He dismissed her with a look and pressed a button on his phone, calling for security. Keeping her on had done nothing but shoot him in the foot. Even if firing her right now was doing more of the same, he couldn't stand to deal with her for another second. She may have been a good assistant for his father, but she wasn't for him. Not when it seemed like she was following the orders of a dead man. Or at the very least, not following the orders of his very live son. The damn CEO.

While Carolyn stood there, her mouth working open and shut, he connected with security.

"Security. Banks speaking."

"Mr. Banks, Roman Sykes here. Please send someone up to my floor to escort a former employee off the premises."

The man on the other end of the line didn't hesitate. "At once, sir."

Roman hung up. "I'd suggest you use your remaining time to pack up your desk. Security is on the way to escort you out." He looked away from her and back to the email that had started all this. "You may go now."

"But…but I didn't do anything wrong. I was following orders and doing everything you told me."

"I do believe you're wasting your valuable time, Carolyn. Whoever Mr. Banks sends up will not wait around for you to pack up your things."

"This isn't fair!" she said, her hands clenched at her sides.

"I gave you every opportunity to acclimate yourself to the changes here. You've squandered them all and done us both a disservice. Now…" He took a deep breath. "I have work to do."

Then, while she went out to her desk in a flurry of waving hands and muttered comments, Roman called HR to let them know he was looking for a new assistant. Within minutes he was promised a temporary one to arrive in less than half an hour. Candidates for the permanent position would be ready for him to interview by Friday. He thanked the woman in HR and hung up the phone.

He did not need this today.

While Roman spoke with his staff regarding other hot issues, he managed to keep his temper under control. In check. Once he was sure he had done everything he could to calm down, he called his brother. The phone rang a few times before going to voice mail. Only on the fourth try did Roman remember that it was barely nine o'clock and his brother was probably still asleep. The fifth time he got Lance's voice mail, he left a message.

"Call me at the office or come in. I have something to discuss with you." His fingers rapped on the desktop, unable to stay still.

His cell phone lay on his desk, face up, occasionally vibrating with an incoming text message. It vibrated again and this time it was a message from Aisha. A photo of her holding a half-empty coffee cup with all her teeth showing in a look of exaggerated mania. Ready to rumble with the office jackals, the text caption read.

She was adorable and wonderful. And she was going to be devastated by what Lance had done.

Roman cursed.

Barely an hour later, with his temporary assistant sitting at the desk that Carolyn had scraped clean under the watchful eye of the security guard, Lance blew into Roman's outer office.

His brother stopped and looked over the young woman at the desk who was professionally turned out with hipster glasses and her straight hair in a tight topknot. Definitely younger than someone Roman would have preferred but, given his recent change of mind where Aisha was concerned, he had to acknowledge that younger didn't also mean inexperienced.

"What do we have here?" Slowly taking off his sunglasses, Lance looked the new woman up and down. "Whatever happened to the other one?"

Roman stood and pushed away from his desk, buttoning his suit jacket. "Never mind that, Lance. Come in, would you, and shut the door."

"Uh-oh, you have your serious face on." His brother pulled a comic expression, looking at Roman's new assistant who didn't as much as look up. Already, Roman approved of her.

Lance closed the door behind him, looking casual and relaxed in slacks and a designer T-shirt, both wrinkled. Roman wondered if that was the style or if the clothes had spent the night on some woman's floor.

"Sit down, please." Roman gestured to the chair in front of his desk.

"No thanks, I'd rather stand for whatever you're about to drop on me."

Sighing, he leaned back against his desk chair and swallowed, trying to control his temper. After getting Aisha's text, he'd scanned the websites of different news outlets as well as social media to see exactly how far the news had traveled. It had gone far. Twitter. Facebook. Even the *New York Times* had a small item about it.

By the time he'd finished assessing the damage and called Aisha, she was no longer available. Probably in a meeting at work. He left her a text just letting her know they needed to talk. He wasn't a fan of giving or getting bad news via text message.

Roman steepled his fingers. "I saw the press release

this morning about the official cancellation of the Sykes Prize."

"Oh, that." A smile twitched across Lance's face.

"Yes, that." A muscle ticked in Roman's jaw. "I didn't tell you to do anything with the prize or the committee."

"Well, that's one of the few things regarding this company that I do have some say-so about," Lance said. "And it didn't seem right that you were handing such a prestigious award to a girl you're sleeping with. It would reflect badly on the company. I'm just looking out for Sykes and its interest since you can't because you're so far up this woman's—"

"Don't say it!" Roman angrily cut him off. Was his brother really doing this? "Aisha won the prize before she and I ever met. What you've done is a supreme overreach, and an unnecessary one."

"Someone has to stop you from making bad decisions," Lance said smugly. "Think of this as a system of checks and balances. That woman may have been a stranger to you before, but she isn't now. I can't allow you to drag the company down in scandal because you can't keep it in your pants."

After he'd seen the press releases and confirmed that nothing could be done, Roman had done some investigating to see what exactly his brother had done. Using his influence at the Sylvia Sykes Foundation where he had the same amount of authority Roman did, Lance had cut the funding to the Sykes Prize. Without the allocated funding, the memorial library couldn't be built.

"You weren't thinking of the company. If you were, you'd realize this petty move of yours would do more harm than good. The project would've provided jobs. It would've injected money into the community."

It wasn't just that. Because the project had already been announced in the local papers, cutting funding and officially canceling the prize made the company, and Roman, seem heartless and indecisive.

"You've damaged this company's reputation, Lance. I just don't see why."

"Why? Have you always been this blind, Roman?" His brother shoved away from the door. "Right now you have everything I want, and the messed-up thing is that you don't even want to keep it. With the money Mom left you and what you're making from your stupid yoga shops or whatever the hell they are, you have everything that *you* want. While I have *nothing.*"

Roman felt his heart plunge to his stomach. This was what his brother thought of as "nothing"? Lance had never had to worry about money. He'd had every chance to start his own company from even just the contacts being a Sykes afforded him.

Instead he'd bet his entire future on controlling Sykes Global even though Roman had been the one sitting, sometimes reluctantly, at their father's knee, learning everything about the company. In the meantime Lance had chosen to only dream about power, all while sleeping with the wives of influential men he should've known better than to cross.

Since they were kids, Roman had been protecting his brother. Shielding him from their father's disappointment, from the men who wanted to skin him alive for sleeping with their wives, from everything that could possibly hurt him. Roman had done everything to keep his brother safe. Now he realized he hadn't been protecting Lance, he'd been enabling him.

Before, even knowing his brother's weaknesses,

Roman had still planned on passing the company over to Lance. To move him from being just a board member with limited power to full CEO by whatever means he had in his control. But now that Lance was petty enough to harm the company over something he thought Roman had done to him, there was no way in hell he was going to hand over Sykes Global.

Roman wasn't going anywhere.

"I'm sorry, Lance."

A look of surprise took over his brother's face. "What are you talking about?"

Roman shook his head, feeling like he was emerging from a fog. "Thanks for stopping by on such short notice. You can get back to what you were doing now. I'll deal with the backlash from the press release."

A look of growing realization, of fury, transformed Lance's face into something ugly. "Wait! You're not— You're taking the CEO position away from me, aren't you?"

"You never had it, Lance. And because of what you did today, you never will."

Chapter 19

Aisha stared at her email in shock.

Oh my God.

She squeezed her eyes shut then opened them again to stare at the computer screen. A sizzle of excitement warming her belly, she reached for her cell. With the phone gripped tightly in her hand, she suddenly realized she was torn between who she should call. Then reality smacked her in the face. Of course there was only one person to call. Opening her list of favorites, she tapped the button and initiated the call.

"Good morning, sister dear." Dev answered right away. "You didn't get enough of me this morning?" Their daily morning call had gone on longer than usual. With dawn still coloring the sky in shades of purple and gold, Aisha, Dev, their mother and then Ahmed, after he'd dragged himself out of bed with his wife, had talked about everything Clark, including Aisha's crazy thing with Roman.

"I could never get enough of you guys!" Aisha said. Although her sister couldn't see her, she fluttered her lashes.

But it seemed like Dev was able to see her anyway, laughing softly in that particular way she did. "What's going on? Aren't you at work?"

"I am at work, and guess what I'm doing."

"Well, what you're *not* doing is working since you're calling me."

"Okay, boss. Get your own gallery all of two minutes and suddenly you're trying to regulate my work output." Aisha laughed.

"Sorry. It just feels so good having my own space now," Dev said, the laughter in her voice giving way to gentle awe. "My dreams are a reality and I can hardly believe it. I'm just waiting for the day when I wake up."

Aisha leaned back in her chair and smiled. "You're awake right now, Devyn. You're just living the life you always wanted."

"Thanks for believing in me and for pushing me," Dev said.

"You did all the work. I knew it would pay off."

Devyn drew a breath full of sentiment and a hint of tears. "Anyway, you didn't call to hear me go on. What's your news?"

Aisha laughed, suddenly giddy again about what she'd just read in her email. "What makes you think I have news?"

"Quit playing!"

"Okay, okay." She laughed again and tilted herself way back in her chair, till she stared up at the ceiling of her office. "Remember when I told you about running into Emersyn Rankin and Patrick Sebastian at your gallery opening?"

"Yes?"

"They just offered me a position at their firm!" Aisha said the last on a little squeal, still unable to believe it. "They didn't ask me in for an interview or anything. It's wild!"

"Oh my God!" Dev screamed so loud that Aisha had to pull the phone away from her ear. "That's freakin' amazing!" She babbled a few more things that kept Aisha alternately laughing and agreeing. "From what you said, the chat y'all had was like a damn interview anyway."

"It kind of was, wasn't it?" That night had been so surreal and wonderful. She'd just been full of happiness for her sister, not to mention thrilled at having Roman by her side all evening. The impromptu gallery tour with Emersyn and Patrick had her practically hyperventilating with excitement. Their interest had been the ultimate in flattery, but the last thing she thought they'd do was offer her a job.

"This is so incredible. No interview. No vetting. At least none that I know of. Just a lucrative job offer and an invitation to come to their offices for a tour and informal chat."

"You're going to accept it, right?"

"Of course!" This time Aisha was the one screaming in excitement.

Devyn laughed. "My sister the shiznit! So brilliant, she doesn't even have to interview for the job of her dreams. The luck of Aisha. No, that's not right, it's more like the Hard Work of Aisha Clark."

"Yeah." She bit her lip, smiling wide. "It's all pretty amazing. The hard work and the luck."

"Obviously, we have to celebrate. Have you told Mom and Ahmed yet?"

"Not yet. They're my next call."

"Okay, good," Devyn said, but Aisha could tell her sister was pleased she'd gotten the first call. "I know of the perfect place to celebrate your brilliance tonight or whenever you're ready."

"Definitely tonight." She and Roman had a date but it felt right to share this with him, too. They could all celebrate together.

"Good. I'll make the reservations."

After instructing her to include Roman in their number, she said, "Thanks, Dev."

"No, biggie. We'll talk later."

Aisha ended the call. Then, as she was quickly scrolling through her missed notifications, she saw an alert she'd set up a few weeks before. It was from Twitter.

It looks like a wrap for the #SykesArchPrize. Although won this year by @AishaTheClark of Wainwright and Tully, a @SykesGlobalCorp news release officially ends the triennial prize that's been a diamond in the architectural world for 15 years. No additional comments yet from SG.

The attached article showed photos of the previous winning designs and the buildings created from them. Aisha was in shock. Her hand trembled and felt cold as she scrolled through image after image on automatic pilot. No way this could be right. The man she was getting to know would never do something like this. Right?

He didn't have any reason to lie to her.

But that was exactly what he'd done. The tweet, the attached article, plus others she rapidly clicked through from other news sources confirmed just that.

Aisha's eyes burned and she blinked quickly, putting down her cell phone with a trembling hand. Just then, it chirped. A message from Roman.

Please call me when you can. There are some new developments with the Sykes Prize.

And that was it. What was he trying to do, get in his apology so they could just get straight to sex when they saw each other that night? Bile rose in her throat at the thought.

He wouldn't do that, though.

She ignored the niggling voice at the back of her mind. She didn't know him. Especially not the version of him that would do this. Lie and betray and send a text after the fact.

A tear splashed down her cheek but she ignored it, turning the phone over on her desk so she didn't have to look at the screen. Her eyes drifted back to the computer and the email she had open there.

The happiness and awe she'd felt when she'd read the email from Emersyn's office felt miles away now, as if it belonged to another person. Another life. She swallowed the lump in her throat and viciously wiped at the fresh tears springing from her eyes.

Maybe...maybe all this is a mistake. Maybe he didn't mean to do this.

It was with this wild hope sitting in her belly that

Aisha finally forced herself to call Roman. He answered on the first ring.

"Aisha, thank Go—"

She cut him off before he could finish. She had to get this out now, all the hurt and disappointment, or she wouldn't be able to say it afterward. Her stomach was sick with it, the bile threatening to erupt.

"How could you do this to me?" she demanded. "Why did you encourage me to keep working on my design— to waste my time—if you were just going to yank it out of my hands anyway? I busted my ass for this prize and this is how you do me?"

The silence on the other end of the line was deafening. Seconds passed before Roman finally spoke. "Is the prize the only reason you called me? Nothing else?"

She swallowed hard, the hurt and betrayal still painfully twisting her insides. "What else is there between us?"

Roman cleared his throat and the sound of it was harsh in her ears. "If you have to ask, then I guess the answer is obvious."

No!

Aisha wished he was there so she could grab him, look into his eyes to see what he was thinking. To read him and ask him why he'd lied to her. But wishes never got anybody fed.

"Yes," she said softly. "I guess it is." Then she hung up.

Chapter 20

The day felt as long as a year. Each minute stretched on like scratches made on a chalkboard with fingernails. Torturous. Seemingly endless. Roman was relieved that it was finally time to go home.

The talk with Lance and the following shouting match between them, which had nearly made him call security, had scorched Roman to a husk of himself.

He couldn't even *think* about the phone call with Aisha. It hurt too much.

He'd sat behind the desk and done the job he'd needed to do because there was no other choice. If it hadn't been for the meetings, and decisions, and talks with lawyers, he probably would have taken himself home and immersed himself in his yoga practice, running through the asanas until his mind calmed and his muscles burned.

But that hadn't been an option. He had to be Roman

Sykes CEO. And although he'd thought before that the job would drain him and leave him with nothing of himself left to spare, the hours he'd spent immersed in work had actually gone a long way toward whiting out his mind. His pain.

Now, though, the workday was over.

Just as he stood to leave the office, his cell phone rang. It was Merrine.

"Roman, what's going on with this damn Sykes Prize that keeps on getting canceled then not canceled then canceled again? Is the committee on coke? Hell, are *you*?"

He wasn't surprised Merrine knew what had been going on behind the scenes with the Sykes Prize. She made it a point to know just about everything that was going on with the people in her life. To her, information was power, and she had a lot of it.

Groaning silently, he dropped into his chair. "Would it do any good if I said I didn't want to talk about it?"

"Nope."

He leaned back in the chair, swiveled it to face the brightening lights of the Atlanta skyline. "It was Lance. He did it to—I don't know—get back at me for whatever he thinks I've done to him."

"You mean for just being a better man than him?"

Merrine had never liked Lance and, over the years, had tried to encourage Roman to be less lenient with him. To treat him more like an equal instead of a child to be protected.

"Don't say that, Merrine. You know that's not true."

"You have your version of truth where your brother is concerned and I and the rest of the world have ours." She cursed softly. "So, what are you going to do? That cutie-pie architect you're falling for isn't going to like this."

His stomach dropped at the thought of Aisha. "She didn't like it, no."

Merrine drew in a sharp breath. "Oh, crap. She didn't…"

"Yep, she did."

"Are you…are you sure that's what happened?" Merrine asked. "I know sometimes you can jump to conclusions that aren't even in the same universe."

"I'm very sure about what happened. Aisha found out the prize wasn't hers. Even though I tried to explain, she basically said we had nothing else to talk about and then she hung up on me."

A stronger curse and then a whole string of them, each more inventive than the last, practically blistered his ear through the phone.

"Pretty much." Roman sighed. He didn't want to talk about this anymore. He really didn't.

"I'm sorry, Roman. I know you really liked her."

"I did. I do." But there was nothing to be done about it now.

"Do you want to come over and drink my liquor and not talk about it?"

The idea was tempting. Very tempting. The oblivion that a good bottle of Jack Daniel's could bring was a powerful seduction to lure him away from his pain. But he'd never been the kind of man to bury his emotional aches in alcohol, sex or anything else that would make him regret himself when he woke up the next day.

"How about a rain check? Tonight I just want to…" Hell. He didn't really know what he wanted. Sighing, he dragged a rough hand over his face. "Let's talk more tomorrow, okay?"

A bubble of silence grew between them and, for a moment, Roman thought Merrine would insist on making sure he wasn't alone. Then the bubble burst.

"Okay, Roman. One night. But if I don't hear from you first thing in the morning, I'm coming over to your house. I don't care if I accidentally get another eyeful of that stupid yoga body of yours."

He gave a weak chuckle, all he was capable of at that moment. "All right. Fine. I'll talk with you in the morning."

"First thing."

"Okay. First thing," he echoed.

It took him a while to get out of the chair again but then he finally forced himself up and out. Briefcase in hand, he locked his office door behind him. His temporary assistant looked up from shutting down the computer and offered him a smile.

"Thank you for being available on such short notice, Olivia," he said.

"It was my pleasure, Mr. Sykes. I can be here as long as you need me." She pulled her purse from the drawer and stood as he walked past. "I've had extensive experience working for a high-level corporate executive, so the work is more or less familiar."

"Really? Who?" He waited as she finished up, curious. She had done an excellent job today. As someone the company had on a list of already vetted temporary employees, she'd come in, taken an hour to acclimate to his particular systems, and pushed through full steam ahead without asking him any questions.

Her cheeks creased in an easy grin. "My father."

"Ah, I see."

Once she was ready, he held the door for her and they walked together to the elevator.

"So, why are you here instead of with his company?" He pressed the down button.

"I'm the last of five, his youngest, and I've mainly been trained to support him instead of *be* him. I'm comfortable with that, plus I'm not that interested in staying in the same place where I was born. Either professionally or geographically."

"Interesting thought process," he said. "Tell me more."

They spent the rest of the ride to the lobby talking about her background and what she wanted from her life, where she saw herself in a few years. Olivia didn't strike him as any older than twenty-five. Roman was surprised how easy it was to talk with her and how deftly she answered his questions. When the elevator stopped at the lobby, he stood back to let her out and held the door open for her.

"It was good talking with you, Olivia."

"Same for me, Mr. Sykes. I'll see you tomorrow."

"See you tomorrow," he echoed and took the elevator further down to the parking deck.

Now that it was just him and his thoughts, Roman felt the discomforts of his earlier conversation with Aisha slither under his skin like hungry maggots.

After she'd hung up on him, he'd asked Olivia to cancel their dinner reservations and then offered her the two tickets he'd bought to a French film that Aisha was interested in seeing. Without a doubt, Aisha didn't want to see the film with him anymore. She didn't want him.

Had she ever? Or had everything they'd shared been a ploy to get what she wanted—the Sykes Prize—and now that there was no way she would get it, she didn't want anything to do with him?

He cursed softly under his breath.

Even if that wasn't the case, he'd never chased a woman in his life. If what they had together was so worthless compared to what Aisha had wanted him to do for her, then she wasn't worth chasing.

The elevator stopped at his deck and he headed to his car. He got behind the wheel and, after giving the car time to warm up, turned the wheels toward home. But halfway there he changed his mind. Instead of turning down the quiet side street leading to his house, he kept going and jumped on the highway. He drove with the music on and his mind empty. Roman didn't know where he was heading until he flicked on the turn signal almost an hour later, getting ready to ease off a familiar exit.

His mother's cabin.

Before making the date with Aisha for the movie and then dinner, Roman had planned to come up to the cabin just to sit and think and remember. Two years had passed since his mother died. Tomorrow would be two years exactly. On the first anniversary he'd been a broken-down mess halfway around the world at a yoga retreat that hadn't been able to distract him from the incredible pain of losing her. The pain was still strong, breath-stealing. But he'd thought that if he had the chance to wake up to Aisha, a woman he lo—

Gravel flew up under the car's tires as he jerked the steering wheel hard and turned toward the cabin. The road ahead of him was dark, illuminated only by the beams from his headlights. Trees crowded in on him from both sides of the narrow road.

This was how it should be. Him. Alone. In the dark. Fighting to get back to a place that kept him steady.

Not rolling around in bed with a woman who only wanted him for his influence or his money, not for who he was. Not for the heart that he'd been about to offer her on a silver platter.

But no. Aisha wasn't like that.

His hands clenched around the steering wheel. If she hadn't been that type, then why had she dumped him as soon as she'd realized the prize was no longer hers as promised?

As *he* had promised.

Cursing, Roman clenched his teeth and kept driving.

At the cabin he pushed open the front door, feeling as if he had a thousand-pound weight on his shoulders. Although it had been days since Aisha had been there in the cabin, he could swear he smelled her. The hint of lemon from the soap on her skin. A suggestion of the coffee beans she loved so much. A shadowy memory of her sex lacing the air like perfume.

To hell with that.

After throwing his briefcase on the couch, he walked through the living room and straight to the bathroom. There he stripped off his clothes and climbed into a blistering-hot shower. He forced his mind to the off position, registering only the sensation of the water running down his body, the steaming heat, the smoothness of the tiles against which he braced his hands. Water sluicing down his back, he sank into the comforting nothingness he held in his mind.

Slow and deep meditative breaths moved his chest up and down in a comforting rhythm. Nothing mattered except his physical body.

Nothing mattered.

It was just him and his body.

Mind blank. Breaths even.

Each movement was a silent meditation.

That only lasted until he left the shower and got dressed in one of the loose pants and T-shirts he kept at the cabin. A gleam of silver atop the fireplace caught his eye and held it.

With more than a little hesitation, Roman went to the large hammered-silver box his mother had bought in India on one of their trips together. It was cool between his palms and he took it with him to the couch.

After another calming breath, Roman opened it.

When the lawyers had read the will, they'd explicitly mentioned the box she'd left for him and him alone at the cabin. The cabin was also his, along with half of the money she'd inherited from her own family. Before he'd fully grown up, Lance had lost all interest in the cabin. He was more city boy than anything else.

Roman, though, liked the quiet. Just like his mother.

He took another breath and slowly opened the silver box.

The scent of Nag Champa drifted up from its long-enclosed interior and slammed Roman in the gut.

Langston Sykes used to tease his wife mercilessly about burning the incense all the time and making her rooms smell like a hippie commune. It was a smell that Roman, though not a fan of incense himself, associated with his mother.

He breathed in the smoky, sweet scent and reached inside the box.

A set of wedding rings, white diamonds set in platinum, winked from atop a stack of letters. He traced the diamonds on the ring, remembering the times he'd touched his mother's hand and felt those rings, warmed by her body heat, under his fingers.

God, he missed her.

Two years. It had been that long since she'd died from a particularly vicious attack of the flu. Two years since she'd left the box for him. But he'd never opened it. He couldn't. Before, every time he'd even thought of opening the box, a sharp pain had lanced through his chest. So the box had remained there, untouched, in the cabin. A gleaming ghost that frightened him. That he couldn't bring himself to touch.

Now, though, with the pain of losing Aisha a more intense hurt than the fear of finally knowing what the last thing his mother had wanted to give him was, he took out the rings, slid them onto his pinky finger and picked up the first letter. He began to read.

Roman, my firstborn. My child of love. I know the last thing you ever wanted was to read anything like this from me. This must be tearing you apart, and I'm so sorry.

A lump rose up in his throat and slid back down. The letter blurred in front of his eyes. He could hear his mother as clearly as if she spoke to him from the other side of the sofa.

I know things are hard for you right now, but they won't be forever. You can choose that it won't be forever. Staying with your father all these years, I know I haven't been a positive example of the way choice can affect a life. But despite how hard things have been for me, I wouldn't have done it any other way. The life I had as your mother isn't one I regret, but I want you to know you don't have to make the same decisions and sacrifices I did.

Sykes Global can be yours, or not.
You can stay in America, or not.
You can commit to and love another person, or
not.
You choose. Grasp the happiness I never had
the courage to take for myself.

Roman put the letter away, his hands trembling.
Courage. The word stuck with him as he read the other
letters, allowing the beautiful lines of cursive to evoke
the woman who had raised him to be the man he was.

The words seemed to float off the page and around
him, filling the cabin with her voice. Without trying too
hard, he could see her sitting by the fire, her favorite blue
scarf around her neck, a long dress down to her ankles
as she sat in the oversize chair and watched Roman with
a tender gaze.

He picked up the last letter.

You're my son, but you're also your father's. I know
you want to push that part of you away, but you
have his mind, his uncompromising brilliance, and
that's what he needs to keep the company moving
forward. He'll ask you to be his successor after I'm
gone, but I want you to know it's possible to be his
heir and to also be yourself.

Roman put the letter down and heard her words echo
inside him. She'd always been so sure of him when he
hadn't been sure of himself. He'd railed at her in the past,
saying he wanted nothing to do with the man who treated
his wife and children like accessories to be put on when
an occasion called for it but otherwise ignored.

The last few weeks had brought a mountain of new responsibility, but at no point had he canceled an outing with Merrine or promise himself that he'd call Aisha later just so he could work more. He went into the office early, but he left himself time to enjoy his life out in the world. The balance he had found had been effortless and surprising.

Balance. Courage.

He thought again of Aisha. The things he'd confided in her. The things she'd shared with him.

No, he couldn't allow the worst parts of his father to shape how he related to the people he cared about.

Langston Sykes had been all suspicion first then verification and then, far, far down the line, forgiveness. Roman couldn't afford to be that man. He wasn't that man.

Aisha deserved an explanation about what had happened with the prize and, no matter Roman's suspicions about her motives, it was a conversation they needed to have face-to-face.

A glance at the clock over the mantel told him it was late, much too late to find Aisha to tell her what he wanted to say.

But an hour later, with a mug of tea and all his mother's letters reread and spread out in front of him, Roman knew he couldn't wait a moment longer. He put the letters and the rings back in the silver box and returned it to the mantel. Some things couldn't wait. And this was one of them.

Chapter 21

On her lunch break, Aisha called Dev to cancel dinner that night. She was just too raw from her conversation with Roman to pretend everything was okay. Her sister tried to change her mind, but Aisha insisted and went home right after work. Her family was aggressive in the way they cared, and each was determined to make sure Aisha was all right.

But she wasn't all right.

Which was why she shouldn't have been surprised when her doorbell rang a few minutes past seven, a courtesy really, before the key turned and all the Clarks tumbled inside.

"If you won't come to the celebration, then the celebration will come to you." Her mother pulled her in for a long hug. "Congratulations, love. I knew you could do it."

From the shelter of her mother's embrace, she looked

over her shoulder at Dev, who shook her head and mouthed *Sorry* as she shrugged.

One by one, they passed her around for hugs, cheek kisses and congratulations. Ahmed and Elle, Dev and Bennett. The family. But none of the friends Aisha partied with on occasional Saturday nights, thank God.

Bennett carried two bottles of red wine and Devyn had a box of cupcakes with Baked Good's logo. Elle had a casserole dish in hand that smelled suspiciously like the roasted cauliflower tossed in garlic sauce that had quickly become Aisha's favorite once she'd gained the businesswoman for a sister-in-law.

Overwhelmed, she sagged into their touch, their warmth, their love, not realizing until that very moment that was exactly what she needed.

But she didn't have to be gracious about it. Wiping at the tears that unexpectedly fell from her eyes, she waved them inside.

"Come on in. You might as well make yourselves comfortable since you're already here."

"Such a great hostess." Ahmed laughed and headed for the kitchen. Moments later he came back with plates and glasses. The food and wine were on the dining room table while Eloise watched it all with curious eyes, too well-behaved to jump up on the furniture and beg for food while other humans were around.

"So, what's up?" Dev pulled her down onto the couch and her mother sank into the cushions on the other side of Aisha. "Why did you cancel on us?"

While the men conveniently made themselves scarce, Elle poured wine for everyone and curled up on the cozy armchair a short reach away. Then she made a soft sound of realization and sat back up. "If you don't want to say what's wrong in front of me, it's okay."

"No, no. You stay," Aisha said, flapping a hand at her. "For better or worse, you're part of the family now."

A pleased smile touched Elle's mouth. She pressed the glass of sweet red into Aisha's hand and Aisha curled her fingers around it before taking a sip.

Spilling the whole story brought a feeling of relief rushing through her, even with the sadness and regret from the end of it all.

"What about the prize?" Elle asked. "Don't you want that anymore?"

"With this new job, I don't need it. It's enough to know that I won it fairly the first time." She tried to shrug it off and be philosophical about it, but, oh God, it hurt so much. Tears burned her eyes.

"Oh, honey…" Like Aisha was still a little kid, her mother scooped her into her arms and rested Aisha's head on her chest. The blouse under her cheeks quickly grew wet with her silent tears.

Dev cursed and gulped from her wineglass. "This sucks. I'm so sorry, Aisha." Aisha felt her light touch on her back, patting her gently.

"Are you sure it's over, love?" her mother asked.

"I'm sure." Aisha pressed her lips together to stop a pathetic cry from spilling out. "He thinks that I…that I…" She couldn't finish what she was trying to say. Just the idea that she had used him to get the prize made her a little sick. How could he even think that? Then again, she knew anything she and Roman had shared would be tainted by what had drawn them together in the first place—the Sykes Prize.

"We know you're not like that," Elle said, looking

ready to cry herself. "And that's the most important thing."

Dev shook her head. "No, the important thing is getting that man to take his head out of his butt and see Aisha doesn't do that kind of manipulative crap."

Just then Ahmed poked his head through the open French doors that separated the living room from the back porch. "Is there somebody's ass we need to kick?"

"Maybe," Elle said at the same moment Aisha shook her head and Dev said, "Yes!"

Bennett, handsome in slacks and a light blue button-up, slid the doors open wider and stood with a whiskey glass in his hand. "We should probably leave the butt-kicking to the women and just show up with bail money."

"Good idea." Ahmed nodded.

"We're fine," Elle said and waved them away.

Like good husbands, they ducked out the door and went back to whatever they'd been doing.

"Honey, look at me." At her mother's command, Aisha slowly lifted her head. "This could all just be a misunderstanding. Try to see things clearly with this man and not allow your assumptions and hurt feelings to cost you that spark I've seen in your eyes over the last few weeks. You love him. Fight for him." Her hand smoothed Aisha's back. "See him in person. Make sure this is what you think it is."

Just then the doorbell rang.

Dev glanced toward it. "This better not be pizza. Ahmed's been threatening to get Aisha some so-called real 'celebration food' ever since we decided to come over." She got up to answer the door and Aisha immediately missed the comforting touch of her hand.

Assuming it *was* pizza, Dev grabbed her purse on her way to the door.

Pizza did sound good, though, Aisha thought. She was never the kind of girl to lose her appetite when she was sad. The more food, the better. More points if it was greasy and really bad for you.

Behind her, Dev opened the door. Her sister's silence immediately warned Aisha it wasn't who they'd thought it was.

"Good evening," a familiar voice rumbled from the doorway. "Is Aisha home?"

Roman.

Aisha stiffened in her mother's lap.

"Is it okay that he's here?" Elle asked, standing. She faced the direction of the door, looking ready to toss Roman out if Aisha so much as hinted she wanted him gone.

"It's fine," she said, clambering out of her mother's lap and feeling color burn into her cheeks. As she spoke, she felt him zero in on her from the door.

Aisha went to the door, resisting the urge to tug down her dress and smooth her hair. In the doorway, Roman looked a lot like he had the day they'd met. Running shoes, dark gray workout pants and a T-shirt showing off his lean and veined forearms.

"Come in," she said and Dev reluctantly stepped back to let him enter.

Behind her, she sensed movement and heard the patio doors open, but she couldn't take her eyes off Roman. She cleared her throat.

"Dev, you remember Roman." Her sister gave him a nod of greeting and moved to stand by her side, a hand around Aisha's waist. "Roman, you remember my sister, Devyn."

Looking both serious and a little nervous, Roman gave an odd, old-fashioned bow. "Good to see you again."

What was going on? Why was he there?

The sudden hum of conversation behind her finally forced Aisha to look away from Roman's intense gaze. The men had come in and, along with Elle and Aisha's mother, were heading toward them.

"I think it's time for us to be on our way and leave you kids to talk," her mother said.

The others didn't look convinced, but they were leaving anyway, propelled by her mother's urging.

Her mother kissed her cheek as she passed. "Call if you need anything, love. I'll be near the phone all night." To Roman, she gave a slight smile then slipped out the door.

First Elle then Ahmed hugged Aisha and she held on tight to each of them for a moment before letting go. Before he left, Ahmed faced Roman. "I'm as mean as I look, so you better watch yourself with my sister."

Bennett's clenched jaw was no less threatening and Dev didn't bother saying anything to Roman after she hugged Aisha tight and walked out. When the door closed behind her family, Aisha turned and headed back into the living room.

"Can I get you anything to drink?" The social niceties seemed like a good place to start because otherwise she had no idea how to act or what to say to Roman.

"I'll take some of that wine over there but..." He scrubbed a hand over his face and looked around, seeming to notice the signs of a celebration for the first time.

"I'm sorry," he said, sounding truly contrite. "I didn't know I was interrupting something."

"That's generally what happens when you drop by unannounced." For want of anything else sensible to do, Aisha grabbed an empty wineglass and poured some of the Shiraz into it for Roman.

Their hands brushed when she passed him the wine, an electric current zapping between them and nearly making Aisha drop the wine before the transfer properly happened. But Roman held the glass firmly, as well as her gaze.

"Thank you for letting me in." He put the wine to his lips.

Hungrily, Aisha watched as his lips parted and red wine flowed between them, leaving the seam of his mouth painted a faint burgundy. Deliberately, it seemed, he licked his lips. She yanked her gaze away, nearly falling over her feet to get away from him. Desperately needing some fresh air, she lurched for the patio doors.

Roman pulled them closed after he followed her outside.

The evening's breeze brushed against Aisha's face, cooling her cheeks. With her wineglass in hand, she crossed the backyard to sit in the hammock under the magnolia tree. The chain of the swing just a touch away groaned when Roman settled into it. Quiet settled between them, making Aisha grip the wineglass tighter.

Roman sighed. "This afternoon wasn't fair. To either of us."

"What do you mean?"

"For my part, I should have made sure we had that conversation face-to-face—"

"The one where you tell me you changed your mind

about the prize, or the one where you tell me you never meant to let me have it in the first place?" Even just saying the words hurt.

"Neither. I should have told you—" He huffed. "Lance was the one who publicly canceled the prize. I didn't find out until this morning when I saw the press release in my email."

What? She replayed his words in her mind. He was saying he hadn't been responsible? It was so far from what she'd thought had happened that it took a moment for her to process his statement. So he hadn't betrayed her? He hadn't lied? A tentative gladness burst in her chest.

"I swear to you, I didn't know he'd done it." He took a gulp of his wine then looked down at it. It was probably sweeter than what he was used to. "You and I had an agreement and I planned to stick with it. But then Lance broadsided me with that underhanded bull and I was angry with him—and then I was angry at myself for not realizing sooner that he and I have different agendas."

Wow. To have your sibling go behind your back and do something like that… "The reactions to the announcement weren't very positive," she remarked instead. "Not on Twitter anyway."

Roman made a noise. "Hell no. After you and I talked, and after I did some investigating, I realized what good the prize has done for the company's reputation. The tax write-off isn't bad, either, obviously. You have to know I wouldn't have made a move that damaged the business my father put in my care."

Aisha quickly turned to look at him. This was new. Before, he'd always seemed to refer to the company as something his father had burdened him with. Now he was referring to it as something he cherished leading.

"I'm sorry." She didn't know what else to say.

"No. I'm the one who should be sorry. I *am* sorry. Promises are serious things. I feel like the lowest because Lance made me break that promise to you."

The moon glowed from behind a whisper of a cloud and glinted in the hints of silver in his hair. He looked so good she cast her eyes away, down to the damp grass that cooled her bare feet.

"Although I can't imagine something like that happening with me and my siblings, I—I feel bad. Maybe if I hadn't been in the picture..." She shrugged and bit her lip.

"There's nothing good that can come from you not being in the picture," he said.

Aisha glanced up to see him looking at her. She licked her dry lips and wet her mouth with the wine. Its faint sweetness rushed over her tongue.

"I'm happy you're in my life, Aisha. For however long that is, especially after this...this ridiculousness with my brother. I'll retract the announcement and tell the press that we made a mistake," he said. "I'll fix it."

Aisha ducked her eyes to her wineglass, thought about taking another sip then decided not to. She didn't want to be compromised in any way for this conversation. "I..." She trailed off and lifted her gaze to the dark sky with the glittering canopy of stars. "It's not the Sykes Prize that I wanted. At least, not the one that has to do with my design."

"What do you mean?" He shook his head, looking exasperated with himself. "I mean... I mean I know what you mean. And you—amazing, gorgeous you—saying that I'm a prize is a bit on the ridiculous side."

Aisha opened her mouth to protest but he put a finger to her lips. "I know you needed the Sykes Prize to secure your future."

"I'm not sure I ever needed it," Aisha said, although maybe that was a lie because she suspected Emersyn and her partners had only noticed her because she'd won the prize. "I don't want you to reinstate it and jeopardize anything else. I don't need it, I don't want it."

"But…" He looked back at the house and through the glass French doors. "You were celebrating something. I'm assuming not the end of our relationship."

"Never that. The end of us is why you found me here instead of the restaurant I was going to invite you to."

"Did you win something else?" His voice lightened with happiness. "Something better than the Sykes Prize?"

She pressed her lips together. "Yes, yes, I did. Something that won't come between us. If you want to be close to me, that is." Her smile broke free. "Rankin, Sebastian and Ziegler want me at their firm."

His eyes widened. "Damn. That's…that's really impressive."

"I know." She giggled, inviting him to share the joke. "I'm pretty amazing."

"You are that." Roman breathed out a soft laugh and leaned down to balance his mostly full glass of wine in the grass near his feet.

"So…" She gave him a prodding glance, a gentle smile on her lips.

He thought she was amazing. He'd offered her the prize. He was here, offering her his love. The real prize that she wanted.

He laughed outright this time. "So, Aisha Clark.

Whether or not the Sykes Prize is something you want, I want *you*. I need you in my life."

Her heart skipped in her chest but she wasn't going to make it that easy for him. "Oh yeah?"

"Yeah." He brushed warm fingers across her cheek and she sighed at the contact, her skin tingling in the wake of his touch.

Even though it had been less than a day since they'd argued, she'd missed him so much.

"You already have me, Roman Sykes. Since that very first day we met."

He smiled, a starburst of lines at the corners of his eyes. "In that case, will you take me in return?"

"Absolutely, Mr. CEO. Forever and for always."

His lips, firm and warm, pressed into hers and sent her heart spinning all the way to the stars.

* * * * *

Rita extended her hand. "All right, Keith. It's been a pleasure. I'll be in touch if I need you. If I need you for anything," she quickly amended, hoping her words hadn't sounded like a come-on. Though she wasn't sure her second version was much better. "But I'm sure I won't have to call."

Keith's eyes crinkled as he shook her hand. "I'm here. For whatever you need."

Slowly, he released her hand, and as Rita gazed up at him, a jolt zapped her chest. This time, there was no questioning the meaning behind his look. The glint in his eyes along with his suggestive words made it clear that he was flirting.

He walked past her then, and a hint of his cologne wafted into her nose. It was a musky scent that made her insides crumble.

The man was fine, no doubt about it. Too fine.

And he knew it. She could tell by that easy smile he gave her, the gleam in his eyes. He probably thought she'd be calling sooner rather than later, trying to arrange some sort of hookup.

Well, he was going to have to wait a long time if that was what he thought.

Kayla Perrin is a multi-award-winning, multipublished *USA TODAY* and *Essence* bestselling author. She's been writing since she could hold a pencil, and sent her first book to a publisher when she was just thirteen years old. Since 1998, she's had over fifty novels and novellas published. She's been featured in *Ebony* magazine, *RT Book Reviews*, *South Florida Business Journal*, the *Toronto Star* and other Canadian and US publications. Her works have been translated into Italian, German, Spanish and Portuguese. In 2011, Kayla received the prestigious Harry Jerome Award for excellence in the arts in Canada. She lives in the Toronto area with her daughter. You can find Kayla on Facebook, Twitter and Instagram. Please visit her website at authorkaylaperrin.com.

Books by Kayla Perrin

Harlequin Kimani Romance

Visit the Author Profile page
at Harlequin.com for more titles.

UNDENIABLE PASSION

Kayla Perrin

For Emmanuel.
Thanks for coming into my life
and being a happy surprise.
I'm glad I finally let my walls down.

Dear Reader,

Welcome back to the world of the Burke brothers and Keith's story!

They say love is complicated. They also say love finds you when you're not looking. I love to combine both of those elements in my stories. Love finding heroines when they have no faith in love. What fun is a story if the characters aren't put through the wringer?

When love is tested and survives, that's when you know it's real. For this book, I wanted to explore a backstory I hadn't before. One that would have significant complications in a person's life. How easy is it to find love when you are the product of an affair and your father has basically disowned you? That's bad enough for my heroine, but worse, her mother has decided after all these years to reconcile with her father. In fact, they're getting married. With Rita believing that her mother has lost her mind, the last thing she's open to is finding love.

But that's the beauty of love. It finds you when you least expect it!

Best,

Kayla

Chapter 1

Rita Osgood pulled up to the intersection of State and Main and stopped at the red light. So this was Sheridan Falls. She glanced around at the antique-looking light posts, the bright awnings over small storefronts and the array of colorful flowers in large wooden pots. A young girl wearing a floral dress and holding a pink balloon skipped happily beside a woman pushing a stroller. Two people on the other side of the street were in an animated discussion as their dogs sniffed and pranced around each other.

Rita chuckled softly. State and Main, the undisputed center of town. The scene before her resembled a Norman Rockwell painting come to life. Could this be more cliché?

There was a coffee shop on the right hand side, a pharmacy on the left. The light turned green and Rita began to drive—only to have to abruptly hit the brakes several feet later when she came upon a car stopped in the live lane. She was about to put her hand on the horn when she realized that the driver, an elderly man, was communicating with someone on the sidewalk.

Really? People just stopped in the middle of the road with no regard for whoever was behind them?

The driver's hand emerged with a friendly wave, then the elderly man continued to drive. Rita rolled her eyes. It was about time. Though the man's *driving* wasn't much of an improvement. He was moving at a snail's pace.

Rita knew from her map that this was the downtown area, the hotspot for all the action.

What action? she thought wryly. The only thing missing was the tumbleweed.

Everybody here was moving slowly, as if they had nothing but time. Sheridan Falls was home to approximately ten thousand people, and Rita could imagine that they all knew each other.

The driver in front of her slowed again, hitting the horn. An older lady watering her flower pots smiled and waved at him.

Oh, good grief. Rita couldn't take much more of this.

Her temples were already throbbing from the long drive. If she was going to deal with the abnormally slow pace here in Sheridan Falls, she needed a coffee.

Rita made a U-turn, and then another one so that she could pull up in front of the coffee shop. That's when she noticed the bridal store. And as her eyes settled on the dress in the window, she recognized it as the one her mother had sent to her asking what she thought. A pure white dress with a fitted waist and lace bodice. The kind of dress a young woman would wear.

Thump.

Rita's heart spasmed, and she quickly slammed on the brakes, realizing belatedly what she'd done. She'd driven right into the car in front of her. And not just any car, but a luxury Audi A7.

"No!" she exclaimed, and closed her eyes for a moment. Then she turned off her car and exited her Ford Fusion, heading out to see if there was any damage. She wondered if the driver was in the coffee shop or nearby.

By the time she was exiting her vehicle, so was the other driver. All six foot one or two inches of him. Possibly six foot three. Her lips parted as she took in the handsome stranger, momentarily distracted from the issue at hand.

"What were you thinking?" the man asked, breaking the spell of her fleeting attraction. He was holding a cup of coffee on which the lid was askew. A wet brown stain formed a huge circle on his white dress shirt.

"I—I'm sorry," Rita sputtered.

"Seriously, I don't understand how you hit me."

"I'm sorry," Rita repeated. She glanced around, noting some curious bystanders across the street. "I..." She didn't know what to say. How could she tell him that she had been distracted by seeing the dress her mother wanted for a wedding that she vehemently objected to?

"This is a silk shirt," the man went on.

"I'll happily pay for it to be cleaned. Or for a new one if it can't be cleaned." Rita held the man's dark eyes, hoping to see a hint of understanding. No such luck.

She walked forward, checking the bumper on his car. There was a scuff of transfer paint between her car and his, but nothing major. Thankfully, it didn't appear to be dented.

"You've scraped my bumper."

"Maybe it's just transfer paint," Rita said, and lowered herself onto her haunches. She fingered the mark, then used the hem of her shirt to wipe at it. Hard. Some of the white paint from his black car began to come off. Relieved, she tried wiping more. She got most of it off, but some did remain.

"I think it's just transfer paint," Rita reiterated. "A bit of solution and the rest of the white will come off. However, if you want to make sure it's perfectly fixed, you can have an estimate done and let me know. I will happily pay."

"Maybe next time you should watch where you're going."

"It was an accident," Rita said.

"It shouldn't have happened."

Rita stared up at the man, whose handsome face was twisted in a scowl. Hadn't she apologized enough? Accidents happened. She knew it was never pleasant to have a fender bender, but it wasn't like there was much damage. Why was he being such a jerk about this?

"Maybe you should take a chill pill," she uttered.

Good Lord, had she really just said that aloud?

The man's eyes grew wide with indignation. "What did you say?"

"I've apologized," Rita said. "Can you rein in your wrath so that we can resolve this?"

"Rein in my wrath?" the man repeated, and chuckled mirthlessly.

"As I said, I'll pay for anything that's necessary. I'd prefer to pay out of pocket, since the damage is minor."

"Don't worry about it." The man's look of distaste

had her swallowing uncomfortably. "I have an appointment I'm late for."

"You don't want my—" the man got into his car and closed the door "—information," Rita finished softly.

Obviously not. The Audi roared to life, and the man drove off.

Rita stood there looking in the direction of the sleek black Audi A7 for a long while, finally blowing out a frazzled breath. She needed to get herself together. She'd let thoughts of her mother getting married be her undoing.

She was glad that the incident hadn't been something major, that she hadn't totally destroyed the man's car or hurt anyone. She was exhausted from the drive from St. Louis.

All the more reason to get some coffee before her meeting with the realtor.

She reached into her car, got her cell phone wallet case, then pressed the remote to lock her door. As she headed into the coffee shop, she could only hope that the small mishap wasn't a bad omen of what was to come in Sheridan Falls.

The sign Molly's Café was in a cursive font, resembling something handwritten. Rita figured that was to make the sign seem more personable. She opened the door to the coffee shop and the door chimes sang. All eyes turned in her direction. Eyebrows rose and curious expressions appeared on the faces of the patrons. People were wondering who the newcomer was. And none too subtly.

Rita strolled up to the counter where there were baked

goods under glass domes and handwritten specials on a chalkboard. Oh, this was cute.

But the aroma and smell were heavenly, and coffee was coffee. She expected that a small town shop like this would do coffee well. And she needed a cup.

More like three—if she was going to get through the day.

She still couldn't believe she was in this small town. Not because Sheridan Falls was beneath her visiting here, but because of what it signified. Her mother, Lynn Marie Osgood, had lost her mind.

Oh, yes, the mother who had been sane until just a few months ago had lost her mind when she decided that she was ready to get married. At the age of fifty-nine, she was now going to wed the man of her dreams. A man who had not thought she was good enough thirty-one years ago.

The warm smile that greeted her from behind the counter was in stark contrast to the negative feelings flowing through Rita's mind. She drew in a deep breath and held it for a moment.

"How are you today?" the woman asked.

"I've had better days, if you want the truth," Rita said. "I need a really strong coffee. Do you have any flavored cappuccinos?"

"We sure do. Caramel, vanilla, hazelnut, Irish cream, pumpkin. We also have the same flavors in our regular brews." The woman gestured to the array of carafes holding each of the various coffees. "And of course, we have our Colombian and Arabian bold and mild brews."

Rita glanced up at the board, her eyes nearly bulging when she saw the reasonable prices.

"If you'd like to sample one of our regular brews, I

can give you a small taste as well," the woman went on. "Whatever you'd like."

Maybe I'm being too harsh, Rita thought as she looked at the pleasant young woman. Small towns weren't her thing, but her negative attitude toward this one had nothing to do with what Sheridan Falls had to offer. It had to do with her mother, the reason Rita was here.

Just thinking about her mother's upcoming wedding had her chest tightening. She still couldn't believe that the levelheaded woman she'd known her whole life was making the rash decision to get married—and to a man who had destroyed her once before.

Rita's own father.

"Do you need more time?" the woman asked.

The question jarred her into a response. "I'll have a large caramel cappuccino. Actually, can I get that iced?"

"You sure can. Would you like one espresso shot or two?"

"Two, definitely."

"Large iced caramel cappuccino," the woman called to the older woman behind her.

Noticing that there were two young women in line after her, Rita stepped to the side so that they could place their orders.

The older woman approached Rita. "Good morning. I'm Molly."

"Oh, so this is your café."

"Indeed." Strands of Molly's grayish-blond hair hung in her face. "Where are you from?"

"St. Louis."

"What brings you to town?" the lady asked. "By the way, do you want your coffee over ice or do you want it to be blended and frozen?"

"Frozen, definitely."

Molly got to work preparing the drink, and Rita answered her other question. "My mom is visiting a friend here. So I decided to come and take a little break and hang out with her. She said it's a nice spot to escape the big city."

"That it is," Molly agreed. "Make sure you visit the lake. If you check out the wall by the door, you'll see information on who offers day excursions on a boat. The fees are reasonable. And it's an experience like no other."

Rita nodded as the blender whirred. "I'll be sure to do that."

Molly poured the blended coffee into a plastic cup. "Whipped cream and caramel drizzle?"

Rita shrugged. "Why not?"

Molly finished making the drink, then passed it to her. Rita had already paid, but she looked into the slot of her phone's wallet case and was glad to see she had some cash in there, a five. She put it into the tip jar.

Molly's warm attitude had helped to take her mind off the unfortunate incident with the man and his car earlier. The memory flooded back as she made her way to a table closer to the back where the café was less populated. The man had been the definition of gorgeous, but those cold eyes and that scowl...

She didn't want to think about him. At least he had driven off, even if he'd been angry. He could have given her a harder time, but he hadn't. The incident was over. No point harping on it.

Rita had about half an hour until her meeting with Keith Burke, the realtor she'd been communicating with. He had the keys for her rental unit, plus the documents she needed to sign. This was as good a spot as any to pass the time.

A solid half of the coffee shop was surrounded by windows, so Rita had easily been able to get a table with a view to the outside. Fiddling with the straw in her cup, she glanced out at the street. A woman in a flowing sundress was walking a poodle with a pink bow on the top of its head. An elderly couple strolled hand in hand. So far, Sheridan Falls seemed like an idyllic little town, one she might enjoy if she weren't here under duress.

Rita sipped her caffeinated drink, and an explosion of flavor caused her to sigh happily. This was just what she needed, a moment to relax and center herself. She drew in a calm breath, then exhaled slowly. She would have to make the best of it. And she hoped that she still might be able to talk her mother out of this crazy idea of marrying her father.

The minutes passed, and Rita checked the time. She'd already put the navigation for the address of Keith Burke's office into her phone, and it was only a five-minute drive from here. With twelve minutes to spare, she got up to leave. Molly waved at her as she headed toward the exit. Rita smiled and waved back.

She took another look at the front end of her car. The small scuff was hardly noticeable. Her ego had been damaged worse.

Forget the incident, Rita reminded herself. Then she got behind the wheel of her Ford Fusion and turned it on. She glanced at the dashboard clock. She would arrive at the realtor's office at least five minutes early.

Palmer Avenue appeared to be a residential street filled with brownstones. Mature trees lined the sidewalks, and their leaves rustled gently in the breeze. Rita found a spot on the street, parked her car, then made her way to the office steps of the realtor's building. Seconds later, she was knocking on the door. Almost immediately, she tried the handle. This was a business, after all.

The door turned, so Rita entered. In the foyer, a receptionist was sitting at a tall desk. The young biracial woman with a mane of thick curly black hair greeted her warmly. "Good morning. I'm Dana. Welcome to Burke Realty."

Rita returned her smile. "Thank you, Dana. I have an appointment for ten o'clock with Keith Burke."

"Ah, yes. Rita Osgood?" the woman asked, though she clearly knew already.

"Yep, that's me."

"Excellent. Have a seat in the waiting room, and Mr. Burke will be out to meet with you momentarily."

The waiting room was a small brightly lit alcove. There was a coffee table with a variety of magazines. Rita sat on a high-back white leather chair and pulled her phone out of her purse. She opened up one of her social media accounts and began to peruse what her friends were up to. She was simply trying to pass the minutes. Then she opened up her texting app and sent a message to her best friend, Maeve.

Hey, Maeve! I arrived safely in Sheridan Falls. Had a small mishap. Bumped into a car in front of me as I was parking. No big deal, no real damage, but the driver was a total jerk. Anyway, I'll call you later.

As Rita pressed Send, a male voice said, "Rita Osgood?"

A voice that sounded oddly familiar...

Slowly, she raised her eyes and looked up at the man standing at the entrance to the waiting room. Her heart went berserk, and she promptly wanted to be swallowed up by a hole in the ground.

It couldn't be.

But it was.

The same man whose car she'd rear-ended earlier was standing in front of her, dressed in a gray suit with a coffee stain on his white silk shirt.

The realtor she was due to meet.

Keith Burke.

Chapter 2

Keith's eyes widened as they settled on the beautiful woman sitting on the chair in the waiting room. Shock hit his body like an electrical current, and for the briefest of moments, he thought his eyes were playing tricks on him. But as the woman's expression morphed from neutral to horrified, Keith realized that this was none other than Rita Osgood, the woman he was meeting this morning to pass over the keys to the rental property.

He should have known. He had never seen her before—and someone like her he would have noticed. That meant she was new to town, and not that Sheridan Falls didn't have any visitors, but the likelihood of seeing a stranger this morning should have alerted him to the possibility that she was likely the stranger coming into his office.

He could see her chest rising and falling. She was

nervous. And he… Well, there was a certain amount of humor to the situation. What were the chances?

"You must be Rita Osgood," he said, stepping forward and extending a hand.

She ignored his proffered hand. "Um…if you'd prefer that I leave…"

"Why?" Keith asked.

"I can't believe this is happening."

He had hoped that his congenial tone would have allayed her unease, but clearly it hadn't. "So you know," he began slowly, "I did take a chill pill. And wouldn't you know, I'm feeling much better." Keith smiled to soften the comment. It was a little light banter, and surely her tension would fade now, wouldn't it? He wanted Rita to know that what had happened was over and done with, and he was holding no grudges.

"Oh, God." She cringed.

"Hey," Keith said gently. "How about we start over. I'm Keith Burke, realtor. I believe you have an appointment for a short-term rental?"

Rita eyed him warily, but after a few seconds, he saw her shoulders relax. "Yes," she said. "I'm Rita Osgood."

"Excellent. Then come with me. I have the documents for you to sign. And of course, the keys."

She eased up off the chair, slowly, clutching her purse to her stomach. Her eyes still registered some level of discomfort, but he was hoping that she would get past it.

Keith turned and led the way into his office, and she followed him. "Take a seat," he said, pointing toward his desk.

She did, and he closed the door. Then he rounded the desk and sat in the chair opposite her. She was biting down on her plump bottom lip, a lip that was colored in a deep auburn. His gaze moved up her round face to her thick lashes. Her hair was two-toned, a dark brown from the top and down to about her cheeks, and from there it was a blondish color. How had he not seen just how beautiful she was earlier?

Keith cleared his throat. "Let's just find a bit of humor in what happened. I hadn't had my coffee yet, and to be fair you hit me. I had a right to be upset, but I came across way too aggressive, and I'm sorry for that. Ultimately like you said, there is no damage. The way I see it, the whole incident is completely forgotten on my part. So no need to look so terrified of me."

"Do I?" she asked, her voice faint.

"Pretty much, yeah." And he didn't want her to be afraid. Keith had a reputation of loving, not scaring, women.

He'd been far too stressed out lately. The deal he'd been working on in Buffalo had been trying his patience, and he'd just gotten the call that it had fallen through minutes before Rita had rear-ended him.

So he'd been aggravated. Not with her, but because he had lost a potentially lucrative deal. She'd been a convenient scapegoat on which to unleash his anger.

The agent Keith was working with in Buffalo assured him that there'd be another building as ideal as the one he'd lost, but Keith had really liked that one. The location had been perfect and the price right for the trendy lofts he'd planned to construct.

"All right," Rita said. "As long as you're sure that you don't need me to pay for your dry cleaning or anything else."

"It never happened," Keith said, meaning the words. He didn't want the unfortunate incident to influence the business they had at hand. She was a client now, and if she enjoyed the rental unit, she would be sure to tell others about it. Much of his business was city folk coming to get a little bit of rest and relaxation in the country.

In fact… An idea suddenly hit him. Rita had chosen the least expensive unit, likely without even looking at the photos he'd sent, based on her lightning fast reply, *Go with the first one*. But he had another property right on the lake that was vacant. Judging by the expression on her face and the reason she'd come to town—"a wedding that shouldn't be happening and hopefully doesn't happen" she had written in her email—he could imagine she would need a bit more of a serene setting. The lake always brought out that reaction in him and everyone he knew.

"You need me to sign some paperwork?" Rita prompted.

"Give me a second," he told her.

On the computer, he opened up his documents for the rental, and changed the address from the unit he'd been going to rent her to the newer one. Then he pressed for the document to print. He got up and left the office, heading into the hallway where the printer was. A minute later, he was back with the revised documents.

"Is there a problem?" Rita asked. "I thought you had the documents prepared already."

"Actually, it was the wrong paperwork," he lied. He had a feeling that if he told her he was going to be giving her a better unit for the same price, she would raise a stink. She struck him as the kind of person who didn't like favors. While this wasn't really a favor, it was a business decision, she might not see it that way.

The bonus was that she hadn't seen the unit she was

originally to have, so the change would make no difference to her.

Keith gave the paperwork a quick glance, made sure that everything was in order, then presented it to her. "If you'll go ahead and read the document, then initial beside each paragraph where noted on each copy," he explained, indicating with his finger. "Then on the last page, I just need your signature. That's it."

Rita nodded, then began to look over the document. She took her time perusing it. When she reached the last page, she made a face. "This says that you need two weeks' notice before cancellation or changes to the reservation. We discussed a possible shorter timeframe, remember? Given the reason I'm in town, I'm not sure if I might need to cancel suddenly. You said that forty-eight hours' notice would be okay."

"You're right, I did. Let me just change that from two weeks to two days." Keith took back the document, crossed out the clause and inserted the new timeframe. Then he did the same with the second copy. "There you go."

"It's just that I'm not sure I will need it as long as I anticipate. I hope this doesn't interfere with your way of doing business. We did talk about that option, though."

"We did," Keith said, noting that she was repeating herself. Was she still uneasy around him?

Rita went back to the beginning of the document and put her initials where required. When she got to the last paragraph, she said, "Are you sure about the forty-eight hours' notice? Do you normally make concessions when it comes to your rental agreements?"

"I'm flexible when it comes to the weekly arrangements. It's really based on the demand, and if you're giving me no notice at all, etc. We're coming up to the end of summer, when it's busier here, so I'm sure forty-eight hours will suffice. However, if you know in advance and can give me more than forty-eight hours, that'd be great."

Rita nodded. "Okay. Sounds fair."

Keith opened his drawer and withdrew the appropriate key. Then he took the large manila envelope he already had on the table and slipped her copy of the signed contract into it. He passed it across the table. "There you go."

"Thank you. I really appreciate it."

"No problem. I appreciate your business."

Rita waited a moment longer, staring at him. Keith stared back, wondering what the look was about. He narrowed his eyes slightly. Was she...flirting?

"Um, aren't you forgetting something?" she asked.

"Am I?" he asked.

"The key," Rita said, gesturing to it.

"Oh." Keith instantly felt foolish. Why on earth would he think she was flirting with him? Just minutes ago, she'd looked terrified.

Rita pushed her chair back and stood. "I'll just take the key and be on my way."

Keith stood as well. Rita extended a hand to shake his, but he said to her, "We're not finished yet."

Her eyes widened as she looked up at him. "No?"

"I'll take you there."

"Oh, I can get there on my own. I'll put the address into my GPS."

"It'll be easier if I take you. Besides, I'd like you to go through the unit and make sure that everything meets with your approval. That way if there are any issues, I can deal with them now."

"Is that necessary?"

"It's how I like to do things," he said. Then he snatched up the keys. "I'll lead the way."

Rita had wanted to protest. She could find the place on her own, and she was certain it would be acceptable. As long as it had a bed, a kitchen and a bathroom, she didn't care how it looked. She wasn't here for the aesthetics. She just wanted the basics.

Besides, spending more time with Keith didn't appeal to her in the least. She just wanted to get to the rental, kick off her shoes and lay her head down.

Yet here she was, following Keith's car. Just about fifteen minutes later after leaving his office, he turned onto a road that led into a forested area. Rita made the turn as well, frowning. Where was he taking her? There was no sign of housing here.

But moments later, a row of cabins came into view. Three modern-looking buildings formed a U-shape around a paved parking lot. One was yellow, one peach and one pale blue. The pops of color reminded her of what she'd seen when she'd vacationed in Nassau years ago. In the distance, she could see the shimmery water of the lake. It was as if they'd magically taken a road into the Caribbean.

Which Rita supposed was the point. This vacation spot seemed like a different world.

But despite the modern look of the cabins, the tall mature trees surrounding the property gave the area a rustic feel. A smile touched Rita's lips as she looked out at nature's beauty. The tension in her shoulders began to ebb away.

Keith pulled into a parking spot in front of the middle building. Rita parked beside him. She looked up at the peach-colored apartment, noting that there were unit numbers on the top and bottom rows.

Keith exited his vehicle, and Rita followed suit. He came around to meet her. "Your unit is on the top level. Number six." He pointed.

Rita looked up in the direction, saw the bold number six on the door, and nodded. "Great."

Keith walked toward the steps that led to the upper level, and Rita followed him. As she did, she tried to avert her eyes from checking out his striking form, but she couldn't. This man was truly sexy. He had a tight behind and muscular thighs. He'd taken off his blazer and she could see the well-honed physique of his upper body. Strong biceps. A wide back that tapered down to his waist.

And below that waist, his perfect behind. As they reached the second level, her eyes narrowed on his taut rear-end again. Heat flooded her cheeks.

What was wrong with her? Shamelessly checking him out like this...

Nothing, a voice whispered in her head. You're still a woman. You're not immune to seeing a gorgeous man.

And there was no doubt about it, Keith was fine. Despite the fact that they'd gotten off on the wrong foot, her body couldn't help responding to him.

"I think you'll love this unit," he said, turning to face her.

Rita jolted her eyes upward, her heart jumping into her throat. She hoped he hadn't caught her checking him out. "I'm sure I will," she said. "The area is lovely. It looks very peaceful."

"It definitely is," Keith said. "There's also a wide range of recreation here for you to enjoy."

As if to emphasize that point, the sound of laughter and splashing filled the air. "Is there a pool?" Rita asked. "Or can I hear all that from the lake?"

"Right in front of this building there's a pool. A hot tub as well. There are also tennis courts down the path to the left. A basketball court, too."

Keith slipped the key into the door. Rita glanced around. It was certainly a lovely spot. "And at such a reasonable price," she said.

"Just make sure you tell your friends about it. This is a hidden gem for many people from the city. Most of my rentals come from word-of-mouth."

He pushed the door open and stepped inside. Rita followed him into the unit. She glanced around, seeing a wide-open space with pale yellow walls, wicker furniture, a large flat-screen TV mounted to the wall and a kitchen to the left. The California shutters were open, letting in the sun. The unit was bright and welcoming.

"Take a look around," Keith told her. "The bedroom is at the far end on the left. From the bedroom, you have access to a balcony that overlooks the lake."

Maybe this would be a good place for her to work. Sitting out on the balcony and looking out at the view. Hopefully she could lose herself in nature and concentrate on editing the articles she needed to. She certainly had a lot to read through and select which ones would be purchased for publication. Without her best friend here to have wine with every night and complain about everything that was wrong in the world, she might just be more productive than she imagined.

Rita gazed around at the dinette area, where there was a four-top wicker table. The small kitchen had white cupboards and a pale peach backsplash. And perhaps more importantly, there was a single-serve coffeemaker and a variety of coffees in the adjacent coffee carousel.

"Very nice," Rita said. She strolled through the place toward the back window. She peered through the blinds. About fifty feet away was the pool area. It had a water-slide, as well as a splash pad for kids. Two young children were running around beneath the spray of water.

"You'll get a much better view of outside from the balcony," Keith told her.

Rita moved to the left and opened the bedroom door. More California blinds let in loads of light. There was a queen-sized bed with a wicker headboard. A ceiling fan was above. The wall behind the headboard was painted in peach, while the other three walls were painted white. A white-knit bedspread gave the room a warm and cozy feel. This room had another flat-screen television, though smaller than the one in the living room. Just below the television and to the left was a small desk.

"It's lovely," Rita said. She opened the door that led to the balcony and stepped outside. She drew in a deep breath of the fresh air. Her mood lifted as she looked out at the large lake, upon which some boats were sailing. There was a trail as far as the eye could see around the lake, and she saw one brave soul jogging in this heat.

"I love it," Rita said, turning to face Keith, who'd entered the bedroom with her. He was standing in the room, several feet away, giving her space. "I can already picture myself sitting here with a coffee in the morning."

"I'm glad you like it."

"What's not to like?" Though she wasn't here for a vacation, this place made her feel as though she were in Sheridan Falls for some relaxation.

"The bathroom is just outside the bedroom," Keith told her. "The door right here."

Rita went and checked it out. It was small and functional. It had a shower, sink, toilet, and was nicely decorated. On occasion she liked to luxuriate in a tub, but this unit didn't have one. It was fine. She would survive.

Rita made a quick turn, then gasped when she realized that Keith was almost right behind her. Her eyes landed on the coffee stain on his shirt…then the bulge of his muscular chest beneath it.

"Sorry," he said. "I was just going to ask if you wanted to go downstairs and check out the amenities."

Rita sidestepped him. "Not right now. But I will."

"And so you know, the lake is perfectly fine for swimming."

"I'm glad I brought my bathing suit." Rita offered him a smile. "Hopefully I'll get the time to swim."

"You said you were in town for a wedding?" Keith asked, narrowing his eyes in question.

A bitter taste filled Rita's mouth. "Yes. Well… Maybe."

Keith's eyes registered confusion. "I don't understand."

"My mother. She's engaged. But I'm not one hundred percent certain the wedding will happen. The decision was made on a whim as far as I'm concerned. I wouldn't be surprised if the whole thing gets called off."

Rita met Keith's gaze, saw that he was studying her. "That's why you said in your email that the wedding shouldn't be happening."

"I want my mother to be happy," Rita said.

"And you don't think that getting married will make her happy," Keith surmised.

"It's a long story, and I'm not certain that I want to

get into it right now. I'm not sure she's making the right decision, no. But I'm here because she's my mother, and I'm not about to let her go through this on her own. And if the pieces of her life fall apart, I need to be here to help her pick them up."

"Ouch." Keith cringed. "You don't sound too hopeful about this wedding."

"It's not really something I want to talk about. I hope you don't mind."

"Hey, I didn't mean to pry."

"I know. It's just…complicated." And stress-inducing. Just thinking about the wedding was causing the momentary peace she'd felt to dissipate. Two months in Sheridan Falls was going to be two months too long. But hopefully her mother would come to her senses before that time.

"The unit's great," Rita said. "Everything looks fine. More than fine."

"I aim to please."

She sauntered through the living room and toward the front door. "This is much more than I expected," Rita told him. And she still couldn't believe the price. It was a steal. "Thanks again."

She looked up at him and he down at her. She waited for him to say his goodbyes and be on his way. But he simply smiled at her. Why wasn't he leaving?

"Well, I do thank you very much for your time," Rita went on, ready to end their time together. "I know you've got to get back to work, but I appreciate you taking me here. I have your card, so if there's any trouble I'll be in touch. But I doubt I'll have any problems."

"I saw some boxes in the back of your car," Keith said. "Let me help you bring your stuff upstairs."

"That's not necessary," Rita said. "I'll bring my stuff up later. Right now, I'm going to take a nap."

"I can help you."

"Oh, I don't expect that. That's above and beyond the call of duty," she said, giving him a little chuckle. "But I do appreciate the offer."

"I insist," Keith said. "Besides, I've got a bit of time before my next appointment."

Rita gave him a quizzical look. Why was he suddenly being so nice to her?

Was he going overboard to prove to her that he wasn't the jerk he'd initially acted like? Was that why he was suddenly trying to win her over with his charm?

If that was the case, then what would it hurt to take him up on his offer? "If you really want to help," Rita said, "then how can I refuse?"

Chapter 3

As Rita watched Keith carry her two large suitcases from the trunk, she couldn't help thinking that he was seriously attractive. He was the kind of guy she could enjoy gazing at. Like someone on a safari checking out the wild animals, she could watch him and not get bored.

However, she knew that wouldn't be wise. Keith wasn't a man on display. And he was the kind of man that she knew it would be risky to get close to. If she had him pegged right, he had an easy way with the ladies, and how many times had Rita seen women fall for guys like that during vulnerable times? She knew her heart was especially weak after her breakup with Rashad a few months ago and the reality that their wedding would have been just weeks away. The fact that her mother was getting married on top of that only made her heart more fragile.

Vulnerable women looking for a way to forget or ease

their pain often brought on more heartbreak. Rita read about it in the various stories sent to her for her magazine, *Unlock Your Power*. The magazine was a voice for women who'd endured devastating situations but were picking up the pieces of their lives. Sharing their stories was a way to help ease their pain and let others in similar situations know that they weren't alone.

So Rita definitely knew better than to think of men as a distraction. She could look at Keith or any other man and leave it at that. It was a matter of choice, wasn't it? Knowing the risks and behaving accordingly.

The first rule of guarding your heart was to not get involved on any level. Keith was simply a man who wanted to help her out—a good guy doing the courteous thing. No need to let herself think that there might be more motives to his actions.

Keith exited the bedroom, where he had brought her two big suitcases. "I know it's a lot, but considering I might be here for a while…" Her voice trailed off. "Speaking of which, are there laundry facilities?"

"Excellent question. Forgot to mention that. There is a stacked washer and dryer in the cupboard in the kitchen. You'll see it."

"Perfect, thank you."

Keith headed to the door again, and Rita said, "I can get the rest."

"You don't have too much more. I'll get the big box I saw in the backseat. Plus, wasn't there a case of water?"

"Yes, but—" Rita stopped when her phone rang. She pulled it out from the back pocket of her jeans and glanced at the screen. It was her best friend, Maeve.

Keith jogged down the steps, and Rita swiped to answer the call. "Hey."

"How's it going?" Maeve asked without preamble.

"Good. I got here okay."

"You said something about a mishap," Maeve said, concern in her voice.

"Yeah, but... It's not really a big deal. It was a small fender bender, but the situation's been resolved."

"Someone hit you?" Maeve asked.

"Actually, I hit someone."

"What?"

"I was distracted for a second when I was pulling up to the coffee shop. And...it was barely a touch. No real damage."

"Did you leave a note for the owner?"

"Actually, he was in the car," Rita said as she watched Keith make his way back up the steps with the box of food items. "There was just a bit of paint transfer." He gave her a little smile as he passed her, and Rita smiled back. Then she stepped outside of the unit to continue her call. "I offered to pay, he refused. Everything's good."

"Okay, that's great to hear. Just make sure you follow up. You don't want the guy to start claiming back pains tomorrow."

"I doubt that's going to happen. Something tells me that people in small towns like this are honest, not opportunistic. And from the sense I got from the guy... I highly doubt he would do that."

"All right, if you're sure, then I trust your judgment."

"I am sure," Rita said. She didn't bother to tell her that the very man whose car she'd hit was currently helping her move in. Maeve would demand an explanation. "Anyway, I'm just getting my stuff into my apartment. The realtor is here with me. He's helping me carry up some boxes."

"Really?" Maeve asked. "You mean he didn't just hand you an invoice and call it a day?"

"No. He's been quite helpful, actually."

"That's a change from St. Louis. I guess you're right. People are nicer in small towns."

"So far."

"Unless he's interested." Maeve's voice rose on a hopeful note. "Is he cute? And is he single?"

"Maeve, seriously."

"I am serious. Lord knows you need a distraction from Rashad and what he did to you."

Rita threw a quick glance at Keith before whispering, "I didn't give him the third degree." Keith took a step in her direction, and Rita quickly changed the direction of the conversation. "It's a totally beautiful unit, and you should see the location." She spoke loudly enough for Keith to hear as he passed her and headed to the steps. "Maybe you can come up for a weekend."

"Mmm, now that's an idea. Maybe I will."

"I could use a friend up here."

"Have you talked to your mother yet?" Maeve asked.

"No," Rita answered. "Not yet. I wanted to make sure I got settled in first before I call her."

Maeve sighed softly. "You know I'm thinking of you and wishing you the best. Remember, you've got to accept whatever decision your mom's making. Just do your best to be there for her."

Rita stared off at the wall of trees as Keith walked past her with her case of bottled water. She knew her friend was right, but still it hurt to think about doing that. But she said, "That's why I'm here. One way or another, I'm going to be there for my mom. Hopefully everything works out the way she wants." Although Rita said the words, she couldn't help secretly wishing the opposite. Because she didn't want to see her mother get hurt. If the relationship fell apart now, it would spare her mother prolonged pain.

"Look, I'll give you a call a little later this evening," Rita told Maeve. "I'm hungry, and I've got to get settled in."

"All right, girl," Maeve said. "Glad you arrived safely and that everything's going okay."

"Thanks."

She ended the call and stepped back into the apartment. Keith approached her. "I just saw one more box in your trunk," he said.

"Oh, that. It's miscellaneous stuff. It can stay in the car for now. You've brought up everything I need, so thank you."

"Any time."

Rita extended her hand. "All right, Keith. It's been a pleasure. I'll be in touch if I need you. If I need you for anything," she quickly amended, hoping her words hadn't sounded like a come-on. Though she wasn't sure that her second version was much better. "But I'm sure I won't have to call."

Keith's eyes crinkled as he shook her hand. "I'm here. For whatever you require."

Slowly, he released her hand, and as Rita gazed up at him, a jolt zapped her chest. This time, there was no questioning the meaning behind his look. The glint in his eyes along with his suggestive words made it clear that he was flirting.

He walked past her then, and a hint of his cologne wafted into her nose. It was a musky scent that made her insides crumble.

The man was fine, no doubt about it. Too fine.

And he knew it. She could tell by that easy smile he gave her, the gleam in his eyes. He probably thought she'd be calling sooner rather than later, trying to arrange some sort of hookup.

Well, he was going to have to wait a long time if that's what he thought.

Rita was glad when Keith finally left, and she laid her head down for a full five minutes. Then she got up abruptly. Before she took a nap, she needed to call her mother. Let her know that she'd arrived safely.

The phone rang twice before her mother answered. "Hello!" she exclaimed in a cheerful voice. "Have you arrived?"

"Yes. I'm here."

"How was the drive?" her mother asked.

"Uneventful. Peaceful." Rita loved long drives. They allowed her time to think. She often came up with her best article ideas when she was driving.

"And you're at your rental unit now?" her mother asked.

"Yep. And it's lovely. Right on the lake. Such a fantastic view."

"Didn't I tell you? You're going to love this little town. You might not even want to leave," her mother added with a chuckle.

"I wouldn't go that far," Rita said. This was a quaint and beautiful spot, that was for sure. But she was a big city girl. Besides, her life was in St. Louis. She wasn't about to move here and play family with her mother and father.

"You know, it's not too late to reconsider," her mother said.

Though her mother hadn't specified what she was talking about, Rita knew. "Mom…you know my position on this."

"We have the room. And that way, you can spend more time with your father. With us."

The very idea caused a lump to form in Rita's throat. "I need my own space. At least to get work done."

There was a soft sigh on the other end of the line. "Well, if you change your mind…"

The invitation hung between them, but Rita wasn't about to take her mother up on the offer.

"You have the address for the house?" her mother asked. "I texted it to you."

"Yep. I got it."

"Why don't you come over for dinner? I made enough to feed—"

"Not today, Mom."

"You must be hungry. Come by, I'll give you a plate to take."

"Another time," Rita said.

"You're going to have to see him at some point," her mother told her.

"At some point, yes. But that doesn't have to be today. I'm exhausted from the drive, and I figure I'll go get some groceries. Plus, I need to check back with my office about some assignments…"

"It needs to be sooner rather than later. We need to get on with the wedding planning. And I'd like you and your father to smooth things over before we walk down the aisle."

Rita wanted to say, *If you walk down the aisle. How*

do you know he won't change his mind again? And how could you be with him after how he abandoned you? He cheated on you, for God's sake. He cheated on his wife. And now here you are giving him the ultimate reward of your love.

But she said none of those things, because she'd said all of those things in the past. Ad nauseam. Until even she couldn't stand to hear those words come out of her mouth again.

"He's really been wonderful, sweetheart. If you talk to him, you'll see."

"Well, that's great," Rita said. But she knew that her tone indicated she felt otherwise. She didn't want to fake it, and for her mother's sake, she did hope things worked out.

She just wasn't banking on it.

Rita's eyes flew open. Glancing around, she felt a sense of panic. She was on a sofa she didn't recognize, and the surroundings were completely unfamiliar.

It took only a few seconds for her to remember where she was. The floral-patterned sofa, the California blinds. The colorful walls and the bright kitchen.

She was in Sheridan Falls.

Rita eased herself up to a sitting position on the sofa. Then she reached for her cell phone on the coffee table in front of her and checked the time. It was 6:28 p.m. Wow, she'd slept for a good couple of hours.

Her stomach grumbled, making it clear that she needed to feed herself. She wandered over to the kitchen table, where Keith had placed the box of her food items. Pancake mix, bread. Peanut butter. A container of almond milk. There was also a box of cereal. If nothing else, she could have cereal and some toast with peanut butter.

But that idea didn't really appeal to her. She wanted a hot, filling meal. A proper dinner.

It was time to venture into town.

Minutes later, Rita was in her car and driving to the center of town to see what Sheridan Falls had to offer in terms of food. She stayed on the main strip, where she saw a place called Sally's Soul Food, an Italian restaurant and a burrito joint. When she saw the Chinese restaurant, she knew that's what she wanted.

She found a parking spot, then went inside. The Asian woman behind the counter greeted her warmly. Rita indicated that she would need a minute, and she began to peruse one of the folded paper menus.

After a few minutes, she went up to the counter to order. "I'll have some lo mein noodles, sweet-and-sour chicken balls and an order of chicken fried rice." It was a lot of food, but at least she could keep something for the next night. It was always good to have something on hand to warm up when she didn't want to cook.

The woman calculated the order and gave Rita the total, which was quite reasonable. Rita reached into her pocket for her cell phone. She opened up her mobile wallet, which allowed her to pay via her phone.

"No, I'm sorry," the lady began. "We need the card. Or cash."

"I have my card on my phone," Rita explained.

"No, that won't work here."

"You're kidding?" Rita said. It had worked at the café earlier.

"I'm sorry. We have an old system. Do you have the card?"

"No. And I don't have cash." Rita hadn't even thought to bring her actual wallet. She was used to using her phone to pay for her items in St. Louis and even carried her driver's license in there. She didn't even consider that mobile pay might not be an option here.

"Maybe you can go get some cash and come back?"

Rita made a face. She'd have to head back to the apartment to get her bank card, then venture back out to an ATM. And she was already starving. "You know what, just cancel the order for now. I'll…come back."

She left, frustrated, and went back to her car. She didn't feel like heading back out once she got to the apartment.

Well, peanut butter and bread it would be.

Putting two slices of bread in the toaster, Rita retrieved her laptop and brought it to the sofa. She opened it up and continued reading the submission for her magazine that she had started before she'd left St. Louis. A harrowing story of a husband's betrayal.

When I realized that he had drained our bank accounts, I thought my life was over. My husband was gone, my house was foreclosed on and I was about to be thrown into the street.

There was a knock at the door. Rita looked in that direction, startled. Was someone knocking at her unit?

Her eyes ventured back to the laptop screen, and then the knock sounded again. Rita moved her laptop onto the sofa beside her and got up. She padded over to the door and called, "Who is it?"

"It's Keith."

Rita reeled backward. Keith! Why was he here?

She ran her hand over her hair, making sure it was presentable, then opened the door. She looked up at Keith with a quizzical expression. "What's up?"

He raised a white plastic bag, in which she could see a brown paper bag. The smell of food instantly wafted into her nose. It smelled like Chinese food, and her stomach rumbled in anticipation.

"The food you ordered," he said. "Keith's Delivery, at your service."

Chapter 4

Keith grinned down at Rita, whose beautiful bright eyes were wide with confusion. "But I didn't order food."

"No, but you were going to." She blinked, completely perplexed. "I happened to see you when you were in town," Keith explained. "You were leaving the Chinese food place just as I was parking. Anyway, when I went in because I was getting some food, Wei—the owner— happened to mention that the previous customer wanted to pay with her phone but couldn't. I was in the right place at the right time, so I paid for the order for you."

Rita looked at Keith as though he had grown two heads.

"You did what?"

"I bought the order you had to cancel. And I de-cided—"

"Why would you do that?" Her tone was accusatory.

"Because you were in a bind. You didn't have cash. I know you had a long drive here—"

"How was I to know that places in this town would not accept mobile wallet payments?"

"However it played out, I happened to be there. So I bought the food for you. I knew where you were staying, so it was no problem for me to deliver it. Then I decided to head across the street and pick up some soul food for variety." He held up another bag. "That way you can sample a couple of the options here in Sheridan Falls." He shrugged. "I thought maybe we could eat together?"

"You make a habit of getting people out of financial binds?"

The question sounded like an allegation of a criminal offense. Had no one ever done anything nice for her before?

"Like I said, I happened to know who you were and where you were staying. And this is the kind of town where we believe in doing favors."

Rita crossed her arms over her chest, but she didn't look happy. Wow, she had a lot of pent-up anger. Was she always like this, or was she offended by his presence?

He hoped it was the stress over her mother's wedding that she clearly wasn't in favor of. In which case, she should want a friend, shouldn't she?

Keith offered her his most charming smile. "Well, are you going to make me eat my food out here? Or are you going to invite me in?"

Rita looked up into Keith's eyes, which held a hint of humor as he smiled down at her. She glanced at the bags he was carrying, and her stomach rumbled.

Why was she standing here frowning at him when

he'd done her a favor? He'd done a nice thing, hadn't he? Why was she so on edge about it?

Because she knew men like Keith. Men who thought a charming smile would get them everything they wanted.

"Listen, if this is some misguided attempt to…"

"To what?" Keith asked. "Make sure my tenant has a decent meal?"

"I'll pay you back. When I get cash. Or I can do an email transfer."

"Just pay it forward. If someone else needs a favor, help them out."

The food smelled good. Lord, did it ever. And she was beyond hungry at this point. Was there a logical reason for her to be refusing this kind gesture? "Are you sure?"

"You know how you can pay me back?" Keith asked. Rita's stomach fluttered. She waited for the inevitable come-on. "You can sit down and have a meal with me. I work a lot, so I typically grab food on the go. Most times when I make a meal, I have only my goldfish for company. So…consider yourself as the one doing me the favor."

The last of her resistance ebbed away. Why was she even giving Keith a hard time? Because he'd bailed her out of a situation? The truth was, she was thrilled that she could actually have that dinner she'd planned.

She stepped backward, smiling awkwardly. "Come in." Keith stepped into the apartment. In addition to the smell of the food, the scent of his cologne flirted with her nostrils.

Apparently it didn't matter what this man was wearing. Because right now, dressed in black jeans and a baby blue shirt that had the two top buttons undone, he looked as good as he had in his business suit.

"By the way," Rita began, "just thinking about it, will my app for food delivery work here?"

Keith chuckled warmly. "We're not that sophisticated. Not enough people in this town to make that kind of thing worthwhile. Besides, folks like to head out, pick things up personally. I don't think they'd trust an app."

Somehow, Rita couldn't quite see Keith being at home as a small town guy. He had a sense of sophistication about him that made her think he would thrive on the excitement and challenges in a big city.

She walked into the small dining area and pulled out a chair for him. "I'm sorry. I don't have anything to drink. Except water."

"I've got it covered," he told her. He placed a six-pack of vodka coolers on the table. Rita hadn't even noticed that he'd been carrying them. "I've got this. If you prefer, I also have some beer in the car."

"The vodka cooler is perfect." She frowned. "Are there plates? Cutlery?"

"That's all there," Keith said, pointing in the direction of the kitchen cupboards, as he took out the bags of food and placed them on the table.

Rita went into the kitchen and opened a cupboard. She found the plates and took two down. Then she opened a drawer in search of cutlery, but it only contained a variety of oversized knives and spoons. By the time she was reaching for the next drawer, Keith's fingers were brushing against hers.

"Sorry," he said, as her eyes flew to his. "This is where the cutlery is."

Keith took a step backward, and Rita proceeded to take out two forks and two knives.

"The coolers are already cold, but do you want yours

in a glass with ice?" Keith asked. He was already opening the freezer.

"Sure, why not?"

Minutes later, the table was arranged with plates,
glasses, cutlery and open cartons of food. Keith twisted
off a cap from a cooler and poured it into an ice-filled
glass for Rita. Then he poured himself one.

"I'm not even sure I said thank you. I do appreciate
you bringing me food. It looks and smells delicious."

Of the containers with the soul food, there was fried
chicken and collard greens and seasoned potato wedges.
And of course, there were the sweet-and-sour chicken
balls, fried rice and stir-fried noodles Rita had originally tried to order. There was enough food for a number of people.

"Let's dig in," Rita said. "Can you pass me the noodles?"

"Here you go." Keith passed her the container, and
Rita used her fork to scoop some onto her plate. Then
she took some of the sweet-and-sour chicken balls and a
piece of the fried chicken.

"If this is how you treat people who bump into your
car, what would you do if someone really smashed it?"
Rita asked, smiling lightheartedly.

"One thing you'll learn about the folks in Sheridan
Falls, we try our best to focus on the good things. Un-
less something is majorly wrong, we don't dwell on it.
Life is short. Why sweat the small stuff?"

Rita narrowed her eyes as she regarded him. "You
don't really strike me as a small town boy with a small
town mentality."

"No?"

"Not really, no. I don't mean that in a negative way."

"I haven't always been," Keith admitted. "I grew up here, but by age nineteen I was itching to get out. Everybody knows you. You can't do anything without people saying something. You hit a point where you want to spread your wings beyond this small town. I wanted to experience something bigger and better."

Rita lifted the chicken thigh. "Did you?" she asked, then took a bite. Her eyes rolled heavenward. "The crispiness. The spices. Oh, my goodness, this is to die for."

"Southern fried chicken is Sally's specialty. Sally's Soul Food is the name of her restaurant."

"I'll have to check it out."

"Like me, Sally grew up here, and had roots in the South." Keith picked up a thigh. "She lived in Louisiana for a while and perfected the cooking. Her restaurant is now one of the most popular ones in town."

"I can see why." Rita took another bite, her stomach doing gymnastics of joy. She hadn't realized she was this hungry. "Anyway, you were saying that you wanted to escape the small town life?"

Keith chewed his morsel of chicken, nodding. "The walls started to close in on me. I think it's tough enough being anonymous in a small town, but that's all but impossible if you have a bit of celebrity."

"Oh?"

"I grew up the son of a fairly famous football player. At least in Sheridan Falls."

"Really?"

"Cyrus Burke, NFL star. He played for a number of years."

"That had to be exciting."

"It had its perks, for sure. But for us, it has always been about family, not fame."

Rita swallowed her mouthful of smoky collard greens before asking, "Big family then?"

"Three brothers. I used to be the baby of us four until my sister, Chantelle, came along when I was nine."

"An oops baby," Rita said, grinning, "or was she planned?"

Keith's expression grew serious, and Rita wondered if she'd said the wrong thing. "Was that insensitive? I didn't mean—"

"She passed away."

"Oh, no." Rita saw a flash of pain cross his face. "I'm so sorry."

"She drowned when she was five," Keith explained. "In the family pool."

Rita placed a hand on her heart. She couldn't even imagine the pain. "Oh, Keith. That must have been horrible for you."

"It was." He exhaled harshly, then scooped out some of the collard greens and a bit of the fried rice. But instead of eating, he set his fork down and met her gaze as he continued talking. "It was very hard for all of us. The worst thing that's ever happened to our family. Honestly, it's a reminder that no matter how much money you have, it can't buy the things that matter most."

Rita couldn't imagine losing someone to a tragedy like that. The thought of anything happening to her mother gave her anxiety.

"What about you?" he asked. "Big family?"

Rita shook her head. "I'm an only child. It was always just me and my mom. I have some cousins, but they live in Chicago, and I didn't see much of them."

"And your mother's living here now?" Keith asked.

"Well…for the time being." Rita pushed the rice

around with her fork. "Who knows what the future holds. But tell me more about you and what it's like to grow up in a small town."

Keith took a swig of his cooler. "It's hard to find your own uniqueness, let's say, when you have three brothers and a famous father. Everyone pretty much looks at you as one entity. So I needed to forge my own way. Like my dad, I was good at sports. I ended up playing semi-pro football. I didn't really make it anywhere, but it was fun. Got me out of Sheridan Falls, allowed me to travel over much of the states. I've been to the best cities, like Miami, Dallas, Los Angeles. And you know what? After a while, you kind of end up missing home."

Rita lowered the morsel of chicken, which she'd pretty much devoured. "Really? You seem like the kind a guy who would love the fast-paced life."

"I did," he said. "Until I was no longer playing football and I realized that some of the people I thought were my friends passed me over for others. It hurt, but I'd much rather know that someone is my real friend than hanging on for whatever breadcrumbs they think they might be able to gather."

"That had to be tough, though."

"It was. And after a friend of mine who'd played semi-pro ball with me, Richard Dawson, was killed in a car crash, big city life didn't have that much appeal for me anymore. I missed the comfort of home, the familiar faces, the people I knew loved me. Not the gawkers in the media."

"I'm so sorry for your loss."

Keith chewed and swallowed some rice. "Thank you."

There was more to him than she had thought. Weird, she'd seen his handsome face and flashy car and thought only of his sex appeal and charm. She hadn't thought about him as a person who'd had his share of trials and tribulations in life.

That's because she hadn't been trying to think about him, period.

"What doesn't kill you makes you stronger, right?" Keith said. "That's what they say."

"I guess it depends on what it is."

"People can go through the worst things. Absolutely devastating stuff. But isn't it your perspective on what's happened that determines how it affects you?"

What are you getting from holding on to anger toward your father? Until you learn to forgive, you're just hurting yourself.

Rita's mother's words sounded in her ear as clearly as if she were in the room. Suddenly, the spoonful of rice in her mouth had no taste.

"I think that's a bit of a simplistic view," Rita said.

Keith's eyes registered mild surprise. "Simplistic?"

Rita took a sip of her cooler. "I understand that tragedies happen, and they're crushing. But you can process it, move on. However, what if someone has gone through something for years? Pain that is constant for years on end. It's not really how you decide to feel about the situation then, is it? It's the reason some people turn to drugs or alcohol to cope. The pain is too much to bear."

"I still think that your attitude determines how that affects your life. You can choose to hold on to the pain or let it go."

"Is that so?" Rita's voice sounded testy even to her own ears. Her chest was getting tight. She couldn't have this conversation with a man who didn't understand what she'd gone through.

"Definitely," Keith said.

"That's easy to say," Rita told him. "But you haven't lived through every scenario, have you?"

"Of course n—"

"Have you had someone disappoint you for your entire life?"

"No, but—"

"Then you really can't speak for those who've gone through that kind of pain."

His eyes narrowed as he looked at her. "Hey." He placed a hand on hers. "I didn't say I could. Why are you getting so upset?"

"People judge others when they really shouldn't."

"You think I'm judging you?"

Rita pushed her chair back and stood. "You know, I'm feeling really tired."

Keith's eyebrows shot up. "Are you asking me to leave?"

"I really need to get a good night's rest," Rita said. "Let me pack up some of this food for you."

"If I said something to offend you…"

Rita closed the container with the chicken and placed it in the bag.

"I don't want any of the food," Keith said. "You keep it."

Rita covered the noodles. She needed to keep her hands busy.

"I don't want the food," Keith reiterated. Then, "Are you okay?"

"I'm just tired." She stopped fiddling with the food and ran a hand through her hair. "It's hitting me all of a sudden."

"You're sure?" Keith asked.

"Yes. I need to go to bed." She didn't quite meet Keith's eyes. "You want the coolers?"

"No, I'm good."

Rita started for the door, making it clear she was ready for him to leave. She opened it, and a few seconds later, he exited.

"Rita—"

"Good night," she said. "Thanks for the food."

And then she closed the door.

Chapter 5

Should he call her?

That was the thought dominating most of Keith's thoughts two days later at work. He'd thought of her quite often the day before, but had decided that calling her was not the smart thing to do. She was a tenant. Nothing more, nothing less. He didn't need her to be nice to him.

That's what he'd told himself yesterday, and yet today he'd woken up thinking about her. About those dark eyes filled with mystery.

He didn't like how things had abruptly ended between them, and he simultaneously felt the urge to reach out to her, and to completely leave her alone.

"Keith?"

"Hmm?"

"Did you hear what I said?" Barbara, his real estate broker, asked on the other end of the line.

"Sorry. I was checking out the floor plan."

"The units are in good shape," Barbara said, "but the location is a little farther west than you'd like."

"How much farther?"

"Twenty miles."

"Too far," Keith said.

"However, I think this is still workable," Barbara quickly said. "It's close to the University of Buffalo, so you'll always be able to rent to students."

"Keep looking," Keith said abruptly.

"You don't want to even come to town and see it?"

"I know there's a better deal to be found. I want you to find it."

"Right now, this is the best deal."

"I've got time," Keith said. "I'm not going to jump on a deal unless it's one I want."

Barbara sighed softly. "Okay."

"Talk to you later." Keith ended the call, and looked at the photo of the building Barbara had sent him on his computer screen. It wasn't half as appealing as the one he'd lost. Students were not his desired clientele. Too much turnover. Too little investment in the upkeep of the property.

His eyes went downward to his cell phone. He strummed his fingers on the desk. Should he call her?

He was in a funk this morning, more than usual. And though he had tried to tell himself it was about business, he knew there was another reason. The beautiful yet serious woman who was renting apartment number six.

She went from hot to cold without batting an eye. What had he said to set her off? And why was it still bothering him a day and a half later?

Keith had been talking about his own experience,

about how moving forward with a positive attitude made all the difference, and she practically lost it on him.

It was obvious that something was bothering her. The wedding? Was her mother's upcoming nuptials really that upsetting to her? Or had somebody broken her heart and left her hateful of all men?

She was hot to handle, no doubt about it, but Keith couldn't help thinking that a man who would break her heart was foolish. She had a lot of passion—that was clear. Keith could only imagine that when she was using that passion for loving as opposed to arguing, the man in her life would be very happy.

"Um, Mr. Burke."

Keith looked up from his desk toward the open office door. "What is it, Dana?"

"There's a problem with the plumbing at one of your units."

Keith groaned. For goodness' sakes. Why today? He didn't need the added stress.

"Call Jake." He was the plumber Keith used. "Have him go over there and fix it."

"It's a little more complicated. I thought you might want to talk to the tenant."

"Why?"

"Because it's Rita Osgood, the woman who rented the unit a couple of days ago. She said she didn't want to disturb you, but she's asking me if I could possibly move her to a new unit. She said if there isn't another unit, she'll need to break her rental agreement."

Keith was out of his seat in a flash. "Is she on the line now?"

"No. Your line was busy when she called, so I told her I would try to solve the situation and get back to her."

"I'll deal with it," Keith said, grabbing his car keys. And then he headed out of the office.

When Rita heard the urgent knocking on her door, she ran to answer it. Thank God, the plumber had arrived.

She swung the door open without hesitation. And gasped when she saw Keith standing there.

One of his arms was raised above his head and resting on her doorframe. He looked down at her with dark eyes, and an unclear expression on his face. "You have a problem with the plumbing?" he asked, getting to the point.

"I… I thought the plumber was coming."

"Why didn't you call my cell?"

"I called your office."

"And when my line was busy, you should have called my cell." Keith stepped forward, and Rita moved backward to let him pass. Was he angry? She couldn't tell.

"What exactly is the problem?" he asked.

"All of the water is cold. I went into the shower, turned it on and I'm sure my bloodcurdling screams terrified some people. I'm not a wimp or anything, but I'd really like to have a hot shower. How long do you think it will take for the plumber to get here?"

Keith looked her up and down, taking in her damp hair and then her T-shirt and shorts. "I called the plumber on the way over here. He's busy right now and can't get here until the end of the day."

"Are you serious? Then you need to call someone else."

"Let me have a look." Keith went into her kitchen and turned on the hot water faucet. He let it run. He placed his hand under the water, and after a good minute, he frowned and shut the water off. As he did, his phone rang. "Dana, hi. Damn, okay. Thanks for letting me know."

"The water's still cold, right?" Rita said.

"Yes, and apparently it's more than one unit. So it's got to be the water heater for this sector of the building."

"This is a huge inconvenience," Rita said.

"I know. I understand you requested a possible new unit, but I'd have to move you to another building altogether. Let me see what Jake can do first, all right?"

"How long is that going to take? I really need to shower now and get on with my day."

"What about going to your mother's place?"

Rita's jaw flinched. "Not an option."

Nodding, Keith placed his hands on his hips. "Why don't we do this? I can take you to my place and you can shower there."

Rita's eyebrows shot up. "What?"

"I can drop you off, let you use the shower and then hopefully by the end of the day this situation will be resolved. Sooner. I'll get right on it."

Rita bit down on her bottom lip. Go to Keith's place? Use his shower? "I don't know…"

"It's the best solution I have for the immediate time being."

Rita needed a hot shower. Cold water just wouldn't cut it.

"I guess I could be quick about it," she found herself saying.

"Get what you need. I'll be downstairs. You can follow me to my place."

Keith spoke in a commanding way, all but giving her no choice. There was something off about him today, and Rita was pretty sure she knew what it was. Their interaction the night before last had gone from pleasant to negative in seconds.

"All right," she said. "Thank you."

"Let me call my plumber again."

As Keith made his call, Rita went to her room and got fresh clothes, a towel and her shower gel. She would be quick at Keith's place.

When she exited the bathroom, Keith said without preamble, "Jake says he'll be able to get here in a couple of hours. Hopefully he can resolve the situation quickly. It might be several hours before you have hot water, though. Do you want to wait, or do you still want to come to my place?"

Rita hesitated only a beat. "I'll go to your place."

Keith's house was a large two-story home on a quiet tree-lined street. It looked modern, yet quaint. The exterior was a combination of gray and pale blue. The white trim around the windows provided the perfect contrast to the color scheme. The lawn was lush and well manicured. There was a white wooden swing that could accommodate two hanging on the porch. The only thing that was missing was the white picket fence.

Rita pulled into the cobblestone driveway beside Keith and parked her car. Was there a Mrs. Burke around? Or had there been one? Rita hadn't seen a ring on Keith's finger.

That didn't mean he wasn't married, though. Did he have any children? This wasn't the kind of home she pictured a bachelor inhabiting.

"Is there someone who's going to wonder why I'm coming home with you?" Rita asked when she got out of the car and met Keith on the driveway.

Keith looked down at her. "You mean like a wife?"

"Yes." Rita paused. "Are you married?"

"No." Keith shook his head. "I'm not. No kids. Only some goldfish."

That's right. He'd mentioned the goldfish two days ago. How had she forgotten?

Keith strolled up the stone walkway and up the steps to the front door. Rita glanced around at the flower boxes hanging from the porch railing and the wind chimes near the door. They sang as Keith and Rita walked past.

"Welcome to my home," Keith said, and opened the door. Rita followed him into the house. Her eyes volleyed back and forth, taking the place in. Like outside, the walls were painted a pale blue. A strip of white-painted wood stretched across the wall about three and a half feet up, separating the blue from the white wainscoting below. The polished dark wood floor provided a contrast to the bright colors.

An open archway to the left led to the living room. A staircase on the right wall led to the upper level. Directly at the back of the house, there was a kitchen.

"The basement's finished, and I have a full bathroom down there," Keith said. "Let me show you."

Keith made the way to the basement steps, where he hit the light and began to descend. The walls were the same pale blue, but instead of the hardwood floor, there was a beige carpet.

"That's the bathroom on the left," Keith said, pointing to a door as he rounded the corner. "The linen closet is right inside, so you'll have access to towels, if you need any."

"Oh, thank you."

"I don't have a hair dryer, sorry."

"I don't need one."

Keith nodded. "I'll leave you to it then. I'll be gone when you're finished. Let yourself out."

"I will, thanks."

Rita stood and watched Keith begin to ascend the stairs. Then she went into the bathroom and closed the door, and released a breath she hadn't realized she'd been holding.

Keith was being so…businesslike. He was upset with her, and Rita didn't feel good about that. Especially not when she was here in his private home to take a shower.

She'd been unfair to him the other night, and she felt the weight of guilt on her shoulders. Her own issues had had her snapping at him and she needed to give him an explanation.

She swung the door open, calling, "Keith!"

His name morphed into a scream on her lips.

Because there he was, standing before her. His eyes widened in surprise. Then darkened with a look that had her heart fluttering.

Rita exhaled heavily. "You scared me."

"Sorry. I just…" He extended a robe. "I brought you this. In case you need it."

She took the robe from his arms, her fingers brushing his hand. And just that simple touch caused heat to spread across her skin. She glanced away, swallowing.

Keith took a step backward. "I'll just be… You know how to reach me."

"Okay," Rita said softly.

He turned and took a few steps, and Rita was going to retreat into the bathroom. But instead she said, "Wait."

Halting, Keith glanced over his shoulder. And Lord help her, there was that look again.

He fully turned. "Do you not want me to leave?"

"Uh…"

One step, two. He headed back toward her. Slowly. Like a jaguar stalking its prey.

"I just…um…" Suddenly Rita couldn't think. She couldn't form the words she had wanted to say.

"Because if you don't want me to leave…"

Keith was right in front of her now, his gaze holding hers. She could see it now, as clear as day. His desire for her.

The same desire she was feeling.

He tucked a tendril of her hair behind her ear, then let his fingers graze her face. More heat filled her body. "Is this what the tension between us is about?" he asked, his voice husky. "Are we fighting something?"

Rita swallowed. And dang it, why couldn't she form a word? This wasn't why she'd called out to Keith. And yet her body was so alive with excitement that she didn't want to stop what was happening.

Keith slipped his fingers around her neck, and she uttered a soft mewling sound. As he urged her toward him, she tipped up on her toes and tilted her chin.

Slowly, his mouth came down on hers. Soft. Warm. And so utterly delectable.

His lips brushed across hers. Once. Twice. And then he softly suckled her bottom lip. Rita leaned into him, placing a palm against his chest. The feel of his muscles beneath his shirt caused her heart to flutter. Lord, this man was sexy.

Rita felt and heard Keith's heavy intake of breath. He snaked a hand around her waist and as he pulled her forcefully against his body, he deepened the kiss. His tongue swept across hers, and Rita gripped his shirt now, needing to hold on to him in order to steady herself.

Keith's cell phone ringing was like a bomb going off, that's how unexpected and intrusive it was. He broke the kiss and stepped backward. He looked flummoxed as he reached into his jacket pocket for it.

"Sorry," he said. He glanced at the phone's screen, then back at her. "I have to take this."

Rita was too shaken to do anything other than nod.

"Keith Burke," he said. "Yes, hi. Oh. Right now? Okay. I'm on my way."

He ended the call and faced her. "I have to go."

Rita nodded. "Right. Of course."

"I'm sorry."

Rita forced a smile. "I'll see you later."

Rita stood under the spray of hot water, wondering what on earth had just happened between her and Keith. Kissing him had not been part of the plan.

There had been no plan, except to shower and apologize to him for her up-and-down behavior the other night. But somehow he'd looked at her with those smoky eyes and she'd been lost.

Honestly she hadn't recognized herself. Keith was not the kind of man she dated.

And yet... The kiss had excited her in a way she hadn't been for so long. A gorgeous man had looked at her as though he'd wanted no other woman but her... How could she not be affected?

Thoughts of Keith consumed her as she lathered up her body. Her nipples were taut, all from that kiss. Maybe it was being in Keith's home, in his shower, but flashes of him naked behind her, his hands smoothing suds all over her, invaded her mind.

Maybe she'd need a cold shower after all...

Rita washed her hair, then exited the large glass stall. The bathroom mirror was steamed, and she wiped a portion of it with her towel so that she could see herself. Her reflection wasn't fully visible through the smoky glass, but was that a satisfied smirk on her lips?

All because of a kiss? Wow, she was becoming a cliché. Angry woman cured by a man's touch.

But still, as she dried off and then dressed herself, she couldn't help feeling a little bit lighter. For that brief moment in time, she had been able to forget about the stress in her life.

She almost wished that Keith were here when she got out of the shower.

"Are you insane?" she asked herself. "The last thing you need to do is sleep with him."

She exited the bathroom and went back upstairs, where she discovered that she was indeed alone. It was just as well.

She didn't need to complicate her life during her stay here in Sheridan Falls.

Minutes later, Rita left the house. Obviously she would not be able to lock the door, but Keith had to have known that. Then again, he would probably give her a spiel about how people in small towns could be trusted not to rob houses.

Rita was making her way to her car when another vehicle pulled into the driveway. She halted. Behind the wheel of the sparkling white Nissan Maxima was a woman with a wild mane of curly hair and dark sunglasses.

The woman regarded her, then glanced around. She put down the window and asked, "Keith's not here?"

Rita shook her head. "No."

The woman smiled and waved, then backed out of the driveway. Just like that, she was leaving. What the heck?

The woman's Maxima went to the right and disappeared down the street.

Chapter 6

Two days later, Keith was perplexed. If he couldn't vividly remember every moment of the amazing kiss he and Rita had shared and the way she felt in his arms, he might start wondering if he'd dreamed the whole thing.

Their connection had been spontaneous and hot, and if not for the phone call interrupting them, he was certain that they would have ended up making love. And yet Rita hadn't responded to any of his calls or texts. She hadn't even responded to say whether or not the hot water was working.

He knew that it was, but given the situation, he thought she would have said something to him.

Once again, she was back to the hot-and-cold routine. She'd been hot in his basement—so very hot—but now she was being cold again.

"Let me get this straight," his brother Aaron said. "A

guy shares a hot kiss with a woman, there's definitely attraction there, but then she doesn't return his calls. And you're asking why not?"

"Yep," Keith said.

"Maybe you're losing your touch," Aaron joked.

Keith was reclining on a lounge chair beside his three brothers, Aaron, Carlton and Jonas. They were on the lower patio at their parents' house, sitting and overlooking the lake.

"I didn't say this was about me," Keith said. "It's…a friend of mine."

"The proverbial friend," Carlton teased. He was the oldest of the four of them, thirty-five. And after a failed marriage, he was the most serious.

"Why would she just go AWOL?" Keith asked. "A total one-eighty from her previous behavior?"

"Ever consider that she's involved with someone else?" Aaron asked. "You ask me, that's the most likely scenario."

Keith frowned, then reached for his beer in the nook of the arm on his Adirondack chair. He took a swig. Before this moment, he would have sworn that Rita was single. But was his brother right? Was Rita's hot-and-cold routine due to the fact that she had a boyfriend?

He took another pull of his beer, his mind playing out the possibility. His jaw clenched. If Rita was married…

"Dinner's ready, boys."

Boys… Keith glanced over his shoulder at his mother, Cynthia, who was approaching the outside dining table with a roasted ham. Would she ever refer to her grown sons as anything other than boys?

Probably not.

Aaron's fiancée, Melissa, was carrying a pitcher of

lemonade in one hand and holding a baby monitor in the other. It had been an eventful and happy year for the Burke family. Last summer, Aaron had reunited with Melissa at their cousin's wedding. Aaron and Melissa had dated several years before when they'd both been camp counselors after their senior year of high school. But life had sent them in different directions. Until last June, when they'd reconnected and fallen in love.

Now they were the parents of a four-month-old baby girl, Kara. The pregnancy had been unexpected, and Melissa had wanted to wait until after she'd had the baby to tie the knot. She and Aaron were in the midst of finalizing the details for their destination wedding in St. Lucia over Christmas.

"Let's say she isn't married," Keith said, as he and his brothers made their way to the dining table. "Why would she ghost a guy then?"

"She's mentally unstable?" Jonas suggested. Aaron had earned the reputation of player among the brothers because he'd played professional soccer and traveled the world. But Jonas, the second oldest brother at thirty-three, was the actual player. He always had an excuse for not settling down, mostly that the women he got involved with were crazy.

"You think every woman's unstable," Keith said.

"Only the ones I seem to find," Jonas clarified.

"You've got to start looking beyond all those pretty faces," Aaron chimed in.

"Who is this guy and what did you do with my brother?" Jonas teased.

Aaron smiled. Then he looked toward Melissa as he took a seat at the table. "I'm a man in love."

"Yeah, well you're lucky," Jonas said. "You found a

great one." He turned back to Keith as he slipped into his own seat. "My advice—don't get emotionally invested. Because when it comes to women, they can change like that." He snapped his fingers. "One minute they're sweet and loving, the next minute you're getting a restraining order against them."

Keith frowned. Was Rita crazy? He didn't think so.

"I've got to agree with Jonas," Carlton said, making a face. "Women have mastered the art of how to keep our heads spinning." After a tumultuous marriage that hadn't lasted more than a few years, Carlton hadn't dated and vowed to stay single forever. "You ask me, they live for it."

There were some chuckles, and Aaron snaked an arm around Melissa's waist and pulled her onto his lap. "I can't say I agree. My lady plays no such games."

"I bet that's not what you said when we first started dating." Melissa raised an eyebrow.

"My therapist said I handled the situation very well," Aaron told her.

There was a raucous round of laughter. Melissa playfully swatted Aaron's arm. Then she stroked his face. "To be fair, I didn't make it easy for him."

"You boys." Cynthia shook her head. "You're never going to settle down if you have such views of women."

"You're one of the few women I know isn't crazy," Jonas said to their mother. "But tell us the truth—did you give Dad a hard time when you started dating?"

"Of course not." She fixed a napkin that was blowing in the breeze. "I was as sweet as apple pie."

"Is that what Dad would say?" Carlton asked.

"Where is your father?" Cynthia glanced around, then called out, "Cyrus? Will one of you go and get him."

"I'll go," Keith said. But no sooner than he was out of his chair his father appeared at the patio doors below the deck. He pulled them open and stepped outside.

"There you are," Cynthia said. "Where have you been?"

"I was resting, that's all." Cyrus made his way to the table and took his place at the head.

"You okay, Dad?" Keith asked.

Cyrus frowned. "Of course I'm okay. Why do people keep asking me that?"

"Because you seem more tired than normal lately," Cynthia replied. She took a seat beside Cyrus and squeezed his hand.

"I'm fine," Cyrus reiterated. "Let me grace the food." Cyrus said a brief prayer, then announced, "Let's dig in."

Cynthia reached for the carving knife. "Sweetheart, do you want to do the honors?"

"Carlton, why don't you do it today?" Cyrus asked.

Keith noticed the frown that marred his mother's beautiful face. His father always carved the roast.

"Are you sure you're okay?" Cynthia said softly.

"Son, will you pass me the lemonade?" Cyrus asked, looking at Jonas and ignoring his wife's question.

Keith could tell that his mother was concerned, but worrying was a part of her nature. Especially after they'd lost his sister, Chantelle. For the longest time after Keith had left Sheridan Falls, his mother insisted on nightly calls from him, just to know that he was alive. She was definitely happier that he was living here again.

And with her new granddaughter, his mother was over the moon ecstatic. So it bothered Keith to see the worry on her face.

He met his mother's gaze, giving her a questioning

look, but she suddenly steeled her shoulders and forced a smile onto her face. "So, Keith, who was the woman seen coming out of your house?"

Keith's eyes bulged. "Wh-what?"

"Ahhh, so that's why you asked that question," Aaron said.

"Hypothetical," Carlton scoffed. "Yeah, right."

"You're seeing someone?" Cyrus asked, looking at him askance. "Why didn't you bring her to dinner?"

Keith held up a hand, hoping to stop the questions being volleyed at him. As if he would invite Rita to his family's weekly Sunday dinner. "I'm not seeing anyone," he said to his father. Then, looking at his mother, he asked, "Who told you a woman was coming out of my house?"

"Deidre said she was pulling into your driveway when a woman was coming out of your place. Her hair was damp. She looked freshly showered. That sounds like you're seeing someone to me."

"Shower," Aaron said, narrowing his eyes. "Just how serious did you two get before she ghosted you?"

"It was a hypothetical question," Keith stressed, but he knew no one would believe him now. Of course, it hadn't been, but he hadn't wanted his brothers to know the truth. Although that was the least of his concerns at the moment. Because he finally understood why Rita was avoiding him.

If his cousin Deidre had seen her, she must have seen Deidre. And she'd jumped to the wrong conclusion.

"Spill the beans, bro," Jonas said. "I thought you burned through all the women in this town."

"No, Jonas," Keith countered, "that was you. Starting with Nora Baxter in fourth grade. Remember her?"

Jonas groaned. "My first stalker."

The brothers chuckled.

"Oh, yes, I remember her," Cynthia said. "Didn't you date her after Jonas, Aaron?"

"Aaron dated all of our girlfriends," Carlton joked.

"Hey," Aaron said. "Don't give my fiancée any reason to doubt me. I assured her our reputations were greatly exaggerated."

Keith shot a glance in Melissa's direction. She turned to Aaron and gazed at him with unbridled love. "Oh, I'm not worried. I know I can trust Aaron completely."

Aaron stretched his neck toward Melissa and gave her a soft kiss on the lips. Cynthia clamped her hands together. She made a cooing sound. "That's what I want for all my boys. True love."

"When did Deidre say she went to my house?" Keith asked.

"A couple of days ago," his mother answered. "I'm surprised she didn't call you about it already."

"Why the secrecy?" Aaron asked. "Who's the girl?"

"Sweetheart, maybe he's not ready to talk about her," Melissa said.

Yes, it totally made sense that Rita had seen Deidre and assumed that she was a woman he was involved with. She would have no reason to think Deidre was related to him.

"I'm not sure I've seen your brother so quiet," Cynthia mused.

"She's one of my tenants," Keith said. "She's visiting from St. Louis."

"I like St. Louis," his mother said.

As if by extension, that meant she would like Rita. Keith shook his head, but he was smiling. He was grateful for his family. He loved them dearly, and didn't know what he would do without them in his life. Every Sunday he had dinner with them, provided he was in town, and every Sunday he dealt with his mother's commentary about how he was too busy to find love, and he needed to stop working so hard and concentrate as much on his personal life as he did on business. His single brothers also got the same questions from their mother.

This family meal was Keith's favorite part of the week. He looked forward to the day when he could bring a woman here to join the family for dinner the way Aaron now had Melissa.

His mother could then concentrate her efforts on seeing Carlton and Jonas married off—though that was bound to be a huge task.

"Why don't you bring her by for dinner one day?" Cynthia suggested. "How long is she in town?"

Keith looked at his mother. "Mom, it's way too soon for that."

"So there is something brewing between the two of you," Cynthia deduced, her eyes dancing with delight.

"I didn't say that."

His mother gave him a knowing look.

"She's just a friend," Keith insisted.

His mother made a little sound of derision, but she was smiling. It was a smile that said, *Are you sure about that?*

Rita was on the balcony of her unit, her laptop open on her lap as she looked down at the people frolicking in the pool. Keith had sent her another text a little while ago, asking that she call him, but she hadn't responded. Seeing that woman drive up to his place when she'd been leaving had been the wake-up call she'd needed.

Not that she was into Keith, or God forbid jealous, but the woman's arrival reminded her that she wasn't in town for a carefree vacation. She was here to deal with her mother and the wedding, not to get caught up in a summer fling.

Though, as Rita looked down at the people jumping around and swimming in the pool, she felt a little wistful. Her mother had invited her for dinner again, and again she had declined. She just wasn't ready to see her mother, because she knew that would mean also seeing her father, or listening to her mother go on about her excitement over the wedding.

Not yet, Mom. I'm finishing some work.

That was becoming her mantra.

She'd heard the disappointment in her mother's voice, but still Rita hadn't acquiesced. Back in St. Louis, she had dinner with her mother once or twice a week. But the idea of breaking bread with her father was still overwhelming for her.

Rita reached for the vodka cooler on the small table beside her. She was looking out at this stunning scene and reading about heartbreak and betrayal. It didn't seem right.

Was that a knock she'd heard at the door? Frowning, Rita threw a glance over her shoulder, as if she could see the front door through the walls.

She was contemplating whether or not to get up when her cell phone trilled. A text appeared on the screen.

It's Keith. I'm at your door. Can you please come talk to me? I have something to explain to you.

Darn it. He would know she was here because her car was parked outside.

Her brow puckered, Rita got up with the laptop, which she placed on her bed. Then she went to the door and opened it.

"Why haven't you responded to any of my calls and texts?" Keith asked.

"I've been busy."

Keith gave her a doubtful look. "I think it's something else. Can I come in?"

"Why don't you just say what you need to say?"

"You saw a woman when you were leaving my place, didn't you? And you assumed the worst."

Of course, this woman had talked to him. Grilled him, more likely. "She told you?"

"It's not what you think."

"It doesn't matter what I think."

"It does. To me. If you thought that I brought you to my place and made moves on you while I have a girl-friend or something, you need to know that you're wrong. That's not how I operate."

For some odd reason, Rita's pulse was beating a little faster. She squared her shoulders. "Like I said, you don't owe me any explanations."

"Deidre is my cousin. She was dropping by to see me because she'd gone to the office and I wasn't there. Some-times I work from home. Anyway, that's who it was."

Despite herself, Rita felt relief. The idea that the woman was a love interest had troubled her.

More than troubled. Rita had been hurt.

And then she'd felt stupid for even caring. After what she'd been through with Rashad, didn't she know better than to trust any guy?

"Okay," she said, trying to inject a nonchalant tone into her voice. "I mean, it's not like we should have been kissing, anyway. I'm not sure what came over me."

One of Keith's eyebrows shot up. "You didn't want to kiss me?"

"We were acting irrationally—"

"Some would call it passionately."

"You know what I'm saying," Rita protested.

"Well, I liked it." He held her gaze. "A lot."

"Of course you did."

"I shouldn't have?"

"You didn't even like me when you first met me. We both know this is just about the chase."

"Is that so?"

"It's classic male behavior. You chase, you win and then your interest wanes."

Keith chuckled, but it was a hollow sound. "You're wrong, but you seem to have your mind made up about me." He paused. "Or is this even about me?"

His question hung between them. He stared, and Rita held his gaze. She was the one to look away first.

"Because everything you said about me seems pretty specific," Keith went on. "And I really don't see how you determined that about me from one kiss."

"It's common knowledge, isn't it? Certain behavior is in a man's DNA."

"So every man's the same in your mind?"

Rita sighed softly. "Maybe it isn't about you," she admitted.

There was a hint of concern in Keith's eyes. "You want to talk about it?"

Rita looked over her shoulder into the unit. "Do I want to? It's not my favorite topic." She frowned. "But...maybe we can sit on the balcony and I can explain some things. It's lovely out there."

Together they went into the apartment. Rita shot a fleeting glance at the bed as she passed it en route to the balcony. She could easily picture Keith naked in bed with her, which was something she didn't want to think about. Especially given how she felt about men these days.

"Would you like a vodka cooler? It's one of the ones you brought."

"I just want to know that you don't think I'm a creep."

Rita sank into a chair. "I don't," she said.

"So that spiel you gave me at the door about knowing my type…"

"If I came across as judgmental, I'm sorry. You could say that these days I'm a bit…jaded. I was engaged."

Keith lowered himself onto the chair beside hers. "Recently?"

"Yeah. Kind of. We broke up four months ago. After we'd been planning our wedding for…well, three weeks from now. Labor Day weekend."

"Oh, man."

"It's the typical story. Really kind of cliché, actually. He cheated on me. I didn't see it coming. The wedding's off."

"Then he's a fool," Keith said.

A smile pulled at Rita's lips, but she held it back. "So I'm taking a break from men, concentrating on me. Plus, my mother's getting married in October." Rita sighed. "She's planning this big wedding, and she needs my help over the next seven weeks."

"What's the deal with that? You think your mother is making a mistake?"

"My mother is marrying my father. The dream of most

kids, right? Except when your father was never in your life. Because your mom was his secret mistress. Only now that his wife has died, he suddenly realizes he loves my mother?" Rita scowled.

"Wait a minute," Keith said, his eyes widening with understanding. "Are you talking about Lance Pritchard?"

"Yes. You know him?"

"Small town. Certain stories don't stay hidden."

"So now I have two brothers. Neither of whom has reached out to me, by the way. They probably hate me, or think all kinds of negative things about my mother. I'm dreading meeting them."

A look passed over Keith's face. He seemed about to say something, but thought better of it.

"What?" Rita asked. "You think I'm being too harsh?"

"You haven't heard from your brothers?"

"No, and I'm sure they have no interest in getting to know me. I wouldn't be thrilled to learn that my father had led a secret life and had an illegitimate child."

"And with what your fiancé did, trusting men is probably challenging," Keith suggested.

"That's an understatement."

"Your last name is Osgood."

"It was Pritchard while I was growing up. But I changed it to my mother's when I turned eighteen. I figured, why should I have his name when he hadn't been a part of my life?"

"That's surprising," Keith said. "From what I know about Lance, I would have expected him to behave better. No contact, no support?"

Rita tipped her head back, finishing off her cooler. "Oh, he sent regular child support checks."

"He did? Well that's posi—"

"What was the point in sending child support and having no contact with me? Not to mention how he destroyed my mother's life. He didn't even tell her he was married until she got pregnant, and for a few months he talked about having a life with her, how he loved her more than anything. All lies. It didn't take long before he claimed he was racked with guilt, that his wife needed him, his family needed him and he couldn't destroy their lives. But what about my mother? What about me? He was just a liar. A selfish liar. He slept with my mother when he came to St. Louis for his job, strung her along and then dumped her when things got real."

Silence passed between them. Rita could hear her pulse thundering in her ears.

"Now his wife has passed away and wouldn't you know it, he wants to be with my mother." Rita grimaced. "And my mother, who has already endured enough heartbreak where he's concerned, said yes to his marriage proposal. Honestly, I think she's having some sort of mental breakdown."

"That's a lot to deal with," Keith said. "I can see why you're hurt and why you're concerned. The only thing I can say is that maybe Lance felt obligated to his wife. Karen had multiple sclerosis, and she really did need help as the disease progressed."

Rita rolled her eyes. "He made his choice. He should have left it at that. If he cared so much about his wife, he wouldn't have cheated on her. And if he cared about my mother, he wouldn't have strung her along."

Keith pursed his lips. He stared down at the happy people in the pool before facing her again. "Have you talked to him?"

"Ever? Sure. But not in years."

"So you haven't talked to him since you've gotten to town?"

"If this is where you tell me that I need to forgive, then I really don't want to hear it."

"I wasn't going to tell you that," Keith said.

"Good." Rita blew out a frazzled breath. "So when you were talking about how people need to make the best of the horrible situations that happen to them, that's why I got upset. I fully believe in what you're saying, and in general I try to live by that code. But some pain is so deep, you don't know how to get past it. Some things are unforgivable."

"I get that," Keith said. "But you're going to have to talk to your father because of the wedding, aren't you?"

"Well… I…" Rita bit down on her bottom lip. Every time she thought about talking to her father, her stomach twisted in a painful knot. "Logically I know I have to. But I'm just not ready."

"You want me to be there with you?" Keith asked. When Rita stared at him in shock, he went on. "Yeah, I guess that'd be awkward. But I know Lance… I could call him on your behalf…drop you off to see him if you think you'll be too upset to drive." Keith shrugged. "Whatever you need. I don't know."

"Why would you…" She looked at him with a quizzical expression. "You can't help me with this. This is something I need to deal with on my own."

"Of course," Keith said softly. "But a word of advice? Don't put it off. Go see him, talk to him and do it as soon as possible. One way or another, you need to know what you're dealing with before you can help your mother plan the wedding."

As Rita digested Keith's words, she glanced down at a

mother, father and their young daughter leaving the pool area. The girl was holding her father's hand and bouncing about happily as they walked.

The picture of the happy family she had always craved but never had.

Chapter 7

It took a couple more days, but Rita finally heeded Keith's advice. Her mother had been urging her to get the meeting with her father underway, so she agreed to a dinner at her father's house on Tuesday evening.

"I'm just about there," Rita said to Maeve, who'd been talking to her on speakerphone for the entire drive. She slowed to a crawl when she reached the address. "It looks nice. Older house, established neighborhood. The perfect house to raise a family."

"Hey," Maeve said softly.

"Yes?"

"This isn't about the past. This is about today. Take it one day at a time. You don't have to forgive him today. You don't even have to hear him out. This is about meeting your brothers and breaking the ice. You can do this."

Rita looked up at the house, saw her mother standing

on the porch, waving. "Gosh, my mother's already out there waiting."

"You can do this," Maeve reiterated. "Call me when it's over. Let me know how everything went."

"I will."

Rita ended the call, then closed her eyes. She drew in a slow, deep breath.

Then she pushed the car door open and stepped out. Her mother was already heading down the walkway toward her.

Rita forced a smile onto her face. "Hi, Mom," she called.

Her mother hustled toward her, beaming. She was wearing a white cotton shirt that had frills around the neck's edge and loose fitted arms. Her capri denim jeans looked spectacular on her slim legs. Her graying hair was out in a soft afro and held back with a hair band. She looked lovely.

"Darling." Her mother had her arms spread wide long before she was close enough to hug Rita. Rita walked into her embrace, and her mother gathered her into a hug. She swayed back and forth with her. "Oh, Rita. It's so good to see you."

Her mother released her, and Rita stood there awkwardly looking beyond her shoulder to see if her father had appeared at the door. So far, he hadn't.

"Everybody's excited to meet you. Let's go inside." Her mother took her by the hand. A short while later, they were walking into the house.

Rita sucked in another breath when she saw one of the two men she knew to be her half brothers. Brandon, she believed this one was. He was tall, definitely attractive, and dressed in denim jeans and a white button-down shirt.

He walked toward her, his smile warm. "You must be Rita."

Rita wasn't sure if she managed a grin or a grimace. She extended her hand. "Hello."

Brandon bypassed her hand and instead pulled her into a hug. He rocked her back and forth in an embrace that said he was happy to see her.

"It's really great to finally meet you," he said as they pulled apart.

Rita looked up at Brandon bashfully. "Nice to meet you as well," she said, hoping she didn't sound stilted. She was nervous, yes. And she really didn't want to be here. Everything about this situation had her on edge.

"By the way, I'm Brandon," he said.

"The younger brother," Rita said.

"And the more attractive one," he joked. "You'll see when you meet Daniel."

Brandon was around six foot one, and light-skinned like their father. His hair was closely cropped, and he had no facial hair. He seemed nice enough.

"Your father's in the sunroom," her mother said. Then she linked arms with hers. "Come."

Rita's heart began to pound. Was it too late to turn around and run? She didn't want to see her father. And why hadn't he come to the door to greet her?

Maybe because he didn't want to see her, either, and it was her mother's idea that they all get together.

Adrenaline was coursing through Rita's veins as she walked with her mother through the house until they rounded a corner leading into the sunroom. His back was to the door, but she knew it was him.

And then he turned, and Rita's chest tightened. Her father—a shorter, older version of Brandon—looked at her and offered her a faint smile.

"Rita," he said, and she could hear the emotion in his voice. Her back stiffened. She felt...ambivalent? Irritated? He cared now, but where had he been all these years?

He walked toward her, and that's when she noticed that he had a gift bag in his hands. As much as Rita wanted to find her footing, she stared at her father, unable to move. When he reached her, he leaned in for a hug.

It was brief and awkward.

"Hello," he said when they pulled apart.

"Hi," Rita responded. She hated how meek she sounded. But she didn't feel as if she were meeting her father. This man was Lance Pritchard, a virtual stranger to her.

"I'm really glad you're here," her father went on. He raised the gift bag. "This is for you."

Rita looked up at her father, at the face that she had not grown up knowing. It was weird, because she could see a little bit of herself in that face.

"Thank you." She accepted the silver-foil bag. It had white tissue paper protruding from the top. She wondered what it was.

Should she open it, or—

"Rita, hello." She quickly looked in the direction of the voice, and saw her other half brother strolling into the sunroom. A woman was walking with him, and Rita assumed she was his wife.

Rita sidestepped her father and walked in Daniel's direction. "So you're Daniel."

"I am. Your oldest brother." He gave her a quick hug. "This is Aaliyah, my wife."

Rita wanted to shake her hand, but a hug seemed more appropriate. "Nice to meet you," she said and gave the woman a hug.

"Very nice to meet you, too. How are you enjoying Sheridan Falls?"

"So far, so good," Rita told her. "It's a lot quieter than St. Louis."

"I can imagine," Aaliyah said.

"Have you always lived here?" Rita asked.

"Born and raised."

"And you like it? I mean, obviously you like it. But have you ever lived anywhere else, or ever wanted to explore different parts of the world?"

"No. I'm fine here. Traveled, yes. But big cities aren't my cup of tea. There's so much congestion and noise and way too many people are impersonal or downright rude. Honestly I'm so happy to get back home when I leave that there's not a chance I would ever consider living anywhere else. That said, I do love Miami. I guess it's the culture, the music, the food and the weather. And of course, the beach. Once you get there after fighting all that traffic."

Rita nodded, but she didn't understand why some people were against big cities. She loved the energy of Chicago, New York, LA. She loved the fast pace, the variety of restaurants and entertainment, and she enjoyed being a number in the crowd. Being invisible had its perks at times. She didn't want to be obligated to stop and talk to everyone she knew every morning at the coffee shop or every time she stepped outside of her apartment. But to each his own.

Rita's gaze wandered to the view outside the windows. There was a large wooden deck with a table and grill. Beyond that, there was an aboveground pool. Massive trees provided shade near the fence. The bit of lawn that she could see was lush and nicely trimmed.

Rita turned toward her mother, then looked at her father. "The house is beautiful."

Her mother sidled up beside her father. "Do you see why I'm not missing St. Louis? I have my own private paradise right here."

"Open your gift," Lance said. "I'd like to see your reaction."

Rita lifted the bag. It wasn't very heavy. What was inside? Jewelry?

Rita glanced around the room and saw that everyone was looking at her. Her mother wore a bright smile of anticipation. Her brothers regarded her with curiosity, and her sister-in-law—gosh, she had a sister-in-law?—also stared at her with wide eyes.

"Okay." Rita took a seat on the nearby rose-colored sofa. She placed the bag on her lap and pulled out the tissue paper. Inside was a long rectangular-shaped case. It had to be a jewelry box.

Rita's heart picked up speed. Why was he getting her jewelry? This was too much. Way too soon.

"Go on," her father urged.

Her mother took a seat beside her as Rita pulled the box out of the bag. She opened it, and her lips parted in surprise. It was a silver chain with three charms—a star, the sun and the moon.

"You used to love your baby mobile with stars and the sun and the moon so much. You won't remember now, but your father gave that to you. It was the one piece of him you had back then that you really loved." Her mother withdrew the bracelet from the box and looped it around Rita's wrist. "Now you can always have a piece of that memory with you."

Her breathing was becoming shallow. She didn't like this. Not one bit. Did her father think that all he had to do was give her a gift and all would be forgiven? This gift was supposed to make up for all the years he hadn't been in her life? Was her mother so blind to this level of deception?

Rita wanted to scream, but she looked up at everybody who was regarding her, and she knew that she couldn't. So instead, she tried her best to smile and said, "This is a surprise. Thank you."

She raised her wrist and looked at the jangling ornaments. "I'll just take this off for now, " she said. She unclasped it and carefully put it back in the box.

She didn't want to be wearing this, not now, not ever. Then she remembered Maeve's words that she needed to be there to support her mother. Especially with her brothers here and her sister-in-law, she knew she had to keep her cool. So she added, "But it is lovely."

"Give your father a kiss," her mother said.

Rita's eyes flew to her mom. She felt sick. Her mother knew that this was hard for her. Why was she trying to force a connection when there wasn't one?

Rita glanced up at her father, saw the smile on his face. She could see regret in his eyes, and a part of her wanted to feel bad for him. But how could she feel bad for him when she had missed him in her life for so many years? He needed to accept that this was not easy for her, and that she needed time.

"Go on," her mother urged.

"It's okay," her father said. "She's not ready."

And with those words, he let her off the hook. She gave him a small smile and said simply, "Thank you. I do appreciate it."

Rita met her mother's eyes then, and she could see the disappointment. But her mother needed to understand that she wasn't just going to come here and pretend that everything was hunky-dory.

"You know," Aaliyah began, "why don't we all head to the dining room? Dinner's ready and we don't want it to get cold."

"Yes, that sounds like a great idea," Rita said. "I'm starving."

Thank God for Aaliyah. She was doing what she could to help relieve the tension. In fact, Rita was glad that Aaliyah was here. The one nonfamily member she didn't know and could make a friendly connection with to get through the hours ahead.

She got to her feet and sidled up beside Aaliyah. "Have you and Daniel been married long?" she asked as they walked toward the dining room.

"We recently celebrated our two-year anniversary." Aaliyah beamed. "And I just found out I'm pregnant."

"Really?" Rita said, her eyes growing wide.

"Well, I didn't just find out. But now that I've reached the three-month mark, we finally decided to tell people. We just told your parents."

Your parents... Hearing that didn't sound right. She'd only ever had one parent, her mom.

"That's wonderful!" Rita said. "Congratulations." She looked over at Daniel. "Congratulations on your pending fatherhood."

As she said the words, a lump lodged in her throat.

Was everything she said going to remind her of her failed relationship with her own father? She certainly hoped that her brother would be a positive influence in his daughter's or son's life.

They got to the dining room, and her father sat at the head of the table. Her mother took a seat to his right. Rita started for the seat beside her mother's, but her mom quickly said, "Sweetheart, why not sit across from me. That way you're close to your father."

Rita felt a flash of annoyance. Why was her mother acting as though she and her father had had a normal father-daughter relationship over the years and that she would just naturally feel close to him? Nothing could be further from the truth. Didn't her mother realize that she needed to warm up to the man? She was here, wasn't she? That in itself was an achievement. She wasn't trying to make big leaps; she was making small steps.

But because her mother was looking at her with such expectation, Rita did as she asked. She went to the seat opposite her mother. And then the situation got more awkward because her mother got up from the table and headed into the kitchen.

Rita whipped her head around, suddenly frantic. She didn't want to be with her father without her mother around. Both Rita's mother and Aaliyah were gone now, no doubt to fetch the food. "Do you need any help?" Rita called out.

"No," her mother responded. "You stay with your father. You two have a lot of catching up to do."

Her father stretched his hand across the table and gave hers a gentle squeeze. Rita's back stiffened. A second later, she pulled her hand free, reaching for the phone in her bag. "Excuse me, I need to respond to a couple of emails."

She pushed her chair back and stood, then wandered over to the window. She looked out at the front yard, with a large oak tree providing ample shade on this sunny day. Had her brothers run around that tree as children, chasing each other? Blowing bubbles? All the things she hadn't?

Rita wasn't sure she could deal with this. She sent a text to Maeve.

My mother is acting like everything is A-OK between me and my father! She's forcing a connection between us as if there's no tension at all. It's driving me nuts!

Her mother breezed into the dining room, carrying a platter of carved beef. Aaliyah quickly followed with some sort of macaroni salad. A bottle of wine was already on the table, as well as a pitcher of water. It was a picturesque scene meant for a family that knew each other well and loved each other.

Rita felt like a stranger here.

Her mother made one more trip to the kitchen, and Rita stayed on her phone, scrolling through messages she'd already read, pretending she was too busy to sit and entertain any conversation with her father. Brandon began to speak to their father about a fishing trip he'd recently been on. Rita was glad for that, because it took the pressure off her to engage in conversation with her father.

Her mother re-entered the dining room with a platter of fried chicken. Aaliyah followed with roasted potatoes.

Were they finished getting the food? Rita hoped so.

"Everything smells delicious," Daniel commented. "I

must say, Lynn, Aaliyah has made a couple of your reci-
pes and I've been blown away."

"Thank you, Daniel." Her mother smiled in Daniel's
direction, then went to her seat, looking at Rita as she
did. "Rita, if you'll put your phone away." Her mother
gave her a pointed look, yet a kind one. A gentle reproach
regarding the use of her phone. "Nothing is so important
that it can't wait a little bit."

Rita returned to the table and put the phone back in
her bag. She looped the strap of her purse over the back
of the chair.

"Let's say grace," Lynn said. She placed both hands
on the table, reaching for her fiancé's on one side and
Brandon's on the other. Brandon took his brother's hand
on the other end of the table, and Daniel his wife's. Aaliyah was sitting beside Rita and they too gripped hands.
That left her father's hand, as he was right beside her.

She swallowed, then reached for his proffered hand.
He gave it a squeeze. Rita didn't look at him, just closed
her eyes in preparation for the prayer.

"Dear heavenly father," Lynn began, "Thank you for
family. Thank you for connections that never die. I'm
grateful that we are all able to be here together at this
point in our lives and that we can move forward with
new bonds. Because family is the only thing that matters." She paused. "Please bless this food before us and
help it to nourish our bodies. I ask this in your holy name,
Lord. Amen."

There was an echo of amens across the table, and everyone released hands. Rita caught her father's glance at
her through her peripheral vision, but she didn't look at
him. This whole scenario felt surreal.

Her mother grinned. "Dig in."

Aaliyah reached for the rolls, then passed the basket to Rita. Rita took one and passed it to her father. He took the basket, and then everyone began to serve themselves from the array of food. It would certainly appear to be a happy scene if anyone were to look at them through the window. They would never know that Rita felt like an outcast.

"Anyway, Dad," Brandon began, "as I was saying, we should plan a trip to Key West for the next fishing trip. My friend down there says the marlin are to die for. Huge, delicious."

"Sounds like a plan," Lance said.

"Have you ever gone fishing?" Brandon asked.

Rita pointed to herself and said, "Me? No. Never."

"Well, maybe you can come down with us."

Rita's eyes grew wide at Brandon's suggestion. "You want me to go on a fishing trip with you?"

"It's a family tradition," Brandon said.

"Even if some of us never catch anything," Daniel said, then laughed.

"It's about being out on the water, spending time together," Brandon said. "If we catch something, that's a bonus."

"You would say that," Daniel teased.

"It sounds like a guy's trip," Rita said.

"It always has been," Daniel said, "but you could certainly join us."

"Fishing is not really my thing," she said. "You guys have been going for years, I take it."

"Dad took us out on the water as small kids," Brandon explained.

"How old are you?" Rita asked. "What's the age difference?"

"Dirty thirty," Brandon said. "I turned thirty in March."

"Same as me," Rita said softly, her mind doing the math. She would turn thirty-one in November.

"And I'm thirty-six," Daniel said. "I was probably three or four when Dad first took me out to go fishing with him."

"Brandon and Daniel are right," Lance said. "You should join us on a fishing trip one day."

"It's your tradition," Rita said. "I'd be out of place."

She didn't quite meet her father's eyes, but she felt his gaze on hers.

"Rita, your father is extending an olive branch," Lynn said.

"And fishing isn't my thing. Besides, a tradition is something people have been doing for a long time. I'm not part of any sort of tradition in this family."

"Rita, you know that's not what I wanted," Lance said.

Rita chuckled mirthlessly. "Really? That's not what you wanted?"

"No. It wasn't."

"Then how on earth did it happen? Did someone put a gun to your head and force you to not be in touch with me?" She met his gaze now, pointed. Accusatory. She waited for him to deny her assertion.

"I'm not saying that," her father began slowly. "But not everything is as easy as you might believe."

"It's not easy to be a part of your child's life?" Rita countered. "I know of people who've had secret lives, and they still managed to maintain some sort of relationship with their illegitimate offspring."

"Rita," her mother said, her tone sharp now.

"Mom, I'm here. As far as I'm concerned, that's more

than enough. You can't expect me to sit here and listen while revisionist history is floated around this table. I was never part of his family because he didn't want me to be part of his family. The idea of a trip somewhere for fishing or anything else for that matter is completely offensive."

"Hey, I'm sorry," Brandon said. "I wasn't trying to offend you."

"It's not your fault," Rita said. She was no longer hungry. This had been a mistake.

"I'm sorry for what happened," her father said. His tone was exasperated.

"Are you? What took you so long to be sorry? Your wife's death? If she were still alive, would I still be your dirty secret?"

"Rita!"

Rita ignored her mother. "Because you can't expect me to sit here and believe that you wanted something with me all along when you never tried to make that happen before your wife died. And this nonsense about you always loving my mother..." Rita scoffed. "You may have brainwashed her, but you haven't fooled me for a second."

"Rita, stop this right now," Lynn demanded.

Rita pushed her chair back and stood. "Oh, I'll stop. Because I can't stay and eat with you guys. This is...a farce. I'm leaving."

"Rita, you sit back down," her mother said.

Daniel got to his feet. "Hey, it's all right. We understand your position."

"Do you?" Rita challenged. "Because the way I see it, how the heck can you? You had your father your entire life. You had him to teach you how to drive, to pick you up when you fell off a bike. To give you advice about dating. I had none of that. So what exactly do you understand?"

"We missed out on having a sister," Brandon said.

At the simple words, a wave of emotion washed over Rita. She swayed and gripped the back of the chair so as not to fall.

Then she steeled her back. She didn't want to feel anything for these people. Nothing at all. Her mother was different, of course, but Rita was pretty unhappy with her at the moment.

She turned on her heel.

"Rita," her father called out to her. There was a hitch in his voice, and she could hear the emotion. Again, she wished she didn't care, but something about the sound of his voice got to her heart just a little.

She stormed through the house toward the front door, not stopping. She pulled the door open and rushed outside, running down the slope toward her car. She nearly tripped, but caught herself and continued going.

When she reached her vehicle, Rita looked back toward the house. Daniel and Aaliyah were standing on the porch, both looking disappointed as she got into her car to drive away.

Well, Rita didn't care.

This had been a mistake. A big one.

Chapter 8

Rita drove back to her cottage, ran up the stairs to her unit, and the moment she was inside, she burst into tears. Her emotions ran hot through her. Anger, frustration, humiliation, regret.

She knew that her mother would be mortally embarrassed, and she couldn't blame her. But all that talk of family togetherness and traditions that didn't apply to her had broken her heart. She didn't want to hear about the father who was a great dad to his sons, taking them on fishing trips, while she'd had to grow up without a man in her life. She could have used a father during the very tough times, but he hadn't been there.

Oh, but he was sorry. Life was complicated. It wasn't his fault.

And now he'd decided that he wanted her and her mother in his life and that was that.

No, he'd decided that he wanted her mother. She was just part of the package deal.

Rita went to the sofa, where she curled up and cried until there were no more tears. Then she got to her feet and went to the fridge. She opened it, seeing the remnants of some pasta she'd made the night before, as well as bread, butter and salad. None of which looked even remotely appealing right now.

She was hungry. She'd left the opportunity for a perfectly good meal and a full belly and now here she was.

Alone.

At least she had some wine.

Just as she started to pour herself a glass, her cell phone rang. Rita assumed it was her mother, probably calling to give her heck. She didn't even bother to go and retrieve it from her purse.

But after a couple of minutes, she knew that she needed to talk to Maeve. So she went to the living room, sank onto the sofa and opened her purse. She pulled out her phone and called Maeve's number.

Maeve answered after two rings. "Dinner's finished already?"

"Everything is a disaster," Rita wailed.

"Oh, no! What happened?"

"I tried to make nice, I really did. But it was such a scene of fakeness, I couldn't handle it. My mother gave this grace about family and new bonds, and then one of my brothers invited me to go fishing with them sometime. Fishing! Of all things."

"Okay, calm down," Maeve said. "Start from the beginning. Tell me everything that happened."

Rita took a deep breath, trying to force herself to be calm. She started to relate the story from the beginning.

How she'd gone to the house with hopes of getting along, but ultimately couldn't cope. How it had all gotten to her. Her father had acted almost like a victim in his own decision to not have her be a part of his life.

"And then I just lost it," Rita finished. "I told him everything I was feeling."

"Oh, Rita."

"No one held a gun to his head and forced him to stay out of my life. I told him that."

"How did your mother react?"

"How do you think? She's upset. I know she expected me to behave better, but… I don't know, maybe the hurt child in me was bound to surface."

"I'm sorry, hon."

Rita sighed softly. "Thanks."

The doorbell rang. Rita looked up, alarmed. Was it her mother?

"Someone's at the door," she said cautiously.

"You think it's your mom?"

Rita got to her feet. "I'm not sure." She started toward the door. "But I'm going to find out."

When she got to the door, she peered through the peephole. She was shocked to see Keith.

And then suddenly relief washed over her. Oh, how she was glad to see him.

"It's Keith," Rita explained.

"Keith?" Maeve asked. "You mean the realtor?"

"Let me call you back."

Rita didn't wait for Maeve to respond, she just ended the call.

Rita opened the door, a smile forming on her lips. "Keith." She sounded a little breathless. "What are you doing here?"

He shrugged. "I don't know. I just had the urge to check on you. Make sure you were okay." His eyes narrowed with concern. "And I think I was right, because it looks like you've been crying."

Rita nodded, and then she stepped forward and threw her arms around Keith. She began to cry again, and she wasn't sure why. It felt good to have someone to hold as she let out her frustration, grief and sadness.

Keith cradled her head as she cried. After a moment, he moved with her into the apartment and closed the door. "Hey, what's going on?"

"I went to my father's place for dinner. I just couldn't do it. All my family was there, so happy. As if all the years that my father wasn't in my life didn't matter."

Rita was tired of crying over this. She was angry at herself for caring. She eased back and wiped her eyes, then she looked up at Keith. At his handsome face, those broad shoulders. She breathed in the scent of his musky cologne.

And then she slipped her arms around his neck. "I don't want to think about my father anymore."

Her voice was low, husky.

Keith's eyes narrowed. "What are you doing?"

"What we both want," she said. She wasn't sure who she was. She didn't recognize this behavior. She wasn't a seductress. And yet she couldn't stop herself. She needed this. She needed a distraction.

She needed Keith's strong arms wrapped around her body, his touches and kisses making her forget.

"Come on." Rita reached for the top button on his shirt. "You keep coming by. I'm sure you don't do this for everyone else."

Keith placed a hand over hers, stopping her. "Rita, not like this."

"Why not?"

"Because right now, you're upset. If I sleep with you, I'll be taking advantage of you. And once it's over, you'll come to that exact realization and hate me."

She tried to undo the button. "You kissed me the other day."

Keith tightened his grip on her hands. "I'm not after a roll in the hay."

Rita tried to pull her hands free, but he wouldn't let them go. So she did the next best thing she could. She pressed her body against his and tipped up on her toes and kissed the underside of his chin. "I promise," she whispered, "that I'm taking full responsibility for my actions as an adult."

A groan rumbled in Keith's chest. He wanted her, she could tell.

She kissed his skin again, then moved her lips to the base of his neck.

Deftly, Keith turned her in his arms so that her back was facing him. "Rita, we're not doing this." He walked with her into the living room, where he finally released her hands and deposited her on the sofa.

Rita looked up at Keith, who was standing tall above her, and giving her a look she couldn't quite read. God, was it pity? She hoped it wasn't pity.

Her sanity returned, hitting her hard. She covered her face with her hands. "I'm so sorry."

"Don't be sorry."

"I've made a fool of myself."

"No, you haven't."

"I just threw myself at you like...like some freak."

"You didn't just throw yourself at me. You're hurting."

"Please don't make excuses for me."

Keith sat on the sofa beside her. "That's the last thing I'm doing. And the truth is, your actions aren't completely illogical. What you said about me kissing you...about me stopping by often... I haven't done a great job at hiding my attraction to you. I guess I haven't managed to be as professional as I normally am."

Rita pulled her hands from her eyes and looked at him cautiously.

He gave her a little smile. "So I can't fully blame you."

"Still, this is not who I normally am."

"It isn't?" he asked, a hint of disappointment in his tone. Then he chuckled softly. "I'm just kidding. Did you leave the dinner before you got to eat?"

Rita nodded.

"So you must be hungry. Why don't I take you out?"

"You don't have to."

"You're upset. I don't want you to be upset. So let me take you somewhere and we can enjoy a meal and I can take your mind off of things. And afterward..." He let the suggestion hang between them.

Rita had sobered from her moment of insanity, and yet her heart began to pound at that unspoken suggestion. What was wrong with her? Yes, Keith was nice. But super attractive men like him weren't her type. He was the kind of guy who had women by the truckload throwing themselves at him. She didn't go for guys whom other women were constantly chasing.

And yet, as she looked at him, she couldn't help thinking that he was seriously irresistible.

"All right. Let's do it. What should I wear?"

"You look fine as is."

"So we should just go now?" Rita asked.

"There's no time like the present."

Ten minutes later, they were at an Italian restaurant named Giuseppe's. Like most of the places in this town, it was a gem of a spot. A mom-and-pop type restaurant, small in size but big in character. In St. Louis, places like this boasted polished marble and statues. They were grandiose and stunning, but lacking inherent warmth.

This place didn't have more than ten tables on the inside and four on the patio, yet it had all the quaintness of what Rita imagined she would find in Tuscany or Florence.

"Keith!"

At the sound of the man's voice, Rita looked in that direction. A robust man with a large belly was making his way over to their table.

"That's Giuseppe," Keith explained.

"*Buona sera*," Giuseppe said as he reached the table.

"Good evening to you, too," Keith said.

Giuseppe took both of Keith's hands in his and shook them vigorously. "I'm so glad you stopped by. It's been a while." His eyes shifted to Rita. "And who is this lovely lady with you?" His tone was ripe with suggestion.

"This is Rita," Keith said simply. "She's in town for the duration of the summer. She's renting one of my units."

The look that the chef shifted between them said he thought that there was a lot more going on than was being said.

Rita offered him her hand. "Nice to meet you."

Giuseppe shook her hand as exuberantly as he had Keith's. "Welcome to Sheridan Falls. Thank you for coming to my restaurant."

He was exceptionally warm, and already she felt better. Yes, she would still have to deal with her mother and what had happened earlier, but she could avoid thinking about that for the moment.

"I'm looking forward to eating your food," Rita told him.

"You will love it. I assure you."

The hostess had led them to a table right by the window, so now Rita looked out and watched the passersby strolling leisurely, stopping to talk to one another. Everyone seemed so warm and welcoming. This small town charm was growing on Rita.

"I suggest anything with the mussels," Keith said. "They're amazing."

"Ooh, I love mussels."

"Giuseppe's are the best I've ever had."

"That's some high praise."

"It's not an exaggeration. And I've traveled to a lot of places."

"Then I will have something with mussels. Is there one thing in particular you suggest?"

"Giuseppe makes a really great dish with mussels and calamari. Why don't we order two different things, and we can share. Is that okay?"

Suddenly Rita was imagining *Lady and the Tramp* when the two dogs were sharing a strand of spaghetti. She could easily picture herself and Keith doing just that, and as the strand of spaghetti disappeared, their lips would meet and they would share a kiss…

Rita suddenly swallowed, then cleared her throat. She needed to move her thoughts in a different direction. "So," she began. "You were lucky enough to travel to a lot of places because of football. Have you traveled extensively overseas?"

The waiter arrived then with a pitcher of water. He filled their glasses, and Keith ordered two glasses of red wine.

"I've been to much of Europe. Australia. Tokyo. The Caribbean. I haven't been to Dubai yet, but that's on the list."

Rita sipped her water, then lowered the glass. "World traveler. Very nice. I'd love to travel more. I've been to the Caribbean. And I went to Europe once, to Spain."

"Barcelona?"

"Madrid. Right after college. It was spectacular."

"I've been there, too," Keith said. "It's an incredible city."

"I've also been to a few other states," Rita went on. "And now Sheridan Falls."

Out of the corner of her eye, she spotted Giuseppe walking toward their table. He was carrying a plate.

Rita shot a glance at Keith as the chef put a plate of bruschetta on the table. "Special delivery from my kitchen to you," Giuseppe said.

Rita glanced down at the appetizer, which smelled delicious. "We didn't order this."

"Eat," Giuseppe said. "You will love it."

"It's the kind of thing he does," Keith explained. "He'll bring you out a sample of food. On the house."

"Really?" Rita had never heard of such a thing.

"Please." Giuseppe grinned brightly, gesturing toward the food. "Enjoy."

As he walked away, Rita picked up a piece of the crispy Italian bread covered with diced tomatoes and herbs. "That was very nice of him. I could get used to Sheridan Falls."

"So our town is growing on you?"

Rita shrugged. "Maybe." She tasted the bruschetta. A mix of delicious flavors exploded on her tongue. "No, wait. With food like this, yes. Definitely."

Keith snatched up a piece of the appetizer and took a bite. He moaned happily. "It doesn't matter where I've traveled," he said after he swallowed. "I always miss Sheridan Falls."

"So there's really no place like home?" Rita said.

"Chicago's a great city. I lived there for a few years. Vibrant, lots to do. Gorgeous lakefront. However, the traffic was a nightmare. The roads were always busy. If I wanted to go enjoy the lake, so did half the city. You'd go there and not be able to find a quiet spot to really enjoy yourself. To hear yourself think. Then it hit me one day. Sheridan Falls had a beautiful lake where I could always find some quiet. Parking was never an issue. Heck, the lake is walkable from many of the homes here, plus the cost of owning a house on the lake won't bankrupt you. So I moved back here. And I haven't been happier."

"I guess I should explore more of this town then," Rita said.

He spread his arms wide. "You've got a personal tour guide with me."

As Rita looked at Keith, her heart began to accelerate. He was so darn attractive and so nice. Everything about him was appealing.

Which was exactly the reason she needed to stop spending time with him.

Rita had learned the hard way that a man could seem

awesome in the beginning, and still turn around and break your heart.

And the last thing she wanted was to get involved with anyone, much less a man who no doubt could have his pick of women. Gorgeous men like Keith typically left a trail of brokenhearted women behind them.

Rita may have lost her senses for a moment when she'd thrown herself at Keith, but she had regained her sanity.

No more spending time with him. No more allowing him the opportunity to get into her heart.

Chapter 9

The next morning came the call Rita was expecting, but dreading. Her mother's face appeared on her ringing phone just after ten o'clock.

Rita swiped to answer the call. "Good morning, Mom."

There was the slightest of beats. "You forgot the bracelet your father gave you."

So her mother was beginning with a benign comment. "That's right," Rita said. "I did."

Her mother sighed. "I want to be angry with you," she began. "And I am. But maybe...maybe I pushed things too soon."

Those were not the words she'd expected to hear from her mother. She'd expected a tirade, but not this. "I'm sorry," Rita told her. "It's true, I wasn't really ready. I arrived at the dinner and everything just overwhelmed me. But I should have kept my cool."

"No, I'm the one who's sorry. I know you're not very good at holding in your emotions, and I know how much you've been hurt because of your father. I just want you to be able to see that your father has changed. I want it so badly that I'm not thinking about how hard it is for you to process and deal with."

"What did my father say about what happened?"

"To give you your space. That I shouldn't force the issue."

"Wow." Rita was impressed. She'd expected him to be angry, perhaps to the point where he didn't want to see her again. She hadn't expected him to be understanding.

"In fact, it's because of him that I'm not more upset right now," her mother went on. "I was so embarrassed, Rita. The way you behaved in front of everybody…"

"I know," Rita interjected. She could just imagine her mother's profound sense of humiliation in the aftermath of her behavior. "I really am sorry that I couldn't keep it together."

"But your father is teaching me patience. As well as… what it feels like to be loved. Now I know you don't want to hear that, or that you don't believe it. But it's true. Sweetheart, everyone makes mistakes. He's not the evil man you believe him to be."

"You really call not being in my life a mistake? It wasn't like it was a month or two and then he came to his senses. It was my entire life."

"Everybody deserves a second chance. All have sinned and fallen short of the glory of God."

Rita rolled her eyes. But she couldn't argue with her mother's logic. Her mother always liked to come at major issues from a Christian perspective, and Rita knew that the words were true. No one was perfect. And yet the idea of simply forgiving her father wasn't so easy.

"Your father loves you. You might not believe it, and he may not have ever really shown it, but he does. That's why this is hurting him so much."

The idea that her father had been hurt by her actions caused Rita to swallow painfully. He really cared that much?

"But he understands completely, and he doesn't expect you to just accept him with open arms. He suggested— and I agreed—that maybe you two ought to meet privately. I can be there if you like. But instead of having a big family shindig like I'd planned, which clearly didn't go over well, why not meet privately to talk. Or yell, if that's what's necessary. But ask the questions that you need to ask."

Rita's chest suddenly felt tight, like a vice was pressing against it. Why did the idea of talking to her father hurt so much?

Because he had never been there in her life. She didn't know how to even begin to talk to him. She didn't know if he would behave the way she'd always imagined a father would, to look at her with kind eyes as she told him what was on her mind. To wrap his arms around her and hold her if that's what she needed. Or if he would be defensive about the choices he'd made and expect her to move on.

"A private talk sounds like a much better idea," Rita said.

"Great." Her mother sounded relieved.

"I'll do my best, but I can't make any promises."

"All I can ask is that you try. I know you're able to do it, sweetheart. And hopefully the two of you can come to an understanding."

"Okay." Tears blurred Rita's eyes. "When do you think we should do this?"

"How's tomorrow morning?"

Tomorrow... The scared little girl in her, the rejected little girl, wanted to put it off. But she knew she shouldn't, and so she wouldn't.

"All right. Tomorrow's good for me. Ten o'clock?"

"Ten o'clock," her mother agreed.

Rita knew that after the meeting with her father, she was going to need to do something to de-stress. She hoped that their talk would go okay, but a part of her was afraid that she would fall apart. However, for the first time since her mother had dropped the bomb about getting married, Rita was feeling a sense of resolve. It was time to face her pain and do her best to come to terms with it. Maybe it was the way she had behaved and the sadness she'd heard in her mother's voice, or what her mother had said about her father understanding her bad behavior, but Rita was coming to the realization that it was time to truly try to see if she could forge a relationship with her father.

She was here in Sheridan Falls, after all, and she owed it to herself to see if they could build something. If she tried and her efforts didn't pan out, she could close the door on him forever without feeling any regrets.

Rita thought about what Keith had said to her earlier. That being out on the water was a wonderful way to relax. So she left her rental unit and got into her car and drove to the center of town. She had noticed signs advertising private boat tours, the ones Molly must have been talking about. Going out on the water for the afternoon, especially in this lovely summer weather, was no doubt the kind of activity that would calm her nerves. From her balcony, she had watched people sailing on boats daily and thought it looked so beautiful and peaceful.

Rita looked out at the happy townsfolk as she got to the downtown area. People with frosty drinks and ice-cream cones and huge smiles. If only Rita's own personal world could be as idyllic.

She searched for the sidewalk sign indicating boat tours, and within seconds, she saw it. Rita quickly pulled into a parking spot and moments later, she was exiting her car.

Door chimes sang as she entered Mike's Bait and Tackle Shop. A silver-haired man who appeared to be in his fifties spread his hands on the counter and grinned at her. "Hello."

"Are you Mike?" she asked.

"That's me."

"I saw your sign outside. You offer boat tours."

"Yes, I do."

"Excellent. Is there any chance you have an avail-ability tomorrow? Maybe around twelve or one in the afternoon?"

Mike walked a few steps to the right and opened an appointment book. "Let me just take a look." His finger scrolled down the page. "Yes, I can get you in at one. There are two evening tours, at five and seven."

"One p.m. will be perfect."

"Okay, one it is," Mike said. "What's your name?"

"Rita. Rita Osgood."

Mike wrote that information down. "The fee is sixty-five dollars for the hour. Eighty for an hour and a half."

"An hour is plenty," Rita told him. And then a thought

occurred to her. "Will I be the only one on the boat, or will there be a group of us?"

"At one, I have five other people scheduled. A group from Indiana."

So she wasn't paying for a solo tour. That made sense. When she'd gone on a glass-bottom boat tour in the Caribbean, others had joined her and Rashad. It was just that she would be alone, while the others would have each other. She hoped she didn't feel too awkward.

"I see."

"If you have others you'd like to join you, I can fit them in. Ten to twelve is a good number."

"It'll just be me," Rita told him.

Mike nodded. "That's fine. You'll make friends."

Rita wasn't so sure about that. She wanted a secluded spot on the boat to let the view of nature take her thoughts away.

"Should I pay now, or tomorrow?" Rita asked.

"You pay now, and I'll print you out a ticket for tomorrow. I'll give you all of the information as to where you need to go. Now, just so you know, you likely won't see me there. I have a few partners. We all own boats and depending on our schedules, either of us will be the one taking you out."

"Oh, okay."

"The meeting spot will be the same either way."

Rita shrugged. "As long as someone is there at one."

Mike rang up the order on the till, and Rita paid. He then gave her a receipt and a printout of the location of where she would be boarding the boat.

"Thanks so much," Rita said, folding the paper into a square. "I'm looking forward to this."

"Oh, one more thing," Mike quickly said.

"Hmm?"

"Don't forget your bathing suit. If tomorrow is going to be as hot as today, there's a perfect spot to stop the boat for a swim. There's nothing like it."

"Sounds lovely," Rita said. "Will do."

Keith was exiting Molly's Café when he spotted Rita walking down the street. He paused, a smile spreading on his face as she headed in his direction.

She was wearing denim shorts that exposed her luscious thighs and a frilly white blouse that scooped low over her bosom. He couldn't see her eyes behind her large dark sunglasses, but it didn't take him long to realize that she hadn't seen him. She was on a mission.

Keith quickly shuffled in her direction when he saw that she was heading to her vehicle. "Rita," he called.

Stopping near the back of her car, she glanced around, then saw him. Her lips parted. "Keith."

He trotted over to her. "Hey. What's up?"

"I was just…checking out the town," she answered. "And you?"

Keith lifted his cup of coffee. "Had to get another cup. It's that kind of day."

"Ahh." Rita walked around from the back of her car to meet Keith on the sidewalk. "I know the feeling."

"Everything okay?" he asked, looking at her with curiosity.

"I took your advice," she said. "My father. I'm going to meet with him tomorrow. See if we can't hash things out."

Keith nodded. "I see. Well, that's good. It's a start."

"I guess, but I'm…scared." Rita's chest rose and fell.

As illogical as it was at that moment, Keith's eyes averted to her cleavage for a nanosecond. Every time he looked at her, all he could see was her beauty. Her incredible sex appeal. His body responded to her no matter the topic of discussion.

"It's okay to be scared," Keith told her.

Rita frowned, then bit down on her bottom lip. And that's where his gaze went, to that full mouth scrunched up in a frown. She hadn't been frowning after he'd kissed her. No, her eyes had been alive with excitement, and her lips had been parted, almost begging for more.

"Are you listening to me?"

Her question permeated his brain. "Sorry." Keith cleared his throat. "Yes."

Rita looked at him with an odd expression. "What is it?"

"Hmm?"

"What are you not telling me?"

Keith's brain scrambled to come up with an explanation. He certainly couldn't tell her that his mind had wandered to the memory of kissing her…

"It'll all go well," he assured her. "Just…try to be gentle with your father. He's had a lot to deal with. The death of his wife, the bankruptcy…"

Even behind the dark sunglasses, he could see her eyes narrow. "Bankruptcy?"

"Right after his wife died, he had to file," Keith said. "You don't know?"

"My mother probably does, but she didn't say anything to me."

"The situation was resolved," Keith said. "The townspeople came together to help him out. He was able to keep the house, get back on his feet."

"Hmm."

"Probably no one told you because it's not an issue

anymore," Keith said. He hoped he hadn't said the wrong thing. "Maybe I shouldn't have said anything. I'm just trying to impress upon you that your father has been through a lot. Keep that in mind."

"Sure."

She smiled, but Keith wasn't sure if it was genuine. Was she wondering if Lance's interest in her mother was financially motivated?

"If you're worried that Lance is interested in your mother for money, I highly doubt it. The man I know would only marry her for love."

"But how well can a person know anyone?" Rita countered. "Anyway," she quickly continued, "I see him in the morning. And we'll see how it goes."

She seemed okay, so Keith didn't push the issue. "I'm heading back to the office," he said. "But if you need me, give me call. Anytime."

Rita started for the driver's side door. "Okay."

Keith stared at her as she got into the vehicle, wondering if he'd just opened a proverbial can of worms.

Chapter 10

A̶ll night, Rita had stewed over what she should do with the information Keith had given her. Talk to her father about it first in order to ascertain his true motives, or talk to her mother?

Maybe she ought to only speak to her mother about this. Her father's affairs weren't directly her business, but her mother had a right to know. And if her father's motives where her mother was concerned were at all opportunistic, then that was Rita's business.

But even as she got ready to leave her place, she wasn't quite sure what she would do. All she knew was that the information needed to be brought to her mother's attention. And she wasn't sure that if she spoke to her father about it privately, that she could trust him to tell her mother on his own.

As Rita's coffee brewed, her phone buzzed. She made

her way to the kitchen table, where she'd rested her phone, and pressed the home button to refresh the screen. She wasn't surprised to find another message from Keith.

Hoping everything's okay. Haven't heard back from you.

Rita wandered back over to the coffeemaker. Keith had already called earlier, then sent a message asking her not to take what he'd told her negatively. Apparently he had realized too late that his news had affected her in the opposite way from what he'd hoped. He hadn't considered that his words would be ammunition for her to use against her father, but that's exactly what they were.

And with good reason. It wasn't that she wanted something negative to bring to her mother about her father, but he had not been honest. Her mother had said nothing about a bankruptcy, and Rita was betting that she had no clue. The one thing Rita couldn't stand more than anything was when people weren't honest.

Rita spooned two teaspoons of sugar into her coffee. So much more made sense now. This engagement was sudden because her father had an agenda. A monetary one.

If he was having financial troubles, marrying someone could help alleviate that problem. Her mother thought she could trust her father's love, but he was likely in this relationship for the cash.

Rita didn't even know all of the details about how her parents had reconnected, but perhaps her mother had shared with him the truth about the severance package she'd received from her job. When the insurance company she had worked for downsized, she'd been let go as a manager and received a fairly decent package. It wasn't enough to have her buying lavish homes in exotic places in the world, but it was certainly enough to make her comfortable. That kind of money would probably go a long way in a town like this.

Rita bit down on her bottom lip as she went to the fridge for cream. What she needed to do was obvious. She had to talk to her mother first. Her mother needed to know.

Better yet, why not bring up her father's financial problems to the both of them at the same time? That way her mother could see her father's reaction…and so could she.

Rita added cream to her coffee, then lifted the mug to her lips for a sip. Yes, she knew now exactly what she was going to do.

Just over an hour later, when Rita arrived at her father's place, she was determined. A sense of calm came with her resolve, and she felt no anxiety. If her father had not been honest with her mother, then he would have to deal with the consequences. Rita would put the truth out in the open, because her mother needed to see the full scope of the situation and know exactly what was going on. Then she could decide for herself what she would do.

Rita was fairly certain that her mother would make the right choice. Staying with her father, knowing that his motives might not be pure, would be massively foolish.

Rita rang the doorbell. Only seconds later, her mother answered the door and looked at her with a guarded expression.

Rita offered her mother a warm smile. "Hi, Mom."

"Hello." Her shoulders visibly relaxed. "I'm glad you came."

"Of course I came. What you said—it makes sense. We need to talk."

Her mother opened the door fully, her eyes brightening. "Your father is waiting in the sunroom. I don't know if you want me there—"

"Oh, I want you there. Yes. Definitely. We should all be a part of this conversation."

"Okay, then." Her mother nodded. "I think that's the best thing. It will be good for all of us to discuss the situation."

"Fantastic, actually," Rita said.

Her mother gave her the oddest of looks, as though she seemed surprised by Rita's new position. No doubt she was. Rita had done a one-eighty and wanted this talk; she was no longer the reserved and anxious person she had been when she first discussed this idea with her mother.

Rita stepped into the house. "You can lead the way."

They walked through the house into the sunroom. Rita noticed that the gift bag her father had given her sat on the coffee table. In that instant, she couldn't help swallowing. The memory of that gift, and what it allegedly signified…

She stiffened her spine. No, she wouldn't let herself be swayed by anything sentimental. Especially not with a man who had not been in her life. Her first obligation was to her mother. If there was any chance that her father was being dishonest and using her mother, the truth needed to come out.

Her father rose from the sofa. "Hello, Rita."

"Hi," Rita said. She saw a little bit of contrition on his face, and for a moment felt a slight niggling of guilt. But why should she? If her father was withholding information, was that not the most important thing right now?

She thought of Keith's words, that he had not told her this information for her to hold it against her father, but rather for her to understand him better. Was she making a mistake?

No. She wasn't. Being soft in the past had gotten her walked over. And being soft had gotten her mother hurt, hadn't it? Besides, the truth always had a way of coming out, and wasn't it better that it came out now as opposed to later?

"Please, have a seat here." Her father patted the spot beside him on the sofa.

Rita walked over there and sat. Her mother sat in the armchair beside the sofa.

"I just want to say," her father began, "nothing about what I'm going to tell you was easy. I made decisions, and I have to live with them. But nothing is black-and-white. I want you to understand that from the outset."

Rita nodded, then drew in a deep breath.

"First of all—"

"Wait," Rita said, cutting her father off. "I have something to say before you begin." She glanced at her mother before meeting her father's eyes again. "It's come to my attention that you filed for bankruptcy after your wife died. If not for the community coming together, you would have lost this house."

Her father's eyes widened in shock. His lips parted, but he said nothing.

"Did you tell my mother this?" Rita asked.

Rita shot a look at her mother, whose own eyes were filled with confusion. Her gaze flitted between her future husband and between Rita, and the answer was clear. Her mother hadn't known.

"What does that have to do with anything?" her father asked.

"My mother came into a sizable amount of money after she was let go from her job. But I'm sure you already know that, don't you? My mother isn't good at keeping info like that to herself."

Her father's eyes registered even more shock. "Yes, but—"

"Mom, did you know about the bankruptcy?"

"What is she talking about, Lance?"

His Adam's apple rose and fell. He seemed embarrassed, but spoke. "It wasn't important to tell you."

"It wasn't important?" Rita challenged. "You lured my mother into this relationship, making her believe that it was all about her and the fact that you never forgot her. But it's really about what she's bringing to the table—and your bank account—isn't it?"

"That is *not* the truth."

"Lance," Rita's mother said. "Why would you keep this from me?"

"Everything is fine now," Lance told her.

"I've told you everything, Lance," Lynn said. "Why would you keep this from me?"

"Exactly," Rita agreed.

Her father's eyes flew to hers. Disappointment mixed with something else on his face.

Rita got up from the sofa. Her stomach twisted, but she felt a sense of relief. Her mother needed to know the truth. "Mom, I can't have any conversation about the past when my father is not even being honest with you. I know you believed that I was simply thinking the worst about him, but that's not the truth. I was concerned, just as you would be if it were me in this situation. You're my mother, and I'm always going to look out for you. And if he never told you about this, doesn't that worry you?"

The look of confusion in her mother's eyes caused a wave of pain to wash over Rita. Knowing that this news hurt her mother also hurt her.

"I'll leave the two of you to talk," Rita said. "Mom, call me later."

"Nothing is as simple as it seems," Lance said.

"Or maybe sometimes it is," Rita countered.

"I wish you had spoken to me about this privately," her father said.

"I wish you'd told my mother the truth." And with that, Rita turned and left the house.

Chapter 11

At 12:50 p.m., Rita was arriving on the dock. She was looking forward to this excursion on the water. After the meeting at her father's house, she needed the cool breeze flowing through her hair and taking her thoughts away.

As she made her way toward the designated area, her heart stopped when she saw that familiar body. And then her legs stopped, too. She blinked a few times, her pulse pounding as that face came into clearer view.

Keith!

How could it be?

It made no sense, and yet that was undoubtedly Keith standing in front of the sign that read Private Tours.

What was going on? Was he joining her? He didn't even know she was going to be here. So why was he here?

And where was Mike?

Keith started toward her. Rita sucked in a breath. "Hello, lovely lady."

"Keith... What are you doing here?" She hated that she sounded breathless. Almost wispy and sexy.

But she didn't understand why Keith was wearing swim trunks and a T-shirt, almost as if he were about to go out for a sail. Surely he needed to be working at this time of the day.

"I heard you needed a boat tour," Keith said.

Rita frowned. "How could you possibly know that?" she asked.

"I'm an avid boater. If Mike himself isn't able to take people out for a tour, I'm one of the guys who works as his replacement."

"What?"

"I work with Mike. I'll take his boat out if he can't, or if there are a lot of tours booked—which is unlikely— then I'll use my boat to take people on tours."

Oh, that's right. Mike had told her that. Rita just hadn't expected Keith to be the one here. "So you're operating the tour. Where are the other people? Mike said something about a group of five from Indiana."

"Actually, they've rescheduled. There's an accident on I-90 and they couldn't make it back from Buffalo in time."

"Oh, no. So do you need me to reschedule?" Rita asked.

"No, definitely not."

"But it's not economically feasible to take one person out."

Keith waved a dismissive hand. "That's not an issue."

"And what about you? Don't you have to work?" Rita asked.

"I was able to reschedule some appointments. And I'm happy to do it. Remember, I told you that if you needed a tour guide, I could show you around. So it's fitting I've gotten the job of doing that today. And I'm actually happier that it's just me and you. I can do the tour my way, with my boat."

Rita blew out a harried breath. What could she say? If she kept asking questions, she'd give Keith the impression that she was afraid to be alone with him.

"All right," she said.

"It'll be fun," Keith assured her.

Rita tucked a strand of her hair behind her ear. "All right, then."

"Right this way," Keith said.

Rita clutched her bag to her side as she followed Keith down the dock. She was already wearing her bathing suit beneath her sundress, but now she wasn't sure she would go in the water. She had her towel in the bag and the undergarments she would need to get dressed afterward, but she'd been open to taking a dip when she thought that there would be other people on board. Now that it was just her and Keith, maybe not.

Keith approached a polished white boat with at least two levels. The name Chantelle was written on the side in cursive black font. The upper level was covered with a black awning, and Rita could see that there was space there for a handful of people to sit. The main level was larger, with an open space at the back and an indoor cabin. There was a metal railing surrounding most of the first level, from the edges of where the indoor cabin began on both sides to the hull. While most of the boat was gleaming white, the bottom half that went into the water was black.

The boat could certainly hold a good number of people, and right now Rita wished that she had a crew of friends to accompany her for this ride. She especially didn't want to be alone with Keith.

"What kind of boat is this?" she asked him.

"It's a trawler," he answered. "The perfect boat for a day of leisure on the water. It doesn't go too fast so most people find the ride comfortable. It's got a couple of beds so you can sleep, if you want to stay out on the water for the night."

"Oh, I definitely don't want to stay out here all day."

"I didn't mean you. I was speaking generally." He paused. "Of course, I'd be happy to take you out for a night sail."

Rita didn't doubt he would… Had he taken other women out? Perhaps wined and dined them. Then seduced them…

She wondered if Chantelle had been a lover, or his wife.

The boat swayed as Keith stepped onto it. He turned to Rita and offered her his hand. "Here, let me help you aboard."

She took his hand, and gasped slightly when the boat moved as she started to step on it. She quickly got her footing and hurried up the couple of steps.

"You want to sit up top?" Keith asked. "The view's amazing."

Rita moved to the nearest part of the boat where she could sit and quickly sat. "I'm fine right here."

"All right. You can move about the boat as you like. But first, New York law requires us to put on life jackets." He walked the short distance to where the life jackets were hung on the wall. He assessed a few, then walked back and handed her one. "This should fit."

Rita put the life jacket on over her dress, while Keith put one on as well. "It fits," she told him.

He nodded. "Good. Are you a strong swimmer? Because you can take it off when we get in the water, if you like."

"I'm a pretty good swimmer," she told him. "My mom made sure I took lessons."

"Can I get you something to drink before we set sail?"

"What do you have?"

"Beer, wine, wine coolers, vodka coolers."

"I'll take a vodka cooler," she said. "Lemon-flavored, if you have it."

Keith disappeared inside the cabin, and less than a minute later reappeared with a vodka cooler for her. "Thanks," she said, taking it from him.

Keith began to uncoil the rope that connected the boat to the dock, and once he was finished, he went into the cabin again. Music began to play, a popular Bruno Mars song.

More shocking was when Keith's voice came over the loud speaker. "Thank you for boarding the *Chantelle* today. The weather is perfect for this tour."

He looked over his shoulder at her, and Rita gave him a thumbs-up.

The boat began to move through the water, and although the speed wasn't especially fast, they were soon a good distance from the shore.

"Remember the movie *Jaws*?" Keith asked. "When I was a kid, someone terrified a group of tourists here on the lake. People were sunning on the beach and the kid yelled, 'Jaws!' I never heard so many screams as people scrambled to get out of the water."

Rita laughed. Then she got up and quickly moved to

the seating inside the cabin where Keith was so he could hear her better. "Is that a true story?" she asked.

"Swear to God," he told her.

"But this is a lake."

"And people often don't think. They heard the word 'jaws' and freaked out. It had recently played on television at the time, so it was fresh in people's minds. Even I remember being a bit scared for a moment. Until I realized that the kid screaming 'jaws!' was Frankie DeLuca, the troublemaker at school."

Rita glanced out at the lake, chuckling. This water was calm, the view scenic.

"Now that we're past the vacation condos, you can see some of the homes here that are on the water."

"Wow," Rita said, spying one that was massive. It was ultra-modern, with sharp edges and lots of windows.

"That owner of that one is an architect. He has a very successful business."

"No wonder," Rita said. "That's a spectacular house. Actually, they're all incredible looking."

"These waterfront houses are high-end real estate. You see that one in the distance? The white one on the right?"

"The big one?" Rita asked as the house came into better view. Situated atop a sloped landscape, it was easily one of the biggest on the waterfront, if not the biggest.

"That's my parents' house."

Though she was wearing sunglasses, Rita held a hand over her eyes to provide more shade so that she could better check out the house. The lawn was pristine, leading to a house that had at least three levels. The bottom was a walk-out basement with a large wall of windows. There was a large deck on the second level that spanned the entire width of the house. On the far left side of the house was a pool enclosed by a gate.

"That's some house," Rita said. "Wow."

"It's where I grew up. Lots of great memories. And..."

His voice trailed off, and Rita averted her gaze from the house to look at him. "And what?"

"This boat is named after my little sister. I think I told you... She drowned in the pool."

"Yes, you did. I'm so sorry. What a tragic loss."

"Thanks. So almost all the memories were good." Unexpectedly he raised his hand and waved. "There's my dad sitting on the deck." A woman came through the patio doors carrying a pitcher. "And my mom."

He blew the horn, and his parents waved. Rita waved as well. Their bright smiles were evident despite the distance.

Rita had had just one glimpse of them, but she could tell that they were a loving, happy couple. "Together a long time?"

"High school sweethearts. Married thirty-seven years."

"That's rare," Rita commented. They were a living example of what she'd never witnessed of her own parents.

"Speaking of parents—"

Rita's phone began to ring. She searched for it in her bag and pulled it out. Her eyes widened when she saw Rashad's number flashing on her screen. She swiped to reject the call.

"Everything okay?" Keith asked.

Rita dropped her phone back into her bag. "Yep."

"How did it go with your parents today?"

"Ugh."

"That bad?"

"It wasn't good."

"Did you bring up the bankruptcy?"

"My mother deserved to know," Rita said.

Keith sighed. "I told you not to say anything. I explained to you that I shared that information with you so you could understand your father a bit more. Not for you to use it against him."

Rita was silent for a moment. Then she said, "How could I not tell my mother something so vitally important? Would you stay silent?"

Keith said nothing as he navigated the boat. After about a minute, he killed the engine. Rita got up and walked to the back of the boat and looked out at the thicket in the distance. There were no waterfront homes on that section of the lake. But people were frolicking in the water and on the sandy beach. Behind them were cabins.

"That's a camp."

At the sound of Keith's voice, Rita whirled around and looked up at him.

"We all went there as kids, and my brothers and I even worked there when we got older." Keith paused. "Okay, so you told your mother about the bankruptcy. How did it go?"

Rita stood. "I can go to the upper level?"

But even as she asked the question, she was walking past him.

Keith watched Rita go, shaking his head slightly. They were out on the lake, and it was a beautiful day, but he got the feeling that if he pressed the issue, things would go sour. And that was the last thing he wanted.

So instead of following her, he merely looked up at

her. She took a seat at the top of the boat and gazed out, as if fascinated by what she was seeing.

Not that the view of Sheridan Lake and the properties and nature surrounding it weren't stunning, but he suspected she was feigning more interest as a way to avoid him.

He had hoped for a different vibe between them, but she had that darn wall up. The truth was, she owed him some answers. He hadn't wanted his words to cause any extra conflict between her parents. Having known Lance most of his life, Keith knew him to be a good man. Maybe one who had made horrible decisions, but he didn't doubt the sincerity of his feelings for Rita's mother.

After a few minutes, Keith made his way up to the top level. Rita didn't look in his direction. Slowly, he blew out a breath. She was a beautiful woman. With her eyes directed off in the distance, he allowed himself the time to take in the sight of her bare shoulders beneath the sundress. Her dark skin was smooth. Her curly hair kissed the top of her back, and he found himself wanting to brush her hair aside and push it over one shoulder.

What would it be like if he planted his lips on her shoulder blades? She was so tightly wound now, back to the closed-off version of herself she'd been when they'd first met. Could he melt her frosty exterior like he had when she'd been at his place? Would she come alive if he touched her?

Why were his thoughts even going in this direction? He should be upset with Rita for doing the exact opposite of what he'd told her. And now she wouldn't talk to him about it.

Keith wandered over to her and took a seat beside her. "All right," he began slowly, "I understand that you felt the need to tell your mother about the bankruptcy. Did you talk to your father as well? You don't want to tell me how it went?"

Finally, Rita faced him. "Are you going to hold me hostage in the middle of the lake until I do?"

Her lips curled in a little smile, and he knew she wasn't being serious. Well, perhaps she was being half serious.

"Actually, this is where we can go for a swim," Keith answered. "If you want."

"I want."

And just like that, she started down the steps to the lower level.

She was shucking the life jacket by the time Keith joined her, and she then pulled her sundress over her head. "You said I don't need to go in with my life vest, but you know what? I guess I will. That way I can relax."

Keith's eyes drank in the sight of her gold bikini, which looked amazing on her perfect body. Narrow waist, full hips, large breasts. The bikini top had straps, which crisscrossed over her cleavage, drawing his eyes to that area of her body.

She was gorgeous.

As she swung the life vest around her body again, Rita's eyes met his. Held.

"I'll just…" Keith's voice sounded like a croak, so he cleared his throat. "I'll go in the water. Then I can help you down."

Keith went to the back of the boat, climbed up onto the edge and jumped into the lake. The cold water was a shock to his system, and also exactly what he needed to halt the rising temperature of his body.

His head burst through the surface of the lake. He swam to the boat and grabbed hold of the ladder. Rita walked to the edge of the boat, and the effects of the cold water on his body immediately faded when she turned her backside toward him and started down the ladder. The view of her plump, luscious behind had him biting down on his bottom lip.

Oh, how he would like to get her naked.

He cleared his throat, then spoke, "You okay to get down? Or do you want to take my hand?"

"I'm okay." She dipped a foot in the water, then quickly pulled it back up, shrieking. "Oh, my goodness, that is cold!"

"You're better off to jump right in. That way you get it over with instead of torturing your body inch by inch."

Selfishly, he wouldn't have minded if she stood right there. Her body was so perfect. He could look at her all day.

He could do more than just look at her. He could *be* with her all day. He wanted to talk to her more, get to know her more. He wanted to know what made her tick. He wanted her to share her frustrations with him. For some reason, he was drawn to her. Even though it didn't make sense. She certainly wasn't opening up to him, which should have had him pulling back, not wanting to get closer to her. But he sensed that she needed someone. And he wanted to be that someone.

Rita dipped her foot with her red-painted toenails into the water again. "Oh, goodness." She let her foot sit there. Let it get acclimatized to the water. Then she looked over her shoulder at him and said, "I'm going to jump. Catch me."

And then she pushed herself backward and plunged into the water, and Keith quickly wrapped his arms around her body as she fell. He slipped into the water with her, and a moment later, they both bobbed upward. Rita giggled even as she squealed.

"How can this water be so cold?" she asked.

"You good?" he asked her. He was still holding her body, though the life jacket was certain to keep her afloat.

She slipped free of his grip and swam a little bit away from the boat. "Yeah, I'm good." She treaded water, making a 360-degree turn. "It really is refreshing. And it's not so bad now."

"I told you," Keith said. "The sooner you immerse yourself, the sooner you get used to the water."

Another boat in the distance was moving in their direction, going at a faster clip. Instinctively, Keith moved closer to Rita. Just in case, he wanted to be able to slip an arm around her and pull her out of the way.

As the boat neared them, he heard the happy screams. A couple of kids were holding onto a tube at the back of the boat and bouncing on the waves the water was creating.

"That looks like fun," Rita commented. "This seems like it would have been a nice town to grow up in."

Keith merely nodded, wondering if she was feeling she had missed out. Was that something she'd wanted? To be here, closer to her father?

"Small town life growing on you?" he asked.

She brushed her hair backward off her face. "It has its appeal. The lakefront in St. Louis… It'd be way too crowded to enjoy. This… It's almost like the lake is our private playground."

Keith swam toward her. "You see why I choose to live here."

She nodded. "Yeah, I can."

"You know what's growing on me?" Keith asked, his

voice suddenly raspy. Perhaps she sensed the direction of his thoughts, because her beautiful eyes widened ever so slightly. And in that moment, Keith couldn't stop himself. He snared an arm around Rita's waist and her body easily glided toward his. "You," he finished.

And then he planted a soft kiss on her lips.

She didn't react at first, but even though her body was stiff beneath his hand, he heard her soft exhalation of breath. That soft breath told him what he needed to know. That she was nervous, but interested.

Placing his free hand on her cheek, Keith deepened the kiss. Slowly, Rita's hand crept up his arm as she opened her mouth wider, allowing him more access. He swept his tongue over hers, enjoying the sweet taste of her.

The faint sound of Rita's ringing cell phone was like an alarm going off. Abruptly, she broke the kiss and forced herself out of his arms. She treaded her arms back and forth in the water. "I shouldn't be doing this."

Keith's heart was pounding. Something about Rita made him come alive in a way he hadn't expected and one he didn't understand.

"Why not?"

"Because."

That wasn't an answer. "You're not interested? Or there's someone else?" he asked.

"I didn't come out on a boat tour to end up making out in the water," she said tersely. "Maybe that was your plan, but it wasn't mine."

"You think I'm playing games?"

"I don't know what you're doing. I just know… I need to leave."

"Leave?" Keith's eyebrows shot up. "Let me at least finish the tour and take you to the waterfall. I'll just have to bring the boat to shore near the camp, then we'll walk up along the river to get there."

Rita didn't answer, and instead began swimming toward the boat. She took hold of the ladder and quickly started to climb aboard.

Keith followed her. Was she that upset by him kissing her? She certainly seemed to have enjoyed it.

Rita withdrew her towel from the bag and began to dry her skin. Her phone began to ring again, and Keith glanced down at her bag. "Someone's really trying to reach you."

She groaned. "I don't want to talk to him."

"Your father?"

Rita unfastened her life jacket. "Can you get the boat started, please? I need to get back."

It was a lovely day, and here Rita was, frowning. The cordial mood had soured.

"I don't know what's going on with you, but whatever it may be, it is clearly upsetting you. My advice... Don't keep it all in."

"We kissed, that's all. That doesn't make me obligated to share all my problems with you."

Ouch. The comment stung. So much so that Keith didn't have a reply. If that was what she thought...

Rita groaned. "Can we leave now?"

Keith started toward the side of the boat where he had tossed the anchor. "Yep. No problem."

Keith had had high hopes for today. He'd been looking forward to spending more time with Rita, and getting to know her better. He'd also hoped that he could help put a genuine smile on her beautiful face.

But that plan had just sunk to the bottom of the lake.

Keith began to retrieve the anchor. He said nothing, and neither did Rita. With the anchor secured, Keith then went and started the trawler's motor. He didn't look in her direction as he began to steer toward shore.

He turned up the music, let it blare as the boat sailed. He passed another boater, an older man he knew from town, and they exchanged a wave. It seemed like the minutes to get to shore were an hour. The tension on the boat was so thick you could cut it with a knife.

Keith looked over his shoulder at Rita. She had taken a seat as far from him as possible, and was staring in the opposite direction. With her dark glasses on, he couldn't tell if she was taking in the view. But he doubted it. With the firm set of her lips, he knew she was simply looking away to avoid him.

Finally, Keith was pulling the boat up to the dock. He set about getting the anchor down and tethering the boat to the dock. Sensing movement, he glanced up, alarmed.

"Hey, wait a second."

Rita didn't listen. She had her life jacket off and her bag slung over her shoulder. Though the boat was unsteady and not secure, she made her way to the exit nonetheless. She put one leg over the side of the boat, and as it moved slightly, her legs split. Crying out, she fell forward onto the dock, her knees landing hard against the wood.

Keith jumped off the boat and onto the dock. "Are you okay?"

"I'm fine," Rita answered tersely. She got up, looked around, brushed off her knees and ran her fingers through her hair. She fixed her sunglasses on her face and started to walk. Keith saw the wince, but despite her obvious pain, she moved forward with purpose, not looking back at him.

He watched Rita storm off, wondering why he had been included in the demons she was running from.

Chapter 12

Well, that had gone horribly wrong!

Rita opened the door to her unit and hobbled inside, glad that she hadn't spotted Keith on her tail. She closed the door and locked it, then rested her back against it. She blew out a frazzled breath.

As if Keith would be following her, after the way she had treated him!

Rita stayed against the door for several seconds, drawing in slow, even breaths. Her right knee was throbbing. She'd come down hard on it, so much so that tears had stung her eyes. As she'd rushed away from Keith, she couldn't help wondering what she was running from.

Certainly not him. The brief moment they had kissed had been exquisite, taking her away from the reality of her current situation and to somewhere magical. But then thoughts of Rashad came rushing into her mind, especially every time her cell phone rang.

She knew it was him. He was the only one who would call consistently when he wanted to reach her. He had done the same thing after she'd found out about his betrayal, and she had stupidly answered his calls, listened to his pathetic pleas, and even found herself wondering if she should give him another chance. The way he had spun the story of why he had cheated, she'd ended up almost blaming herself for his affair.

But then she'd come to her senses, realizing that he had never been who she thought he was. It was amazing how you could not see the forest for the trees sometimes. In the stories that women wrote to her for the magazine, it was easy to identify that the man was a lying jerk who they should have moved on from. But in her own life, she had wondered. Doubted herself.

"Why couldn't you keep it together?" she asked herself.

It had been all of Keith's questions, and telling her that he was willing and ready to listen. She knew what Maeve would say, that she'd completely overreacted. Keith had presented himself as a caring man, in addition to his sexiness. Why was she always running from him?

Because he has the power to destroy your heart...

The reality shook her. There was something about him, even though she hadn't known him long, that truly spoke to her. Something about the way he looked at her, something about how she felt when their hands did something as simple as brush against each other. Her attraction to him was fierce and inexplicable.

And it scared her to death.

Unlike Rashad, Keith was gorgeous. He could easily have thousands of women throwing themselves at his feet. And she was sure he had. A guy like him couldn't

walk down the street without women breaking their necks
to look back at him. And men who could have easy access to women often couldn't be trusted. Why choose
one when you could have several?

At least that had been Rashad's thinking, hadn't it?
The moment he'd been able to, he cheated on her. Then he
blamed her for her busy schedule, her lack of passion...

But the beginning had been wonderful. Rashad surprising her with a trip to Mexico. Weekends away. Maybe
that was what bothered her most about her time with
Keith. He seemed like the kind of man who enjoyed win-
ing and dining a woman. It would be so easy to fall under
his spell. But how long before she was heartbroken?

Rita eased herself off the door, and limped to her living room sofa. Her knee hurt even more now. She would
need ice. She barely sat for a moment before getting back
up and heading to the kitchen. At least there was ice in
the freezer. But even better, there was a pack of frozen
peas. She snagged it and went back to the living room.
She elevated her leg, placing her foot on the coffee table.
And then she put the bag of peas on her knee.

She remembered the smile that had come on Keith's
face when he had first seen her walking down the dock.
It was a smile that even now made her heart race. Every
time he looked at her, she felt butterflies in her stomach.
Especially when she could see that he was looking at her
as though she were a hot biscuit and he wanted to eat her
up with some butter.

The look she hadn't quite seen in another man's eyes,
and one that touched her in a way she couldn't describe.

She just knew that he was the kind of man who could
make her lose control, and she hated it. She didn't want

to lose control anymore. Losing control had done nothing but cause her pain.

Maeve would tell her that she had a bad attitude toward love, and it wasn't entirely untrue. But it wasn't that she had never tried. She wouldn't have dated Rashad if that were the case. And of course, there had been bad boyfriends before Rashad. All of her relationships had ended in disaster. And now her mother and her father? If those weren't enough to leave a woman feeling scarred about love, then what was? Her mother agreeing to marry the man who had lied to her for so long had really sent Rita's life into a tailspin.

She thought about the look on her mother's face before she'd left the house, the confusion. The disappointment. Her mother would be contacting her soon. Rita was going to give her at least a day to digest the information she'd learned. Then she would be there for her mother, help her move out of Lance's house and then they could move on with their lives. That was the other reason there was no point in even entertaining any sort of flirtation with Keith. Rita wouldn't be in town for much longer, not after her mother broke things off with her father. But Rita would be lying if she told herself she wasn't going to miss this place. Small towns weren't her style, but something about Sheridan Falls was growing on her. There was a certain peace here, even if she knew in her heart that she wasn't allowing herself to fully grasp it. Maybe if she'd come here under any other circumstance, she could enjoy the place. Relax, truly let go. Maybe even flirt and mean it.

Perhaps have a no-strings-attached affair...

The setting had certainly been perfect out on the water today. Her alone with Keith. The stunning scenery. A man who was attracted to her. She knew that Maeve would tell her she had hit the jackpot—a hot guy who was interested in her. And Maeve had certainly been encouraging her to at least find someone who could be a palate cleanser after Rashad.

Rita heard the sound of scuffling outside of her door, and quickly jerked her head in that direction. Her heart pounded. Keith?

The sounds of laughter quickly followed, and Rita's heart deflated. It wasn't Keith, but other vacationers. She was disappointed, which was irrational. Part of her was hoping that Keith would come to see her.

"Are you crazy?" she asked herself. As if Keith would come to see her. Not after how she had behaved. If nothing else, she owed him an apology.

So what if Keith had kissed her? Why had she pushed him away as if he'd been trying to assault her? Obviously he hadn't planned for there to be an accident that prevented the other guests from making the reservation. They'd had a spontaneous moment, and Rita had fully enjoyed the kiss. The moment he'd given her that look that said he wanted her, then slipped his arm around her waist, she had come alive.

It had been exciting...until her phone had started ringing and she'd known it was Rashad. Then she'd gotten in her own head, remembering how all her relationships had gone completely wrong.

Rashad, computer engineer. Verified nerd. He even had the glasses to prove it. In other words, safe.

Safe men were supposed to have lower than average sex drives, and not seek out other women to sleep with. Safe men were supposed to be available every time you called. Safe men were supposed to let you know where they were at all times.

Safe men weren't supposed to be in bed with other women when you showed up at their place unexpectedly.

Rita pulled her leg onto the sofa with her, then winced. Her knee seriously hurt. But her pride hurt more than anything. In her effort to get away from Keith, she'd made a fool of herself.

Because in that instant, Keith had represented every bad man in her life she'd ever dealt with.

Or was it that he was entirely too tempting?

Keith was so darn attractive. The kind of man she could easily lose her mind over. But men like that tended to break women's hearts.

Rita snorted. Who was she kidding? Rashad had been *safe* yet he'd also broken her heart.

She'd met Rashad when he'd come into the coffee shop and she'd been in line waiting for her morning fix. He'd been behind her, and had struck up a conversation about the shopping app she'd been using on her phone. It had been bizarre, and yet intriguing. She just knew that any man who was so overly obsessed with technology would not be overly obsessed with women. They ended up having a coffee date right then and there.

It had been a pleasant surprise. Rita had laughed more than she had in ages. She'd found Rashad quirky and funny. But mostly, she had thought about how different he was from the other men she'd dated in the past. How different he was from the men that women wrote to her about. The ones who tore hearts to shreds and left lives destroyed.

When seven months later, Rashad had proposed, of course she'd said yes. At nearly thirty years old, it was finally time to get married. Finally, Rita had found the kind of man she could trust to be faithful to her. And she would never cheat on him. She thought she'd found her perfect match.

Until she'd found him in bed with another woman…

"Why are you taking this trip down memory lane?" Rita asked herself. It was pointless.

So she thought about Keith, about him taking his shirt off on the boat. Of the way he looked at her with such intensity. The little smirk on his lips told her that he knew he had an effect on her.

And he did. Just looking at him had her heart beating faster, her skin becoming flushed. Men like Keith had the tools to seduce a woman with just a look, and they knew it.

Which was exactly why she needed to stay away from him.

A mix of bittersweet emotions washed over her. She felt a little disappointed that he hadn't come to check on her. And a lot of guilt for how she'd reacted.

Was it wrong for a man to be attracted to a woman, or to even want a fling with her? Most of her single friends went on vacation with eyes open for a hottie whom they could pass the time with. Maybe even some of the single women who rented Keith's units had hoped to get lucky with him. She couldn't really blame him for thinking she might be hoping for a little vacation action.

Rita looked in the direction of the door again. One thing was certain. She would never survive her time here if she went around biting everyone's head off.

Maybe you need to get laid…

The thought popped into her head, and sounded suspiciously like Maeve. Oh, that was what Maeve would tell her all right. But getting laid was *not* what she wanted.

But that didn't mean it wasn't what she needed.

Rita closed her eyes tightly. She was over Rashad, but knowing that he was suddenly trying to reach her was taking her back to their relationship and the pain it had caused.

She hoped that at least she'd accomplished the one thing she'd set out to do. Let Keith know that she wasn't interested in a one-night stand, nor a vacation fling.

Pursuing her would be a waste of time.

"Oh, boy," Maeve said half an hour later. "Girl, you're falling apart."

"That's what happens when you have a mother who's lost her mind."

"Are you sure that's what it is?" Maeve asked.

Rita frowned. "What do you mean?"

"Don't be offended by what I'm about to say. I'm just wondering… Your wedding to Rashad was supposed to be in a couple of weeks. Maybe what's bothering you is the fact that your mother is getting married and you're not."

Rita opened her mouth to protest, then Maeve's words truly sank in. "My God."

"Like I said, I'm not trying to offend you. And I'm sure you're over Rashad, but I can't help thinking that your mother's wedding plans are a reminder that your own wedding fell apart. On a subconscious level."

The words ruminated in Rita's brain. And suddenly they seemed to fit. "You may be right," Rita said softly. "Like you said, it's not that I'm not over Rashad, but maybe psychologically something is triggering me. It makes a lot of sense."

Was that where Rita's extra stress was coming from? Was there a bitter taste in her mouth, knowing that her own love story had crashed and burned? Was that why she couldn't be happy for her mother?

"That's why I'm your best friend," Maeve said proudly, and Rita could hear the smile in her voice. "Who knows you like I do?"

"It's also knowing that some guys have no qualms about lying to you and breaking your heart. Like what my father did to my mother. So the fact that she was so ready to trust him with her heart again…"

"But you can't stop it," Maeve said. "If she's determined to—"

"Well…" Rita interjected sheepishly.

"What?" Maeve asked, sounding suspicious.

"Right now, my mother may be packing her things and leaving my father's house. At least I hope she is."

"What happened?"

Rita filled her in on the meeting and how she'd brought up her father's bankruptcy. "I'm sure that my mother is seeing the situation in a different light. She's got to realize that my father has ulterior motives."

"My goodness," Maeve said. "Have you talked to your mother since?"

"No. I'm giving her time and space. She'll reach out to me when she's ready."

"All right, well let me know how things go. You know I got a dress for this wedding…"

"Keep the receipt," Rita said. "You might just have to return it."

Chapter 13

Keith ditched the idea of going back to the office because he was in no mood. The pressure in his head made him feel like it was going to explode. He'd probably lose his cool with his receptionist and anyone he had to deal with.

All because of Rita.

Had he really been a jerk? For her to act as if he'd taken her out on the boat as a deliberate ploy to seduce her, then to run off as if she were afraid of him…

She'd even hurt herself trying to get away from him as quickly as possible. He wondered if she was okay.

Keith grabbed a beer from the fridge and went to the back porch. He took swigs of the cold beverage, hoping his mood would improve. Instead, he sat there seething.

Two beers later, he was coming to the realization that what had happened was for the best. Rita freaking out the way she had was sending him a clear sign to stay away.

He'd treat her with professionalism, like the renter she was. That was it. Hadn't he learned his lesson after Maya?

Maya. Beautiful and into him, Keith had fallen for her fast. She'd been in town for the summer because she'd needed an escape from her life in New York City. She'd rented one of Keith's units, and they'd gotten to know each other. Unlike Rita, Maya had tried to develop a relationship with him. She had flirted, conversed and their romance had blossomed quickly.

She'd had a recent ex, but that was part of why she'd come to Sheridan Falls. Under a moonlit sky, Maya had assured Keith of her love for him, that she was done with big town life and her career as a B-level actress, and that she wanted a future with him in Sheridan Falls.

Next thing Keith knew, Maya was gone—and quickly marrying her ex-boyfriend, some big shot producer.

When the pounding started, Keith jerked his head up. It took a nanosecond for him to realize that it was the door.

He scrambled to his feet and went through the house and to the front door. He swung it open, and then his heart stopped.

Rita looked up at him meekly. "I'm sorry."

Keith said nothing. He was too stunned.

"What I said to you… It was wrong. It was offensive. I have no reason to think that you're anything other than a great guy."

"Mm-hmm."

"Can I come in?" she asked. "Can we talk?"

Keith drew in a deep breath, then stepped backward and opened the door wide. With her head hanging low, Rita walked past him into the house, moving with a slight limp.

Keith closed the door, then turned to face her. She was

looking up at him with sad eyes. "How's your knee?" he asked.

She waved off his concern. "Mildly irritated. I'll be fine." She drew in a deep breath, then continued, "I've been stressed out. My mother and her sudden relationship with my father. My ex-fiancé who's suddenly desperate to talk to me. He's been calling me all day…and when the phone rang when we were kissing, I freaked out."

Though he knew that the situation with her parents had to be weighing on her mind, Keith's heart thudded at the comment about her ex-fiancé. "He's been calling you? Why?"

"I don't want to talk about him," Rita said. "I don't want him occupying any more space in my mind."

She pressed her hands on Keith's chest, then slowly crept them around his neck. His breathing stopped as he looked down at her, wondering what she was doing.

"You don't?" Keith asked, his voice a croak.

Rita shook her head, biting down on her bottom lip. "No. I want to do something else."

Despite his earlier pep talk to keep his emotional distance from Rita, Keith cautiously looped his arms around her waist.

"I'm not running," Rita said softly.

Where was this coming from? Why the sudden about-face?

Yet he pulled her closer, enjoying the feel of her soft breasts as they pressed against his chest. "Why not?"

"Because no matter how hard I try, I can't stop thinking about you."

Keith swallowed.

"I went home and was miserable. I feel awful for the way I treated you, but I thought that I could finally put you out of my mind. Instead, all I've been able to do is think about you. About the way I felt when you kissed me. Heck, even when you just look at me, the way you are now."

Keith's heart pounded. "Hmm… I haven't been able to stop thinking about you, either."

Rita began stroking the back of his neck with her fingers. "I like you," she said. "I'm definitely attracted to you. But… I'm not good at relationships."

"Okay…"

"Maybe we can… I don't know…" She shrugged. "Do what comes naturally?"

The way Rita was looking up at him with lust-filled eyes while stroking the back of his neck, it was obvious what she wanted.

"No strings attached," Rita said. "Just sex."

He should pull away. Right now. His brain was screaming that, telling him to steer clear of any romantic involvement with Rita. She was up and down, all over the place.

But the way she was looking at him, and touching him, and biting down on her bottom lip… Damn, he was lost.

He slipped his hand into her hair and pulled her head closer. As he did, Rita eased up on her toes. Keith captured her lips and kissed her fiercely. She moaned against his mouth, her fingers digging into his shoulder blades. Rita was different. She was no longer reserved, holding back. She wanted him.

Fire consumed him. He smoothed his hands over her arms, down her back. Their lips were locked, their tongues swirling over one another's, Rita's fingers still gently stroking his skin. It was driving him wild.

Keith's pulse was racing, his breathing heavy. He tore

his lips from hers and looked into her darkened eyes. As much as he wanted to get naked with her immediately, he had to know that she truly would have no regrets.

"Are you sure?" he asked.

Leaning her body into him, she stroked his face. "Yes."

He kissed her again, his tongue sweeping across the moist recesses of her mouth. Then he pulled back and took her hand in his. Gazing up at him, she giggled, then bit down on her bottom lip. The sound turned him on, made him know that she was looking forward to being with him.

Keith led her up the stairs, trotting once he reached the top. Rita's happy laughter followed them. His bedroom was at the end of the hall, and he hurried into it.

Once inside, he turned and swept Rita into his arms. His mouth came down on hers with urgency. The little sighing sound she made caused his groin to tighten.

Oh, he was looking forward to this.

Her fingers caressed his face in soft tantalizing strokes. Who knew that such light touches could create such fire?

Keith slipped his hands beneath her shirt, feeling her warm smooth skin. Rita nibbled on his bottom lip before easing back so that she could pull her shirt over her head. A slow breath oozed out of him when his eyes took in the sight of her in her bra and skirt. Her breasts were large in her black lace bra, and they jiggled when she moved. She was so incredibly sexy.

Looking into her eyes, Keith stroked her face. Then he pulled her bra strap down one shoulder slowly, and planted a kiss on her bare shoulder. He did the same with the other side, and Rita reached behind her back to undo her bra. As it loosened, Keith groaned, anticipating the moment he would see her fully topless. He pulled the bra straps down her arms and off her body.

Her breasts spilled free, and Keith's gaze lowered. A jolt of desire hit him hard as he took in the sight of her full breasts. The areolas were large, her dark nipples flat. She was perfect.

He let a slow breath as he ran the pad of his thumb over one of her nipples. It hardened beneath his touch, and desire pulled at his groin again.

Slipping an arm around her waist, he gripped her against his body, holding her tightly. He lowered his head and kissed her again. This time more slowly, because he wanted to savor every moment. It had been a while since he'd had a woman in his arms. And he wasn't going to rush this.

As he kissed her, he urged her backward toward the bed. He came to a stop at the edge, and Rita tightened her arms around his torso. It was as though she never wanted to let him go.

She flicked the tip of her tongue over his, while slipping her hands beneath his shirt. She splayed her palms over his abdomen, sighing softly as she did. That little sound, coupled with the way she was touching him, was fuel to his desire.

He covered both of her breasts with his hands, and tweaked her nipples, guiding her backward onto the bed as he did. Once she was on her back, he positioned himself over her. He massaged the full mounds of her breasts, then took one of her nipples into his mouth. He suckled her softly, and she moaned in response. He ran the tip of his tongue around her erect peak, then flicked it back and forth, his shaft straining against his jeans as she reacted to what he was doing.

He drew her nipple fully into his mouth and suckled slowly, softly, and she dug her fingers into his shoulder blades. He glanced at her, saw that her eyes were tightly shut, her lips parted. She was a vision of sexiness.

Keith moved his tongue over her other nipple before shifting his mouth to the center of her body and kissing a path down her belly. She shuddered beneath his kisses. He dipped his tongue into the groove of her belly button, all the while tweaking her nipples. Her erotic sounds grew more intense.

Keith pushed his hands beneath the hem and bunched the skirt up around her waist. He planted a soft kiss on her pubic area with her panties on. She moaned deeply, and he knew that she was ready for what he would do next.

Taking her panties off would take too much time, so Keith simply used his fingers to push them out of the way. And then there she was, her beautiful womanhood. He stroked her with his finger, and her hips bucked. Oh, yes, she wanted this.

He caressed his tongue over her sensitive flesh, and Rita gasped. He did it again, and she gave the same response.

And then Keith was pleasuring her sweet spot with gentle suckles and twirls of his tongue. Rita writhed beneath him, her pleasure undeniable. She was moaning, her head rocking back and forth.

Keith kept up the pressure until her sensual moans came in a steady rhythm. He could sense the building of her climax. He suckled her softly, noting the way her hands were gripping the bedsheets. She was a vision of absolute beauty, and she was hot for him.

"Oh, baby!"

Her back arched, her hands grabbed fistfuls of the

bedsheet, and she released a rapturous cry. Keith's lust charged through his entire body, and he needed to be inside of her. Now.

He eased his body upward, kissing her as she breathed raggedly. And then he hastily undid the clasp on his jeans and quickly dragged his pants and briefs down to his knees. He wanted to make love to her right then and there, but somewhere his senses came to him. He couldn't risk an unwanted pregnancy.

"Do you have a condom?" she asked, clearly thinking the same thing.

"Yes," Keith rasped.

He hobbled off the bed with his jeans around his knees, and when Rita chuckled, so did he. Then the smile on her face morphed into a look of desire, and she sank her teeth into her bottom lip as her eyes lowered to check out his hard arousal.

Keith stepped out of his jeans, found a condom and quickly put it on. By the time he turned back to the bed, Rita had stripped out of her skirt and was slipping her thong over her ankles.

How had Keith gotten so lucky to have Rita here naked in his room?

He rejoined her on the bed, spreading his body out alongside hers. He slipped his hands into her hair and drew her face to his. He kissed her slowly, as if they had all the time in the world.

And as far as he was concerned, they did.

Rita trailed her fingers down his side and over his hips and along his thighs. Keith played with her nipples as he kissed her, then slipped a hand between her legs. As he fondled her, he urged her onto her back and then settled himself between her thighs.

She broke the kiss and looked up at him, now softly stroking his face. She gave him a little smile, just a subtle sign of encouragement.

Keith didn't need any more urging. He guided his shaft inside of her, moving slowly as she gripped his back and mewled. As he went deeper, she gasped. Keith kissed her, taking her mouth with all the fervor he could muster. He wanted to make her feel the way no one had ever made her feel.

He moved inside of her, his strokes slow and deep. She rocked her hips up and down, matching his movements. The crescendo between them built, until Keith's thrusts were faster and faster. Rita was kissing him, and sighing, and gripping his butt. She wrapped her legs around him and held on as Keith sped up the pace.

"Keith… Oh, my God…"

He swallowed her cries of pleasure, and feeling her body tighten, he allowed himself the release his own body craved. He came, groaning loudly and burying his face in her neck.

"Yes," Rita rasped. She stroked his back, her fingertips eliciting even more sensation as he enjoyed the wave of his climax.

And then they were both still, the heavy sounds of their breathing filling the room. They lay there like that for a while, Keith's face in her neck and inhaling her sweet essence.

He wanted her in his bed all the time.

Finally, he eased his body off hers but instantly thought to put his hand around her waist. He wanted to be touching her always.

She looked at him, a twinkle in her eyes and a coy smile on her face. "Wow," she said.

"I have to admit, I did not expect to be doing this to-night."

She slung a leg across his thighs. "You're not complaining, are you?"

Keith stroked her nipple, and was rewarded when she began to purr. "Not at all. And trust me, I'm going to make the most of the fact that you're here in my bed to-night. All. Night. Long."

Chapter 14

Rita had never felt better. She'd had some pretty good sex in her life, but she finally knew what it was to have amazing sex.

Keith had lived up to his word. All night long, he had thrilled her. He had played with her body and teased her and brought her to more climaxes than she thought possible. He'd made love to her slowly, as though what was happening between them was something special. He made love to her hard and fast, like a man starved for her affection.

Now, as morning had come and sunlight spilled into the room, Rita was barely rested but oh so satisfied.

"I really hate to do this," Keith said, "but I have to go to the office. I've got people coming in to sign a rental agreement. You can stay here if you like."

"Really?" she asked, a smile on her lips.

"Sure," Keith told her. "As long as when I come back here, you're naked on my bed just as you are now."

Despite the level of sensation her body had experienced for the night, clearly there was more to be had. Because she felt another jolt of desire. It surprised her that she could want another human being this much.

She leaned forward and kissed him, and then Keith rolled off the bed. Rita's eyes wandered around the room. There were various pictures on the walls, and she got out of the bed and began to take a closer look.

"Your brothers?" she asked, stopping in front of a large framed photo over his dresser.

Keith was taking a suit from the closet. "Yep. Aaron, Carlton and Jonas."

They were all very attractive and it was clear they were related. "Oh, I bet you all caused some trouble growing up. Broke some hearts."

"I don't know why everybody says that."

She looked over her shoulder at him, smiling. "Maybe you'll share some stories one day."

Keith's eyes darkened with an undoubted look of desire. "Are you standing around naked like that as a ploy to get me to skip work?"

Rita felt a surge of feminine power. It was nice to know that she could tempt him to stick around. "Maybe…"

He walked toward her, slipped his arms around her from behind and nuzzled his nose in her neck. "Want to hop in the shower with me?"

"You won't get to work…"

He smoothed his hands over her hips. "You're right. Bad idea."

Rita smiled at him as he headed off to his en suite bathroom. She would shower after he was gone. Continuing to wander around his room, she noticed a picture on a small table near the window.

Her stomach sank.

Keith exited the bathroom with a towel around his waist and drew up short when he saw Rita sitting on the edge of his bed, fully dressed. She had a sour look on her face. What had happened to change the mood since he'd gone in the shower?

"You knew all along, didn't you? You knew that Brandon was my brother."

Keith noticed that she was holding the photo from his table in his hand. A photo of him and Brandon on a boat when they'd gone on a fishing trip. "I'm not sure what your point is."

"All this time I've talked to you about my father, you never once said that you were friends with his son. Small towns." She snorted. "I should have known."

Keith said nothing.

"You're out in a boat in this picture with Brandon. Holding a fish. You've probably been out with my father, too, haven't you? Yet you didn't say a word about being close to them. Why not?"

"Brandon and I go way back."

"That doesn't answer the question," Rita said.

"I grew up with Brandon. Yeah, we're friends."

"So when you were giving me the whole spiel about how I shouldn't tell my mother about the bankruptcy, that I needed to give my father's family a chance, you had an agenda."

"Not a nefarious agenda. I know the family. I know they're good people."

"So why didn't you tell me that?"

"Because… Because I figured you'd react like this. Think that I was too biased to give you an honest opinion."

Rita's gaze fell to the photo. "You and Brandon look like best buds in this picture."

"He is one of my best friends. Which is why I know he's a good guy. That's why I tried to influence you by saying what I did, without explicitly telling you that he was my friend. Because if I told you that he was my friend, you would have dismissed what I said out of turn."

Rita shook her head. "You know what I can't stand? I can't stand when people aren't honest with me. You've been trying to influence my feelings about my father, without being honest with me as to why."

"You're blowing this out of proportion."

"Am I?" Rita met his gaze with a steely one.

"Would you have listened to me had I told you anything otherwise?" Keith challenged.

"That's not the point."

"Isn't it? You came to town with a certain frame of mind, a certain position, and it was really clear that getting you to be open-minded was going to be very hard."

Rita's eyes grew wide. "What do you mean, getting me to be open-minded? Did Brandon put you up to talking to me on his behalf? God, of course he did."

"Brandon put me up to nothing. All I've done as a friend is vouch for his father. Your father. I've known him practically all my life, and obviously he did you wrong, but he's not a monster—"

"No, he's a great guy." She rolled her eyes.

"Life isn't always black-and-white, Rita. Good people do bad things."

Rita put the photo down beside her and shot to her feet. "Last night was a mistake."

She scooped up her purse and started for the bedroom door.

"You're just going to run off like that? You have your own preconceived notions and no one can talk you out of them?"

"I have my truth," Rita said, spinning around to face him. "You have the fairytale version of the story, which is not even remotely realistic. If I need to check out of the cottage sooner than later, I hope you're not going to expect me to forfeit my deposit. After all, deceit should be a good reason to end my contract earlier than anticipated."

"Rita…"

She hurried out of the bedroom. Keith went to the door and saw her rushing down the hallway. Several seconds later, he heard the chiming sound his front door made when it opened.

Keith went to his bedroom window that overlooked the front of the house. He saw Rita getting into her car. She slammed the door, then sped out of his driveway, her tires squealing as she turned onto the road.

Rita's hands were shaking as she drove away from Keith's place.

Not him, too. Why had he lied to her?

Their amazing night of carnal bliss had ended in abject disappointment. One minute, Rita had felt incredible. Now she felt…

Deceived.

Was she overreacting? Of course, Keith knew Brandon, her father. What he'd said made sense. If he had told her that he was friends with Brandon, she wouldn't have given any credence to what he had to tell her.

Rita sucked in a deep breath, trying to calm herself. Keith wasn't the issue. It was this entire town, and her mother's plan to marry her father. Rita felt like she was losing it.

She was driving with no real destination, but soon she saw the sign for the interstate. Heading west.

She hit her indicator and got to the right. Maybe she ought to head back home to St. Louis.

Keith felt out of sorts, a feeling he wasn't quite used to. As though he'd just survived being on a roller coaster caught up in a twister.

The look on Rita's face before she'd taken off had stung. The betrayal. She had spent the night clinging to him and crying out his name, only to turn around and act as though she wanted nothing more to do with him.

How had things gone from bliss to hell so quickly?

Keith looked at his reflection in the bathroom mirror. Stress lines were etched on his face. He dragged a hand over the stubble growing from his chin. He didn't even feel like shaving.

"Didn't you tell yourself to stay away from her? Didn't you know that she was too unpredictable to get involved with?"

No strings attached, she'd said… Yeah, right.

He had no doubt that Rita was back to thinking that he was some sort of bad guy. He could have tried to reason with her until he'd passed out, but it had been clear to him in that moment that nothing he said would change her mind.

It was also clear that no good was going to come from

reliving what had gone wrong. So he got dressed and went to work, figuring that the best thing to do was to give Rita space. He didn't want to regret their night together, but a part of him did. She hadn't been ready. Certainly not for a no-strings-attached relationship as she'd suggested.

He knew that she was struggling with some demons. And while he couldn't understand fully what she was going through, he realized it wasn't easy. She'd been a secret love child, never really acknowledged by her father. Growing up in a small town, secrets came out more often than not, and Keith had learned early that not everything was what it seemed despite the happy exterior people might show to the world.

Rita wasn't the only one who'd gotten the shaft in life. Of course, he couldn't tell her that. But she needed to learn that carrying anger around all the time was completely unhealthy. She couldn't spend her entire life not trusting anybody.

Even though he had told himself that he would give her space, by the time he got to the office, he called her. Her phone went to voice mail.

"Hey, Rita. I'm sorry you left my place upset. Just know that I wasn't trying to deceive you. I just… I didn't want to interfere one way or another. Maybe that doesn't make sense, but I hope it does. Look, please—"

The knock on his door caused Keith to drop the phone from his ear. He looked up to see his receptionist standing there. She was regarding him with concern. "Mr. Burke? Are you okay?"

"Yeah." He nodded. "Fine."

"Your ten o'clock appointment is here."

Keith pressed a button to end the call, then slipped his cell phone into the desk's top drawer. "Send them in."

Of course, going back to St. Louis had been an illogical thought, so Rita had dismissed it shortly after she'd started driving. But what she did like doing when she was upset was going for a long drive. With the music blaring, she drove with no particular destination. So she traveled on I-90 until she reached Buffalo, then she decided to get off the highway and explore the downtown area.

She found a section of Main Street with boutique shops and restaurants and occupied herself window shopping and indulging in an oversized waffle cone. She had turned her phone off so that she would have no distractions, but after a couple of hours without technology, it was time to get reconnected with the world. Mostly because she wanted to use her phone to find the nearest burrito shop.

Her phone trilled almost immediately, letting her know that she had some missed text messages. She saw Keith's name pop up on her screen. Then she saw her mother's. Moments later, she saw that there were four missed calls from her mom.

Feeling a spate of anxiety, Rita quickly dialed her mother's number and put the phone to her ear.

"Rita?" came the reply on the other end of the line.

When Rita heard the male voice, her back stiffened. Was that her father? "Yes?"

"It's your father."

Rita's heart stopped. "Is my mother okay?"

"I've been trying to reach you."

"What happened?"

"Your mother fainted. Blacked right out."

"What?" Rita shrieked.

"She's okay now. I brought her to the hospital, and they're taking good care of her."

"Oh, my God. Which hospital?"

"There's only one in Sheridan Falls. On State Street."

Rita began walking in the direction of where she'd parked her car. "I'm in Buffalo, but I'll head back now. Tell my mother I'm on my way."

Chapter 15

By the time Rita was arriving in the Sheridan Falls town limits, her phone was ringing again. The screen on her car's dashboard display said that the call was from her mother's cell.

She pressed the talk button on her steering wheel. "Mom?" she answered, hopeful.

"It's your father," came the reply.

"God, please tell me she isn't worse."

"She's not. I'm calling to tell you that she's home now. Please come here instead of the hospital."

"Does that mean she's okay?"

"Please don't worry. We'll explain everything when you get here."

Her father's words didn't alleviate her fear. Only when Rita entered his home and saw her mother lying on the sofa, looking a little tired but otherwise okay, did she relax.

"Mom." She rushed to her mother's side. "Are you okay?" Rita wrapped her arms around her mother and squeezed, never wanting to let go.

"Sweetheart, I'm fine." Her mother patted her back to soothe her, much as she'd done when Rita was a little girl. "I hope you weren't too worried."

"You passed out. You had to go to the hospital. That doesn't sound fine."

"I told Lance he shouldn't have taken me. He's like you… He worries over every little thing."

"If you blacked out, he was right to take you." Rita turned to her father. "What did the doctor say?"

"Turns out she's dehydrated. Burning the candle at both ends, not taking care of herself."

"A little fainting spell," her mother said. "It's no big deal."

"Thankfully the cause wasn't more serious," Lance said. "But of course, I was worried."

Lynn waved a dismissive hand. "Oh, Lance. I told you it was nothing."

"It's taken me this long to have you in my life again. I'm not nearly ready to lose you."

It dawned on Rita in that moment that her mother and father were still speaking as two people in love. She'd expected her mother to have her bags packed by now. But apparently that wasn't happening.

Rita turned to Lance. "Um, do you mind giving me a moment with my mother?"

Lynn sat up straight on the sofa, pulling the afghan up to her belly as she did. "Yes, please. I'd like a word with Rita alone."

Lynn's tone was suddenly serious, and Rita could tell

that she needed to have a serious talk with her. Finally, she'd get to the truth.

"All right, dear," Lance said.

Once he was out of the room, Rita looked at her mother with concern. "You *are* all right, aren't you?"

"I'm fine," her mother said. "They gave me fluids at the hospital and I'm as good as new."

"So you want to talk to me about my father," Rita surmised. Her mother had come to her senses. She'd taken the information Rita had given her and had made the hard—but sensible—decision to call off the wedding. "I'm here for you," Rita told her. "No matter what."

"Are you?" her mother asked, a challenge in her voice.

Rita narrowed her eyes, not understanding. "Of course I am."

"That stunt you pulled yesterday—I'm not happy with you."

"*Stunt?*"

"Yes, stunt. I was already stressed enough trying to plan this wedding. Today I had to call the florist, caterer, try to do everything myself because I couldn't count on you."

Reality hit Rita with the force of a tornado. "Are you saying you fainted because of me?"

"I'm saying that I can't handle you questioning my decision anymore. If you can't be in Sheridan Falls and help me with the wedding, then you need to leave."

Rita gaped at her mother. Surely her ears were playing tricks on her. "What?"

"Are you going to stay here and support me—or are you going to return to St. Louis?"

Rita had to take a moment to process the question. Was her mother actually giving her an ultimatum?

"I asked you a question."

"I... You're going through with the wedding?"

"Of course I am. The question is, can I count on you or not?"

Rita stared at her mother for several beats. When she realized that she wasn't kidding, Rita said the only thing she could. "You can count on me. Of course."

"Good. Because as of this moment, I don't want to hear anything else negative from you about your father."

"You're not going to fill me in on what happened? I mean, the bankruptcy—"

"What did you just agree to?"

Rita shut up.

"Your *news* didn't change anything. I'm still going to marry your father."

Rita stared at her mother, so wanting to say something, but knowing that she couldn't.

"We spoke about the bankruptcy. And I'm completely comfortable with his explanation."

"And the fact that he never told you about it?" Rita couldn't help asking.

"Is irrelevant. Rita, I'm certain that you told me that information with a little bit of glee, didn't you? You wanted to believe that your father was using me and that I would immediately drop him."

"I wanted you to be aware. So far you've jumped into this relationship completely blindly. I learned some information that was important, and you needed to know. What you do with that information is your choice."

"Life isn't about money. It's not about how many cars you have, how many trips you can take."

"I know that. I'm not that kind of person."

"Life is not defined by your failures, either. Things

happen in life and you make the best of them, and sometimes you make mistakes and you screw up royally, but you move on."

"So my father explained the bankruptcy and you're not concerned."

"After everything he'd been through, do you think that for one moment he wanted to appear weak when we got back together? Do you think that admitting to me he nearly lost everything and had to turn to the town for help was going to make him feel good about himself? And yet you took the opportunity to rub it in his face. You could have talked to him first, gotten more information, but instead you dropped your little bomb, hoping that it would explode and destroy everything we've been building."

Rita said nothing. What could she say? It was exactly what she had hoped. Not because she wanted to see her mother unhappy, but because she wanted to save her mother from future heartbreak.

"His wife's medical bills were expensive," Lynn went on. "He lost so much because of that. He did everything throughout the progression of her illness to make her life bearable and easier in her final days. He should be commended. Instead, you're treating him like a villain." Her mother's eyes narrowed. "And I won't have it. Not anymore."

"I… I didn't think about that."

"Of course you didn't. You were too busy thinking the worst of him. You have a horrible inability to forgive people who've hurt you. Look how you treated Rashad. He apologized, but you wouldn't hear it."

Rita's jaw dropped. "Are you actually saying that you think I should have forgiven Rashad?"

"He said he made a mistake and that he regretted it. He wanted another chance—"

"He didn't *deserve* another chance!" Rita shot back. Now she knew for sure that her mother had lost her mind. For her to act as though Rashad's betrayal, so fresh, should be forgiven because he'd realized the grass wasn't greener on the other side... Rita was flummoxed.

"Whatever happened with my father, that wasn't Rashad's issue. He didn't face the same kind of dilemma. All men who cheat don't deserve a pass. Seriously, Mom— don't you remember that Rashad and I were supposed to be getting married in just weeks?"

"I know, and I'm not saying that you should forgive him as a way to say that what he did was okay. But forgive as a way to let go of the pain. And who knows, maybe you two could actually work things out."

"Please stop. You want to talk about my father, your wedding... Fine. But Rashad..." She shook her head. "I won't hear it."

"I'm just saying forgiveness is the way forward."

Rita knew all about her mother's views on forgiveness, but she didn't share them. At least not in this case. What Rashad had done to her was unforgivable.

"Maybe I'm interfering where I shouldn't," Lynn continued. "All I know is that forgiving your father has made all the difference for me. He doesn't deserve any more hurt in his life. Not after all he's been through. We both deserve to be happy."

"I wasn't trying to hurt you. And I wasn't trying to hurt him."

"Good. Then you can tell him that."

Rita's eyes widened. "What?"

"Now. Clear the air with your father."

Before Rita could say anything, her mother was calling her father back into the room. Moments later, Lance appeared.

"Lance, sweetheart. Rita has something she'd like to say to you."

Rita's gaze volleyed between her mother and father. Then she said, "I'm sorry about yesterday. I'm sorry I didn't talk to you first."

"So your mother explained the situation."

"Yes. She did. And I... I can't imagine how hard that must have been for you. Losing your wife and not being able to do anything about it."

A flash of grief passed over his face. "Thank you. It was very hard. But I want you to know that your mother is everything to me. I love her, and I want to spend the rest of my life making her happy."

Rita swallowed.

Lance stepped into the room and took a seat beside her. "Ask me anything. I'll answer."

"First and foremost, my concern is that your feelings for my mother are real. I worry that your relationship with her is a rebound thing, especially after losing your wife. I don't want my mother to get hurt."

"I'm not going to hurt your mother. Never again."

Rita drew in a deep breath. Emotions were clogging her throat when she asked, "Did you ever love me?"

"Of course I did!" Lance responded without hesitation. "I always have."

Rita steeled her back and cleared her throat. She didn't want to cry. "You have a funny way of showing it."

"You're right. I do. It's a long story, and I can't sugarcoat what I did. My behavior was in many ways unforgivable. I took the coward's way out. I met your mother and I fell in love with her the moment I saw her, but I was already married. I'd already had a child. I wanted to leave then, but my wife... Well, she didn't make it easy."

"You told her you wanted to leave?" Rita asked, surprised.

"I did. I came home one day and told her that we both deserved something better. We were young when we got married, and she'd been pregnant. I was trying to do the right thing. Well, she had a meltdown. And I don't mean that she yelled and screamed. That I could've dealt with. But it was the talk of suicide that had me pausing."

Rita narrowed her eyes as she looked at him. But she didn't speak.

"She asked me if there was someone else, and I didn't want to hurt her feelings, but at some point she realized that there was. She said she knew it in her gut. Could see that I was slipping away. That's when she told me that if I left, there was nothing for her to live for. That she would kill herself. That she'd already thought of the ways when she'd considered that I might be seeing someone else. I told her not to be stupid, that of course she wouldn't kill herself. But after a night spent crying, I found her the next day in the tub. An empty bottle of pills was beside her."

"Oh, my goodness."

Lance nodded. "Scared me half to death. I called the ambulance and she was rushed to the hospital. It turned out she hadn't taken enough pills to kill herself, but close. Anyway, I realized then that she wasn't kidding. That she really was going to fall apart if I left her. I still loved your mother, of course I did. And all this was right after I'd found out Lynn was pregnant—which is why I wanted to leave and be with her. But with my wife's threat of suicide and our young son, I knew I couldn't risk it. If that's me being a coward, then call me a coward. I accept that."

Rita took a moment to digest what he'd told her. It certainly changed things. She still had questions, and it wasn't as though this explanation simply made all of her pain and sadness go away.

She looked at him. "What about over the years? Why did you never see me?"

"I don't know." Her father shook his head. "My wife ended up being diagnosed with multiple sclerosis, and she needed me more and more. I knew that I had to get a different job, which meant I couldn't travel anymore. I considered telling her about you, but I knew in my heart that it would be the wrong thing to do. That it would send her into a tailspin."

"Are you trying to say that you were in a loveless marriage? Because Brandon's birthday is several months after mine. If you had the one son, I could see it. But you got your wife pregnant again after my mother was pregnant. To me, it seems like you were having your cake and eating it, too."

"Once I told your mother it was over, I figured I needed to try to make a go of it with my wife. What would be the point of being in a marriage that was completely loveless? I tried. She got pregnant again and, for a time, things were happier. But then she got sicker, and never seemed fully satisfied. On another occasion, she talked about wanting to end it all, and I knew that if I left, she might do something very stupid. And if she did do something stupid, it would be something that haunted me for the rest of my days."

Lance sighed, his shoulders trembling beneath that heavy breath. "I never forgot your mother over the years, and I never forgot you. That's why I always sent money, even though I couldn't be a real father to you. Your mother..." He threw a glance in her direction. "Obviously she was quite devastated by my decision as well. I just thought that coming around to see you, to see her when I knew I couldn't be with you both as a real father and family, would hurt her more. So that's why I stayed away totally. And maybe this won't make any sense, but I knew your mother was strong enough to handle living without me."

Lance paused. "I realize now that it wasn't the right thing to do. That a child needs her father. That I should've told my wife the truth and tried to get her help for her emotional issues. Now that she's gone, I think back to the first suicide attempt. The doctor said she didn't take enough pills to kill herself, and I had thought that it was a miscalculation. It really hadn't occurred to me until recently that the threat of suicide might have been a ploy for her to control me. In any case, she succeeded."

"So you see," Lynn interjected. "It wasn't that your father didn't want to be with me, or with you. It was the situation. He didn't want his wife's suicide on his conscience."

Rita nodded, processing the information. "I understand that you were in a tough predicament. And the choice you made was because of that. But I find it hard to fully believe that you kept loving my mother over those years when you had vowed to move on. Can your feelings stay strong for a woman you've left behind?"

A genuine smile lit up her father's face. "Your mother has always had a special place in my heart. I gave up believing we could be together, but then my wife died. I looked your mother up on Facebook. Sent her a message. Said I'd never forgotten what we'd shared and that I wanted to talk."

Her mother smiled from ear to ear. "I fell in love with him all over again."

Her mother sounded like a gushing teenager in love. Rita couldn't deny it. She also couldn't deny that her mother had been a rational adult, not the type of woman to fall into relationship after relationship. Indeed, Rita had never known her to be pining away for her father.

Her biggest objection to her parents getting back together had been the thought that it had been too easy for her father, after the pain he'd caused.

She thought of Maeve's words, that she needed to trust her mother's decision-making. Maeve was right.

But still, she said, "This all just seems so easy."

"Easy?" Her father's voice cracked with emotion. "Nothing about this has been easy. Living a life you didn't really want... I had my boys, yes, and that's the only thing that kept me sane. But once my wife died, I didn't want to waste any more time."

"And neither did I," her mother chimed in. "You remember how Betty Caldwell was alive and well one day, the next day diagnosed with cancer and gone in six weeks? There are no guarantees at my age anymore. At any age," her mother stressed. "If the love was still there for us, why should I make him suffer to prove it? I could feel it in the words he spoke to me, the way he looked at me, and I could feel it in his heart."

Despite herself, warmth spread through Rita's heart, melting the ice that had built there over the years regarding her father. If this had been anyone else's love story, would she question it?

Keith had pointed out that Lance had been a respected

citizen in the town, not known to be some sort of uncouth womanizer. Of course, not everybody knew what people were up to. Some men and women successfully led secret lives for years.

And yet…her father's story didn't sound like that.

"None of this takes away from the fact that I should have been there for you," Lance said. "The pain I've caused you is immeasurable. I just hope that it isn't irreparable."

Her father offered her a faint smile, then reached for her hand. He gave it a gentle squeeze. "Please know that I always loved you, even if I felt I couldn't be with you. I know I can't really walk into your life and be an instant father, but I'm hoping you'll be willing to get to know me as a person. And hopefully one day as a friend."

A tear slid down his cheek then. Rita wanted to be unaffected by her father's words and emotions, but the little girl inside of her who'd always wanted to know that her father loved her was coming to life. Right now, she wasn't thinking about the pain he'd caused her; she was feeling regret. The pain wasn't going to simply disappear, of course. But she could finally understand that her father had been in a tough predicament. In fact, she could see why he had made the decisions he had.

"I wish you'd found a way," Rita said, her own voice ripe with emotion.

"So do I. And I'll live with that guilt forever. I don't expect you to forgive me right away, but we can move forward, can't we?"

Rita looked into her father's eyes, into a face that held guarded hope. And darn if his words didn't hit a bull's-eye, landing in her heart. Unexpected emotions swelled inside of her, and she could feel the walls around her heart starting to crumble. It would take time to develop the kind of relationship she wanted with her father, and maybe they would never have that traditional father-daughter relationship. But she was confident in this moment that they could at least be friends.

Tears blurred Rita's eyes. She fully meant it when she said, "I'd like that."

"Can I hug you?" he asked.

Rita nodded, then allowed her father to wrap her in an embrace. As she let him hold her, her hands slowly moved upward to clutch his back.

Something had shifted between them. Rita felt her anger ebbing away. All of her fighting over her parents getting married—it suddenly seemed senseless. Her father's statement about how much he loved her mother had the ring of truth, and Rita could suddenly see why her mother had believed him.

Keith had told her that life wasn't black-and-white. Good people did bad things.

"I do believe that you love my mother," Rita said, easing back and offering her father a smile. "And there's a lot of planning left to do for the wedding. Can't have my mother stressing herself out over all that needs to be done." She clapped her hands together. "So where do we start?"

Chapter 16

Rita spent the next few hours helping to finalize the wedding plans. She secured the DJ, spoke with the florist and narrowed down the list of photographers. Her mother hadn't asked for one, but Rita also booked a videographer for the event. That would be her gift to her to capture every moment of the special day forever.

It was just after three when her mother came into the study where Rita had been looking up all things wedding on the internet and making calls.

"I just spoke to Enid at the bridal shop. She said she has time for us if we want to go in now."

"But shouldn't you be resting?"

"I've rested enough for one day. The wedding is in two weeks."

"Two weeks! It's supposed to be—"

"We decided to move up the date."

"But all the guests—"

"Have been contacted. That's what I was doing today."

"Why are you moving up the wedding date?" Rita asked. She was going to have to call the DJ, florist and videographer to make sure they were available for the new date.

"We decided we didn't want to wait. Plus, you have your life to get back to."

Rita couldn't argue with that logic. But still, this was unexpected.

"Given the new wedding date, it's imperative that you try on your dress selections and choose one. I'm getting anxious."

Rita nodded. "Okay, that makes sense. If you're up to it, I guess we could…"

"I told Enid we'd be on our way."

"Oh," Rita said. "All right, then."

Minutes later, they were in Rita's car and heading to the center of town. Rita parked in front of the very bridal shop she'd seen when she'd first arrived in Sheridan Falls. A pure white dress with crystals on the bodice and heaps of organza stood proudly on a mannequin in the window. It was a stunning dress.

As Rita and her mother got out of the car, Lynn broke into a smile. "What do you think of the dress? The one in the window?"

"It's gorgeous."

"That's the one I want."

Rita gaped at her mother. "That one? I thought you'd settled on a different one. The one displayed in the window when I first got to town."

Lynn's smile faded. "But this one is even more beautiful. You said it's gorgeous."

"Yes, but don't you think it's a bit much? I thought you'd go for something simpler, less princessy."

"You mean for my age? So because I'm fifty-nine, I shouldn't want to look like a princess on my wedding day?"

That had been exactly what Rita was thinking. As a mature woman, she expected her to choose something simple and elegant. But…it was her first wedding. And the excitement in her eyes was obvious.

It's not your choice, Rita reminded herself. *You're here to support your mother.*

Rita squeezed her mother's hand. "I look forward to seeing it on you."

"Really?"

"Absolutely."

Rita and her mother went into the store. A red-haired woman approached them with a huge grin. "Hello, Lynn." She turned to Rita. "And you must be her daughter, Rita."

"Yep, that's me. Nice to meet you."

"Nice to meet you as well. I have the dresses all set up for you to try on in the back."

Enid led the way to the dressing area. The same dress in the window hung on a hanger.

"Wow, it's spectacular," Rita said.

Lynn started into the dressing room, and Rita asked her if she wanted any help. "No, I want you to stay out here. I want you to see me once I have it on."

"I'm quite excited about your mother's wedding," Enid said softly. "I'm excited about all weddings, but your mother's is extra special. I guess it's her story of finding love at any age that's so touching."

Rita smiled softly. "It sure is."

"Your mother has chosen a few options for you. All

yellow, to go with the color scheme. She said you love the color yellow."

"I do."

"I have three options for you in your dressing room. They're quite beautiful. They range from the simple to the more elaborate. And nothing too bright. We're not talking canary yellow, but something paler."

"I'm sure I'll love all of them."

Enid let out a little sigh. "It's so much easier having only a maid of honor to dress."

"Enid," Lynn called.

"Coming right in."

Rita looked away so that she didn't get a peek at her mother in the dress. And then she waited.

When, a few minutes later, her mother emerged from the dressing room, Rita gasped. And then a bubble of excitement spilled from her throat.

"Mom... Oh... You're so beautiful!"

Her mother's eyes met hers, and both of them started to cry at the same time. Rita had not expected to feel this overwhelming emotion, but seeing her mother looking like a bride caused a joyful sensation she hadn't been prepared for.

Lynn did a slow twirl, allowing Rita to see the back of the dress, with its crystal-encrusted netting. "You love it?" she asked.

"You look breathtaking." Rita got up, taking a closer look at the gown. The low bodice highlighted her bosom without being too revealing. "Like a princess."

"And this is the veil we were thinking of," Enid said.

In keeping with the princess theme, the veil was attached to a bedazzled low crown.

"You are going to be the envy of all brides this summer," Rita said with confidence.

"Go try on your dresses," Lynn said. "I want to see which one looks the best."

Rita tried on the three dresses, and the satin one that flared from the waist and stopped just above the knee was the clear winner. It had short sleeves and a scooped neck. Enid suggested a string of pearls would complete the outfit, and Rita agreed.

"I'll just make the few alterations to your dress, Rita, taking it in at the waist. And yours fits well now, Lynn?"

"It's perfect. And I won't be eating until the wedding day." She chuckled.

"It's been such a pleasure serving both of you, ladies," Enid said. "I'll see you next week."

It was dark when Rita pulled up to the cabin she was renting, but she was fairly certain that there was a shape on the step leading up to her unit. Someone sitting there. She squinted, and as her headlights focused on the form more fully, she realized that it was Keith.

She felt a modicum of relief, quickly followed by regret. Once again, she felt silly for how she'd reacted with him this morning.

She glanced at the clock on her dashboard. It was 9:14 p.m. Ever since getting to her father's house, she'd all but forgotten her phone, and the battery had died at some point. How long had Keith been waiting for her?

She parked her car, then exited. She started straight for Keith, asking, "How long have you been sitting there?"

"A while," he answered.

He was wearing dress pants and a dress shirt, and Rita wondered if he had even gone home.

"I've been calling. And texting. And calling."

"I'm sorry. My mother ended up in the hospital."

Keith got to his feet, worry creasing his forehead. "Oh, no. Is she okay?"

"She fainted due to dehydration. Thank God, it wasn't anything too serious. Anyway, I ended up spending the day with her, finalizing wedding plans. And... I talked to my father."

"Oh? And...?"

Rita gripped the wrought-iron railing. "And we hashed things out. He told me everything. Why he did what he did, how he felt he couldn't leave because of his wife. Let's just say, I understand a lot more, and it became clear to me that holding on to anger is only bringing me down. My parents love each other. That's as clear as day." Rita let out a breath. "I'm sorry if you were worried about me."

Keith stepped toward her and wrapped an arm around her. "I'm just glad you're okay."

As he held her, her insides grew warm. It felt good, knowing that he cared.

"I'm really sorry about this morning. My reaction was... Well, quite frankly, it was juvenile. I'm embarrassed. I was just—"

"Surprised," Keith interjected. "Maybe I should have told you," he added with a shrug.

Rita eased back and looked up at him. "Everything you wanted me to understand makes sense to me now. You said that good people make bad decisions, and you're right. I guess I always internalized my father's rejection, made it about me. But it really wasn't."

"Maybe we can talk inside."

Rita offered Keith a small smile. Then she looked up

at the sky. The stars were numerous and easy to see, so unlike the city.

Sheridan Falls was growing on her.

Or maybe it was Keith. The man whose arm was still casually wrapped around her.

She and Keith started up the stairs together. When they reached the upper level, he twirled her until her body was against his. Then his lips came down on hers. Hard. She felt an electric jolt, a shock to the system. She was so stunned, she didn't process what was happening for a good couple of seconds.

Keith was kissing her, and not just an I'm-happy-you're-okay kiss. This was slow, hot, sensual. Keith was holding her body against his, splaying his hands over her back, rubbing them up and down. Slipping his hands into her hair, holding her face to his as he ravaged her mouth.

It was as if he needed to verify for himself that she was alive. That she was really here.

Her body erupted in flames. She looped her arms around his neck and surrendered fully to his kiss.

The sound of a door opening had them both pulling apart. A woman walked by, a knowing smile on her face. Once she was partway down the stairs, Keith whisked Rita to her doorway. "Let's continue this inside."

The next morning, Rita felt like a whole new woman. Another incredible night with Keith. The way he made her feel… She giggled as she drank the last of her coffee, remembering how he had touched and kissed every erogenous zone of her body.

They'd been even more in sync last night than the first time, and she knew that sex between them would just get better and better.

She could certainly get used to this.

Rita got dressed in a Lycra tank top and leggings. She was energized and wanted to do a run. The path around the lake would be the perfect spot.

She headed downstairs and started off by walking briskly, and taking in the sights of the towering oak trees, the blue jays, the robins and the squirrels scattering about. She smiled, her shoulders feeling truly light for the first time. This place was idyllic. A perfect place to unwind and let your problems go.

And it felt really good to have done just that yesterday. Her parents were getting married. She was vowing to move forward from the pain of not having her father in her life. She breathed in the fresh air and looked up at the blue sky and the sun shining through the leaves. Here she was, a small part of this big magnificent place.

She walked for ten minutes, then started jogging, passing some of the beautiful homes that bordered the lake. Everyone she passed raised a hand in a wave. She did the same. These people no longer seemed weird. They seemed wonderfully human.

After thirty minutes, Rita stopped running. She bent over to catch her breath. Then she started to make her way back. She never would have considered this—but wouldn't it be nice to have a cottage in a place like this? A small town with friendly people, where crime was basically nonexistent and you didn't have to worry about locking your doors? Where nature resembled what God intended? The high-rises and concrete jungles were just not what the soul needed to rejuvenate.

Rita found herself chuckling. "Who have you become?"

She was suddenly someone she didn't recognize, and she couldn't have been happier about that.

Her happiness faded when she went into her apartment and saw Rashad's face flashing on her phone. He was calling again!

She snatched up the phone, determined to put an end to Rashad's calls once and for all.

Rita swiped to answer the call. As she put the phone to her ear, she was unable to stop the groan that slipped from her mouth. "What do you want, Rashad?"

"Is that how you greet me now?"

Rita didn't say anything. What was the point? She had answered this call in the hopes that Rashad would finally leave her alone. "Why are you calling?"

"Because I want to speak to you."

"That's obvious," Rita said, her tone holding a hint of snarky. She wasn't interested in any cute banter with her ex.

"Hopefully in person," Rashad added.

"I'm out of town," Rita told him. It was a convenient excuse, but not the reason she wasn't interested in speaking to him. Their relationship was over, and after what he'd done, they could never be friends.

"For your mother's wedding?"

"How do you..." She frowned. "How do you know about that?" Had she told him and she couldn't remember? Their engagement had ended before her mother had announced that she was marrying her father.

"I spoke to your mother," Rashad answered.

"What? When?"

"When I couldn't reach you. I wanted to make sure that you were okay."

The little weasel! No wonder her mother had started on about how she should have given Rashad another chance. "I'm fine," Rita told him tersely, knowing that she sounded anything but fine. "If that's all—"

"Whoa, whoa, whoa," Rashad interjected. "Hold on there a second." He chuckled softly. "Will you please give me a few minutes of your time?"

He was using that soft pleading tone, the one she had found endearing and hard to ignore. "Three minutes," she told him. "Not a second more."

"All right. I messed up. I know I already told you that. But I want to make sure you know that I realize that. What happened had nothing to do with you. It was all on me."

Rita said nothing. There was nothing to add. Besides, she didn't care to rehash any of this.

"It took me losing you for me to know that I will never do anything to hurt you again. Ever."

"You can't hurt me anymore," Rita chimed in. "Because we're not together."

"But we can be. If you'll give me another chance."

"That's not happening."

There was a soft sigh on the other end of the line. "Rita…"

"Why is this so hard for you to understand?" Rita asked him. "When you had me, you betrayed me. It's over."

"I made a mistake, baby. Please forgive me."

Again with that tone. The one that he thought would get her to bend to his will. "Rashad, don't call me again."

Then she ended the call and tossed her phone onto the sofa.

About a minute later, when her phone began to ring,

she looked toward it with a sense of trepidation. But seeing Keith's name on her screen, she perked up. She snatched up the phone and answered it.

"Hey, you."

"What are you doing tomorrow?" he asked without preamble.

"Nothing in particular."

"Great. Keep it that way."

"Why?" she asked.

"Because I have a surprise for you."

Chapter 17

Rita thought about Keith all night, excited over what his surprise could possibly be. When she woke up, she checked her phone to see if he had sent another message. When she found that he hadn't, she called him.

"Rita," he answered, a smile in his voice.

"You know the suspense is killing me, right? You haven't told me if we're going to the surprise, if it's coming to me, anything."

"I was just going to call you. How about I pick you up at three?"

"Three," Rita repeated, silently wondering what could possibly be happening in the afternoon. "Do I need to wear anything special?"

"Something nice," he told her. "But also comfortable."

Rita frowned. "That could be two completely different outfits."

"It could be," Keith agreed. "But I'm sure you'll figure it out."

"That's it?" Rita asked. "That's my only instruction?"

Keith chuckled softly. "See you at three."

Rita was ready before three o'clock, and when Keith knocked on her door, she swung it open almost immediately. She had been standing there, waiting.

"I'd ask if you're ready," Keith said, "but the answer is obvious."

Rita started walking out the door. "I'm anxious to know what this surprise is."

"You look nice," Keith said as she began to lock her unit. "That's a pretty blouse. It goes well with your jeans."

Rita glanced over her shoulder at him. "Thank you."

"Can I kiss you?" Keith asked.

The door locked, Rita turned to face him. "That depends. Is it a good surprise, or a bad one?"

"Why would it be a bad one?"

Rita shrugged. "I don't know."

"You really don't trust easily, do you?"

Averting her gaze, Rita shook her head. "I've been disappointed a lot."

Keith leaned down and gave her a soft peck on the lips. "You won't be disappointed today."

A short while later, Keith was pulling into the parking lot of the Sheridan Falls Community Center. He exited the car, and Rita followed suit. She looked up at him with a curious expression, but he offered her no answers.

She followed him to the door, surprised that this was where they were. She had thought for sure he was going to take her somewhere romantic.

Keith opened the door to the building and led the way inside. It didn't take long before the sounds of happy children's laughter filled the air.

"What is this?" Rita asked. It was obvious what it was, but she was really asking why they were there. Did he have a child he hadn't told her about?

Keith's expression was playful as he opened the door to the gym. Rita looked inside. She saw the group of children immediately, but it took her another couple of seconds to realize that they were physically challenged. Some had artificial limbs and some were in wheelchairs. They were all involved in a lively game of basketball.

Keith stepped into the gymnasium and Rita sidled up beside him. They both stood outside the court, watching the children play.

One of the boys glanced to his right and noticed Keith. He quickly wheeled his way over to him, his eyes alight and a huge grin on his face.

"Keith!" the boy exclaimed.

Keith lowered himself so that he could hug the boy, who looked to be about ten. Others then came to greet him, throwing their arms around his legs and giving him high fives.

Rita noticed a man across the room, obviously the leader of whatever this group was. He raised a hand in a wave and began to cross the room with the discarded basketball under his arm.

The boy who had first greeted Keith looked up at Rita from his wheelchair and offered her a bright smile. He extended his hand. "I'm Simon. What's your name?"

"I'm Rita."

"Nice to meet you, Rita."

"It's a pleasure to meet you, too, Simon."

Simon had pale skin and raven-colored hair. Rita wondered how long he'd been in a wheelchair.

He must have sensed the direction of her thoughts, because he said, "I was in a car accident when I was seven. I'm paralyzed from the waist down."

Rita bent down and took Simon's hand. "Oh, Simon. I'm so sorry."

He shrugged. "At least I didn't die."

A simple statement, but it exemplified such a positive attitude that Rita couldn't help feeling silly for letting so much in her own life get her down.

"I'm glad you didn't die," she told him, squeezing his hand affectionately.

She stood tall, and Keith said into her ear, "When I'm feeling down, I like to come and spend some time with these kids. They remind me what's important in life."

As Rita looked around at the physically challenged children, she knew exactly why Keith had brought her here. She had spent so much time in Sheridan Falls whining about what was going on in her life. The circumstances in her life were not permanent; they weren't challenges that would always hold her back. These children had real challenges to face for the rest of their days. And yet, looking around at the smiling faces, you could see that they weren't letting their circumstances keep them from being happy.

Rita faced Keith. "Thank you."

"I find giving back always helps. Plus, these kids are like little brothers and sisters to me." Keith wandered over to a girl with an artificial arm. He ran his hand over her hair affectionately. "This is Olivia. Olivia was born without a right arm. But wow, you should see the paintings she creates."

Olivia shook Rita's hand with her left arm. "What's your name?"

"Rita."

"I'm seven," Olivia announced proudly.

"She kind of reminds me of the little sister I lost," Keith told Rita. "She has the same bright eyes and look of wonder."

Rita swallowed, suddenly feeling emotional and unsure why. No, she knew why. She was seeing an entirely different side to Keith that she hadn't expected. "You come here often," she surmised.

"Of course. And not just for them."

Simon wheeled himself over to them again. "Rita, do you play basketball?" he asked.

Rita made a face. "Not hardly."

"Then you'll fit right in."

Rita giggled. And the next thing she knew, she was amongst the group, trying to catch the ball, catching the ball, trying to throw it. Making an attempt to score and failing.

But most important of all, she was laughing.

Keith eyed her from across the court. He winked at her.

Butterflies went wild in her stomach. There was something extra special about this man.

Something she could fall for easily.

"There's one more stop we have to make," Keith announced when they were back in his vehicle.

Rita faced him, her beautiful eyes narrowing. "Where are we going? Or is it *another* surprise?"

He chuckled softly. "You're starting to figure me out."

"Is it as good as this one?" she asked. "Though I doubt it."

"It's even better."

"Better? This was pretty incredible. And you got me thinking about my life, the anger and resentment I've been holding on to. Yes, I just made amends with my dad but this was a good reminder that I need to stick with the plan to move forward, not let the past hold me back. If those kids can be so happy despite their circumstances, what's my excuse?"

"I'm glad to hear you say that," Keith told her. He wouldn't be able to understand the depth of the pain she had endured, but he was glad to know she and her father had made real strides toward resolving it. Carrying that pain around with her for the rest of her life would lead to a miserable existence.

"I'm focusing on the future," Rita said. "The positive things it may hold for me."

She held his eyes for a long moment, and he could see the hint of excitement. Was she including him in the positive things that were to come?

"The only downside to today…"

Keith made a face as he regarded Rita. "Downside?"

"I just wish you'd told me to wear sneakers instead of sandals."

Keith laughed, relieved. "Your footwear is perfect for the next stop."

"No hints at all, hmm?"

She really didn't like surprises. "Then it wouldn't be a surprise, would it?"

Rita pouted a little, but Keith could tell she wasn't being serious. She angled her body toward his in her seat, getting comfortable, and Keith could imagine her like this all the time. Riding shotgun as they went on road trips or, heck, just traveling together to pick up dinner.

She looked content, happy even, and his heart fluttered. And suddenly he was reaching for her hand. He linked fingers with hers, and a small smile touched her lips before she glanced away.

Keith ran the pad of his thumb over her skin. He hadn't known her very long, but already he couldn't imagine her being gone out of his life.

Minutes later, when they arrived at the hotel, Keith saw the confusion in Rita's eyes. "Oh…a hotel…?"

"Get your mind out of the gutter," he quickly told her.

"I wasn't thinking *that*," she added with a smirk. "But…what's here? Full body massage? An evening of pampering?"

Keith pulled the car into an available spot near the front entrance and parked. "You're just going to have to find out."

A minute later, they were heading inside. Rita was looking around with confusion. Keith took her hand and led her down the hallway to where the boardrooms were. Then he started to open the door to the conference room named Daffodil.

Rita gripped his hand, pulling him back several steps from the door. "Keith?"

He paused. He saw alarm in her eyes. She'd no doubt caught a glimpse of who was sitting inside the room, and now she was freaking out.

"My brothers are in there?" she asked, needing verification that her eyes hadn't been playing tricks on her.

"Yes."

Rita bit down on her bottom lip. He couldn't imagine

the thoughts running through her mind, but it was obvious she was a little spooked.

"You should have told me," she said.

"I didn't want you to stress. Because this *is* a good surprise, Rita." He gave her hand a reassuring squeeze. "They're expecting you. They *want* to see you. They know that things got off on the wrong foot through no fault of your own. Brandon's talked to me about how bad he feels that you've been hurting all these years. I figured I'd help facilitate a meeting where you guys could clear the air."

Keith took a step toward the door again, but when Rita didn't budge, he stopped and looked down at her, saw the worry on her face.

"Do you trust me?" Keith asked her.

One second passed, then two. Keith held his breath. He hoped to God that the strides he'd made with Rita didn't die an instant death now.

"Yes." Her reply was faint. "I trust you."

"Then believe me when I tell you that your brothers love you. They want a relationship with you. More than anything."

Seconds passed, and finally Rita nodded. Keith moved toward the conference room. Rita positioned herself behind him as he fully opened the door. Brandon and Daniel looked first at him, then at Rita. Their expressions projected affection and warmth.

Keith felt Rita's body sway. She glanced up at him, and he saw that her eyes were glistening with tears.

"It's okay," he told her. "I'll be waiting right out here. If you need me, I'll be here."

She nodded. And then she drew in a deep breath. Her

shoulders visibly relaxed. She faced Keith again and mouthed the words, *Thank you.*

Then she released his hand and stepped fully into the room.

Chapter 18

Hours later, as Rita lay in her bed, she couldn't sleep. She was tossing and turning, an emotional ball of energy.

The day of surprises had been more than she'd ever hoped for. It had been a day of love like nothing she'd ever imagined.

The heart-to-heart with her brothers would be a memory she would always cherish. They'd laughed and they'd cried in that room. They listened to what she'd gone through without her father in her life, acknowledging her pain. And Rita had listened to them, learning that they too had felt cheated and hurt by not having had her in their lives. It had been a surprise to her to learn that they felt they'd missed out by not getting to know her.

In that room, as they tore down the barriers of the past, they became a real family.

And she had Keith to thank for that.

She wanted to call him, but it was minutes to eleven o'clock. Too late?

She picked up her phone, determined to chance it. If he was sleeping, he simply wouldn't answer. And she would leave him a message. He'd dropped her home after her emotional time with her brothers, leaving her to be alone with her thoughts. It was what she'd needed, but right now, she needed Keith.

The phone rang once, twice...

"Hello?" He sounded a little groggy.

"You're sleeping."

"I was starting to doze off," he admitted. "What's up?"

"I was thinking... Maybe we could go back on the boat?" Rita suggested. "This time I can act like a proper tourist and let you give me a real tour."

She winced, awaiting Keith's reply. She knew that she'd been a tumultuous bag of emotions since getting to Sheridan Falls, and if he said no, she'd understand. But the fact that he'd facilitated the meeting between her and her brothers... Did he feel more for her?

He'd gone above and beyond, and Rita's heart was starting to feel things it hadn't in a while. She was falling for Keith, and it was a scary reality.

"Tomorrow?" Keith asked.

"Whenever's convenient," Rita told him. "I can make some food for the trip... I make a very good mac and cheese."

"Is that so?"

"The best in St. Louis," she told him. "At least the very best in my apartment," she added with a little chuckle.

"I have a better idea," Keith countered.

"What's that?"

Keith left her in suspense, telling her to bring her bathing suit, a towel and comfortable shoes. "I'll pick you up tomorrow at one."

When Rita opened the door and looked at Keith, her breath caught in her throat. He was so darn handsome. She wondered if she would always have this heart-palpating reaction to him.

"Hi," she said, sounding breathless.

"Hey, yourself." His smile was endearing. There was a big part of Rita that wanted to throw her arms around his neck and pull him into her unit and have her wicked way with him. But she imagined the boat would be a more romantic setting. The two of them out on the middle of the water, the blue skies above them—

"You ready?" Keith asked.

Rita cleared her throat, hoping he hadn't been able to sense the direction of her thoughts. "Yep."

A short while later, they were in the car, but they didn't head toward where the boat was docked. Was Keith going to get there another way?

Apparently not. Because Keith drove farther to the outskirts of the town where the wooded area became more dense. He took a winding road into the thicket of trees, then pulled up on a patch of gravel.

"I thought you were taking me out on the boat," Rita said.

"I have something better in mind."

Rita knew by now not to ask what that something was. Keith was fond of his surprises. Today she really hoped that the surprise would involve just the two of them.

Keith parked the car. As Rita exited, she looked up at

the tall trees that had to be hundreds of years old. They seemed to touch the top of the sky.

"Grab your bag with your towel," Keith told her.

"Why would I need my towel here?"

"You'll see."

Once Rita had her bag, Keith offered her his hand and she took it. They walked together into the woods. A few minutes later, they were crossing a footbridge over running water. A river.

Rita looked ahead at the direction of where the water was coming from. It flowed over rocks. And now she understood.

"Sheridan Falls. You're taking me to a waterfall, aren't you?"

Keith looked down at her and nodded. "It's a beautiful spot. You can't get to this one on the boat. Well, you can get to a certain point, but then I'd have to stop the boat and we'd hike to the falls. This is easier. There's more than one waterfall here, and this one's a bit more private."

Keith winked, and Rita's pulse began to race. He had romance on his mind. She felt a rush of excitement.

"We just have to walk a bit to get there. But trust me, when we're there, it'll all be worth it."

For about fifteen minutes, they followed the narrow path along the river. Finally, the waterfall came into view. Rita actually gasped; it was that breathtaking. The sky opened up above and the rays of sun shone down, giving a heaven-like aura to the falls, which looked to be about a hundred feet high. Mist hung in the air. There was a deep pool of water at the base, and a small bit of shelter beneath the falls.

"This is incredible," Rita said.

Keith placed his towel on a large tree stump. Then he

pulled his shirt over his head and tossed it on top of the towel. Rita began to do the same, taking off the dress that she wore over her bathing suit. She was wearing water shoes, and she was glad for that, because even as she took a step onto the rocks bordering the river, she found them slippery because of the mist.

Keith took her hand. "Ready?"

"Let's do this."

He walked the stone path along the perimeter of the shallow pool, and Rita thought at first that he was going to lead them right into the waterfall. But there was a bit of an alcove beneath it, and he took her there. The thundering water crashed down against the rocks, splashing them beneath the alcove, but for all intents and purposes, it was a little haven from the falls. Rita stood there, looking through the cascading water and out at the world. At the trees, the rocks, the beauty of this place.

And then Keith was securing his arm around her waist and pulling her close. Her lips parted in surprise just as his mouth came down and claimed hers.

He kissed her slowly, his hands now moving over her slick body. He kissed her until she was breathless.

Then he took her hand. He led her through the cascading water and she giggled as it splashed down onto her hair and body. It was cold, and her back arched in protest, and then she laughed even harder.

Keith moved forward, his body disappearing into the shallow pool. Then he lowered the rest of his body and swam the breadth of the area, moving to what appeared to be the deepest part of the water. He looked at her, standing on the rocky ledge. "Come on. Join me."

Rita took a tentative step in, found it slightly deeper than she'd expected. "Whoa," she said, spreading her arms wide to balance herself. But she soon found her footing. Then she did as Keith had and lowered herself totally into the water. She swam toward him.

He snaked a hand around her waist again and pulled her close. "How is it?" he asked.

"A little cold, but…lovely. Magical."

And it was. It was their own private paradise.

Keith put his other hand beneath her thighs and held her as though he was carrying her. He twirled her around in the water, grinning at her. Rita knew she was safe, but she secured her arms around his neck. Unexpectedly, Keith dipped her backward and submerged her whole body. When he pulled her up, Rita was gasping and laughing.

As her laughter faded, their gazes locked. In an instant, the playfulness in his eyes changed to something else.

To lust.

When Rita had come to Sheridan Falls, she never imagined herself frolicking in a waterfall with a gorgeous man. Her heart began to beat faster as her fingers stroked the nape of his neck. Keith's fingers tightened on her back.

"I really like you," he said, his voice husky.

"I really like you, too," she replied.

Rita edged her lips upward. He met her partway, their mouths coming together with heavy sighs. Desire exploded in her body, like a volcano erupting.

God help her, this man… He was gorgeous. He was a gentleman. Everything about him turned her on.

His tongue moved over hers wildly, their lust an entity all its own. Slowly, he let go of her thighs and her legs went down. As soon as Rita was standing firmly on her feet, Keith pulled her against himself, their wet bodies connecting.

He held her close, smoothing his hands over her back. Rita leaned into him, loving the feel of his hard muscles against her. She trailed a hand down his arm, caressing his strong bicep and sighing as she did.

A lustful groan rumbled deep in Keith's chest, and he deepened the kiss. His fingers slipped into her hair, holding her head as his mouth ravaged hers. Rita dug her fingers into his arm, needing the support of his body as the onslaught of dizzying sensations made her weak in the knees.

How was she so completely attracted to Keith? And why wasn't she afraid of what she was feeling? Instead, she wanted to explore everything possible with him, do everything possible with him.

Starting with sex in a waterfall.

Breaking the kiss, she glanced around. If she and Keith had ventured to this place, what would stop anyone else from coming here?

Keith held her, his fingers running up and down her back as he too looked around. "We're fine," he told her. "But come."

He took her hand and led her toward the waterfall. Keith then climbed out of the shallow pool, and helped Rita do the same. Carefully, they made their way onto the stone ledge beneath the spray of water. Rita giggled as they went through the waterfall and into the alcove. She knew what he was doing. Here, they would be afforded some privacy if anyone came along the path unexpectedly.

Keith looked down at her, and her laughter subsided. He placed a gentle hand on her face and Rita curled her cheek into it. Her heart was thundering in her chest, much like the water around them. She honestly couldn't remember feeling this excited about a man, ever. And everything he had done for her, being patient with her, listening to her, helping her smooth things over with her brothers... Her feelings for him were growing by the second.

"You're incredible," she said, the words spilling from her mouth unintentionally.

Keith kissed her. As he did, he slipped a hand beneath one bathing suit strap and pulled it down over her arm. Then he did the same with the other one. Both straps now hanging down, he tugged on them, pulling the bikini top from her breasts. They fell free.

Keith eased back and looked at her body. "Damn."

The way he uttered the word and looked at her made Rita feel as though she were the most beautiful woman in the world.

He covered both breasts with his palms, then tweaked her nipples at the same time. Rita's lips parted, and she sighed softly, enjoying not only the sensation, but the thrill of being out in open nature like this.

Keith lowered his head and brought his mouth down on one of her nipples. He drew it into his mouth deeply and sucked softly. Rita moaned in delight, and as his tongue worked its magic, she looped an arm around his neck and held on to him. He slipped a hand beneath her bathing suit bottom, finding her center. Rita gasped at the exquisite feeling. Then she leaned into his hand, urging him to stroke and explore.

His lips moved to her other breast as his fingers tantalized her sensitive flesh. "I need you out of your bikini," he growled, a sense of urgency in his voice as he tugged the material over her hips. Rita helped him, bending to pull it off her body. Then she unfastened her bikini top and let the material fall to the ground.

Standing there in front of Keith, totally naked, she could see the look of lust and awe in his eyes and that had heat surging through her body. She would never tire of seeing him look at her like this.

Keith stripped out of his own black swimming trunks, and Rita shamelessly checked out his large shaft. She bit down on her bottom lip.

Stepping backward, Keith leaned against the stone wall. Then he took Rita's hand and pulled her toward him. He kissed her, then lifted her into his arms, as though she weighed no more than a feather. He hooked her legs over his arms, and Rita looped her arms around his neck. She braced her feet against the wall for support.

With skill, Keith guided his arousal to her center. And then he was thrusting inside of her, and kissing her, and bringing Rita to a height of ecstasy she hadn't known was possible. With the water crashing around them, they found their rhythm with each other and nature.

And Rita knew in her heart that she was falling in love.

Chapter 19

"Wow, Mom—you look beautiful," Rita said. And she meant it. Her mother looked absolutely stunning.

"My hair—"

"—is perfect," Rita told her. "But your makeup… If you don't hold back those tears, it'll be ruined."

Lynn dabbed at the edges of her eyes with a handkerchief. "I know, sweetheart. I'm just… I'm so happy."

The words hit Rita in the chest, causing warmth to spread within her. Her mother *was* happy. Rita could see it, feel it. And unlike weeks ago, the fact that her mother was about to marry her father didn't fill Rita with a sense of anxiety. Instead, Rita felt a sense of peace. Love was a magical thing, wasn't it? It always found a way.

As that thought popped into Rita's head, she couldn't help thinking of Keith. Keith, with his broad shoulders and that knowing smile. The past two weeks since their adventure at the waterfall had gone faster than Rita had thought possible, faster than she would have liked. For once, she wished that she had the power to suspend time.

Because the time she'd spent with Keith had been the most amazing weeks of her life. Between helping her parents plan their wedding, Rita and Keith saw each other almost every day, talking, sharing a meal and, of course, making love. He'd turned something on within Rita, something that was insatiable when it came to him.

She would never tire of making love to him. But more than that, she simply wanted to be with him.

What would happen now, though? It was her parents' wedding day, and after this, she was supposed to be heading back to St. Louis. She and Keith hadn't discussed a future, though he had asked if she thought she would ever be able to live in a small town.

"Yes," she'd told him, surprised at how she'd changed. Sheridan Falls had grown on her. But mostly Keith had grown on her.

"Sweetheart," Lynn said, her eyes suddenly filling with a sense of panic. "Do I have everything? I have something old, something new, something borrowed, something—"

Rita took her mother's hands in hers and squeezed them reassuringly. "You have everything."

"Is everyone here?"

"It was a pretty full house when I took a peek a while ago, but let me check again. I'll be back."

Rita left the room and made her way to the church vestibule. She peered through the glass in the back doors and into the church. Her eyes landed on Keith, who was standing at the front with Brandon. Rita's pulse quickened just looking at him, and she swallowed. Good Lord, he looked delectable in a black suit that appeared to be tailor-made just for him. Wide shoulders that tapered beautifully down at the waist. A black bow tie that looked so much sexier on him than the traditional tie. She could ogle him all day.

Keith caught her eye, and smiled. A smile that always made her feel giddy.

Brandon looked over his shoulder in her direction. Seeing her, he waved.

Her brother.

Rita felt overwhelmed, but this time with happy emotions. The future was going to be different, because she had changed her view of how it would play out. No longer a burden or a curse, she saw her new family members as a blessing. The brothers she'd never had.

Keith stepped back for a moment, and then her father came fully into view. He looked dapper in his double-breasted black suit with a yellow kerchief in the pocket, and his gleaming leather shoes. The look of excitement in his eyes was undeniable. Rita saw a man who was looking forward to marrying the woman he loved.

Finally.

Keith headed down the aisle in her direction, and within seconds, he was opening the back doors that led into the sanctuary. The way his eyes swept over her had her feeling another unexpected emotion. Desire. She was suddenly wishing this day would hurry up and be over so that she could skip to later when she could spend the night in Keith's arms.

"Wow," Keith said. One word, but it filled her with a sense of elation and confidence. He thought she was sexy, beautiful.

"You're looking pretty sexy yourself," Rita told him.

"How's your mother doing?" Keith asked. "Is she ready?"

"Yes. Please tell the organist to begin."

"Will do."

Keith gave her a quick peck on the lips, then Rita shooed him away. They'd been keeping their relationship hush-hush, as there was no need for anyone to know about them, considering they weren't an official couple. After the wedding, they would figure out what their relationship was and where it was going.

"Hey, Keith."

Both Rita and Keith turned at the sound of the voice, and the moment Rita saw the man walking up behind them, she knew that he *had* to be Keith's brother. He looked so much like him.

"Aaron." Keith hugged the slightly shorter man, then turned to the woman by his side who was holding a sleeping baby. "Melissa, it's good to see you as always." He kissed her cheek. "Aaron, this is Rita. Rita and I—"

"I'm the daughter of the bride," Rita quickly interjected. "I'm in town for the wedding and I'm renting one of Keith's units."

"Ahhh," Aaron said. He readjusted the baby bag on his shoulder, then offered her his hand. "Nice to meet you. This is my fiancée, Melissa. And our daughter, Kara."

"My goodness," Rita cooed, looking at the small baby decked out in a cute pink dress and matching pink shoes. "She's so precious! How old is she?"

"Five months," Melissa responded.

"Have you enjoyed your time here in Sheridan Falls?" Aaron asked.

"Yes," Rita answered. "Surprisingly."

"I came back to Sheridan Falls," Melissa began, "and

this is what happened to me." She indicated the baby in her arms, then glanced up at Aaron and grinned playfully.

"Wow," Rita said, and laughed. She didn't look at Keith. But she was suddenly thinking about her future with him.

"We'd better get inside," Aaron said.

"Mom, Dad and the family are halfway up on the right," Keith told him. "Saving you a seat."

Keith opened the door for them, then gave Rita a little smile before he, too, went back into the church. Rita watched him to speak to the organist. Then he went to one of the church deacons, an older man Rita had met earlier named Stan. Moments later, Stan headed to the sanctuary doors and began to prop them open.

It's showtime, Rita thought to herself. Then she returned to the bridal room.

Her mother looked at her expectantly. "Is everyone here?"

"Looks like it, yes. The church is pretty full." The ceremony was open to anyone who wanted to attend, and it appeared that quite a number of the townsfolk had shown up.

Lynn visibly swallowed, and her eyes widened with panic. "Oh, God. Is everything going to be okay?"

Just weeks ago, if her mother had asked that question, Rita would've seen it as an opening to talk her out of getting married. Now she knew the question was simply one that many a bride had on her wedding day. Nerves. She wanted everything to be right and for there to be no complications.

The organist began to play the traditional "Here Comes The Bride." Rita walked toward her mother and looped her arm through hers. "Yes. Everything is going to be perfect."

Her mother smiled, and seemed to truly relax.

Feeling a sense of contentment Rita never thought was possible, she straightened the train on her mother's dress as she made her way toward the head table. Her parents had entered the reception hall only minutes ago, had their first dance as a married couple and now the reception festivities could begin. Her mother was undeniably glowing. She was happier than Rita had ever seen her.

From the weather to the ceremony, the day had in fact been perfect.

Perfect… Rita made a face as she remembered what her mother had said to her when they'd been leaving the botanical gardens where the photographer had taken photos. "This day has been perfect, sweetheart. And it's going to be perfect for you, too."

Rita had looked at her mother with curiosity. "Hmm?"

Her father had slipped his arm around his wife's waist at that moment and pulled her close. The photographer had been right there, ready to snap some impromptu shots of the cozy couple outside of the limousine.

The day had been busy, and Rita had put her mother's cryptic statement out of her mind. She had probably been alluding to the fact that Rita, her father and brothers were all a real family now.

Rita continued to fix the train as her mother got to the head table. Instead of climbing the platform to get to her seat, her mother stopped to talk to yet another guest.

Rita glanced around. And her heart nearly flatlined when she saw him entering the banquet room. Suddenly, she understood the meaning of her mother's mysterious words.

Rita stared, horrified. She blinked, confused. Maybe she was seeing things. Maybe...

"No," she uttered.

As each second passed, there was no mistaking what she was seeing. And then her stomach bottomed out. Because walking toward her with a smile on his face, wearing a black suit and tie, was Rashad.

Rashad's smile grew as he neared her. What the heck was he doing here?

Rita wished she could disappear into the ground. God help her, she hoped that Rashad wasn't here for the reason that she thought he was here. How was she going to explain this to Keith?

As Rashad closed the distance between them, he opened his arms. Rita stood paralyzed as he wrapped her in a hug.

"Rita." He said her name with meaning, as though they were reuniting after not having seen each other for years. He held her close, hugging her, letting his hands familiarize themselves again with the skin on her back. Rita was mortified.

She extricated herself from Rashad's grasp and threw a glance in Keith's direction. He was looking at her with a curious expression.

"What are you doing here?" Rita demanded.

"Your mother invited me."

Lynn turned from the person she'd been talking to and beamed at Rashad. "Rashad! I worried that you might not make it."

"Of course, I'd be here," he said. He leaned in and hugged the bride. "And wow, Lynn, you look ravishing."

"If everyone can settle into their seats, please," the emcee said into the microphone.

Rita sidestepped Rashad and her mother. Then she hurried out of the banquet hall and into the bathroom.

Keith's breath quickened as he watched the scene before him. Who was this man who had practically had his hands all over Rita?

Rita had looked at him, pulled away from the guy, then raced out of the banquet hall, looking extremely uncomfortable.

Because she didn't want to be around this guy, or because her relationship had just been outed?

A huge knot formed in Keith's stomach. He thought about the way Rita had quickly introduced herself to Aaron as his tenant earlier, clearly not wanting his brother to know that there was a relationship between them. He'd believed it was because she didn't want to go public with their relationship yet. But had she been lying? Did she actually have a relationship with someone else back home?

The last couple of weeks Keith had spent with Rita had been incredible. Had he been foolish to believe that they'd become an item? Or had she just been passing the time, having a summer fling until she left Sheridan Falls for good?

Questions raced through his mind. He needed to know what was going on.

The stranger had just finished talking to Rita's mother, and now he was looking for a place to sit. Keith headed the man off, extending a hand as he stepped in front of him. "Hello. I'm Keith Burke."

The man took his proffered hand and shook it. "My name is Rashad. Rashad Williams."

The blood drained from Keith's face. Rashad? Rita's ex-boyfriend who'd been calling her constantly a few weeks back. What was he doing here?

"You're Rita's ex," Keith supplied.

Rashad gave him a curious look then, suddenly sizing him up. "Well, technically yes. But we're trying to work things out."

The words were like a blow to Keith's stomach. "Are you?"

"That's why I'm here."

The man's smile was way too syrupy. Keith disliked him.

"Excuse me," Rashad said. "I've got to get to table seven."

Keith forced a jovial demeanor, grinning at the man. "Of course," he said.

Keith walked back to his table, which turned out to be adjacent to Rashad's.

So he was here to rekindle his relationship with Rita. The question was, did Rita want the same thing?

What man would come all this way to attend a wedding and see a woman he'd dated if he *didn't* have the go-ahead of that very woman? It would be insane to simply show up on a whim, wouldn't it?

The pain that streaked through him with that thought was intense. Had Keith, once again, fallen for the wrong woman?

Chapter 20

Rita sucked in a startled breath when she heard the bathroom door open. But seeing Maeve, she immediately relaxed. She was so glad that her best friend had been able to come to Sheridan Falls for the wedding. She desperately needed her right now.

"Oh, thank God," Rita uttered.

"That's actually Rashad?" Maeve asked, but the question was sarcastic. "My eyes aren't deceiving me?"

"Can you believe it?"

"What's he doing here?"

"Heck if I know," Rita quipped. "I think he's lost his mind."

"He didn't tell you he was coming?"

Rita loosened her grip on the edge of the sink she'd been holding. "No! I had no idea. And now… Oh, my God, what's Keith going to think?"

"That your ex is a nutcase?" Maeve supplied.

"I hope so." Rita looked at her reflection. She saw a frazzled woman staring back at her. "I can't believe he showed up here."

"You said he'd been calling you. He didn't give you any hint at all?"

"Nada. He said he was sorry for hurting me and wanted another chance. I told him I wasn't interested. I thought that was the end of it. But get this—my mother just said that she was glad he could make it, and something about fearing he wasn't going to show up. I think the two of them conspired to have him surprise me."

"No, your mother wouldn't do that."

"I wouldn't have thought so either, if not for something she said earlier today. She said the day was going to be perfect...for *me*."

Maeve's eyes widened. "No."

"Not too long ago, she was talking about how I ought to have forgiven him. Some nonsense. My mother knows how Rashad hurt me... If she conspired with him to do this, what was she thinking?"

"Don't let him rattle you. Be cordial, obviously, but don't let him see that he's even affecting you."

"I'll try."

"And that starts by going back out to the reception. You can't hide in here."

"I know." Rita shouldn't have been letting Rashad's appearance affect her at all, but it was such a shock to see him here in Sheridan Falls. And the big concern was how Keith would react.

She stood up straight, smoothed her hands over her dress, then looked at herself in the mirror again. She took a breath and willed herself to relax. "It doesn't matter why he's here. He wasted his time if he thinks this stunt is going to win him any points."

Maeve smiled at her. "That's my girl."

Leading the way, Maeve headed out of the bathroom. Rita followed her. Once in the banquet hall, it took a moment before she saw Rashad sitting at a table beside Keith's. He turned as she neared him, meeting her gaze.

Rita quickly looked at Keith. He, too, was regarding her. She saw a mix of confusion and concern on his face.

She tried to smile at Keith, give him some sort of re-assurance, but she felt so sick that she wasn't sure she succeeded.

Throughout dinner, Rita was able to relax for the most part. She avoided looking in Rashad's direction, making sure to keep her eyes on the guests near the front. She kept telling herself that it didn't matter why he'd shown up here, and that Keith would obviously understand.

"...so join me in a toast for the happy bride and groom," Brandon was saying when Rita tuned back in to his words.

People raised their glasses and toasted the new couple.

"And now the daughter of the bride will say a few words," the emcee announced.

Drawing in a deep breath, Rita forced a smile. She was nervous about speaking in front of the crowd, especially since she hadn't written anything down. But what she was going to say would come from the heart.

She made her way to the podium. Once there, she glanced down at the bracelet her father had given her, now adorning her left wrist. Warmth filled her heart.

She cleared her throat before speaking. "When my

mother first told me that she was going to marry my father, I thought she had lost her mind." There were a few chuckles. "Now, I know that most of you would think that that's crazy. Children usually are thrilled with their parents getting back together. But all of you in this room know the reality. How my parents were involved briefly decades ago and then parted ways. I'll skip over the nitty-gritty. That's not the point now. The point is that despite all odds, love found them again."

Rita glanced toward her mother and father. Her mother's eyes were alight with love. Her father gave her a little nod and smile before she continued. "I'll be the first to admit that I didn't trust this," Rita went on. "Not after everything they'd been through. I just didn't see how this union would work now. I didn't believe that the love was real. To be honest, I came to this small town kicking and screaming," she added with a chuckle, and some in the crowd laughed with her. "But not only has this town grown on me, so has the relationship I see between two people who clearly love each other. Maybe they never stopped loving each other, even though life and circumstances got in the way.

"So today, I am here to say that I wholeheartedly support the newest couple in Sheridan Falls. I've seen their love with my own eyes and if I can give it my blessing, everyone else can. I know that my father loves my mother. And I know that she loves him deeply. And I'm confident that they will live out the rest of their days making each other happy. If this kind of love story doesn't give you hope that love finds a way, nothing will." With that, Rita's eyes ventured toward Keith. She offered him a little smile, and she felt a wave of relief when he smiled back. Thank God. Hopefully he hadn't even realized who Rashad was.

"Will you all please raise your glasses in a toast for this very special couple who have finally made it official! Mom and Dad, I love you."

The guests raised their glasses and sipped their wine. Then the clinking of glasses began and without much more prompting, Rita's father leaned forward, gently stroked his wife's face and planted a soft and sensual kiss on her lips.

There was a raucous round of applause.

"We've heard from the best man and the maid of honor," the emcee said when the applause died down. "Now the floor is open for any of you who'd like to say a word or two. I ask that you please keep your speeches to two minutes or less."

The guests glanced around the room, waiting to see who would be the first to speak. No more than a few seconds passed before Rashad jumped to his feet and started for the podium. Rita swallowed, fear making her body tense. What was he doing?

Rashad offered a charming smile to all of the guests and raised a hand in a wave. Then he stepped behind the microphone. "Evening, ladies and gentlemen. I know that most of you don't know who I am, and that's okay. I'm a friend of the bride and her daughter. It's my pleasure to be here in your town today." Rashad surveyed the room, then continued, "I have to say that I absolutely echo what Rita just said. About love finding a way. This occasion also gives me hope about love, and second chances." He paused. "I'm not a perfect man. I've made a lot of mistakes. And the biggest mistake was letting the most amazing woman in my life go because I was stupid. I hurt her. I betrayed her. And I'll always be ashamed of that fact."

Rita began to slink down in her seat. *Please, Rashad... Stop.*

"She did the right thing when she dumped me. But like her own parents were able to find each other after challenging circumstances, I'm hoping that my being here today will prove to her—" Rashad turned to look at Rita "—the woman I love, that I'm fully ready and willing to commit. I'm sorry, baby. And I hope to God this finally proves it to you."

Rita glanced around the room, saw that some of the guests' eyes were alight with curiosity and even excitement.

No! she wanted to scream. *You have no clue!*

And then Rashad did something that absolutely mortified her. From his jacket pocket, he withdrew a small box. Obviously the man had lost his mind. This wasn't happening.

It *couldn't* be happening.

"You gave this back to me after we broke up," Rashad said, "and I never returned it. I always knew that one day I would give it to you again." He inhaled a deep breath. "Rita, will you marry me?"

People began to clap. Rashad started up the mounted platform and toward the head table, making his way toward her. Rita, like a deer caught in the headlights, sat there like a fool. She wanted to scream, she wanted to say something.

Rashad reached her and took her hand. "Rita—"

She pulled her hand from his and pushed her chair back. Then she rushed out of the room.

As she did, she saw Keith's eyes. Saw and understood clearly the emotion on his face.

Betrayal.

Chapter 21

Keith watched Rita go. Then he looked at Rashad's stunned face. It didn't take long for Rashad to quickly scurry after her. Keith sat there, watching the man run out of the banquet hall. The wedding guests did the same, mouths wide, eyes bulging.

Obviously there was unfinished business between Rita and Rashad. Their relationship wasn't truly resolved. And Keith didn't need that complication in his life. He'd been falling for Rita, yes, but she was a woman who still had an ex in her life. An ex who wanted her back.

Keith had been down this road before, with Maya. She'd said that she loved him, wanted to spend her life with him, but how long had it been before she'd changed her tune and left town? Barely after she had left Keith brokenhearted, he'd read of her marriage to a movie producer, the man she'd been seeing before getting involved with Keith.

Keith would be an absolute fool to not run from Rita as fast as he could.

But apparently his brain was at odds with his heart, because suddenly he was getting to his feet. And then he was heading out of the room in search of Rita. He looked left, then right, but saw her nowhere.

Seconds later, it was the sound of a male voice that directed him where to go. "How could you do that to me?" Keith overheard. "Humiliate me in front of everyone?"

Keith quickly ran to the left. As he rounded the corner to where the sitting area was, he saw Rita standing near the wall. She met his gaze, looking terrified.

Keith stepped forward. Following Rita's line of sight, Rashad whirled around. He glowered at Keith.

"This is not your concern," Rashad said. "Leave us alone."

"Rita, do you want me to leave?" Keith asked.

Keith looked at her, and could see in that moment that she was relieved. Even though she still looked horrified, she was glad that he was there. And for that reason, Keith was going nowhere.

Her lips parted, but she didn't get to speak before Rashad took a step toward Keith. "I'm not sure what your problem is, buddy. Do you make it a habit to intrude on people's privacy?"

"Do you make it a habit to cheat on women?"

An expression of understanding came over Rashad's face. "So my feeling was right about you. You've got a thing for my girl. I guess I can't blame you. She's beautiful. But whatever you're thinking, forget it. Rita and I are going to work things out."

"Last I checked, a woman needs to have a say in working things out. And I haven't heard Rita say that's what she wants."

"So you think you're some kind of knight in shining armor?" Rashad chuckled. He took a few steps forward. "You need to back off."

"Rashad, stop it," Rita told him.

Keith stepped toward Rashad. Now they were practically toe-to-toe. "I'm not going anywhere," Keith said. His voice was cool. He wasn't sure why he was doing this. Maybe he was getting himself involved where he shouldn't, but he didn't want to leave Rita alone with this man. No matter what history they had.

"You're the one who let her go. You were stupid enough to not appreciate her."

Before Keith knew what was happening, he heard Rita's scream. Then he saw Rashad swinging his arm. Keith deflected the blow, then threw a right hook that connected with Rashad's nose. The shorter, thinner man quickly doubled over, whimpering.

When Rashad looked up, Keith saw blood streaming from his nose. "Damn you, I'm bleeding!"

"Keith!" Rita yelled. "What did you do?" And what she did next annoyed him. She ran to Rashad. "Rashad, are you okay?"

"Are you serious?" Keith asked.

"I think my nose is broken," Rashad whined.

"You're not a fighter, Rashad!" Rita said. "What were you thinking?"

Watching the two of them, Keith's stomach sank. "So he was right," he said. "There's still something between you two, isn't there?"

Rashad began coughing. So much so that he sounded

as if he was going to die. Keith caught on quickly. Rashad was hamming it up for more attention from Rita.

Pathetic.

He was gripping Rita's arm, and working this moment for as much leverage as he could.

"You know I would do anything for you, Rita. Even take blows from some guy to prove that I love you."

"Rashad." Rita sounded pained. She shot a glance at Keith, looking as though she were about to say something. Rashad spoke first.

"Please, I need some water," the man pleaded. "And… I'm seeing stars."

Keith glanced around, noting with horror that a crowd had formed around them. Their eyes were volleying from Keith to Rashad, their concern for Rashad clear.

Surely everyone in this town had to know that he wasn't a violent man. That if he'd hit Rashad, there had to be a good reason.

"Please, can someone get him some water?" Rita called out.

Keith looked at her, and all he could do was shake his head. This was Maya Part Two, and he wanted nothing to do with it.

He turned and started to walk away.

"Keith!" Rita called.

Keith kept walking.

Rita watched Keith leave, feeling a sense of helplessness. Everything had gone horribly, horribly wrong. She wanted nothing more than to run after Keith, explain to him that there was absolutely nothing between her and Rashad. But Rashad was bleeding and clutching her arm. How could she leave him when he was hurt like this?

She may not love him anymore, but she wanted to make sure he was physically okay.

"Rita," Rashad said, gripping her arm harder and pulling her down toward him. "I meant it when I said I still love you. That I'm done being a jerk. I just took a punch in the face to prove to you that I'll do anything to fight for you. From this moment on, I'm yours forever."

"Stop talking," Rita told him. She saw Brandon standing a few feet away. "Can you call an ambulance?"

Brandon gave Rashad a distasteful look. "I'm sure he'll live. Probably his ego is bruised more than anything." He paused. "Where did Keith go?"

Rita shook her head. "He left… I…"

Rashad placed his hand on Rita's face, forcing her to meet his eyes. "Please, don't leave me. Ever again."

Rita wasn't sure why, but as she looked at Rashad, she got the slightest feeling that he was enjoying this…. Was he not as injured as he was appearing to be?

"Is your nose broken?" she demanded.

"I… Maybe… I think so," Rashad croaked.

Rita knew for sure then. As Brandon had said, Rashad's ego was more hurt than anything else. He was probably glad that he was bleeding, because the fact that he'd seemed so hurt was what had her sitting by his side.

Like a fool.

Rita looked down at her dress, now splattered with blood. She glanced through the crowd, hoping to see Keith somewhere. But she didn't.

Rita pulled her hand free from Rashad's grip and quickly got her feet. "Brandon, can you see that Rashad gets what he needs?"

Rashad's eyes widened. "What? Where are you going?"

"I need to find Keith."

* * *

But Keith was nowhere to be found. Feeling a sense of resignation, Rita moved through the hotel corridors back to the ballroom. Someone other than Brandon had offered to take Rashad to the hospital. Oh, he had begged her to go with him. But she hadn't. He didn't need her there.

Rita wanted to apologize to the crowd for the spectacle that had disrupted this special occasion. But the DJ was playing music, and people were dancing, and interrupting the happy flow now made no sense.

Spotting her mother across the room, Rita walked straight toward her. She needed answers.

Lynn was standing at a table, talking to some guests. Rita touched her mother's arm, then guided her to the side of the room where they could have some privacy.

"Is Rashad okay?" Lynn asked without preamble.

"He's gone to the hospital, but I'm sure he's okay." Rita frowned. "Mom...you told him he should come here and do this?"

"Well, not exactly this." She paused. "You weren't happy to see him? At all?"

"No, I wasn't happy. I was mortified. Why would you think that him proposing to me, putting me on the spot like that, would be a good idea?"

"I didn't know he was going to do *that*... He asked if he could come to the wedding, surprise you."

"And you thought surprising me was a good idea?"

"He said you weren't listening to him when he'd called you. He told me that he very much wanted to apologize to you, make you understand that he'd changed. And I more than anyone understand that people can change. I saw no harm in him coming here and talking to you."

Rita shook her head. "What about the fact that *I* didn't want that?"

"I figured you might have a change of heart. You've come around to forgiving your father..."

"My situation with Rashad isn't the same thing. You should have told me. Better yet, you should have told him to stay away."

"Were you really not swayed by anything he had to say?"

Rita squeezed her forehead. How could her mother not understand? Why did she believe that every guy was worth another chance, even when he betrayed you?

"I never told you, Mom, but I've been involved with someone else." Perhaps she should have mentioned this to her mother before, but she'd had no idea she would invite Rashad here.

Her mother's eyes narrowed. "What? Who?"

Her father appeared at that moment, placing an arm around Lynn's waist. He must have heard what Rita had said, because he responded. "Keith Burke, right?"

Rita looked at her father, her heart beating a little faster. "Yes."

"Keith? That young man who punched Rashad? Oh..."

"I thought I saw something between the two of you," Lance said. "Didn't I tell you that, sweetheart?"

"Yes, but I didn't think it could be anything serious. Rita, you've just met him. Rashad, on the other hand, you have history—"

"Enough about Rashad!" Rita whipped her head around when she realized she'd raised her voice more than she'd wanted to. Thankfully no one other than her parents had heard her above the music.

"Mom, I know you like Rashad. I know you thought

he was a great guy. And I'm sure in many ways he *is* a great guy. He just wasn't a faithful guy. What you and my father have is completely different from what Rashad and I had. There isn't going to be a reconciliation. So please…forget about Rashad. If he ever talks to you about me again, tell him I've moved on."

Understanding registered in her mother's beautiful eyes. "Okay, sweetheart. I'm sorry. I only want you to be happy."

"I know that." She squeezed her mother's hands. "I'm leaving, okay? I need to find Keith."

"So it's serious with him," her mother surmised.

"It is," Rita said.

And she was going to search the streets until she found him, make him understand how deeply she felt for him.

The only problem was, she couldn't find Keith anywhere. Not at his house, not at the office. She'd called him a few times, but his phone was going straight to voice mail.

Rita texted him, hoping that he would respond.

He didn't.

His family had been at the wedding, but it wasn't impossible that he'd gone to one of their homes to be alone.

And then it hit her. The boat.

Rita drove to the area of the lake where she'd boarded the boat. Her heart filled with hope as she parked. His car was in the lot.

Rita quickly made her way down to the dock. People regarded her with concern in her bridesmaid dress smeared with blood. "I'm okay," she announced to the spectators before anyone could ask.

She'd been hoping against hope that Keith was simply on his boat, but it wasn't there. She looked out in the distance, saw a couple of boats out in the middle of the lake. It was dusk, so it wasn't easy to make out either of the boats in particular.

Keith was out there, she knew it.

But it wasn't like she could swim to him.

No. All she could do now was wait for Keith to reach out to her. To respond to her messages. She would keep texting and calling him until he responded.

Keith saw the latest let's-get-together-so-we-can-talk text and quickly tossed his phone onto the bed. He'd done the only thing he could to escape, which was to head out on his boat. Out on the water, he could disappear from the world.

He cracked open a beer and sat, mulling over his life. He wished he didn't care, but he did.

Because he loved Rita.

And he'd never felt so scared by that emotion in his life. Because he could see the exact thing happening with Rita that had happened with Maya. And God help him, he didn't want to go through that again.

"It's too late for that, you fool," he chastised himself. Something about Rita had had him diving into a relationship with her with both feet.

He took a swig of his beer. He needed to harden his heart, forget she ever existed. She didn't know what she wanted. That was as clear as day. And heck, hadn't she tried to let him know that in the beginning? Every time she had run from him, she'd been making it clear that she wasn't ready for a relationship. But no, Keith hadn't paid attention to the glaring red flags. Instead, he'd chased her, feeling a sense of closeness as she'd let down her walls.

As she'd started to trust him. And every time they'd made love, Keith had felt as though he were getting more and more of her heart.

Foolishly Keith had allowed himself to believe that because they'd been as intimate as two people could be, she had moved on from her past.

Even if she wasn't confused about her ex and had feelings for Keith, was she really going to give up the big city for small town Sheridan Falls?

It was unlikely.

So why bother investing any more time in her?

"It's over," he said aloud. But then he remembered how she kissed him, touched him and the sweet sounds she'd uttered every time they made love. And his heart didn't want to believe that what they had was over.

Keith's chest tightened. Maya leaving had crushed him. But what he felt for Rita was stronger, their connection deeper. From the feisty girl carrying so much pain on her shoulders to the happy woman whose laugh made his heart soar, she fit into his world effortlessly. The time she'd spent here this summer had seemed like forever, and he wasn't ready for her to be out of his life.

But what if the connection had been one-sided? Maybe for Rita, she'd simply needed someone to help her forget about her ex.

Keith downed his beer. Then he went to the fridge and got another.

He had to stop thinking about Rita immediately. He would be a fool to believe that he could have a future with a woman who was most likely going to run back into the arms of the very man who'd hurt her.

Didn't they all?

Chapter 22

The next morning when Rita drove back to Keith's place and saw that his car was finally there, waves of relief washed over her.

He was home.

Rita rushed from her car and to his door. She rang the doorbell. She barely waited a beat before she began to knock.

Moments later, her hand was raised to knock the door again when it suddenly opened. And there he was, looking haggard, as though he had hardly slept. He was wearing boxers and the shirt he'd had on last night at the wedding, minus the tie. The shirt was crumpled now. His face was drawn. He was upset. It was clear. And it was because of her.

Rita expelled a breath she didn't know she'd been holding. "Have you eaten?" she asked.

Keith frowned. "What?"

"I've been worried sick," she went on.

"Why?"

"*Why?*" she countered. "Because you left the reception, and you haven't responded to me."

"I got out of the way."

"What do you mean, you got out of the way?"

"So that I wouldn't be a distraction."

What was he going on about? "Can I come in?"

"I'm not sure that's a good idea."

"We need to talk about what happened."

"Do we?" Keith gave her a pointed look. "It seems pretty self-explanatory to me."

This was just as she'd feared. Keith was thinking the worst. "It isn't. Nothing about this is self-explanatory. Rashad... I don't know why he got it in his head to come here to the wedding. To humiliate me like that. But obviously he thought it was going to score him some points."

"And did it?" Keith asked.

"Of course it didn't!"

"The moment I hit him, you jumped right to his side. You chose him."

"That's because he was bleeding." And then his words registered. "I didn't choose him. I just... I thought he was seriously hurt. Rashad isn't a fighter."

"You did see him raise his hand to me?"

"I saw. I'm not blaming you for hitting him. It's just... I didn't want him to be hurt. It's okay that I still care about him, isn't it?"

"Hey, whatever you feel for him is completely your business."

Rita's heart began to pound. "What do you mean by that?"

"Only that it's not up to me to tell you whom to care about or not care about. I can't make anyone do anything."

Keith was speaking in a monotone voice, as though he was catatonic. Rita blew out a frazzled breath. "Can we at least sit down in your living room? I don't want to be talking about this on your doorstep."

Keith hesitated, and Rita's heart sank. Had his feelings for her changed so radically over night? Just a few days ago, they'd been making sweet love here. Now he didn't want her around?

But finally Keith stepped backward, then started for his living room. Rita entered his house and closed the door behind her.

"I spoke to my mother," she explained as she sat on the sofa in his living room. "Rashad apparently called her. She thought I would appreciate him coming here, trying to make amends with me."

"Because you never told her you were seeing me, right?" Keith surmised.

"Well..." she hedged. "I didn't, but the wedding was her focus."

"I told Brandon."

"And I told my best friend, Maeve. Keith, it's not my fault that my mother thought she could play matchmaker. No matter what I said about how he hurt me, she felt I needed to forgive Rashad."

"Maybe you do."

The words were like a bomb. They shattered her. "Excuse me?"

"He came all this way," Keith said, shrugging. "Maybe there's still something between the two of you, even if you're too mad at him right now to see it."

How could he say this to her? After the time they'd spent together, how connected they were when they made love? She'd given herself to him so completely. Didn't he realize that?

"You think I spent the night trying to contact you, driving around to find you, getting no sleep, because I want to be with Rashad?"

"Relationships are complicated," he said, his expression was blank. His face unreadable. "Your own parents' relationship proves that, doesn't it?"

"My mother's situation is her situation. I came here not expecting to make any connection to this place, or to like anybody. And I most certainly didn't expect to like you. But…" Her voice trailed off. She wanted to see something from him, a flinch, the shifting of his eyes. Anything. But he continued to regard her with a blank expression.

"I think what happened between us was very clearly a case of passing the time."

Never had words hurt her so completely. "*Passing the time?* You think I slept with you because I was bored?" She couldn't prevent the rising sound of hysteria in her voice. Her heart was breaking, and Keith didn't even seem to care.

"Maybe a better word is that I was a distraction. Look, I fully understand you're angry with Rashad. You *want* to move on. But how many times do people get sucked back into the vortex of a relationship with someone because it's familiar?"

This wasn't the man she had fallen for. The man who had understood her pain and talked her through it. This one wasn't even listening to her. "What exactly are you saying?"

"You have unresolved issues with your ex. Whether you realize it or not."

A feeling of horror filled her belly like a lead ball. It was dawning on her, really hitting her, what he was saying. She wanted to resolve things, but he was telling her that he didn't trust that she had moved on.

Maybe she was being irrational, given how everything had played out, but she wanted him to fight for her, not just give up.

Unless there was nothing for him to fight for in his opinion. Maybe he had just been *passing the time*…

Rita swallowed, doing her best to keep her tears at bay. "I think I'm getting it now. You said passing the time, basically saying that was *my* motivation." Slowly, she got to her feet. "But that's what *you* were feeling. That's what you were doing."

"I didn't say that."

"It's what tourists do, isn't it?" she said, her voice cracking a little bit. "They come to town and have a summer fling. Meaningless, right?"

"I'm not saying that what we had—"

"Do you want a relationship with me?" Rita asked. She needed a direct answer.

Finally, she saw his jaw flinch. It took a beat before he spoke. "You need… You need to work things out with Rashad."

Rita's body actually swayed, as though the ground beneath her had shifted.

And it had. Keith had just pulled the proverbial rug out from under her.

"Oh, my God."

"He still loves you. And he made a comment that I can't refute. I'm involved where I shouldn't be."

"So what we had…"

"I've played this game before, Rita. I know how it ends."

Rita took a few steps backward, disoriented. "*Game. Passing the time.* My God, I've been an idiot."

For the first time, she saw a look of pain cross Keith's face. "Rita, please—don't misunderstand and don't make this harder than it needs to be."

"Make what harder than it needs to be? You dumping me?"

"You owe it to Rashad—"

"Oh, stop using Rashad as an excuse." Rita blinked back her tears. "I have to get out of here."

She turned as fast as she could, and stumbled to the door, tears in her eyes. She barely made it onto the porch before she was crying. She had come here to make him understand that Rashad was her past, that she felt bad for letting him walk away yesterday. Instead, he was telling her that she needed to give Rashad another chance.

He would never tell her that if he loved her. Never.

Passing the time.

He had been projecting onto her the very thing *he* had been doing. And oh, God, it hurt. It hurt so much.

She loved him, but he didn't love her. It was as simple as that.

Rita got behind the wheel of her car, and cried for a good few minutes. Then she wiped the tears from her eyes so that she could see to drive.

She started the car, then looked toward Keith's front door.

He wasn't there.

And that told her everything she needed to know.

* * *

A good twenty minutes after Rita had left, Keith stayed seated in the same spot on the sofa, pain whirling inside him. The look on her face kept flashing in his mind. The look of pain and betrayal.

He should have gotten up and chased after her. But he hadn't. He let her go. He let her think the worst, because it was the best way.

The only way.

He'd chased Maya, assured her that they would have an amazing future. But she'd left anyway. Married her ex.

No, Keith had to let Rita go. But watching her leave had been the hardest thing he'd done in a long while.

He got up and went to the kitchen, trying to ignore the stabbing pain in his chest. He had told himself that once she left he would feel a sense of acceptance, that he would know in his heart he had done the right thing. Instead, his heart felt like it was splitting in two.

Maybe a walk around the lake. Maybe a visit to the community center. He swallowed. He'd done those things with Rita. How could he do them now without thinking of her?

He grabbed a beer from the fridge, then put it back. It wasn't even eleven o'clock. He couldn't start drinking. Besides, it wasn't going to numb the pain.

"It hurts now," he told himself, heading instead to the coffeemaker. "But it's like ripping off a Band-Aid. The pain will subside soon enough."

But three days later, the pain hadn't subsided. If anyone were to see him now, they would think he was a homeless person. He hadn't shaved; he looked unkempt. But he didn't care.

He was working from home—allegedly. Instead, he was right now sitting in his armchair with his laptop, looking over the details of the same property he'd been looking over for the last twenty minutes.

The knock at the door had his heart filling with hope. He put the laptop on the coffee table and quickly headed to answer it. He flung it open, and though he didn't think he'd see Rita there, he felt a sense of disappointment more profound than he expected when he saw Brandon.

"Don't look so happy to see me," Brandon quipped, a wry smile on his face.

"What's up?" The words barely croaked out of Keith's throat.

"Shouldn't you be the one telling me what's up? You look like death warmed over." Brandon lifted a six-pack of beer. "Why don't you invite me in and tell me all about it."

"Yeah." Keith cleared his throat. "Sure."

Though sitting back and having a beer was the last thing he wanted. He wandered into the living room nonetheless. He didn't want to talk; he just wanted to forget. Sooner or later the days would pass and he would eventually feel better.

"Have you talked to Rita?" Brandon asked once they were in the living room.

Keith shrugged. "Not really."

Brandon placed the six-pack on the coffee table. "You either have or you haven't."

"Are these cold?" Keith asked, reaching for a beer.

"Yep."

Keith discovered that they were in fact cold the instant he bent over to pluck a can from the box. As he stood tall, Brandon clamped a hand down on his shoulder. "You hear what happened to that Rashad guy?"

The question piqued Keith's interest. "I heard he packed up and left town. That's all I know."

"The big baby was practically laughed out of the hospital. They gave him a Kleenex and a Band-Aid and sent him home."

"Really?"

"That might be a bit of an exaggeration, but the point is, he wasn't really hurt."

Keith popped the lid on the can and drank some of his beer. Three days after the wedding, that scene had yet to stop playing in his mind. That and Rita rushing to his side...

"Did Rita tell you what happened when she went to see him?" Brandon asked.

"She went to see him?" Keith asked.

"I assume she did." Brandon narrowed his eyes. "Haven't you talked to her?"

Keith slumped onto the sofa. "Man, what's with all the questions?"

"So you haven't? You just let her leave town?"

Keith's jaw tightened. "She—she's gone?"

"Keith... What the heck are you doing? You just let her leave without talking to her?"

"We talked. I told her to work it out with her ex."

Brandon looked at him as though he'd grown horns. "Are you out of your mind?"

Keith drank more beer. "You don't remember Maya?"

"Come on, Maya was always a flake. Didn't I tell you that? Rita isn't. And I'm not just saying that because she's my sister."

"Mark my words. She's gonna get back together with the dude. They always do."

Brandon shook his head. "You really love her, don't you?"

Keith shrugged, trying to appear nonchalant. But the question had his heart stirring, a fresh wave of pain hitting him.

"And you just let her go."

Keith said nothing.

"So you, a six-foot-three strong guy, were too much of a coward to talk to her. That's what you're telling me?"

Keith shot his friend an irritated glare. Brandon was his best friend, so he knew him well. He knew what he'd gone through after Maya. "Did you expect me to chase her? Make her believe for a moment that she wanted something she doesn't want? And then after couple of months, she decides she's out of here?" He shook his head. "Naw, I've been through that before. Played that game. It was best that she left now."

"Best for whom?"

"For both of us," Keith replied, but the words lacked conviction.

"Keith, you love her. I can see that as plain as day. And the Keith Burke I know doesn't let some other guy dictate his future. You're making a whole lot of assumptions based on your experience with a girl who was never that into you. Yeah—" Brandon said, holding up a hand when Keith opened his mouth "—I'm saying it. Maya wasn't the one for you. Rita… I think she is."

Despite himself, Brandon's words gave Keith the slightest hope. Was he sitting here holed up in his house being a coward? Because he didn't want to get hurt again?

No one wanted to get hurt.

Rita certainly didn't want to get hurt, either. But Keith had not been able to stop thinking about the look in her eyes when he'd sent her away. Maya had never looked at him like that. Damn, his friend was right.

"I don't know, Brandon. I guess I was thinking… You know how the saying goes… If you love something set it free, and if it comes back to you—"

"But what if it's too injured to come back to you? Did you ever think of that?"

Brandon's words hit him like a ton of bricks. God, what had he been thinking? If Rita didn't want Rashad, how would she ever want him after how he'd treated her?

She wouldn't. And suddenly Keith knew what he had to do. He got to his feet. "Brandon, I'm gonna have to ask you to leave. There's something I need to do."

A slow smile spread on Brandon's lips. "That's it, my friend." He stood up. "Stop sulking and go get your girl."

Rita returned to St. Louis, vowing to get over Keith, but two weeks later, she couldn't deny that her heart was still broken. She'd allowed herself a few solid days to mourn, then had gotten back to work. But she was only working from home, mostly so that she could eat tubs of ice cream in bed and cry whenever she wanted. The office had strict word to tell anyone who called for her that she was on a cruise.

"Maybe you ought to try talking to him again," Maeve suggested. She was sitting beside Rita on her sofa, looking at her with concern. "Honestly, I don't even remember you being this upset when things ended with Rashad."

"I blocked him," Rita said. "I've had some calls from unknown numbers, but I'm not answering them."

"You think it's him?" Maeve asked.

"I don't care." It wasn't entirely true, but it needed to be true. If Keith could so easily disregard what she had to say to him, she needed to move on. Her view that men were unfeeling beings had been solidified the day she'd left his place, heartbroken. It was time she concentrated on her career, on moving forward and forgetting that men ever existed. Her life would be better off for it.

"I think you need to at least have a conversation with him. You're sitting around here, gaining weight from all the ice cream you're eating. You need closure."

"I'm gaining weight?" Rita asked.

"Well, maybe not yet. But you will." Maeve sighed. "Just talk to him. And for God's sake, reactivate your social media accounts in case he's trying to reach you."

"Then what would be the point of blocking him?" Rita countered. "I'm fine. All I need is a bit of time. I'm not the first woman to be heartbroken. I won't be the last. Maybe I'll even write a story about it for my magazine."

Maeve shook her head at her. "Maybe this is what you wanted. With all those stories of gloom and doom and heartbreak, maybe there's a part of you that doesn't *want* to be happy."

"What?"

Maeve got up from the sofa. "I've got to go."

"Where are you going?"

"Somewhere where I can smile, laugh. Maybe even flirt. And when you're ready to do the same, call me."

Rita's heart slammed against her rib cage as Maeve walked to the door. "You're leaving me? We didn't even order takeout yet."

Maeve continued to the door. Rita thought she was

going to leave without a word, but she paused and looked back. "You know I'll call you tomorrow," she said, and gave her a smile.

Maybe it was Maeve's frank words, but Rita got up the next morning and went to the office. She needed a change of pace. She needed the sunshine on her skin, the wind in her hair.

She had alerted the senior editor that she would be arriving around eleven o'clock. They needed to have an editorial meeting about the next issue.

When she arrived, her coworkers looked at her from wide eyes, as if they were stunned to see her, even though they should have known she was coming in. Rita offered them a tight smile, continuing to her office without breaking stride.

"Madeline," Rita said, addressing the junior editor who was standing near the water cooler. "I'll be in the boardroom in ten minutes. Please make sure everyone's there for the meeting."

Madeline hurried over to her. "There's a story that was submitted to me and I'd really like it included in this issue."

"You know I've already approved the stories for the next issue. There's no room for any additions."

"Before the meeting, I think you should read it." Madeline looked at her with a pleading expression. "You're always telling me I should stand up for the stories I believe in, take some initiative. Well, I want you to read the story before the meeting. It's interesting because it's from a man's perspective."

Rita was about to say no, but she glanced at her watch. She had fifteen minutes before the meeting was to begin.

She could start going through the story, and if it caught her fancy, she could continue reading it. This way she could at least honestly tell Madeline what she thought of it.

"Okay. You're right—I am always telling you to take some initiative. I'll have a glance at it. But I'm still not sure it can fit into this issue."

Madeline smiled. "Just read it, then tell me what you think."

Rita went into her office and sat behind her desk. She saw the printed sheets of papers there with the title, "A Fool's Regret."

Interesting title, she thought. Then she began to read.

Sometimes a man has everything he wants, everything he needs, and still he lets it slip out of his hands. My story begins one day in the summer, in early August. I wasn't expecting the woman of my dreams to come into my life at that moment. There was nothing especially significant about that day. Nothing to prepare me for the way my life would irrevocably change.

Nice opening, Rita thought.

I was simply stopping for a coffee at a shop in town when the car rear-ended me. Not the greatest start to most romances, I guess.

Rita dropped the paper. She looked around the office, as though expecting Keith to appear. Was this... No. It couldn't be.

Maybe I should start before that. To the time when another city girl had come to my small town and I fell for her. I thought we would have a future to-gether. She seemed enamored with me, as I was with her. But she had unfinished business in her life. A career in New York, a former lover there. Long story short, she made promises to me, told me she wanted to spend her life with me. But be-fore long, she left me abruptly. Went back to the city and to her ex.

I guess that made me jaded. Made me unpre-pared to deal with a similar situation when it hap-pened a few years later.

I'm not like most men. I can admit, at least now, that I was scared. No one wants to get hurt. And when I fell for this woman who rear-ended my car, it was significantly more intense than the love I'd had for the woman before. I had no reason to be-lieve that anything would come between us. Until I learned that her circumstances were much like my ex's. She had a man from the past, one who wanted her back. And yeah, that terrified me. So I said some things and pushed her away. Not because I wanted her to go. Because I couldn't stand it if she stayed and then broke my heart.

"Oh, my God." Rita couldn't read anymore. Her eyes were welling with tears. This was clearly not a random story from a random man. This was from Keith.

She left the story on the desk, and got up, and opened her office door. She was about to go in search of Made-line, but stopped short when she nearly ran into the wall of his chest.

Keith...

Here. In the flesh.

She looked up at him, and he down at her. With the pad of his thumb, he wiped at the tear that had escaped the corner of her eye.

"Hi," he said softly.

"Keith... I... You're here..."

"I've been coming to the office every day for the past three days. When I got here, I found out that you weren't away, but working from home. I figured at some point you had to make an appearance, so I was going to keep coming by until you did."

Rita's lips fell open. "Are you serious?"

"About day nine of me calling and getting the she's-on-a-cruise line, I started to doubt you were actually away. In fact, I was pretty sure you were avoiding me. That's when I knew I had to come here to see you."

Rita looked beyond Keith, saw her coworkers staring, smiling. They had been in on this. They had to have been. "So you're saying that you have been coming to the office, and no one told me? But my staff must have been in on this. They gave me the story..."

"Let's just say, Madeline and I are BFFs now," Keith said, a smile touching his lips. "I told her what I wanted to do, and she's been excited to put the plan into motion the moment you came back."

He wasn't joking. Rita pulled him into the office and closed the door.

"I read your story—"

"I should never have pushed you away—"

They spoke at the same time.

The faintest of smiles tugged at Keith's lips, one filled with regret. "I'm sorry. I was a fool."

"Is it true what you wrote? That someone left you before?"

Keith nodded. "It was pretty much the identical situation, except for the wedding and her ex showing up."

"Oh, Keith." That explained a lot.

"Look, I know I shouldn't have judged you based on her actions, but the thought of you staying with me, then leaving... Rita, I couldn't take that. Not with you."

"So all that nonsense about me working things out with Rashad—"

"I thought it best for you to resolve your feelings for him one way or another. You know, the whole if you love something, set it free. No?"

"Except I told you that I didn't want Rashad. I wanted you, you doofus."

"Doofus, fool, moron. Wait a minute—*wanted?*"

Rita's expression softened as she looked up at him. "Have you really been coming by the office for the past few days?"

"I'd come for a hundred more, if that's what it took to make you see me. I needed time, Rita. Time to get over my fear and to let you figure out what you really wanted."

"You, Keith. You're the one I want. Rashad is my past. You need to believe that."

"I do." He inhaled deeply, then smoothed a hand over her hair. "I'm sorry I hurt you. But I promise that if you give me the chance, I'll spend the rest of my life making it up to you. I love you, Rita. And I hope to God you love me, too."

Her lips trembled. Was this really happening?

She looped her arms around his neck. "I love you, too, Keith. My heart is yours. Please believe that."

A smile spread across his lips. Then he drew her close, lowered his head and kissed her.

He kissed her until she was breathless. Rita pulled away first. With a serious expression, she looked up at him and said, "I do have some bad news for you."

Keith frowned. "Oh?"

"I'm not going to publish your story."

They both laughed.

"Because I want it for me, only me," she went on as their laughter subsided.

Keith stroked her cheek. "That's okay, baby. As long as you'll be my girl. Then one day my wife. My everything."

"Oh, Keith. Yes. Always."

How had she been so lucky to meet him? To meet the man of her dreams when she'd least expected it?

"But that brings me to my good news," she told him.

He raised an eyebrow. "Better than you loving me?"

"I'll live in Sheridan Falls with you." She grinned up at him, nodding when he gave her a look of disbelief. "After all, I can work anywhere. I can come to St. Louis when necessary. It's a quick flight."

The emotion that flashed in his eyes was a mix of happiness, love and awe. "I love you, baby," he said, his voice raspy. "So much."

"I love you, too."

And then she tipped up on her toes, and he edged his mouth down to meet hers. And this time when they kissed, it was slow, deep, tender. A promise.

A promise of the kind of love that would last forever.

* * * * *

Soulful and sensual romance featuring multicultural characters.

Look for brand-new Kimani stories
in special 2-in-1 volumes.

Available October 15, 2019

His Christmas Gift & *Decadent Holiday Pleasures*
by Janice Sims and Pamela Yaye

Her Christmas Wish & *Designed by Love*
by Sherelle Green and Sheryl Lister

Christmas with the Billionaire & *A Tiara for Christmas*
by Niobia Bryant and Carolyn Hector

She took another step closer. "Mr. Millner—"

"I'm sure Annalise explained to you that I need an assistant for the weekends only. Your main priority would be typing my handwritten book, updating my social media accounts and running errands," he said, turning to stride across the room to stand next to the lit fireplace.

"You write by hand?" she asked, unable to hide her amazement and forgetting the reason for her visit.

"Yes," he said, his voice deep.

"And you've finished your new book in the Mayhem series?" she asked.

"So, you're familiar with my books?" he asked, his attention locked on the crackling fire.

Samira wished she could see his face. She felt almost like he was hiding it from her intentionally. "Yes," she finally answered. "My favorite is *Vengeance*."

He grunted.

She eyed him. There was something so powerful but still sad about his stance. The way he moved. The way his stare was downcast. She was surprised at how strongly she needed to know what gave him such a demeanor. It, plus the dark interior of the home and neglected exterior, was all so mysterious—maybe even more so than one of his novels.

The man was an enigma. How could someone so abrupt and insolent write with such emotion and rhythm that she was forever transformed by his words? The two did not match.

"I assume since you're here you made Annalise's round of cuts," he said.

Annalise? As in Annalise Ray?

"Absolutely," she lied, completing winging this unexpected interaction.

"I like that you don't talk much."

She pressed her lips together.

"Do you want the job?" he asked, crossing his strong arms over his chest.

She didn't miss the way the thin material stretched with the move. "Wait. What?" she asked, forcing her attention from his fit form framed by the light of the fire and on to his words.

A billionaire heiress working as an author's weekend assistant. The thought actually made her smile.

The smile widened.

And maybe a better chance to get to know him and just what his reservations are about selling the land.

She contemplated all the pluses and minuses of the ruse. Some work related.

Samira eyed the fine lines of his taut body and her body instantly responded to him.

Some not.

"Yes or no?" he asked, his tone brusque.

Is this crazy? Am I?

"Yes, Mr. Millner, and thank you," she said.

Will this work?

"Good. Ms.…"

She opened her mouth but closed it as she almost supplied him her real name. He might very well know the Ansah name. "Samantha Aston," she lied, pulling the name out of the air.

Ding-dong.

She briefly looked over her shoulder to the front door at the sound of the doorbell.

"Your first duty is sending away all the other applicants," he said, turning and leaving the room with long strides.

What the hell have I gotten myself into?

Don't miss Christmas with the Billionaire
*by Niobia Bryant, available November 2019
wherever Harlequin® Kimani Romance™
books and ebooks are sold.*

Looking for more satisfying love stories
with community and family at their core?

Check out **Harlequin® Special Edition**
and **Love Inspired®** books!

 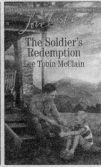

New books available every month!

CONNECT WITH US AT:

Facebook.com/groups/HarlequinConnection

Facebook.com/HarlequinBooks

Twitter.com/HarlequinBooks

Instagram.com/HarlequinBooks

Pinterest.com/HarlequinBooks

ReaderService.com

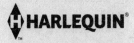

**ROMANCE WHEN
YOU NEED IT**

Reward the book lover in you!

Earn points on your purchase of new Harlequin books from participating retailers.

Turn your points into **FREE BOOKS** of your choice!

Join for FREE today at **www.HarlequinMyRewards.com.**

Harlequin My Rewards is a free program (no fees) without any commitments or obligations.

MYR18